# THE
# OREGON TRAIL

# THE OREGON TRAIL

## WILLIAM W. JOHNSTONE
### AND J.A. JOHNSTONE

**KENSINGTON**
PUBLISHING CORP.

www.kensingtonbooks.com

KENSINGTON BOOKS are published by

Kensington Publishing Corp.
900 Third Avenue
New York, NY 10022

PUBLISHER'S NOTE: Following the death of William W. Johnstone, the Johnstone family is working with a carefully selected writer to organize and complete Mr. Johnstone's outlines and many unfinished manuscripts to create additional novels in all of his series like the Last Gunfighter, Mountain Man, and Eagles, among others. This novel was inspired by Mr. Johnstone's superb storytelling.

KENSINGTON BOOKS and the WWJ steer head logo are trademarks of Kensington Publishing Corp.

ISBN: 978-0-7860-4982-0 (ebook)

ISBN: 978-1-4967-4037-3

First Kensington Trade Paperback Printing: May 2024

10 9 8 7 6 5 4 3 2 1

Printed in the United States of America

# THE
# OREGON TRAIL

# Chapter 1

"Who is it, son?" Garland Scofield called out to his son, Robert, who was standing at the kitchen door. "I hope it ain't somebody I'm gonna have to get up for." He, his brother, Clayton, and his nephew, Clint Buchanan, were still sitting around the supper table, drinking coffee. Garland's wife, Irene, his daughter, Janie, and Ruby Nixon were clearing the table and getting ready to wash the dishes. The men had just had a full day recovering some horses that had wandered away from a herd they had moved to new pasture, and Garland didn't want to get up to talk to anybody.

"It's Spud Williams," Robert answered his father. "He's ridin' up to the back door."

"Well, good," Garland said. "I don't have to get up for Spud. Tell him to come on in."

Robert held the door open for the round little man who removed his hat when he stepped inside out of respect for the ladies. "Hope I ain't intrudin', Miz Scofield, I just wanted to tell Clayton that I got his message sent to Peter Moreland in Independence."

"Of course not," Irene said, "come in, Spud. Are you just getting back from Sacramento?"

"Yes, ma'am, just this minute," Spud answered.

"You must be hungry," Irene replied. "We're just getting ready to dump the leftovers, so you got here just in time. Set yourself down at the table and we'll fix you a plate."

"I don't know, Irene," Clayton japed. "You sure you wanna cheat the hogs outta them leftovers?"

When Irene gave Clayton a scolding frown, Spud said, "Pay him no mind, Miz Scofield, I never do. And when we start back from Independence with another wagon train, I'll have all kinds of opportunities to spike his food with gunpowder."

"So that's what causes all that rumblin' I hear in my belly when we're on the trail," Clayton said, chuckling. "I wondered why Clint never complained about it."

Ruby set a cup of coffee on the table for him and said, "Here's your coffee, Spud. Janie's fillin' a plate for you." She looked at Clint then. "You want more coffee?" He shook his head. She aimed at Clayton and Garland. "Anyone?"

"Thank you, Ruby," Spud said. It always did his heart good to see how compassionately Ruby had been accepted into the Scofield family, much as they had Clint many years before when Clayton found him living in a Crow village. He wondered if any other young woman had suffered the loss of two husbands on a single crossing of the country before, like she had. It seemed an odd thing to look at her experience as good luck. But in a way, Spud thought you could call it that because it caused her to end up with this family. And to him, that looked like the place she ought to be. At first he, like many others on that wagon train, thought Ruby and Clint had a special attraction for each other, but it proved to be more like brother and sister. His wandering thoughts were corralled then by a question from Clayton.

"That operator send that whole message, just like I wrote it?" Clayton asked.

"Well, he said he did, and he charged me for every word of it," Spud replied. "I just had to take his word for it. I sure couldn't understand that clickety-clack he was doin' on that thing."

"I wanna be sure Moreland knows we're gonna get to Independence by the fifteenth of March, so I can have a couple of weeks to get our wagon ready and meet the folks Moreland's signed up to go. That's about what it took me and Clint to get ready for an April first departure last year. I want this one to be a good one 'cause I ain't plannin' to make another'n after this 'un."

"That's what you said last year," his brother was quick to remind him.

"I know, but this year is gonna do it for me in that business. Hell, look around us. This valley ain't got that much cheap land left. Folks ain't got the fever like they did when I first started guidin' wagon trains out here. And the way the railroads are layin' track, it ain't gonna be long before folks back east can take a train out here. I'm gettin' too blame old to put up with the hardship of the trail. I've got to spend what time I've got left to helpin' you keep this ranch growin'." He reached over and poked Spud on the shoulder. "Besides, when Spud told me he was quittin' me after this next run, I figured it must be time for me to move on to homesteadin', too."

An interested listener, Ruby wondered what plans Clint Buchanan might have after he helped Clayton and Spud bring another train of hopeful settlers out to the Willamette Valley. Unlike Spud or Clayton, Clint was still a young man. She found herself hoping he would remain here with his uncles and work with the horses and cows. He was the dearest friend she had and she didn't like the thought of losing him. Finally, she asked him, "When are you leaving to go back to Independence?"

"First of February," Clint answered. "That'll be next Tuesday. Uncle Clayton wants to plan for two months to make the trip on horseback. It normally wouldn't take but about a month and a half, but this time of year, we're gonna catch a lot of snow, and we'll lose some time huntin' for food."

"That's just a week away," she replied, "the first of February. When I think of some of those mountain roads we came over on our way out here, I don't see how you could even get through some of those passes."

"On horseback, we'll be able to ride around some of those

wagon roads," he said. "We've always managed to find a way to get around some of the worst spots. Like Uncle Clayton said, though, this is our last go-round with the wagons, and I want to say goodbye to Yellow Sky and Mourning Song and Broken Wing if he's there. Then I reckon we're back here for good."

"The three of you better be careful," she cautioned. "Your Uncle Garland needs you to help him run this ranch." She paused, then slipped, "I'll miss you . . . all three of you," she quickly added.

"We'll miss you, too," he replied. There followed an awkward silence until he said he'd best get moving if he was going to get any work done on his cabin tonight. "I'm hopin' to get the inside finish on the walls before we have to head out for Independence. I'm tryin' to make it look more like a house, instead of a huntin' cabin."

"How long have you been working on that cabin?" she asked.

"This is the third year, since I first built it." He chuckled. "I thought they'd kick me outta the big house before now, but they didn't."

She laughed with him. "I'm just wondering how long it'll be before they kick me out. They've treated me so nice since you brought me home with you and Clayton, after Cal was killed. But I can't expect them to keep me forever."

"That's where you're wrong," he quickly objected. "They've accepted you like family, and they know your husband was a friend of mine. So you're stuck with us from now on. Besides, everybody in the whole family is crazy about you."

The days that followed were spent in great part on preparation for the challenging trip across the divide in the midst of wintertime. It is a trip that Garland Scofield maintains is undeniable proof that his brother and his nephew, and Spud Williams too, were certifiably insane. Clayton never tried to refute the claim, but said that, unfortunately, wagon master was one of only a few things he was good at. So his inclination had been to stay with it until he thought he couldn't do it anymore. He didn't admit the fact that he had to rely on the young eyes and skill of nephew Clint Buchanan, but it was a secret he never tried to hide from himself.

Always of concern in planning the upcoming trip was the condition of their horses. They all three had favorite horses, but a trip across the country they would be crossing in the dead of winter could tear the heart out of a good horse. So they were giving special attention to the condition of their hooves and any signs of a lack of spirit. Each man would lead a packhorse that was equal in condition to the one he rode, in case something happened to his favorite horse. Clint declared his Palouse gelding he called Biscuit in prime shape and ready to get started. Clayton made the same judgment for the dark Morgan he favored. Spud decided his dun gelding he'd ridden the past couple of years was showing signs of aging recently, so he decided he'd best not make the trip this year. He picked out a younger bay gelding with Clint's help.

"You gonna name him?" Clint asked Spud when he decided on the bay. Spud looked at him as if he didn't understand. So Clint said, "I call my horse Biscuit. Uncle Clayton calls that Morgan Blackie. What you gonna call that bay?"

"Horse," Spud answered, "same as I called the dun."

"That's a good name for a horse," Clint remarked. "Easy to remember." *I should have known better than to ask*, he thought.

The week went by in no time at all and on Tuesday morning the three travelers were saddled up, packhorses loaded as planned. Only a light snow covered the ground, but there was promise of possibly more in the clouds lying low over the valley. Looking more like Eskimos than horsemen in their heavy buffalo coats, they climbed up into the saddle and said their goodbyes to Garland and the family. Clint motioned for Ruby to come to him, and she ran tiptoeing in the thin layer of snow. "Sorry, I meant to give you this before I left the house." He handed her a key. When she seemed puzzled, he said, "It's the key to my cabin, if you ever need it for anything. I sure won't need it till I get back."

"Is there something you need to have me do? Do you want me to check on it to make sure it's all right?"

"No, nothing," he replied. "It's just in case you need it for something, maybe if you need to get away from my crazy family for some peaceful time alone. Whatever you might need it for, consider it yours."

"All right," she said, still confused. "I'll take care of it for you. You come back safe, you hear?"

"I hear and obey," he said with a grin. "See ya in the fall." And he was off after Clayton and Spud.

She stood and watched until they rode out of the front gate before turning to tiptoe back to the porch, already feeling the void created by their departure. It would be a long time before next fall. She permitted her mind to fantasize for a few moments to wonder if giving her the key to his cabin held an implied meaning. Like the giving of a ring, she thought. Surely he would have given some indication, if that was the reason behind it. *Put it out of your mind*, she warned herself. *Don't destroy a good friendship.* She knew she could not willfully put it out of her hopes and wishes, however.

Watching her from the other side of the porch, Irene Scofield imagined she could feel the young woman's emotions. She spoke softly so that only Garland standing next to her would hear. "You know, it'll be a downright shame if those two don't get married."

Garland gave her a look of surprise. "What makes you say that? They ain't give off no kinda sparks like that. Hell, they's just good friends. They told you that."

She reached up with a closed fist and tapped his forehead with her knuckles. "Men!" she huffed. "Hard as a rock."

Upon their arrival in Independence, Missouri, they checked into the Henry House Hotel where three rooms were reserved for them. It was close to suppertime by the time they parked their saddlebags and rifles in their rooms. They went straight from there to the stable where they made arrangements to leave their horses as well as their packs. Then instead of returning to the Henry House for supper, they went to a little place called Mama's Kitchen where they always ate when in Independence. It was good, solid home cooking, and was always satisfying, but Clint was convinced his Uncle Clayton insisted on eating there because they always remembered him. The woman for whom the restaurant was named was Polly Jenkins. She, of course, did the cooking. Her husband, Tom, owned the place, and their two daughters waited tables and helped in the kitchen. Clint liked to eat there because the food was all right and it was a family affair. Maybe Polly remembered his uncle after a year's absence, Clint couldn't say, but she always pretended to, and it was no different this April.

"Lookee here, Mama," Tom Jenkins sang out when they walked in. "Look who's back."

"Well, my stars," Polly responded on cue and walked out of the kitchen to greet them. "We was just talkin' about you the other day. Thought you mighta found another place to eat."

"No, indeed," Clayton said. "We just got back in Independence tonight, and this is the first place we hit. It takes half the year to lead a bunch of wagons out to the Willamette Valley, or we'da been back sooner."

"Well, we're glad to see you again," Tom said. "Mama does a lot of braggin' about how she cooks for the best wagon master in the country. We 'preciate your business. Pick you out a table and one of the girls will fix you up with some coffee."

Grinning wide with satisfaction, Clayton picked out a table and sat down. "Beats me how these folks always remember a customer, don't matter how long he's been gone. They even remembered I was a wagon master and was bragging to their other customers about me."

"Yep, that's something, all right," Clint remarked, content to let him think that, since he seemed to enjoy it so much.

Spud, on the other hand, was not of such a benevolent nature. "I swear, Clayton, them folks ain't remembered you from doodle-dee-squat. Hell, you just told 'em you was a wagon master. They're just tryin' to get you to keep comin' back. Can't blame 'em for that. Oh, you mighta looked familiar, like they'd seen you somewhere before. But it mighta been on a Wanted poster at the post office, for all they knew."

"Jealousy don't look good on you, Spud," Clayton replied.

"In less than two weeks, we'll be back on the trail," Spud said. "I'll be doin' the cookin' again and I'll try not to forget to tell you I remember you every time you set down to eat."

"Evenin', my name's Bessie. Everybody want coffee?"

"Yes, ma'am," Clint answered at once. "You came just in time. I thought I was gonna have to take a switch to my two young'uns here."

She laughed. "Actin' up, are they?"

"It's gettin' where I can't take 'em out in public no more," Clint said. "We'll all take coffee and just bring us the special, whatever it is tonight."

"Three specials," she said, but waited for a few moments in case one of his companions wanted something different or at least wanted to know what the special was. No one said anything, so she shrugged and repeated, "Three specials." Then she was off to the kitchen. She couldn't know that for days they had been living off whatever game they happened upon. And they were to the point of not caring what the special was. It was bound to be better than what they had been eating. It turned out to be pork chops, so there were no complaints.

After the supper was consumed, the conversation turned to business. Clayton said he would go to Peter Moreland's office in the morning to make all the arrangements for getting his wagon and selecting the horses to pull it. He would also pick up the money to buy the supplies they would need, so they could load the wagon. "I expect he'll have a list for me of the families who have signed up for this trip. After you get everything you're gonna need to cook with," he said to Spud, "we'll take the wagon across the river and pick a spot to circle our wagons. In the next week or so, we'll get a chance to meet the folks we're gonna be livin' with for the next five or six months."

"In other words," Spud commented, "same as last year and the year before that. I'm damned glad this is my last year in this business."

"What are you gonna do when we get back to the Willamette Valley?" Clint asked. He had never heard Spud talk about anything but driving the lead wagon and doing the cooking.

"Same thing you did, I reckon," Spud replied, "build me a cabin on that piece of ground next to your'n. I know I ain't gonna keep livin' in my tent. Maybe I can help you raise them horses you're always talkin' about, since you'll be usin' the Scofield range to raise 'em. We'll be neighbors, anyway, since I'll be right down the creek from you and Ruby."

"Me and Ruby?" Clint responded.

"I swear, Spud," Clayton interrupted. "Every thought in your head just drops right outta your mouth."

"What?" Spud replied. "Hell, ever'body knows them two young people is s'posed to get hitched. Ain't that right?"

"I reckon me and Ruby don't know it yet," Clint declared. "Are we ready to go back to the hotel now? Or are you thinkin' about stoppin' in the Gateway Saloon before you turn in for the night?" He directed his question at Clayton. "Maybe they won't remember the little ruckus you stirred up there last year."

"Well, he was cheatin', and he was so bad at it that I thought I was doin' him a favor when I told him just how bad he was at it. Then it was his idea to wanna have a shootout with me, and me so drunk by then I could hardly stand up. So I just gave him a little tap on the side of his jaw."

"And laid him out cold," Clint finished for him. "Maybe we'd best just go on back to the hotel."

# Chapter 2

After breakfast at Mama's Kitchen the next morning, they walked up the street to a small white house that served as Peter Moreland's law office. Realizing that Moreland probably didn't start his day as early as they were accustomed to, they waited until eight thirty and were told by Moreland's clerk that his boss wouldn't arrive at the office until nine. "But Mr. Moreland has been expecting you to show up any day now," Jacob Moore told them. "He said that you would probably show up a little early and that I should offer you some coffee while you wait." To Clint, it sounded as if he said it hoping they would decline the offer. To his probable disappointment, however, they accepted.

"That sounds like a good idea," Clayton said, "even though I just drank a gallon of it at Mama's Kitchen."

"Well, I didn't," Spud spoke up. "I'd appreciate a cup, young feller."

So the three of them were sitting, drinking coffee, in Moreland's waiting room when the attorney came in at a quarter after nine. "Well, Clayton Scofield," he announced when he walked in. "I see you brought your partners with you. I'm guessing this young man is your nephew, Clint Buchanan. You'll have to tell me who this other gentleman is." He reached out to shake Clint's hand.

"That'll be Spud Williams," Clayton said. "He drives my wagon and does the cookin' for the three of us. And he ain't no gentleman."

"Well, I'm pleased to meet you, Mr. Williams," Moreland said. "I see Jacob made you some coffee. I hope you haven't been waiting very long. I stopped by the post office to see if there were any late commitments to go to Oregon with you."

"How many have we got so far?" Clayton asked, since his contract with Moreland called for him to be paid by the wagon. He was most comfortable taking twenty-five to thirty wagons. That was not too many for him to handle, and it paid him enough to make a good profit after allowing for Clint and Spud. At least it had when he did all the work that Moreland was now doing for him this year.

"I've got twenty-eight confirmed with the deposit. They've signed their agreements on the wagon train rules and regulations, along with the restrictions on their wagons, and they've all gotten the suggested food and supplies list. If you want to come into my office, I'll show you the file of applicants, and I'll advance you the money for your initial expenses so you can get your wagon ready to roll. They all have agreed to arrive during the last week of March and not after April the first, or they lose their deposit."

They went inside his office then, leaving Clint and Spud to work on the coffee. Inside the office, he handed Clayton a stack of folders that contained each applicant's information. "There's already half a dozen of these wagons across the river right now, and I expect more of them will start showing up every day, if it's like it usually is." He walked over to a closet and pulled out a board. "I got a sign made up for you." He held it up for Clayton to see. It read simply, *Scofield*. "When you move your wagon across the river and find the place where you want to circle up your wagons, fix this on your wagon so you can see it. Every family knows their wagon master's name is Scofield."

"That's a good idea," Clayton said. "That woulda come in

handy last year when we had three different trains makin' up on that prairie across the river."

"You can get to know that half dozen right away and you'll practically get to know the ones who aren't here yet just by reading these folders. That's just one of the benefits you get by working with me. I know that you always handled all the arrangements for the train yourself before this year. But you had to spend half the year back here to do it. Am I right?"

"Ain't no doubt, it's a lot easier on me not havin' to line up all the people to ride with me."

"Now, when you leave here, you've got your expense advance. You can go right to J. C. Evans and Sons and pick up your wagon that's already paid for. But maybe you'd better go to the stable and pick out the team you want to pull it first." He chuckled in appreciation of his humor. "So whaddaya think, Clayton? This arrangement made it a helluva lot easier on you, right?"

"I reckon it did make it easier, but I'm takin' home less than I did last year when it was just me linin' up all the customers," Clayton said. "We'll see how we end up money-wise when the last wagon shows up and we settle."

"It'll be worth it, Clayton," Moreland insisted. "This arrangement this year added years to your life."

"Maybe so," Clayton allowed. "I'll go along now and pick up my wagon. You know where I'll be if you need me for anything." He didn't tell Moreland that this was his last trip on the Oregon Trail. He didn't think it a good idea until he got the rest of the money he had coming under their deal. He hadn't admitted it to Clint or Garland, but he must have been drunk when he agreed to let Moreland handle all the selling of the wagon train. Moreland's percentage off the top was going to leave him with a lot less money because he was still giving Clint and Spud the same as he did last year when he handled the whole thing. *Never too old to learn a new lesson*, he thought and left the office.

They went from Moreland's to the stable, where they got the horses they rode in on and then selected a team for the wagon from the corral. Once that was done, they walked all the horses over to J. C. Evans & Sons to claim Clayton's wagon. In a short time, Spud was driving the new wagon back up the street to Appleby's General Store to buy his supplies for the trip. They parked the wagon in a vacant lot behind Mama's Kitchen and tied the other horses to the wagon. Then they went inside for one last meal at Mama's before taking the ferry across the Missouri River to Kansas.

Once they picked a spot on the prairie with room for twenty-eight wagons to circle up, Scofield fixed his sign on the side of the wagon. On a good-sized board, it was easy to read the bold letters from way across the prairie. And before long one of the wagons already there hitched their horses up and drove over. A man and a woman sat in the driver's seat and three children walked along beside them. They pulled up beside Scofield's wagon. "How do?" the man called out. "I see by your sign there that you must be Clayton Scofield, the fellow who's gonna lead us to the Willamette Valley."

"I've gotta plead guilty, I reckon," Scofield responded. "Who have I got the pleasure of meetin'?"

"We're Tracy and Ada Bishop from Springfield." He climbed down from the wagon, then helped his wife down. Scofield shook hands with both of them and welcomed them to the train. "This is Tim, Lucy, and Bo," Tracy said.

"I'm proud to meet you all," Scofield said, "and welcome to the Oregon Express. Those two fellows you see down there by the water with the horses will be leading the way with me. The young fellow is Clint Buchanan. He's the guide and he ain't never led me wrong in the three years he's worked with me. The other fellow is Spud Williams. He drives my wagon and cooks for me and Clint. You'll get to know both of 'em pretty well before we get very far up the road."

"I'm a little worried about having enough supplies," Tracy said. "We got here so early we're eating up a lot of food just sitting here waiting for everybody else to show up. How long will it take us to reach Fort Laramie? I understand that's the place to re-stock on anything you're short of."

"Well, I can't predict what weather and whatnot we might run into between here and there," Scofield answered. "So I always figure close to two months. Then if we get good weather and no problems, we'll make it in a month and a half. But if you're really runnin' low, you can buy what you need at Fort Kearny. That's about half the distance to Fort Laramie, and we'll be staying overnight there. The government sets the prices on food stocks at Fort Kearny, so settlers like you don't get overcharged."

"I declare, that makes me feel a lot better," Tracy said. "Did you hear that, Ada?"

"I did," she replied. "I know we'd have run short of flour and coffee before we got to Fort Laramie."

"So, are you gonna have the wagons form a circle right here?" Tracy asked.

"That's right," Scofield replied. "We'll do that at the end of every day's travel. Spud will park this wagon facin' the direction we'll start out the next mornin'. And I'll point the wagon tongue in the direction of the north star, so you can always know which way's north the next mornin'. We'll change the order of travel in the train, so that nobody gets a face full of dust every day. If you want to, you can go ahead and park your wagon behind mine. I see another wagon headin' this way. He can park behind you." Tracy said he would do that and climbed back up in his wagon. While he was moving it into position behind him, Scofield was thinking that sign Moreland painted for him was a good idea, but maybe not worth the money it cost him. *Maybe one of us, me or Clint, would have thought of it*, he thought, although they hadn't in the years prior to this.

He went through the same welcoming with Will and Angel Tucker then. They looked to be a younger couple than the Bish-ops. They had two children, but they were younger, a boy, Billy, who was three, and the youngest a baby girl, still on her mother's breast. The Tuckers not only met the wagon master but they got acquainted with the Bishops as well. Scofield went through the same routine every day after that as more of the contracted families showed up. Everybody got acquainted and were soon socializing every evening after supper, waiting for that final starting day. It wasn't long before the musicians showed up, Henry Abbott with his fiddle, Lucien Aiken with a guitar. It was a disappointment for Spud, but he was contented again on the final day before the starting day when Tiny Futch showed up with a banjo. Spud was partial to the banjo, said it lifted his spirits.

With only one day left before the deadline, the last wagon rolled in. Like Scofield's wagon, it was brand-new and fitted out for the trail by J. C. Evans & Sons. It was driven by a brute of a man named Roy Leach. But it was owned by Bass Thornton, a man who looked to be in his mid-forties. He was accompanied by his wife, Violet, who appeared to be half his age and there were no children. Far in appearance from the typical settler, Bass Thornton was not on his way to Oregon to build a farm. That much was easy to assume, and when Scofield shook his hand, the softness of it confirmed his assumption. And wife Violet's dress seemed more suited to a dancehall or saloon. "But this ain't the Mormon wagon train," Scofield told Clint and Spud. "It ain't up to me to say we don't need saloons and dancehalls and such in the Oregon country. My partner, Moreland, approved him and took his money, so I reckon he's all right."

"Hell, why wouldn't he be?" Spud piped up. "Maybe he's figurin' on buildin' a saloon out there, and Lord knows we need 'em."

As for Bass Thornton, however, he seemed friendly enough, and he and Violet made sure they joined the after-supper get-together with their fellow travelers. It being the final night before starting out for Oregon, Scofield made it a point to call everybody's attention to the start of what was to be their daily routine for the coming months. "I've already told all of you what the daily schedule will be, but for the benefit of our newest arrivals, Bass and Violet Thornton, and their driver, Roy Leach, I'll go over it again. Four o'clock tomorrow mornin' you'll hear my bugle announcin' time to get up. That'll give you time to get up and get your cows if you've let 'em graze. So by five thirty, the women oughta be up and fixin' breakfast 'cause we'll be pullin' outta here at seven. That oughta give you enough time to pack up all your beddin' and such. Like I said, I'll blow my bugle at four o'clock in the mornin', but don't be expecting no fancy bugle calls like the soldiers get. Last year on that first mornin', I got some complaints on my talent with a bugle. I'm just warnin' you. So go back to your dancin'. Just remember four o'clock comes pretty early in the mornin'."

Evidently, Scofield's reminder of the importance of keeping on schedule the night before was taken to heart by all the wagons because everyone was in place and ready when an excruciating blast from the bugle sounded at seven o'clock the next morning. Once again, Clayton, Clint, and Spud began the first mile of a long, hard journey to test the strength and fortitude of the people and horses under their care and supervision. For the twenty-eight families that trusted them for their safe deliverance, it was the start of a new life and maybe a chance for a start-over for one that hadn't worked out so far.

Clint rode out ahead of the wagons for no other purpose than to make sure there were no recent obstacles in the trail that weren't there before. Other than that, there was little need for a scout on the obvious trail to the Kansas River crossing. Back with the wagons, Scofield rode his dark Morgan gelding up and down the line to keep it closed up and offer encouragement where it was needed. They would only travel about six days before undergoing their first river crossing where the trail crossed the Kansas River. This was time enough to become used to the daily routine. It took only a day or two of the constantly rough, bumpy ride in the wagon boxes for passengers to prefer walking over riding. So, for the most part, the children and most of the women seemed destined to walk to Oregon. The springs under the driver's seat took some of the roughness out of the ride, so some of the wives rode beside their husbands much of the way, occasionally leaving the wagon to walk with the children.

The one exception to this was Bass Thornton. He remained in the driver's seat beside his driver, Roy Leach. Violet, his young wife, walked cheerfully along with the children of the other families, seeming to have more in common with them than she did with their parents. It was quite natural that Bass Thornton quickly became the mystery of the wagon train. He was just out of place, to say the least, so there was much speculation about him in the smaller conversations at evening time when the music cranked up. Even more mysterious was Bass Thornton's man, Leach. As far as anyone could tell, he might be a mute, for no one ever heard him say a word. He was a powerfully built man whose hairless face wore no expression and his short-sheared hair on the top of his head gave it a flat appearance. Will Tucker whispered to his wife that Thornton kept him clean-shaven to keep everybody from discovering that Leach was actually an ape. Angel giggled and suggested that they should watch when they stopped for the night to see if Thornton took a cage out of the wagon for Leach to sleep in. They were disappointed when they made camp to see Leach unroll his bedroll under the wagon while Thornton and Violet retired to their tent.

Scofield was satisfied that everyone's attitude seemed lighthearted and confident, but that was fairly common the first few days. Their confidence would be tested soon enough, however, when they reached the Kansas River, and their first river crossing. On the day before they expected to arrive at the river, the crossing was naturally the topic of discussion at the social hour after supper that night. Since the creek they stopped to camp by that night offered plenty of wood for fires, they built one big fire in the middle of the circle and the folks gathered in small groups to sit near it. Tiny Futch tuned up his banjo and started picking out a few tunes, which was enough to entice Henry Abbott to bring his fiddle from his wagon. Wilma Aiken prodded her husband to get his guitar, and before long the dancing started. Scofield looked at Clint and commented, "I swear, every year it's just like the year before, ain't it?"

"Yep, I reckon it is," Clint answered. "I don't know what we woulda done to entertain 'em if the musicians hadn't showed up."

The folks who were not dancing were at least nodding in time with the music as they sat on a blanket on the ground, not really concerned with what the children were up to. Before long, however, someone brought up the river crossing the next day. Ada Bishop started the discussion with a question. "Do you think those wagons will really float? I don't see how they can. You think we're going to have to unload it before it'll float?"

"If you do, how you gonna get everything you unloaded across?" Levi Watkins asked. He let Ada think about that for a second, then said, "Heck, no, we ain't gonna unload 'em. They'll float loaded just like they are."

"I hope you're right," Tracy Bishop commented. "I was told my wagon would weigh fifteen hundred to two thousand pounds loaded like it is. That's a heck of a lotta weight. If it starts sinking, I might have to throw Ada in the river to lighten the load."

"That'ud save you fifty pounds right there," Levi joked and dodged to avoid the little stick of wood the tiny woman threw at him.

"Mind if we join you?" They looked up to see Bass Thornton and his wife standing behind them.

"Glad to have you," Levi replied at once. "Move over this way, Ella," he told his wife, "and they can set down there." Ella made a place for them.

"Did you bring something to sit on?" Annie Futch asked as she moved over on the other side of the space. "Here, I'll unfold this blanket and you can sit on it."

"That's mighty kind of you," Thornton said. "We should have thought about that, shouldn't we have, Violet?" Violet didn't say anything but smiled and nodded her head in response.

Ella could see that the young woman was uncomfortable with

the situation, so she patted the blanket and motioned for her to sit down, as she would have for a child. "Here, sit down beside me where you can feel the fire a little bit." Violet smiled at her and nodded again as she sat down, although looking back at her husband as if for permission.

"Violet and I don't get the chance to get out and socialize very much," Thornton said. "We got here late, so we haven't gotten around to meeting everybody yet."

"Well, you've just met the most important people on the train right here," Tracy joked. "So you don't have to waste any more time meeting the rest of them."

"Please ignore him," Ada said. "We're glad to have you join us. Where are you folks from?"

"Indianapolis," Thornton replied. "At least we had a farm near there." He quickly changed the subject then. "I couldn't help hearing your questions, ma'am, when we walked up. And I can tell you for certain that these wagons will float, loaded as they are. Did Mr. Scofield give you some wax like he offered me?" She and Tracy both nodded. "Then it would be a good idea to use it on any cracks you might have in your wagon box. It'll help keep the water out."

"Please call me Ada," she responded. "Yes, he did give all of us some wax, but I don't think Tracy put any of it on our wagon."

"I was gonna put it on before we got started in the mornin'," Tracy claimed. She gave him a look and shook her head, knowing he was lying. "Sounds like you've made a river crossin' before with a wagon, Mr. Thornton."

"Please just call me Bass," Thornton replied. "No, this will be my first river crossing with a loaded wagon, too. I said what I did because I've dabbled a little bit with flatboats and barges in the past, so I've seen small flatboats carry some pretty heavy loads. But I have heard of some large wagons with really heavy loads that had to have a couple of tree trunks tied to them before they could be floated across. At any rate, I'm sure Mr. Scofield will get us across the river safely. He has an excellent reputation."

His comments served to reassure the small group of folks around him and lessened the worry of the women who were concerned about driving their wagons with all their possessions out in the middle of the river. Will Tucker decided that maybe there wasn't really anything mysterious about Bass Thornton, after all. So he asked, "Who's the fellow that drives your wagon? Is he kin? He don't mingle very much, does he?"

Thornton gave him a patient smile, then answered. "His name's Roy Leach. No, Leach is no kin of mine. He's just a man who wants to go west and he didn't have the money to buy a wagon and supply it. So I let him go with Violet and me as our driver and hired hand. He's not the kind to mingle very much, just likes to keep to himself." They didn't linger long after that, even though the music and the dancers were still going strong. "Well, tomorrow's a big day," Thornton said. "I think Violet and I will turn in early so we'll be ready when Scofield blows on that horn of his."

"I can see why," Levi whispered to Tracy, as Thornton extended a hand and helped the young woman to her feet. Ella reached over and hit Levi on his shoulder while he and Tracy snickered. When they had left, Levi remarked that maybe Leach and Violet were both mutes. "You know, she never opened her mouth to say a blame word. Maybe they're deaf and dumb."

"You'd best watch what you say, Levi Watkins," Ella warned him. "You're liable to get struck down by lightning one of these days. Then what am I going to tell the kids when they ask me why their daddy had to get hit by lightning when there wasn't no storm anywhere?"

"Tell 'em the Lord needed some help, so he sent for me," Levi said. Ella hit him on the shoulder again.

Seeing young Will Tucker grinning at them, Ella asked, "Where's that pretty young wife of yours? Why isn't she out here listening to the music?"

"She's in the wagon, feedin' the baby," Will answered.

"Well, she shoulda come on out with the rest of the folks," Ella said. "She coulda fed the baby out here. What's the baby's name?"

"We're still decidin' on her name. Angel can't feed her out here with all you folks, 'cause she's still feedin' her, herself."

Ella didn't understand at first and started to offer her help, but then she realized what he was saying. "Ohh," she said. "You mean her baby's so young she ain't on the bottle yet."

"Yes, ma'am," Will said. "So she stayed in the wagon, and I reckon I'd best get back to the wagon, too. She might be needin' me for something." He got up then and said goodnight to the little group he had been sitting with.

"Tell Angel we missed having her visit," Ella called after him. Then to Ada Bishop, she said, "That little wife of his just had that baby. Heck, she could have nursed her out here and just thrown a blanket over her shoulder. Nobody woulda thought nothing of it." Then she turned her attention to Wiley and Maggie Jones, another young couple who were sitting close by but not really participating in the conversation. "What about you two? I haven't seen any children around your wagon, either. Are you like Will and Angel, just getting ready to start your family?"

Wiley and Maggie looked at each other as if they suddenly smelled something unpleasant. "I reckon we ain't thought much about it," Wiley said. "We're mostly just thinkin' about gittin' ourselves out to the Oregon country."

"Well, I guess you're young enough to take your time thinking about a family," Ella said.

# Chapter 3

They had traveled almost fifteen miles the day before, due to excellent weather and good condition of the road. Scofield thought it was especially good considering how little experience his greenhorn travelers had. As a result of that good day's travel, they were going to strike the Kansas River earlier in the day, in fact, only an hour and a half past the nooning. So instead of camping on the south bank that night as he had originally planned, and crossing in the morning, he decided to cross that afternoon and camp on the north bank that night. Clint had already ridden out ahead of the train to scout the site of the crossing. He found the site in much the same condition as it had been the year before. He had scouted up and down the river two years before that to see if there was a place any better than the commonly used one. And he found at that time that there was no better section of the river than the one he was looking at now. The slope of the banks, both entering the river and leaving it on the other side, was not steep, this in spite of the deepest water running closer to the far side. The only difference from last year's crossing was a shift downstream about thirty-five yards, according to the many tracks left behind by others. Clint felt reasonably certain that his uncle's wagon train the year before was responsible for the new entry point. He remembered the trouble they had encountered when a partial collapse of the bank under the water occurred after most of the wagons had crossed over. It had left a wider channel and a soft bottom that made it harder to pull the wagons up on the other side. He wanted to avoid any possibility of that on this trip.

To make certain that he gave his uncle an accurate report, he rode Biscuit down the slope to the water's edge, judging the firmness of the slope. He rode the Palouse gelding slowly into the water and halted him after he'd gone about four yards out into the shallow water. Then he just sat there for a few minutes to test Biscuit's reactions. The horse remained perfectly still and started drinking the water. Clint noted that Biscuit showed no indication that the river bottom was soft or yielding under his hooves. So Clint gave him a touch of his heels and started the horse to the other side. Making note of the point where the horse started swimming, he estimated the distance to the point where Biscuit's hooves were back on the bottom. In his mind, he saw it as a little longer than the typical wagon box, by a couple of yards possibly. *Hasn't changed much from last year*, he thought and climbed out of the water and up the other bank. "Shouldn't be any trouble a-tall," he told the Palouse. So he turned the horse around, entered the water again, and crossed back over. With wet buckskins from the seat of his pants to his moccasins, he rode back to intercept the wagons.

"Yonder's Clint," Spud said to Scofield, who was riding beside the wagon. When Scofield turned to look, he started to ride out to meet him but changed his mind and just kept pace with the wagon. He figured he might as well wait and let Clint come to them, so Spud could hear what he had found at the crossing. He would be the one driving the first wagon across. "How's it look, Clint?" Spud asked when Clint wheeled his horse around and rode along beside Scofield.

"Looks like everybody's been crossin' in that same section of the river as before. There's just a slight change." He went on to tell them about the shift of the entry point and that served to revive the episode of the prior year. "I checked both sides of the river, and everything seemed solid under Biscuit's hooves. The deepest part still ain't but about twelve feet across. That's about how far Biscuit had to swim before he struck bottom again. So, I don't see any reason why we can't make a trouble-free crossin' this afternoon. We oughta have time before supper."

"Good," Scofield said, "then that's what we'll do." So Scofield and Clint rode back along the column to prepare everyone for the crossing.

Upon arriving at the river, everyone began preparing their wagons for the trip across, removing any objects that were not secure on the sides or the backs of them. All children had to be accounted for and safely on board. Scofield recruited a team of volunteers led by Tiny Futch and Levi Watkins to take a team of horses across to be used in the event a wagon had difficulty pulling out of the water. Spud drove Scofield's wagon across first to demonstrate how smoothly it could be done. As Scofield and Clint expected, Spud had very little trouble, and his horses were able to pull the wagon out without requiring help from the extra team Tiny and Levi brought over. Lucien Aikin was first in line and he confidently drove his horses into the water. But he promptly drew some concern from the anxious onlookers when his wagon swayed as it struck the current in the middle of the channel. Thinking his wagon was going to overturn, he frantically began whipping his horses to pull him out. It caused the horses to rear up in confusion until their hooves struck bottom once again. Tiny Futch waded out to take hold of the bridle on one of the horses and led the team at an angle to counteract the uncooperative wagon. It caused the wagon to straighten out and the horses pulled it up on the bank. After that, a couple of the heftier volunteers went into the water to help hold the wagons that came after his against the current.

One by one, the wagons followed, and there were no real problems until the middle of the line when Bass Thornton's wagon started across. As it entered the water, those in line behind him noticed his wheels sank a little deeper into the bank of the river. It caused Henry Abbott to wonder aloud, "What in the world has he got loaded in that wagon?" Thornton's man, Leach, drove the horses aggressively toward the deep part of the river, intent upon building momentum evidently. It worked to a point, for the wagon had less time to sink than the other wagons driven at a slower pace before the horses found traction again. But then, the left rear wheel either found a hole or made one, bringing the swaying wagon to a halt. Leach flailed the horses with the reins, but the wagon wouldn't budge. So he handed the reins to Thornton and jumped off the wagon and went to the back of the wagon, where he disappeared under the water. After what seemed a long time, the left rear corner of the wagon began to rise a few inches at a time until, finally, the wagon became level again. Tiny took hold of the bridle and pulled the team forward, and they pulled the wagon out of the river. Like a huge sea creature, Leach came up out of the water and walked up the shore after the wagon. "Damn," was the only word uttered by someone in the group of onlookers awaiting their turn. It only added to the mystery already growing around Leach.

Tracy Bishop was next, and he was directed by Scofield to enter the river farther downstream so as to avoid the hole left by Thornton's wagon. Expecting the worst, Bishop drove his team into the water where Scofield indicated. And much to his surprise, he made the crossing without a speck of trouble. The next few wagons followed Bishop's example and crossed without a hitch until it was young Will Tucker's turn.

Just like those before him, Will popped the reins over his horses' rumps and drove them forward into the water. Beside him on the wagon seat, Angel clutched her baby girl close to her breast. "I don't like this," she muttered to Will. "We should never have left my father's home. He would be angry if he saw what we are doing here."

"Don't worry yourself about this little river, honey." Will tried to calm her. "We're gonna be fine." He had the immediate concern for getting their wagon safely to the other side, and he really wished she would pick another time to bemoan her leaving Daddy's house. He had tried to make a decent living in Columbia, Missouri, as a lamp maker, a trade his father taught him. He tried for three years without success before finally persuading Angel their best chance was in the new country in Oregon, where he would be among the first in his trade. The trip in the wagon from Columbia to Independence, however, was more a shock to her than she had anticipated. Giving birth to a baby on the way made it so much worse. They had planned to get to Independence before the baby came, but the child came early. She bewailed the fact that she had given birth to her daughter like an Indian squaw by the side of the trail, when actually, they had been fortunate to find the services of a midwife at a trading post. Although she was unhappy, she didn't begin predicting their certain misfortune if they didn't turn around and go home, until they crossed the Missouri. "Maybe you and the baby would be better if you got back in the wagon, so you wouldn't see the horses swimmin'," he finally suggested.

"Not as comfortable as I'd be if you could turn this cursed wagon around and take us home," she said, but she got up off the seat.

"Be careful," he warned when he saw that she was going to get in the back of the wagon. "I'd hold the baby while you do that, but I've got my hands full with these horses."

"I can hold my baby," she said, clutching the baby tight against her breast while she held on to the wagon seat with the other hand to steady herself against the rocking motion of the wagon when it was hit by the current. When she started to step over into the back of the wagon, it dipped when it suddenly started floating, catching her with one foot in the air and off balance. In her efforts to grab on to something to stay upright, she began to fall over backward. Will dropped the reins and tried to grab her, but it was too late. She screamed as her baby slipped out of her arms and dropped into the river with Angel following right on top of her.

In a panic, Will dived into the river after them, leaving three-year-old Billy in the wagon alone. The horses stopped where they were, their feet on solid bottom, but the wagon was still floating and being pulled by the current. Deep under the dark water, Will found Angel flailing about wildly, looking for her baby, but there was no sign of the baby. When he could hold his breath no longer, he pulled at her to come up, but she fought his efforts. Totally out of breath, he rose to the surface and gulped for air. Then he held his breath again and, determined to pull her up regardless, he went back under to find her motionless, gradually moving along with the current. Horrified, he caught her and pulled her up to the surface.

Only then aware of the trauma taking place, the people on both sides of the river responded to the emergency. Men from both banks plunged into the river to swim to the stricken couple. Clint, on horseback, rode out into the river to Will's horses, grabbed one of the team's bridles and led them toward the bank. Tiny came out to help and between them they managed to get the wagon out of the water and up on the riverbank. "There!" Someone on the opposite side shouted and pointed at a small object floating slowly down the river. Clint looked where he was pointing and realized it was the baby. He immediately turned Biscuit and went down the river at a lope to head the infant off. Riding out into the water again, he stopped just before the bottom fell away to the deep part. Then he waited until the baby was almost there before he signaled Biscuit forward and caught the baby as it floated to him. One look told him she was dead, but he turned his horse around and returned to the side of the river where they had taken Will and Angel. Once out of the water, he took a closer look at the infant to see if there was any possibility she could be alive. He pressed an ear to the baby's chest to listen for a heartbeat. All he heard was the gurgling sound of the little one's lungs full of water. He was at once struck with the tragedy, absolutely unexpected on this, one of the simple river crossings these people would face on their journey. With the baby in one arm, he rode back up the river expecting to find the mother dead as well.

When he got back to the others, he found that Ada Bishop and Ella Watkins, having already unofficially claimed the roles as senior mother figures for the whole company, had taken charge. Angel was lying on a blanket on the ground and Ada and Ella were taking turns trying to start her heart pumping again. Will was sitting on the ground close by, his arms wrapped around his legs, his head down on his knees. When someone said Clint was back, Ada went to meet him. "Did you get the baby?" she asked.

"Yes, ma'am," Clint answered, "but she's gone. Her little ol' lungs are full of water."

Ada took the infant from him to see for herself. Like he had, she listened for a heartbeat and pressed the tiny breast below her ribs, forcing some water out. "You're right," she said, "she's gone." She turned then when Ella called.

"She's coughin' up water!" Ella exclaimed. "She's gonna make it!" Will scrambled over on his hands and knees when he heard Ella. When Ada rushed back to her, Ella looked up and saw that she was holding the baby. "You got the baby," she said, but Ada quickly shook her head and Ella understood. "We need to give her a little time to come back from wherever she's been," Ella said to everybody standing around them, but more directly to Will. "You keep holding her hand. I think she needs to feel somebody that ain't pushing on her like Ada and me. Don't worry about Billy. One of the other ladies got him out of the wagon and she's watching him."

Will was in the midst of expressing his heartfelt thanks to the two women when Angel suddenly opened her eyes and looked up at the circle of faces looking down at her. "My baby," she uttered.

Still holding her hand, Will said, "You're gonna be all right,

Angel. You was in a bad way for a while there, but you're gonna be all right."

She jerked her hand out of his and demanded, "My baby!"

He looked up at Ada, who was still holding the dead infant, but Ada said, "You need to rest a little bit first, honey. Let us get you into some dry clothes and maybe make some coffee for you. You need to save your strength."

"I want to see my baby!" Angel demanded. "Give me my baby, you old hag!"

"Angel, honey," Will confessed, "the baby's gone. You gotta let her go." He looked up apologetically at Ada for his wife's outburst.

"What do you mean, she's gone?" Angel demanded. "I see her holding my baby right there in her arms!" She began to try to get up. "That's my baby." Will held her down, but she still struggled against him.

"Here," Ada said. "Here's your baby." She put the infant down on the blanket next to Angel and she took it at once and held it tightly up against her breast.

"You're just cold, poor little dumplin'," Angel cooed. "Let Mommy warm you." Will looked at her, then up at Ada helplessly. "I know what you need," Angel declared. "I bet you're hungry." She pulled her wet blouse apart and placed the dead infant on her breast, causing Will to quickly fold one side of the blanket over her. Ella and Ada immediately shooed all the male spectators away.

"Will," Ella said, "we need to take her to your wagon and get her out of those wet clothes. We'll help you get her there. She just has to rest and get her mind straight again. It's a wonder she ain't dead, anybody stay underwater as long as she did. When she comes to and realizes that baby is dead, we can have a ceremony for the child and bury it."

"I don't know how I'll ever thank you for your kindness," Will told her. "I feel so bad about how she talked to you and Miz Bishop. I don't know what brung her to talk like that."

"Don't you give it a thought," Ada said. "She's just outta her head right now. She don't know what she's saying. She just needs to rest up. When you get your wagon placed for supper and get your tent set up, you can put her to bed, and tomorrow mornin' she won't remember a thing about what she said."

"I sure hope you're right," Will said.

Meanwhile, in spite of the traumatic mishap, it was Scofield's responsibility to make sure the few remaining wagons all crossed over the river and the line of march was established for the next day. So Will carried Angel, still holding her baby to her breast, to their wagon, which Tiny Futch had driven into position for him. He quickly set up their small sleeping tent and got their bedrolls and blanket from the wagon. Then the two women persuaded Angel to put the baby down long enough to get her out of her wet clothes and into her nightgown. While they did that, he got the tiny baby crib out of the wagon. The women hung the clothes up to dry before they left to take care of their families. "You can send Billy over to our wagon for supper, if you want to," Ada said as she was leaving.

"Thank you again," Will told her, "but I oughta be able to cook us up enough to keep the sides of our bellies from rubbin' against each other."

Meanwhile, Clint helped Scofield get the last of the wagons in camp and the Kansas River crossing was completed in time for the usual five o'clock supper. The events of the day supplied plenty of fuel for conversation around the campfires that night. And out of respect for Will and Angel, the musicians and the dancers took the night off.

Will built a fire for Billy to sit by and eat some crackers to hold him until he could cook something for them. "Is Mama sick?" Billy asked as Will opened a jar of preserves to put on his crackers.

"She just had a bad time of it when she fell in the river," Will told him. "She just needs to rest up. I'm gonna see if I can get her to go to bed. Then I'll fry us up some bacon and hardtack. All right?" Billy said it was.

When Will went into the tent, he found Angel standing there staring at him as if seeing him for the first time. "What do you want?" she asked him.

"I'm gonna fix Billy something to eat, but I wanted to make sure you're all right first. Let's put the baby in her little crib while you crawl into bed."

"She fell in the river," Angel said, "and she wants me to hold her."

Feeling exasperated by her insistence to deny the truth, he nevertheless tried not to upset her. "I know she does," he said. "But I think she would like for you to get some rest." She looked as though she might be considering that, so he said, "I'll put her in her crib for you." She let him take the baby. He put the infant down very gently, then made a show of pulling her baby blanket up around her. "How's that?" he asked, and she nodded. Then she stood there while he straightened out her bedroll, watching his every move. "I need to get outta these wet things of mine, too," he said then and started unbuttoning his shirt.

"No!" She blurted so forcefully that he stopped at once.

"Angel, I'm your husband. Don't you know me?"

"I know you," she stated accusingly.

"I just wanna get into some dry clothes," he pleaded. "Then I'll get outta here, all right?"

"Get out of here now!" she demanded. "You're scaring my baby!"

In total frustration at this point, he couldn't resist saying, "Ain't nothin' liable to scare that baby now. You go to bed and get some sleep." He decided there was nothing he could do with her in the state of mind she was in, so he left her to crawl into her bed while he got some dry clothes from the wagon.

In a dry shirt and trousers then, he got out the frying pan, took the butcher knife and sliced some bacon off to fry. He served that up to Billy and himself, then fried the hardtack in the grease. It wasn't as good as a regular meal like Angel would have fixed, but it would keep them from starving. At least the coffee was as good as usual, and that was because he usually made that, anyway. And maybe Angel would be back in her right mind tomorrow.

While he and Billy were eating, Henry Abbott walked by their wagon. He was on guard duty that night and he stopped to ask about Angel. Will told him she was still a little mixed up and shaky, and he had put her to bed. "Too bad about the baby," Henry said. "That was a terrible thing to happen."

"Yes, it was," Will replied, "and right now, she don't wanna let the baby go. I'm hopin' she'll let me bury it in the mornin' when she's thinkin' right again. Least, I got it outta her arms. She let me put it in the crib."

"Well, I hope she has a good night, and you do, too," Henry said, then nodded toward Billy, who was still chewing on a tough strip of bacon. "Looks like the boy is doin' all right."

"He's like me, I reckon," Will replied, "a little shook up by the whole thing, but everything will be better in the mornin'." Henry nodded in agreement, then walked away to continue his rounds as night guard.

After a little while, Will decided he'd look in on Angel to see if she was sleeping soundly. Being as quiet as he could, he pulled the tent flap aside just far enough to permit him to see her bedroll on the opposite side of the tiny tent. The bedroll was empty. Surely he would have seen her if she had come out of the tent, he thought, so he bent over and pushed on through the entrance of the tent. She was not there! He started to turn around but was startled by her voice behind him. "Something's wrong with my baby. She won't take my milk." He looked behind him to discover her sitting in a front corner of the tent, holding the dead infant up tight against her.

"Angel, honey," he pleaded. "You've got to accept it. Our baby is gone. She's been called back to heaven. You have to let her go."

"No, she's not gone!" Angel insisted.

"Angel," he said bluntly, thinking he had to force her to think rationally. "The baby's dead! Look at her! She's stone cold dead!

I'm gonna bury her in the mornin' before we start out again." She glared at him as if he was the cruelest man on earth, but he knew he had to stop her illusion somehow. "Give her to me," he said and reached out and took the baby. She reluctantly released it. "I'll let her sleep right here in her crib, and tomorrow we'll give her a decent burial. All right?"

She took a few seconds to think about it before she finally asked, "Where's Billy?"

"He's out there settin' by the fire. He didn't wanna bother you while you was restin'."

"Can he come in to see me?" she asked suspiciously.

"Well, of course he can come in to see you, Angel. He's your son and he's been worried about you. I'll tell him you wanna see him and I'll fix you something to eat while you're visitin' with him if you want me to." He went out of the tent and told Billy his mother was asking for him, so Billy ran to the little tent at once. Will stood by the flap for a few seconds to watch Angel embrace her son. The sight gave him hope. He felt that his wife was finally returning to reality. Eager to encourage the progress the sight of her son seemed to generate, Will hustled to the fire to get some more meat and hardtack frying. *Wish I had something a little better ready to cook*, he thought, *but this'll have to do*. It was a terrible tragedy, the loss of the baby. But the loss of his wife was something he wasn't sure he could have survived. Maybe they would have more babies when they reached the Willamette Valley. That thought was still in his head when he heard the gunshot. He was startled because it sounded like it was right behind him. Indians? Were they under attack? His next thought was his wife and child, so he dropped the frying pan and ran to the tent. His shotgun was in the wagon and he didn't know if he should get that first but decided to make sure Angel and Billy were all right. So he ran to the tent. When he threw the flap back he was stopped cold, stunned by the sight of his son lying on the ground, his chest torn apart. The small lantern hanging from the center pole offered enough light to reveal his dead baby daughter's body that had been placed under Billy's arm. Reeling then with the magnitude of the horrible scene, he turned to see his wife, holding the barrel of his shotgun under her chin. He took two staggering steps toward her before she calmly said, "Goodbye, Will," and pushed the trigger with her toe.

# Chapter 4

The first shot was enough to alert the whole camp. Not sure where it had come from, Clint and Scofield split up and ran along opposite sides of the circle of wagons, all of which were alert as well. When the second shot was fired, Lucien Aiken, whose wagon was parked behind Will's, yelled, "Here! It's Tucker's!"

Clint was the closest and it was his lot to be the first to arrive at the gruesome scene inside the little sleeping tent of the Tucker family. Thinking them all dead at first, for Will was lying unconscious just inside the tent flap, Clint was stopped cold, unable to think for a moment. And then Will, lying at his feet, began to stir, so Clint immediately dropped on one knee beside him. "Are you shot? How bad are you hurt?"

"No, I ain't shot," Will stuttered. "I reckon I musta passed out when I saw 'em like that." He tried to get up, but his legs refused to support him, so he sat back down. "I heard the shot when she killed Billy and I saw her put my shotgun under her chin." He suddenly got sick. "I gotta get outta here." Without waiting for help from Clint, he crawled out of the tent and heaved the contents of his stomach out on the ground behind the wagon as Scofield and people from the other wagons came running.

One look told Clint there was nothing he could do for the victims, so he turned around and went outside to stand before the entrance flap of the tent as the others arrived. Scofield pushed his way through the small crowd already gathered, some of them trying to ask Will what happened. "That ain't a pretty sight in there," Clint told Scofield. "I reckon she went completely outta her mind."

Scofield nodded solemnly, ducked his head and went into the small tent. He came back out after a short time. "I swear," he bemoaned, "she took the boy with her, too. What a mess. Where's Will?" He hadn't seen Will when he ran up, since there was a small gathering of people around him, and he was still sitting on the ground.

"He's over there," Clint said and pointed to the small gathering around Will. "He got sick when he saw it and he had to get outta there."

Other folks were gathering now, even women and children, and they started pressing for information. "Like Clint said," Scofield announced, "that ain't a pretty sight inside that tent. Mrs. Tucker and her son, Billy, are both dead—two shotgun blasts. And it's the kind of picture a young'un could see in their dreams for a helluva long time. So make sure don't none of your young'uns try to sneak in there to take a look. If there's any of you adults with a strong stomach feel like givin' us a hand, we could use some help gettin' the bodies ready for burial. And we'll need some volunteers with shovels to dig a grave in the mornin'." He turned back to Clint then and asked, "You have any reason to believe Will shot 'em?"

"I don't think he did," Clint answered. "When I went in there, I almost tripped over him. He was passed out just inside the tent. I think he was cookin' something for them to eat when he heard the shot. When he came to inside that tent, he couldn't stand lookin' at 'em. Made him so sick he crawled outside and puked. Besides that, did you look at the way she was shot? She held that shotgun up under her chin and blew the top of her head off. She was still holdin' on to the barrel of that shotgun when she was layin' on her back."

"I reckon you're right," Scofield said. Then Lucien Aiken yelled to say that he had pulled Will's frying pan out of the fire with some burnt-up bacon in it. So Scofield looked back at Clint and said, "That sounds like he was surprised by the shots, all right." He went to talk to Will then. As soon as he and Clint left, the more curious of the spectators took turns sticking their heads inside the tent to get a look at the grisly scene. Some came away wishing they hadn't looked.

For a little while, Scofield thought he was going to have another lunatic on his hands when he started talking to Will. At first, Will could barely hold his head up to talk, but he eventually made an effort to face the facts that were obvious to everyone else. He confessed then that Angel had decided she didn't want to go to Oregon. She wanted to go home. He really thought that she loved him and would be happy with him wherever they ended up. That's why it struck him so hard when she preferred death rather than continuing on with him. And she took the children with her in her sick mental condition. "Looks to me like that was her test," Scofield said. "Now, I reckon this is your test from this point on. I think you ain't got no choice but to do the best you can and go on out to Oregon to set up your lamp-makin' business."

"I reckon you're right," Will admitted. "I ain't got nothin' to go back to. I'll get Angel and Billy ready to bury."

"I think you're gonna need some help with that," Clint said. "I don't think you wanna remember Angel and Billy like they are right now. It'd be better if somebody else got them ready."

"Clint's right," Scofield said. "I'll ask for some volunteers from the women to take care of Angel and Billy. Ada Bishop and Ella Watkins come to mind right away."

"I truly would appreciate that," Will said. "I don't know if I could stand to look at Angel and Billy like that again."

"It's my responsibility to keep this wagon train on schedule, so we don't get caught in the Blue Mountains by the first snowfall," Scofield advised. "So I'll be blowin' my bugle at four o'clock in the mornin' as usual. We'll take the time to bury your family, but then we'll be on our way. So you'll be ready to roll. Right?"

"Yessir," Will replied. "I'll start diggin' a grave tonight."

"I'll help you with that," Clint volunteered.

"I'm obliged," Will said.

"I expect there'll be other volunteers," Scofield remarked.

As Clint and his uncle expected, Ada and Ella were quick to volunteer to clean Angel and Billy up as best they could for their burial. There wasn't much to do for the baby except to clean some of Billy's blood off her little body. And there were so many volunteers with picks and shovels that it was necessary to limit the number who could dig at the same time. There was a brief ceremony the next morning, after which the grave was filled in, and the wagons got underway again at seven on schedule. Nothing was left at the campsite but a small sleeping tent with blood-spattered canvas walls and sleeping bag, and a small baby crib.

The wagon train moved along over the prairie with no troubles worth mentioning for the next three weeks. A good portion of the trip followed beside the Little Blue River, so good water for people and animals was not a problem. The tragedy of the Kansas River crossing soon melted away and spirits were high once more for the after-supper social time each night. Most everyone on the train spent some time listening to the dueling between Tiny Futch's banjo and Henry Abbott's fiddle and watching the buck dancing competition between their wives to the beat of their husbands' music. Several of the other men had guitars and would often accompany Tiny and Henry. Most often it was Lucien Aiken and his wife. Wilma liked to sing, mostly the slower songs. Her voice was not especially pleasant to the ear, but she sang loud and no one was unkind enough to complain. And as Scofield commented to Clint and Spud, "She ain't all bad. I think it keeps the Injuns away."

There were two souls who never attended the nightly social gatherings, however. One was Will Tucker, and everybody knew why he kept almost totally to himself. The other was Bass Thornton's ape, named Leach, and no one had any idea what his story was. And ever since the crossing of the Kansas River, when he remained under the water for so long, and then lifted Thornton's wagon up to solid ground, no one approached him. Leach had tiny ears for such a big head and Levi Watkins confided to Tracy Bishop that they were really gills. And that was the reason he could breathe underwater.

Shortly before reaching Fort Kearny, they left the Little Blue River and struck the Platte River and the first stop on the Platte was a nooning. Scofield had told them when they left Independence that the rivers and streams they would access were all good water with the exception of the Platte. Most of the emigrants had forgotten that by this time, so they tasted the silty water and spit it out in alarm. Scofield had to assure them that there was nothing wrong with the water except the taste. "It won't hurt you. It always tastes like that. I don't know why. Maybe it's because it's so shallow and full of sand islands, but get used to it because we're gonna be followin' it till we reach Fort Laramie. And that's a long way." When someone asked how long a way, he replied, "About three hundred and fifty miles." Then to the chorus of groans, he said, "You'll strike a fair amount of creeks and streams along the way where you can refill your water barrels."

"Look!" somebody exclaimed. "Leach is leading Thornton's horses to the river. Thornton's kind of particular. Wonder if his horses are?" They all turned to watch as the mysterious man walked into the shallow water with the horses. "Yep, they're drinking it." Then Leach dipped into the water with a cup he was carrying and filled it. He tipped it back and drained the whole cupful of river water, wiped his mouth with the back of his hand, and filled the cup again, and drained it. The expressionless face they had come to find a constant never changed.

"I swear," Levi uttered.

\* \* \*

They rolled into Fort Kearny before suppertime on a day that had threatened rain all day but failed to deliver. Scofield led his wagons to his favorite camping spot not far from the fort beside a nice little creek that would provide his people with some sweet drinking water. It would be well received by them after having been subjected to water from the Platte. From the looks of the new grass, it was apparent that they were among the first, if not the first, settlers on the trail this year. After the wagons were circled on the prairie next to the creek, some of the settlers went into the fort right away to buy the supplies they were already short of. Scofield told everybody they would camp there an extra day, so they had plenty of time to do what buying they needed to do. The fort also offered a blacksmith as well as other tradesmen if wagons needed repairs of any kind.

Clint made it a point to check on Will Tucker after the wagons were all in place in the circle and the horses were unhitched to graze. He knew the man had to be going through a great deal of pain, so he wanted to help if he could. Will had completely withdrawn from the nightly gatherings after supper, so Clint decided to go to Will's wagon before he built his fire to cook supper. Will was just walking back from the trees by the creek with an axe in one hand and an armload of wood for his fire. "How's it goin', Will?" Clint called out as he approached.

"Can't complain, Clint," Will returned. "Somethin' I can do for you?"

"I just wanted to see how you were gettin' along," Clint replied. "I see you ain't started your supper yet, so I thought I'd see if you'd like a good home-cooked supper tonight." Will looked puzzled by the question, so Clint was quick to explain. "I ain't talkin' about eatin' Spud's cookin'. Spud ain't gonna cook tonight, anyway. You see, there's a place a little less than a mile up this creek called Leo's Road Ranch. A fellow named Leo Stern owns it, and it's really what the soldiers call a hog ranch." Again he saw an instant negative reaction in Will's expression, so he said, "I'm not talkin' about havin' anything to do with the women that work there, except one, a lady named Lulu Belle. She's the cook, and it'd be hard to find a better cook anywhere in the territory. Uncle Clayton and I always eat supper at Leo's every time we hit Fort Kearny and we ain't ever been disappointed. I thought you might be interested in goin' with us and eatin' a good supper tonight."

Will, already having decided to avoid all contact with his fellow travelers, if possible, had to stop and think about it. The thought of a big supper, fixed by a woman, would sure be welcome after the past days of his own cooking. But he was still reluctant to have contact with anybody. Sensing that and more convinced it was just what Will needed, Clint continued to push. "It'd just be you, me, and Uncle Clayton goin' over there to fill our bellies, have one drink maybe, then come back here and go to bed. Whaddaya say? Spud might decide to go this time, hard to say, but there wouldn't be nobody else."

Will had to consider it. He was almost to the point of going out of his mind with the loneliness of his life without Angel and Billy. And every time his mind returned to his final moments with her, he thought about taking the same departure from this life that she had taken. At the same time, he couldn't help wondering if in her final moments of apparent insanity, she might have been telling him what she truly thought of him. And she killed herself to escape a life with him. Possibly, she had come to agree with her father's opinion of him. He looked at Clint, patiently waiting there for an answer. "Are you sure Mr. Scofield doesn't mind you askin' me to go with you?"

"I don't know why he would," Clint replied. "I didn't tell him I was goin' to ask you. But if he minds, then he can go by himself, and you and I'll go over there."

"I wouldn't wanna go, if he'd rather I didn't," Will said.

"For Pete's sake, Will," Clint said, beginning to become impatient. "It's a public place. He can't tell you not to eat there."

Will cracked a smile. "I reckon you're right. I'll go with you."

"Good. Uncle Clayton and I will have to make sure the men

on guard duty tonight are all set and everything looks like he likes it, and I'll give you a holler. All right?"

"All right," Will answered, still not sure he wanted to.

On his way back to the wagon, Clint had some second thoughts about what he had just done on the spur of the moment without checking with his uncle first. If it was like previous occasions at Leo's, his uncle would not come back to the wagons with him after supper. Since he had a special relationship with Lulu Belle, she usually made some time to visit with him. He had to wonder how this visit was going to go, since his uncle swore this was his last wagon train he was going to lead. They had stopped in at Leo's just a short time before on their way to Independence to pick up their wagon. Uncle Clayton had spent some time with Lulu Belle on that occasion. Spud asked him the next morning if he had told her he'd visit her one more time and that would do it. Scofield said he didn't mention it to her, the evening had been too nice to spoil it with talk of farewell. When Clint and Spud had talked about it later, they agreed that the relationship between Scofield and Lulu Belle was more than casual, as his uncle contended.

When he got back to the wagon, he found Spud cooking a small pan of chipped beef and beans. "Thought you might go over to Leo's Road Ranch with Uncle Clayton and me," he said.

"Nah, I reckon not," Spud replied. "I ain't that hungry. Besides, we ate there on the way down here. She's a pretty good cook, but she ain't the cook Scofield says she is. That's just the excuse he uses to go see her."

"Well, it does give you a chance to eat something different," Clint said, thinking he detected a little competitive attitude from one cook to another. He saw Scofield approaching then.

"You ready to go to supper?" Scofield called out as he walked up.

"Yep, I'm ready," Clint answered. "Spud said he ain't goin', but I asked Will Tucker if he wanted to go with us."

"You did?" Scofield responded, genuinely surprised. "What did he say?"

"He said he did," Clint replied and waited for his uncle's reaction.

Scofield didn't say anything for a few seconds while he thought about it. Then he said, "Good idea. That boy needs to come back to the world of the folks that's livin'. It'll be good for him to get outta that wagon for a spell."

"That's what I thought," Clint said. "Maybe it'll get him to thinkin' about Oregon again and a whole new life for him out there. If you're ready, I'll go get him."

"I'm ready," Scofield said.

While the three of them walked along the path by the creek, Scofield and Clint did most of the talking, with Will still having a little trouble breaking out of his shell. When they got to Leo's, Scofield took them to the side door that led into the saloon and dining section, which was just a line of tables at the back of the saloon. Clint smiled because prior to this night, his uncle always entered Leo's through the front door. He liked to look at the merchandise in the parlor, even though he never did any business there.

"Howdy, Scofield," the bartender, Floyd Trainer, greeted them when they walked in the saloon, "Clint, and I don't know this gentleman."

"Evenin', Floyd," Scofield returned. "This is Will Tucker. He's one of our company of wagons. Me and Clint decided we'd introduce him to the best cook in the territory."

"Glad to meetcha, Will. Welcome to Leo's Road Ranch. You fellers want a drink before you eat, or you gonna wait till after?"

"I believe I'd like to have a little shooter before my supper," Scofield said, "kinda let my belly know to get ready. How 'bout you boys?"

"Before's all right with me," Clint said and turned to look at Will.

"It don't make no difference to me," Will said and started digging in his pocket for change.

"I got the drinks," Scofield said and stopped him. He felt like he owed him a drink, after the ordeal he had just endured.

"I'll go tell Lulu Belle you want supper," Floyd said after he poured their drinks. "Just set yourselves down at one of the tables, and she'll be with you in a jiffy."

There were two men sitting at a table in the corner of the back wall. They weren't soldiers. Clint figured they were cowhands from one of the several ranches around Fort Kearny. Although there were just two of them, Clint noticed there was a third plate on the table. He also noticed that both men looked them over quite thoroughly. Scofield picked the table in the opposite corner and sat down. Feeling the burn of the whiskey in his belly now, Clint was ready for the coffee that was always brought right away.

# Chapter 5

"Lulu Belle, you've got three more customers out there that want some supper," Floyd said when he walked into the kitchen.

She was talking to a heavy-set man wearing a gun belt with two matching Colt Army .45 handguns. He was an outlaw who went by the name of Jack Dalton and he had a hankering for more than Lulu Belle's cooking. "Tell 'em I'll be with 'em in a minute, Floyd. Take 'em their coffee, if you don't mind."

"All right," Floyd said and went to the table with the cups. "One of 'em's Clayton Scofield," he said casually while he put three cups on a tray.

"Oh, hell," Lulu Belle muttered. "Tell him I'll be there quick as I can get finished with something on the stove."

"Clayton Scofield!" Jack Dalton exclaimed. "Is that the sorry dog that's beatin' my time with you?"

"Now, Jack, there ain't never been nothin' between you and me and you know it. You just decided to come in here and own me just because I was nice to you that one time. I ain't a money sack you can just grab off the stagecoach and say it's yours. So I'd appreciate it if you get outta my kitchen now so I can wait on my customers."

Dalton wasn't hearing any of it. "Clayton Scofield, huh? You're pickin' him over me, are ya? Well, I know how I can make it easier for you to make a choice—when there ain't but one to choose from."

"There ain't no use for that kind of talk, Jack. I don't know how you got to thinkin' there was anything goin' on between you and me. But just listen to me now, there never was anything and there ain't never gonna be anything. So you know where you stand. Now let that be the end of it. Get your two friends and get on outta here."

"You lyin' hussy!" He backhanded her hard across the side of her face, knocking her over a kitchen chair. Floyd set the tray back down and started for him. Dalton turned back to meet him with a wicked grin on his face. "Come on," he coaxed, motioning him forward with his hand.

Floyd thought better of his decision to defend Lulu Belle. He stopped, knowing Dalton would destroy him. Away from his bar and his shotgun he had no defense against an animal like Dalton. "You had no call to strike that woman," he finally managed to say. "You've done enough harm. Why don't you and your friends just leave now?"

"Because I ain't through here with what I'm gonna do," Dalton told him. He walked up into his face before shoving him aside and storming out of the kitchen to stop and glare at the three startled faces at the near-corner table. "Clayton Scofield!" he roared.

Already puzzled by the noises coming from the kitchen, Scofield unwisely answered. "I'm Clayton Scofield," whereupon Dalton promptly pulled one of the Colts he wore and shot at him point blank. With reactions quicker than the angry outlaw's, Clint yanked the table up off the floor and caught Dalton's shot with it. Then using it as a shield, he charged into the surprised assassin, driving him backwards and unable to shoot a second time. In a fit of angry frustration then, Dalton dropped his pistol back in his holster so he could wrestle the table out of Clint's hands. There followed a short test of strength for possession of the table, but Dalton was clearly the more powerful man, and he gradually forced the table from shielding him. When he finally forced Clint far enough aside to give him a clear shot again, he was stopped cold by a shot in his chest from Scofield's Colt Navy revolver. While the table and Dalton both dropped to the floor, Clint and Scofield turned quickly to meet the response from Dalton's two friends. There was none, however, they having been taken by surprise as well by Jack Dalton's actions. And now, they were discouraged from taking any action because the shots had drawn the owner, Leo Stern, as well as several soldiers from the parlor in the other side of the establishment.

Clint looked at Scofield and said, "I didn't think you were ever gonna shoot. That man was a helluva brute. He was about to twist me right down to the floor."

"Hell, I had to wait till he turned that damn table outta the way to give me a clear shot. You shouldn'ta fought him so hard for that table. Besides, I had to keep an eye on his two friends over there. And Will didn't even bring a gun with him. But it looks like his friends were just as surprised as we were."

"What the hell happened here?" Leo Stern demanded, and Floyd told him what had taken place and could give him no reason for it other than possibly Jack Dalton was insane.

"Where's Lulu Belle?" Scofield asked, and Floyd said she was in the kitchen, so Scofield didn't wait for any more questions but went straight to the kitchen. "Lulu Belle!" he called out as he walked through the kitchen door.

"I'm right here, Clayton," she answered, standing back by the pantry door where she had been examining the black bruise rapidly forming around her right eye. "Ain't that a pretty thing?" she asked as she turned away from the mirror on the back of the pantry door.

"He did that?"

"Yeah."

"I swear, I oughta go back in there and put another bullet in him."

"Is he dead?"

"Yes, ma'am, he's dead all right, but I still oughta go back and put a bullet right between his eyes."

"What about those two saddle tramps who always ride with him, Shep Grice and Bob White?" Lulu Belle asked. "They were dipped from the same pond scum as Jack."

"They didn't make a move," Scofield said. "We figure they were as surprised as I was."

"Is your nephew with you?"

"Clint? Yeah, he's with me. He's the only reason I'm standin' here talkin' to you now." He told her then that Dalton just pulled his gun and shot at him and how Clint saved his life.

She smiled when he told her that, even though she grimaced as if it hurt her to do it. "I always liked that boy," she said. "I'm real sorry your supper was interrupted like that. If you still wanna eat, it won't take me but a minute or two to get something for you. It's on the stove."

"Oh, yes, it'd take more'n that to kill my appetite. Clint's either."

"Floyd said there were three that wanted supper," she said.

"That's right," Scofield replied. "We brought one of our wagon owners with us. Name's Will Tucker. He's had a terrible piece of bad luck hit him when we crossed the Kansas River. We invited him to come to supper with us, to get his mind off his troubles. I expect we did the job already. I'll tell you about him and how he lost his family."

"My goodness," she joked. "Ain't this a happy little supper we're havin' here tonight? Here, I'll put you to work. Pour some coffee in those three cups Floyd started to take out to you, and you can start on that while I fix up three plates for you."

"Yes, ma'am," he responded politely and got the coffeepot off the edge of the stove. He had waited as long as he thought he could before asking, so he posed the question while he was filling the cups. "Did you give any thought to the proposition I mentioned when we passed through on the way to Independence?"

"Yes, I gave it a lot of thought," she answered. " 'Course, I have to say you surprised the hell outta me at the time. You oughta know I've always liked you from the first time you came in here to eat. But are you sure you're really gonna make this trip your last one across the country?"

"This is my last trip," he said. "I just came back this time to get you. And from the looks of the way your eye is swellin', maybe I shouldn't have waited so long. Like I told you on the trip down with Clint and Spud, I'm lettin' the wagon train stay over here for an extra day, so you've still got all day tomorrow to make up your mind. And if it ain't convenient for you tomorrow, I'll come back for you after I take these folks to Oregon. I know it don't seem like much of an offer, but you ain't exactly no spring chicken either. And I can offer you a home on a nice piece of land in the Willamette Valley and a family that would welcome you to boot. I'm sorry I ain't more romantic, but I mean what I'm sayin' when I say I'll take care of you."

"Does Clint know about your proposal?" Lulu Belle asked.

"No, so you don't have to be embarrassed, one way or the other," he assured her. "I reckon I'd better take this coffee out there before it gets too cold to drink. You just think about it, all right?" He started for the door with the tray, but she stopped him.

"Clayton, I have been thinking about it. And I'm tempted to take you for your word and go to Oregon with you. You're a fine and decent man. You deserve better than me, but I can't leave Leo without a cook for his saloon. I reckon we met just a little too late in life, so I guess my answer is no, but I think the world of you for asking me." He didn't say anything, just looked at her and nodded his understanding. Then he turned and took the coffee to the table.

When Scofield went back into the saloon, he found the two friends of Jack Dalton's gone and Leo was still talking to Floyd to make sure he got the whole story. "Say, Clayton, I sure am sorry you had to walk into an ambush like that. That Dalton fellow was a maniac. I'm just glad you didn't get shot. Is Lulu Belle all right?

Floyd said Dalton hit her a pretty good lick. I better go in to talk to her." Scofield told him that she was going to have a black eye, but she was okay otherwise. "Those two that were in here with Dalton carried him outta here," Leo continued. "That was three rough-lookin' men. They just started comin' in here about three or four weeks ago. I hope they don't come back. But they're gone now, so maybe you boys can enjoy your supper." Before going to the kitchen to check with Lulu Belle, he turned to Floyd and said, "There's no charge for their supper tonight."

When he left, Clint couldn't resist asking, "Well, Will, what do you think of Leo's Road Ranch so far?"

"Before you make up your mind," Scofield interrupted, "wait till you sample the cookin'."

"I swear," Will said, "when that big fellow came out the kitchen door shootin', I thought bullets would be flyin' all over this room and I didn't even have a gun, and there weren't no place to hide." Clint didn't comment on it, but he thought it a good sign that Will was concerned about saving his life. After his experience at the river crossing, he and Scofield had both feared that Will might take his life as well. "Does something like this happen to you two at every army post you stop at?" Will asked.

"Yep, every one of 'em," Scofield said, then he quickly confessed, "Nah, I was just japin' ya. If you stay away from the hog ranches and the saloons, most of the folks you meet are friendly, includin' the Injuns. Ain't that right, Clint?"

That's right, Will, I expect you'll meet a lot of hardworkin', honest folks on the way out to the Willamette Valley. Here comes one of 'em now," Clint said when Lulu Belle came out of the kitchen carrying a supper plate in each hand and one riding on her forearm.

"Howdy, Clint," Lulu Belle greeted him. "Glad to see you again."

"I swear," Clint gasped when he saw her face. "Is that what that fellow did to you?"

"No," Lulu Belle said, back on her game, "that's what Clayton did to me just now in the kitchen. Who's this you brought with you?" she asked, smiling at Will.

Scofield answered her. "This is Will Tucker. He's another young fellow who's headin' for a new life in the unspoiled Oregon country and leavin' the cramped-up country back east."

She gave Scofield a raised eyebrow and said to Will, "Welcome to Leo's Road Ranch. I hope you enjoy your supper."

They took their time eating and afterward sat a while drinking coffee. There were only a couple more customers who came for supper, so Lulu Belle found time to sit and talk with them while they ate. Will declared that all the bragging on her cooking Clint and Scofield did was wholly justified, and she thanked him for the compliment. When Clint looked at Will and asked if he was ready to go back to the wagons, he said he was. Scofield commented that it was time for all of them to get back. There were some things he needed to check on. "That's right," Clint said, at first surprised because Scofield always stayed with Lulu Belle until later. Then it occurred to him that his uncle was going back with them, then would come back to see her after that. That way, Will wouldn't know he had something going with Lulu Belle.

Lulu Belle was somewhat surprised, herself, but she understood that Scofield might be feeling a strain on their relationship after she had refused his marriage proposal. She walked them to the door and expressed her concern for their safety. "Listen, Clayton, I know those two friends of Dalton's left the saloon. But you boys be careful. Those two are as evil as the man you killed tonight. So please watch your backs."

"We will," Scofield said. "And thank you for the fine supper." He paused, then added, "And all the fine suppers we've enjoyed at your table over the years. Good luck to ya." Then he led them through the door to the parlor, so Will could get a glimpse of what else went on at Leo's Road Ranch.

"I declare," Clint said, "you told her goodbye like you weren't ever gonna see her again."

"I did?" Scofield responded, then shrugged and said, "Well, I reckon we ain't gonna see her again. I ain't plannin' on eatin' here tomorrow night. Matter of fact, if everybody gets all their supplies and repairs done by noontime, we might as well pack up and leave. No sense in just hangin' around here when we could pick up a half a day."

"Makes sense to me," Clint said, even though he had to wonder what was going on in his uncle's head. He must have his reasons for passing up an opportunity to spend some private time with Lulu Belle.

"What if he don't come out this door?" Bob White questioned Shep Grice as they waited across the road in front of Leo's Road Ranch.

"Why wouldn't he come out this door?" Shep replied. "He went in this door. We was settin' right there in the saloon when he walked in the outside door to the saloon."

"You're most likely right, but if he takes a notion to take a look at the women, he might go through the parlor and come out the front door."

"Well, hell, there's two of us," Shep said. "It you want to, go on over there and watch the parlor door."

"That's what I'm gonna do," Bob declared, "'cause that's the way I would leave." He moved off into the darkness, his rifle in hand.

"Make sure your first shot is at that big feller," Shep called after him. "He's the one that shot Jack."

Inside the building, Scofield led Clint and Will through the parlor where the ladies of the night were sitting awaiting customers. Scofield only chuckled in response to their crude remarks and their attempts to entice the three men. Still chuckling, Scofield walked out the front door to the porch. He had taken no more than half a dozen steps before Clint suddenly launched his body into Scofield's ankles, cutting his legs out from under him causing him to drop with a heavy thud on the porch. The report of the rifle and the sound of the bullet smacking the siding where Scofield's body would have been seconds earlier was heard at almost the same time.

"Stay back, Will!" Clint yelled. So Will, who had not come out on the porch yet, slipped back inside the parlor.

Out on the porch, Clint and Scofield, flattening themselves as much as they could manage, dragged their bodies over to the edge of the porch and dropped off to the ground. The porch was only four steps above the ground, but that was enough for cover. Both of them ready to fire now, Clint with his rifle, his uncle with his Colt Navy .45, watched for a muzzle flash. It was not long in coming and they both used it for a target. Firing as quickly as they could when they saw the muzzle flash, they both sent two shots at it. They waited only a short time before deciding they'd be better off if they crawled under the porch. No more shots came from the spot where they had seen the muzzle flashes, but they had no way to determine if the shooter had been hit or not. But they agreed that there had been only one shooter, and it was reasonable to believe the two outlaws had split up with one watching the front door, while the other watched the outside door to the saloon. If that was the case, they might have a second shooter gunning for them from that direction. And the cover they had taken behind the side edge of the porch left them vulnerable to an attack from that direction. That was the reasoning that caused them to be crawling under the low porch now, a task that was considerably more difficult for Scofield due to the size of his body.

It had been a good decision, however, because in the next few seconds, a string of six shots were thrown at the edge of the porch where they had been. They could hear the bullets striking the edge of the porch. "He ain't sure where we are," Scofield said. "He's just firin' blind, hopin' to hit meat."

"We need to know if that first shooter got hit, or if he's movin' to a better place," Clint decided. "You watch for the fellow that's reloadin' his six-shooter right now. I'm gonna go see if I can find the one with the rifle." He started crawling toward the other side of the porch.

"You be careful," Scofield cautioned. It wasn't all level ground under the porch and he didn't like the thought of getting stuck while trying to crawl over a hump in the ground.

"Always am," Clint responded and crawled out from under the porch on the other side. Kneeling beside the porch now, he peered into the darkness across the road from where the first shots had come. It was impossible to make out any distinct shapes. All he could tell was that there was a line of low bushes on the far side of the road and the shooter was no doubt behind them. And the only way to find out if he was or not was to get behind the bushes himself. If he was still there watching, Clint was counting on his not noticing that he had crawled to the other side of the porch. Knowing the shooter couldn't see in the dark any better than he could, he slowly crept a dozen yards or more away from the porch to increase the distance even more. Then he stopped and prepared to run across to the other side of the road. Holding his rifle in both hands before him, he sprinted through the black empty darkness, halfway expecting to hear the report of a rifle—at the same time telling himself if he heard the sound of the rifle, it would mean the shot had missed him.

When he reached the bushes on the other side of the road, he stopped to make his way through them quietly instead of plunging through them as he would have preferred to do. Assuming he was now on the same side of the bushes as the man who shot at them, he cautiously started back toward the spot where they had seen the muzzle flashes, watching for the image of a man above the tops of the bushes. There was no sign of him, even as he was almost to the spot he estimated he had shot from. *He's moved!* he thought at once, and that meant he had no idea where to look for him. The game must start all over again, and with Uncle Clayton stuck under the front porch, he couldn't help thinking, it would have been funny had it not been a game of life and death. He had no option but to continue along the line of bushes, so he started forward, only to stop immediately when he discovered the body he was about to stumble over.

He approached the body carefully to see if there were any signs of life and found there were none, and the only wound he could find was one shot in the middle of his forehead. He and Scofield had thrown four shots at his rifle flash and one shot hit the target, and it was a perfect kill-shot. There would be an argument over whose shot it was. *If we take care of the other fellow*, he immediately reminded himself. The job was only half finished. Chances are, he figured, the other shooter was also behind these same bushes, only a little farther over. *Got to be more careful*, he thought, *because this one's on the move.* But he found he was not going to be hard to find when he heard a loud whisper.

"Bob, you think we got the reprobate? There ain't been no more shots."

"No," Clint answered him. "I think they got me."

"You got hit?" the voice asked, getting closer now.

"Yeah," Clint answered, down on one knee with his rifle ready to fire.

"How bad?" The man was close enough to make out his form now.

"I'm dead," Clint answered.

"What the hell are you talkin' about?" Shep demanded, then stopped dead still when he realized what he had walked into.

"You're dead, too," Clint said. Shep raised his pistol to fire, but Clint pulled the trigger before Shep could aim and cock it.

Clint's shot hit the would-be assassin in the chest, killing him almost as instantly as his outlaw partner had died. He slumped down to his knees before he dropped his pistol. Then he keeled over on his side, clearly finished. Clint rose from his knee and picked up the pistol. Then he took a closer look at the dying man, whose eyes flickered open briefly and he pleaded, "Finish it, man. Don't leave me like this." Feeling compassion, as he would for a deer he had just shot, Clint walked around behind him, cocked the pistol he had just picked up, and put him out of his misery.

He walked back across the road to the front porch and told Scofield it was all over. "You can come out from under there now."

"You got both of them?" Scofield asked.

"Yeah, they're both dead. Come on outta there."

"I can't," Scofield said.

"Why not?"

"Somethin's got me caught. I'm hung on somethin' that's got me by my belt, I think, and I can't move an inch. Well, damn it, it ain't funny," he said when he heard Clint laughing.

"Well, I'll go tell Will it's safe to come out now, then I reckon me and him will go on back to the wagons 'cause I don't think I can crawl under that porch again." He chuckled again. "I'm just japin' ya. I'll crawl back under there and get you loose."

"You better be japin' me, or I'm fixin' to come up from here and bring this whole damn porch with me," Scofield threatened.

"Can I tell Will first?" Clint asked, still japing.

"I'd druther you didn't, if you don't mind," Scofield replied.

"I reckon it ain't a fittin' position to see the wagon master in, is it?" Clint came back. He crawled back under the porch and freed his uncle from the nail driven only halfway into the floor joist that had snagged Scofield's gun belt. By the time Clint went back inside to get Will, there had been a long enough time with no more gunshots that some people were coming outside to find out the cause. One of them was naturally Leo Stern. Scofield told him about the attempted ambush, and that it was all taken care of. Leo's only request was that they should drag the bodies away from his establishment, and they said they would.

"They've gotta have some horses around here somewhere," Scofield said. "Most likely over there by the path down the creek."

"I'll go look for 'em," Will volunteered, feeling as if he should be doing something to help. So while he was doing that, Scofield and Clint went to the spot where the bodies were and did a search for anything worth keeping. They found a small amount of money, and when Will returned leading their two horses, they gave him his third of the cash. He didn't want to take it but they insisted. They loaded the bodies on the horses and led them back down the path along the creek. About halfway back, they led them off into the woods and dumped the bodies.

"You know, I was kinda suspectin' those two jokers would be waitin' to ambush us along this path on our way back to the wagons," Scofield said. "But they sure caught us by surprise when they was waitin' right outside the door at Leo's." He thought about that for a moment, then he thought of something else. "How'd you know they was waitin', when you cut me down on the porch?"

"I didn't know," Clint said. "When we walked out the door, I heard a rifle being cocked."

"We just walked outta that noisy parlor and you heard somebody crankin' a shell into a rifle?" He looked at Will then. "Did you hear a rifle bein' cocked?"

"No," Will replied. "Like you said, there was so much noise in that parlor."

Scofield looked back at Clint as if expecting him to explain. "It wasn't noisy on the porch," Clint said. "Whaddaya think? I just decided to see how hard you'd hit the floor if I cut your feet out from under you? I heard a rifle gettin' cocked." Scofield just shook his head in wonder.

They led the two horses back to the wagons, figuring they'd just add them to their horses. When Scofield and Clint were telling Spud about it later, they were undecided what the effect of their evening might have had on Will Tucker. But his attitude seemed to be all right when they left him. He even thanked them for inviting him along. "The next few weeks will tell if he's gonna get past his loss or not," Scofield said.

Like Clint, Spud was surprised that Scofield came back with him and Will, instead of lingering a while in the company of Lulu

Belle, but he decided not to ask him about it. "If everybody fin-ishes up in their dealings with the fort by noonin' tomorrow, I'm figurin' on movin' us outta here in the afternoon," Scofield told him, and that was another surprise.

"Well, ain't nothin' holdin' me here," Spud said. "I'll be ready whenever you wanna go. The social hour's still goin' strong. Maybe you can find out tonight if they'll all be ready."

# Chapter 6

Not everyone was gathered around the fire that night at the singing and dancing, but everyone who was had no objections to leaving Fort Kearny a half day earlier than originally announced. So Scofield figured he and Clint could get around to the others in the morning to let them know of the change in plans. The night guards were set and Clint called it a night while his uncle took his usual last walk around the wagons to make sure everything looked all right. When they left Fort Kearny the next day, they would begin a journey along the Platte and North Platte Rivers for maybe three months before the train reached the Sweetwater. For the most part the terrain would not be difficult for the horses and wagons, but Clint and Scofield knew the people would soon become weary of the dryness, the foul taste of the Platte River, and the lack of firewood, causing them to hunt each day for dried buffalo and cattle chips to use for fuel to cook their food. It would be their first taste of that form of weariness, but in a couple of weeks or more, there was an oasis of sorts in the form of a place called Ash Hollow. It was where they left the Platte and continued along the North Platte.

At breakfast the next morning, Clint and Scofield walked the wagons again to make sure everyone knew to be ready to roll after the nooning time. So most of the morning was spent packing up and getting ready to start out as soon as they had eaten the noon meal. Spud checked his horses over that morning and decided he needed to change one of the horses, and Clint and Scofield were helping him pick a good horse when Spud poked Clint on the arm. When Clint looked at him, Spud motioned toward the creek with his head. Clint looked where he motioned and saw a woman coming off the path that ran beside the creek. She was wrapped up in a coat with a scarf around her head and she was carrying what looked like a carpetbag in one hand and a larger suitcase in the other. At that distance, it was difficult to tell much more about her, but she appeared to be coming straight to the wagon train. Spud and Clint watched her for a few minutes until she got closer. Then Clint suddenly said, "Uncle Clayton." Scofield, who was in the midst of examining a dun horse's hoof, looked up and Clint motioned with his head, just as Spud had done.

"What?" Scofield asked and Clint didn't answer. He just motioned again toward the woman approaching the wagons. This time, Scofield turned to look. He dropped the dun's hoof and uttered, "This'un's all right." Then he stood up straight and stared at the woman for several long moments as if waiting to see if she was a mirage that would disappear any second if he even blinked.

"Want me to go tote those bags for her?" Clint asked.

"No," Scofield answered and started walking to meet her.

Clint and Spud grinned at each other. "We gonna have to repack that wagon," Spud said.

"I reckon I'll be movin' out," Clint declared. "Maybe I can move in with Will. We'll work something out 'cause this might be the best thing that could have happened on this trip."

Lulu Belle stopped when she saw Scofield walking briskly toward her. She put her bags down and waited for him, wondering if she was making a foolish mistake. She studied his intense expression as he approached and when he reached her, she said, "I'm lookin' to find a ride out to the Oregon country."

"I can fix you up with one, but there's certain restrictions.

Number one is we don't take single women, married women only, unless they agree to marry somebody on the train."

"I'll agree to do that," she said, "if that's what the fellow really wants. Like you said, I ain't no spring chicken, but I think I've got a lotta years left in me."

"I ain't the youngest rooster on the farm, either. That's why I think you and me are a perfect match. And God's honest truth, you're the only reason I agreed to come back for one more of these trips. Will you marry me?"

"I sure will," she answered and threw her arms around his neck. He picked her up in his arms, lifted her off the ground, and spun her around a couple of times.

Watching from back at the wagon, Clint let out a loud, "Whoop!" and declared, "I reckon we can go carry her suitcases now." He ran out to meet them. "Welcome to the family, Lulu Belle! Here, let me tote those suitcases for you." He picked them up and led the happy couple back to the wagon, thinking it the best thing that could ever have happened to his uncle. He pictured the re-action of Uncle Garland and Aunt Irene when Uncle Clayton showed up with a wife. Aunt Irene, especially, was always concerned about Clayton growing old alone. He smiled to himself then when he remembered it was Aunt Irene who was foremost in pushing him toward Ruby Nixon. She just didn't seem content unless everyone was paired up.

When they got back to the wagon, Spud gave her a big welcome smile and told her that when they had packed the wagon in Independence, they had saved a space for her belongings. His comment caused Clint to give him a startled look and demand, "You mean you knew about his plans to kidnap Lulu Belle the whole time and you didn't tell me?"

"I didn't see no need to, in case she turned him down," Spud said. "Wasn't no need in lettin' folks know he got turned down, if she hadda."

"Well, hell, Spud, I ain't just folks, I'm his nephew," Clint complained.

Spud shrugged. "I reckon he'da told you if he wanted you to know. Weren't my place to go blabbin' it around."

Clint shook his head in frustration and went to the back of the wagon where Scofield was showing Lulu Belle where her belongings were going to be kept. "So you told Spud you were plannin' to trap Miss Lulu Belle this trip and you didn't even tell me."

Scofield looked at him and chuckled. "I was afraid it was too much for you to handle," he said. "Mighta took your mind off scoutin' and other things I pay you for."

"Are you gonna make it legal?" Clint asked.

"That was my plan," Scofield answered. "Ain't that what you're thinkin', honey?"

"That would be my preference," she said, laughing. "I wanna tie you up in a contract for life."

"You gonna wait till you get to Oregon to find a preacher?" Clint wondered. "You bein' the wagon master, it might be legal for you to marry two people in the wagon train. But I doubt it's the same for the wagon master to marry himself to somebody." He could tell by Scofield's expression that he hadn't thought about that.

"There's no cause for worry," Lulu Belle told him. "Lots of people get married without a preacher around. We can just exchange our vows and jump over a broom together in front of some witnesses."

"There you go," Clint said. "And I know the place to do it, tonight at the social hour. Whaddaya think?" He expected Scofield to protest, but he said it was fine with him. He wanted everybody to know. "Lulu Belle, I never have heard your last name," Clint confessed. "Or is Belle your last name?"

"Come to think of it," Scofield confessed as well, "I've never heard it either."

"I reckon if you're willing to marry me, you should at least know who you're marrying," she said. "Lulu Belle is a name I started callin' myself when I got into the business of cookin' in a saloon—to keep anybody who knew my family from hearing where I was. So I have to inform you, Mr. Clayton Scofield, you will be wedding Miss Lily Bellmont."

"Damn, Uncle Clayton, I ain't sure you're high class enough to marry a woman with a name that fancy. You sure you still wanna jump the broom?" He hoped his uncle was enjoying this as much as he was.

"I wanna do it tonight," Scofield said. "I want everybody to know Lulu, I mean Lily, as soon as possible. Is that all right with you, Lily? Damn, I like that name, Lily." He gave her a grin. "Clint's right, though. If I'da known your real name before, I might notta had the nerve to ask you to marry me."

Lily laughed with him, but she had a pretty good idea what her family back in New Orleans would think of her progress in this life. And then she laughed again when she realized she really didn't care. She was confident that at last she had made a contract with a solid, dependable man who would take care of her. And in her mind, they were a perfect match, both well past the fickle youth of their lives. And to think, she had almost lost this chance when she turned him away last night. She had been honest when she told Clayton of the obligation she felt for Leo Stern, and she did not like to leave him in a bind for a cook. But last night she confided in Leo that she had been sorely tempted to accept a proposal of marriage from Clayton Scofield. She turned it down because it would leave him shorthanded. To her surprise, Leo told her to go with Scofield. "I think a lot of you, Lulu Belle," he had said. "There ain't gonna be many men come through here as decent a man as Clayton Scofield. My advice to you is, if you love him, you go with him. I'll find another cook— won't be as good as you, but the food business is a small part of my profit." So now, she was sure she had met two of the most decent men in this part of the country.

"Am I seein' things?" Levi Watkins exclaimed to Ella. They were sitting in the driver's seat of their wagon, third in line of travel for the day, waiting for the "Wagons ho!" call from Scofield.

"I don't know," Ella answered. "Whaddaya think you see?"

Levi stood up, trying to get an unobstructed look at Scofield's wagon. "I swear, is that a woman settin' beside Spud Williams?"

"What would a woman be doin' settin' beside Spud Williams?" Ella asked. "You must be seein' things. You can't see whose settin' in the seat anyway from behind the wagon."

"I know what I saw," Levi insisted. "You can't see the driver's seat now, but the wagon was turned a little bit back there."

"Whatever you say, love." Ella dismissed the thought.

At the signal, the wagons rolled out of the campsite by the creek and started out along the Platte for a stretch of about two weeks that would be a poor introduction to the Oregon Trail for Lily Bellmont. Scofield, Clint, and Spud had all made an effort to prepare her for the long monotonous days of the wagons rumbling over the treeless prairie. She got a fair taste of what it was going to be like on that first half day of travel. Being a strong woman, she remained cheerful throughout the rest of the day, but informed them that she would be walking on the morrow. "I know now why so many women and children were walking," she said.

They went to camp by a small creek about six miles from Fort Kearny. The horses could have gone a little farther, but Scofield knew the next good water was at least five miles beyond and it was close to five o'clock anyway. After they circled the wagons and took care of the stock, the women cooked supper. "Now tell me I'm crazy," Levi said to his wife.

She looked where he was pointing and saw Lily helping Spud cook supper. "As I live and breathe . . ." she started. "How in the world did Spud Williams get a woman to come with him?"

"She ain't bad-lookin', either, from what I can see from here," Levi commented. "I wonder if he'll bring her out to the social hour tonight." There were like comments from some of the other

wagons as well. They were all in for some quite different entertainment than what they were accustomed to that night.

Henry Abbott's fiddle and Lucien Aiken's guitar started the
evening off, and it wasn't long before Tiny Futch joined them
with his banjo. Some of the women started dancing by the time
the wagon master arrived in the center of the circle with the
strange lady on his arm. The three musicians stopped simultane-
ously without anyone giving an order. "Folks, I don't wanna interrupt your evenin' long, but I'd like to ask you to do us a favor."
He had everyone's rapt attention. "Maybe you noticed, my
nephew is comin' along behind us totin' a broom. Now, I wanna
introduce you all to Lily Bellmont, a lady that has finally agreed
to marry me after quite a few years I've called on her. So I'd like
to ask you folks to witness our marriage by jumpin' over this
broom tonight and a few short vows we'd like to say to each
other. Will you do that?" He was answered by a tremendous cheer
from the entire audience. "Looks like we're gonna get married,
honey," he said to her. When the raucous cheering died out, he
gave a short speech in which he vowed to take care of her all her
life and do his best to never cause her pain. She vowed to honor
him and to be the wife he deserved to have. Then Clint and
Spud held the broom and Scofield and Lily jumped over it together to a volley of cheers. Afterward, the music started up
again and Scofield spent the rest of the night introducing Lily. At
eight o'clock, as on all nights on the trail, the night guards went
on duty, to be relieved by other guards at midnight, while everybody else went to bed at eight.

Promptly at four o'clock the next morning, the rude screech of
Scofield's bugle announced that it was time to begin another day
on the Oregon Trail. Lily joked to him that had she known he
had a tendency to blow that thing in the middle of the night, she
might have reconsidered her decision to follow him out west.
"You'll get used to it," he told her, "and pretty soon you'll be
wakin' me up to tell me it's time to blow my bugle." He tried to

prepare her for the next couple of weeks of traveling across a seemingly endless prairie where trees refused to grow. There was grass for the livestock and there were dried buffalo and cow chips to use for fires. The latter chore provided a competition for the children on the train to see who could provide the most fuel. It took Spud to convince Lily that the substitute fuel burned clean and was odorless. And Scofield promised her there was a Garden of Eden awaiting them about two weeks away, with trees and bushes and flowers, and best of all, a spring with sweet water. He told her that they would camp there for a couple of days for their honeymoon. Clint could have told her that they always camped there for a couple of days to give all the folks a chance to enjoy some relief from the dry prairie crossing, but he didn't.

The Eden he promised her was a place called Ash Hollow and it was somewhat of a miracle. It was located at the point where they left the Platte River and continued on to the North Platte. Up to this time, they had followed a trail along the south side of the Platte, so it was necessary to cross the river to continue on to the North Platte. This was actually the easiest place to cross the Platte because the river was only one to two feet deep at this point, although it was about a mile wide. Scofield usually broke the train up into four or five columns so as not to churn the bottom up too badly for wagons near the end of a single column. As in years past, the crossing was accomplished without incident. However, the entrance into this Garden of Eden Scofield promised Lily was not one without risk. To reach it, the wagons had to leave the high table lands they had been traveling for forty or more days and descend almost three hundred feet to the North Platte river bottom.

Ash Hollow was, in fact, a deep, wooded canyon about four miles long. And there was only one possible entrance, a steep hill that was in later times called Windlass Hill. But to these travelers it looked so steep as to be impossible to descend. Yet it was the only place that was not a steep bluff with rocky ridges that absolutely denied descent in a wagon. The many ruts of prior wagon trains were easily distinguishable down the steep slope. Most of one whole day was spent lowering the wagons down the steep slope after the horses were unhitched and the wheels were locked by tying them to keep them from rolling. After that every man who could get a rope on the wagon pulled back to try to keep it from crashing down the slope.

When the descent was finally accomplished, the travelers found themselves in a cool, shady canyon with trees and bushes, and the fragrance of roses and jasmine and many other flowers. There were several springs with cool, sweet water and grape-vines and currant bushes that soon attracted the attention of the whole wagon train. "I have to admit," Lily said to Scofield, "I thought you were exaggerating a bit when you told me about this place."

"I don't know why you woulda doubted me," he joked. "I hadn't never lied to you before."

"Yes, but now we're married, and most husbands are liars," she said. "Any wife will tell you that."

He chuckled in response. "Maybe so, but sometimes we have to lie, to keep from gettin' hit over the head with a rollin' pin." On a more serious note then, he changed the subject. "Last year when we camped here, Clint managed to kill a couple of deer. I expect he'll be huntin' again this time. And a little fresh venison would sure help out with the vittles. As attractive as this spot is to us, it's just as attractive to deer and other animals. And that made it a favorite place for the Sioux Injuns to come to hunt."

"Do you think there's a chance we might see some Indians here?" Lily asked, somewhat concerned now.

"Not much of one in recent years, but this was the sight of a big battle back in fifty-five where a whole lot of Brulé Sioux were killed, a lot of 'em were women and children. I don't look to find any here. We'll see some as we get closer to Fort Laramie, but they'll most likely be friendly."

"Is Clint a good scout?" Lily asked.

"The best," was Scofield's brief answer.

"He seems to get along in the outdoors pretty well," she commented.

"He ought to," Scofield replied. "He was a Crow Injun for three years until I found him in a Crow camp. His name was Crawls Through Fire. He was seventeen when I found him in that camp. Took a helluva lot to convince him to come home with me." He went on to tell her how Clint happened to be with the Crows after a Sioux war party killed his parents. "And I'll guarantee you, if there's a deer out there in them woods, we'll be havin' venison for breakfast."

"I hope he doesn't resent me for taking his space in your wagon," she said.

"Don't worry yourself about that for a minute," he assured her. "He's actually got more room for himself since he moved into Will Tucker's wagon. And Will seems glad to have him help with his chores."

Even though everyone had put in a pretty hard day getting the wagons down into the canyon, almost everyone turned out for the social hour after supper. Since firewood was plentiful for the first time in quite a number of days, some of the men built a nice big fire in the center of the wagons. No one was concerned about the usual eight o'clock bedtime except those men unlucky enough to have guard duty that night. They knew there would be no bugle blast at four o'clock in the morning. Scofield looked around at the gathering, divided up into individual groups rehashing the perilous trip down Windlass Hill. The only missing faces, as far as he could tell, was Bass Thornton's man, Leach, and Clint. Not even a joyous occasion like tonight could bring the solemn Leach out. Clint, on the other hand, had saddled his horse and ridden down the canyon a mile or two to the place he found the deer last year. He took his bedroll with him to sleep there that night, so he would be in position when the deer came out of the woods to go to water.

With help from a three-quarter moon to light his way, he made his way along the same game trail he had followed a year ago. He could still hear the sound of the fiddle and the banjo behind him as he continued down the narrow game trail until it finally faded away when he came to the point where the canyon turned at a sharp angle. Just beyond that was the pond he remembered from before. It looked to be bigger than last year, he thought. It was fed by a strong spring that came from somewhere in the steep bluff above the canyon. Picking the same spot that had been successful for him the previous year, he pulled Biscuit's saddle off and let the horse go to the pond to drink. He spread his bedroll, using his saddle as a pillow, checked his rifle to make sure it was ready for deer in the morning, or whatever during the night. Satisfied then, he lay down to sleep. Within a minute or two, he was asleep, awakened a few minutes later when Biscuit returned through the bushes to stand beside him while he slept. He was disturbed no more until the horse whinnied softly just before daylight. Alert at once, for he knew what that meant. So he very carefully rolled out of his blanket, holding his rifle in his hand, and carefully parted the laurel bushes that hid him from the pond. There were six that he could see and probably more that he could not see in the darkness of the forest. He could imagine they had not been hunted in a long time as their dark forms took shape when they came out of the trees.

He wanted two deer, so he picked the last two does following a big buck to the pond. Just enough light was filtering through the branches of the trees surrounding the pond now to permit him to place his shots. He aimed for lung shots right behind the front leg because he didn't want to risk having to go in the pond to get the deer. He braced himself for the shot, aiming at the second from the last and squeezed the trigger. Anticipating the doe behind her to rear up in surprise, he quickly chambered another round in the Henry rifle and caught the second deer right behind her front leg as well. The two sudden cracks of his rifle sent the rest of the deer to scatter into the woods on the other side of the pond.

Moving quickly now, he hurried to finish them with his knife. Both deer had staggered no more than a few feet before they dropped, so he was on one and then the other to end their suffering. With keeping the meat fresh and cool in mind, he used the two coils of rope he brought to string both deer up from the limb of a large tree. Then he proceeded to cut the hides away and gut and bleed them before he backed his horse up next to the tree. He swung one over and dropped it across his saddle. When he was satisfied it would ride all right, he dropped the other doe behind the saddle. When they seemed secure, he retrieved his ropes and started walking back to the wagons, leading Biscuit and his load of meat.

Long his custom, Clayton Scofield was up before the break of first light, even though he was not going to awaken the camp at four o'clock as usual on this morning. He had been in the process of lighting a fire to make some coffee when he heard the first shot off toward the other end of the canyon. *He got one*, he thought. When it was followed almost immediately by a second shot, he grinned and said, "He got two of 'em."

"Got two what?" Lily asked, surprising him.

"I'm sorry, darlin'," he said. "I tried to slip outta the wagon without disturbin' you. I'll have you a little coffee in a minute or two." He answered her question then. "Deer," he said. "Clint got two of 'em."

"He did?" Lily asked. "How do you know that?"

"'Cause I heard two shots from that Henry rifle of his. We'll have fresh deer meat for breakfast. I need to get ready to help him butcher them deer, the sooner, the better."

"How do you know he got two deer?" Lily wanted to know. "Maybe he shot at the same deer twice before he knocked him down. Or could be, he missed when he shot at two deer."

Scofield stroked his chin thoughtfully and grinned at her before he answered. "Darlin', when you get to know Clint a little better, you'll learn not to ask silly questions. I need to roll Spud outta his blankets 'cause he's gonna be helpin' with the butcherin' and the cookin'." He went over to the wagon to wake Spud, who was sleeping under it. Lily couldn't hear exactly what words passed between the two men, but Spud rolled out of his blankets right away and hurried down the creek to a thick stand of fir trees that the men favored to greet the new day. She watched the two of them when Spud came back as they decided on a tree close to the wagon to begin the butchering. She was amazed when, a few minutes after that, Clint came walking back into the circle of wagons leading his horse carrying two deer carcasses.

"I guess I'll learn not to question anything Clint attempts," she announced to no one.

It didn't take long for the word to travel the circle of wagons that the three men were butchering two deer to be cooked for breakfast, and they were sharing the fresh meat with anyone who wanted some until it gave out. So the early risers held an advantage in securing a share. Clint and Spud tried to butcher the meat in reasonable-sized portions to make the meat go as far as possible. But for the hosts of this venison breakfast, those riding the wagon master's wagon, Clint took their cuts from the backstrap, that part of the deer that sits on each side of the spine and includes the loin. He also took cuts from the tenderloin, which he especially liked. It was a little more work to get to, since it was beneath the spine, along the insides of the ribs, but well worth the trouble in his opinion. Will Tucker was included in the select group who got first choice of the cuts, since he was sharing his wagon with Clint.

Although they took their favorite cuts of the deer, they were not greedy. They only took enough for the one big feast, for they wanted everyone to share in the breakfast. The meat would spoil quickly, anyway, and they could not take the time to smoke a quantity to preserve it. There were plenty of good parts of the deer in the rump and the sirloin. No one complained. It was a welcome change from the salt pork and the beef chips.

# Chapter 7

After a couple of days of rest, the settlers set out on the trail along the North Platte, and the harshness of the prairie once again reminded them of the challenge they had undertaken. All the delights of Ash Hollow were distant memories by the time they reached Courthouse Rock four days later. Another day found them camping within sight of Chimney Rock. Both of these were checkpoints along the trail that they had read about when planning their trip to the Willamette Valley. Leaving Chimney Rock, they reached Scotts Bluff in just under three full days. It was actually an area of many rugged bluffs, and Scotts Bluff was the highest of them. At the social hour after supper that night, Scofield informed those who were interested that they had completed about one third of their westward journey. It was meant to be encouragement, but it received a fair amount of groans with a few suggestions to turn around and go back to Ash Hollow. Scofield told them they would strike Fort Laramie in about four days, where they would stay over an extra day so they could take advantage of the blacksmith and harness maker if they were in need of their services. And they could replenish supplies that had been exhausted at the post trader's store. So that was enough to award him a faint cheer. "Tiny," he called out to Tiny Futch, "maybe you'd best warm that banjo up. These folks need something to pick up their spirits."

"We ain't all newlyweds like you and Lily," Levi Watkins yelled.

"It'd take a heck of a lot more than Tiny's banjo to pick up your spirits," Ella Watkins commented.

"Is that so, old woman?" Levi came back. "As I recollect, there was a time when I used to dance you till you dropped."

"As I recollect," Ella responded, "I had to work twice as hard as you, just tryin' to keep you from stomping on my feet."

"I don't believe either one of you can dance a lick," Tracy Bishop said. "Crank that banjo up, there, Tiny. Give 'em somethin' to make 'em high-step it."

Tiny accepted the challenge and started flailing away on a lively tune that some of the women liked to buck dance to. Henry Abbott picked it up with his fiddle, so Lucien Aiken joined in with his guitar. "Come on, Ella!" Ada Bishop called out. "Show him how it's done!"

"It ain't the same, tryin' to do the steps on the ground like this," Ella said. "You need a good wood floor to buck dance." Nevertheless, she didn't back away from the challenge and started doing her steps in time with the music. "Come on, old man," she goaded her husband.

"You just remember, you asked for this," Levi told her. Then he walked out to face her and began to make a series of alternate up and down movements with his toes and heels, combined with a shuffling move with both feet. It was hard to describe it. It most resembled a man who had stepped in something and was having a helluva hard time wiping it off his shoes. And all the while, the expression on his face was one of judge-like concentration. The small crowd of spectators were not sure which was appropriate, to cheer or jeer, so they remained quiet.

Of all those watching, the most surprised was his wife. This was her first time seeing her husband perform that particular routine. He ended his performance with a final stomp of the ground and a double click of his heels, still maintaining the deadpan expression on his face. Then he returned to the stool he had been sitting on to a light patter of applause. "What in the big blue-eyed world was that?" Ella was prompted to inquire, still puzzled by the ultraserious expression still in place, like that of a man who had proven himself when challenged.

"Maybe there's still some things you don't know about me," he replied, smugly.

"I reckon you're right about that," Ella said. "I didn't know you were crazy, but I know that you still can't dance worth a nickel."

Scofield laughed at the exchange between them and announced, "Well, I don't reckon I'll hang around to see the fight. Four o'clock still comes pretty early in the mornin'. Lulu"—he slipped then recovered quickly—"Lily's most likely already gone to bed." No one seemed to notice, so he figured no one was listening, anyway. He was not sure if any of the men on the train had visited Leo's Road Ranch when they were parked at Fort Kearny. But he knew it would be an embarrassment to his wife if they knew she worked there under the name of Lulu Belle, even though she was only a cook and not one of the doves.

At seven the next morning, the wagons started out on Mitchell Pass, which was a road between Scotts Bluff and South Bluff and a shortcut from the original trail that ran farther south. It was a fifty-four mile journey to Fort Laramie at the confluence of the Laramie and Platte rivers.

It was almost suppertime the day Scofield led his wagon train to his usual camping ground a short distance up the Laramie River from the fort, to find Clint waiting for them. He had ridden on ahead of the wagons to make sure their favorite camping spot was not occupied. Biscuit whinnied a greeting to Scofield's Morgan to officially welcome the wagon train to Fort Laramie. Maybe the Palouse gelding knew about the pleasant surprise awaiting humans and animals alike at this camp. It didn't take long after the wagons were circled up and the stock unhitched that the travelers discovered that the water in the Laramie River was sweet and clean for drinking, washing, and cooking. It was only minutes before over half the folks on the train were in the river, clothes and all, with the first real chance to wash the dust from their clothes and bodies. Walking sometimes as far as fifteen miles a day over the hot, dry prairie dried out their lips so badly that some resorted to using axle grease on them. "That'll raise everybody's spirits for a little while, at least till we get to South Pass," Scofield told Lily. "Tomorrow, we'll go over to the post trader's store and pick up anything you're runnin' short of."

"There's not much of anything I need," Lily said. "I'm sure Spud has his own list of supplies we need." She gave him a helpless look and commented, "You know, I try to help him any way I can, but he makes it pretty plain that cooking is his job, so I try not to get in his way."

"I know that, honey, and I appreciate it," Scofield said. "I think he was expectin' me to tell him that you would do all the cookin' when you came with us. He's pretty rough around the edges, but he gets his feelin's hurt awful easy." He chuckled then and said, "I know Clint is probably wishin' you would make some of your biscuits. You're the reason he named that Palouse he rides, Biscuit. Couple years back when we stopped at Leo's, Clint snatched a biscuit off a tray on our way out the door. When he got outside, his horse started nosin' around his hand, wantin' to see. Clint opened his hand to show him and his horse snatched it right outta his hand. So Clint named him Biscuit."

He got a healthy chuckle from Lily in response to the story. "I wish I could make some biscuits for him," she said. "But you know you need a good oven to bake good biscuits, and I plum forgot to bring one with me."

"If we were gonna be in one place for any length of time, Clint would most likely build you an oven," Scofield said. When she asked how he could do that, he said, "He'd dig it outta the ground like the Injuns do."

\*    \*    \*

After supper was finished and the usual couples began to as-semble in the middle of the wagons, Clint went back to Will's wagon to get several boxes of cartridges he had transferred there from Scofield's wagon when he moved out to make room for Lily. The cartridges were to be a gift to the old chief, Yellow Hand, to fit the Sharps Model 1853 Sporting Rifle he had presented him with the year before. When he got back to Scofield's wagon, he checked with Spud to see if he still had any unopened sacks of coffee and flour. When he found that he did, he asked if he could buy them from him.

"Buy 'em from me?" Spud asked. "What are you talkin' about?"

"I'm goin' to see my Crow friends tomorrow and I'd like to take my Crow mother something. I'd just go to the post trader to-morrow and buy 'em, but that village is twelve miles from here. And I gotta go up there and back tomorrow, so I'm leavin' here before Seth Ward opens his store in the mornin'. If you'd let me buy that stuff from you, it would sure help me out."

Spud scratched his chin as if considering it. "I might could do that," he said, "if you was to do me a favor in turn."

"Sure, whaddaya need?"

"I've had me a cravin' all day for a drink of likker," he said. "You know where that saloon is up the river someplace?"

"Jake's Place," Clint replied. "Yeah, I know where it is, 'bout a mile and a half up this river." He corrected himself. "About a mile from our camp here. You can't miss it. Matter of fact, if you was to walk over to the riverbank and follow that path, it'd take you right to it. You'd most likely see some soldiers goin' up that path. Just follow them."

"I was wonderin' if you might wanna go with me," Spud said. "Whaddaya say? Could you use a little drink? Scofield used to go with me, but he's a married man now."

Clint realized then, that for whatever reason, Spud didn't want to go by himself. "Yeah, I reckon I could use a drink. Just one would be about all I'd want, though. If you're thinking about having just one or two, I reckon I could go with you for that. Like I said, I'm plannin' to leave early in the mornin'."

"Let's go then," Spud said, "so we ain't too late gettin' back."

As a matter of habit, Clint picked up his rifle and they started walking toward the riverbank. Still sitting by his supper fire, Will Tucker saw them and called out, "Hey, Clint, where you goin'?"

"We're gonna walk up to Jake's Place for a drink of whiskey," Clint answered. "You wanna go?"

"No, I reckon not," Will called back. "I'm fixin' to go wash some clothes in that river."

"Well, I reckon that is a lot more enjoyable," Clint japed.

"It's a good idea if he don't get into drinkin' too much, anyway," Spud remarked. "After the hell that boy's been through, it'd be too dang easy to get sucked into a likker bottle for good."

"I expect that's true," Clint said, somewhat surprised that Spud cared one way or the other.

When they reached Jake's Place, it appeared to be fairly busy at this early hour. As expected, most of the customers were soldiers from the fort, but there were a few non-military— cowhands, trappers, drifters, typical for a saloon close to an army post. The far end of the bar was the least crowded, so Clint and Spud went down there. Clint recognized the bartender as the same fellow that tended bar last year. He even remembered his name, Elmo. "Whaddleya have?" Elmo asked.

Before Clint could reply, Spud said, "Give us a bottle of corn whiskey and two glasses." He had his money in his hand and when Clint started to protest, Spud said, "Put your money back in your pocket. You said you didn't want but one drink, and I'm gonna take most of this bottle back to the wagon." When Elmo came back with the bottle and the glasses, Spud paid him and poured two drinks out of his bottle. "You can gimme two bits for that drink if it'll make you feel any better."

"Right," Clint said and gave him a quarter.

They tossed that drink back and Spud poured himself another, then held the bottle over Clint's empty glass and waited for him to say. "All right, one more," Clint decided. "That first one didn't taste bad a-tall."

"Keep your money," Spud insisted when Clint started to dig for another quarter. "Let's sit down and enjoy these," he said when three soldiers vacated a table in the back of the room. So they hurried back to take it before someone else did. To Clint, this was not a good sign. He was already thinking he would have to leave Spud there if he intended to finish the bottle here instead of taking it back to the wagon as he had said.

*I'll sit with him for a few drinks*, Clint thought, *but then I'm going back, whether he does or not.* So he sat at the table, watching the other drinkers in the saloon, while Spud downed a couple more shots. Then a familiar face appeared in the doorway and walked to the bar. Clint nudged Spud's arm to get his attention. When Spud turned to look at him, he had big tears rolling down his cheeks. "What tha . . . ?" Clint started. "What's ailin' you?"

"Nothin'," Spud answered and put his arm over his face and wiped his eyes on his shirtsleeve. "What did you poke me for?"

"I wanted you to see who just walked in," Clint said and nodded toward the front end of the bar.

"I swear," Spud remarked, "it's Bass Thornton's ape." He craned his neck in an effort to see Leach more clearly. "I wanna see if he talks to the bartender, or if he tries to make sign language." After a few moments, he said, "It's hard to tell, but he ain't makin' no sign language, and the bartender's gittin' a bottle of whiskey for him. Bass musta sent him up here to get a bottle for him."

Since it didn't appear that Leach saw them sitting in the back of the saloon, they didn't try to get his attention, assuming he would take his bottle and turn around and leave. But he didn't do that. When Elmo gave him his change, Leach pushed some of it back and Elmo poured him a drink from the bottle on the bar. "Bass bought him a drink for himself," Spud said, still commenting on the incident. Leach, being the brute-like figure that he was, was not the type to go unnoticed in a rowdy barroom. Clint had to admit that the man did remind him of pictures he had seen of a great ape. Not particularly tall, but with broad shoulders and big hairy arms, the similarity was completed by a large, round head that seemed to have been placed on the shoulders with the neck having been forgotten. "Uh-oh," Spud uttered when one of three men sitting at a table close to that end of the bar made a comment that brought a laugh from his two companions. Clint and Spud were too far away to hear what he said in the noisy saloon, but it caused Leach to turn to stare at the table. "Somebody's fixin' to make a big mistake," Spud said, thinking back about Leach lifting the rear end of a loaded wagon out of a hole in the Kansas River. Leach didn't say anything. He just continued to stare at the three men, his face barren of any expression, as usual. This seemed to irritate one of the three men to the point where he pushed his chair back and stood up. He was not a soldier, probably a drifter, and Clint could see that he was wearing a handgun. All the noise in that part of the room stopped when those around them sensed something was about to happen. Consequently Clint and Spud could hear the drifter order Leach out of the saloon or pay the consequences.

Clint started to get out of his chair, but Spud grabbed his arm to stop him. "Let's just see if he gets out like the feller told him before we get into it." Clint let himself be restrained, but he was still wary, afraid that Leach was really mentally impaired, and he didn't want to see him harassed because of it.

"I told you to get your ugly face outta here," the drifter yelled at Leach, loud enough for everyone in the saloon to hear it.

Leach didn't say anything. He turned around and pushed some more of his change toward Elmo, and the bartender poured him another drink. Then Leach turned back to face the big drifter and held the glass of whiskey up toward him as if saluting him. Then he tossed it back and wiped his mouth with his sleeve. The gesture was enough to infuriate the drifter. He immediately charged the bar and Leach, whose back was turned to him again. Not willing to watch Leach taken advantage of, Clint got up from his chair. But Leach spun around in time to meet the drifter's charge. With one handful of the drifter's shirt and the other hand clutching the crotch of his trousers, Leach lifted him up off the floor and threw him in the middle of the table, knocking it and the two seated drifters over backward. All three came up from the floor with six-guns drawn, facing the stoic Leach, who was unarmed. "You just signed your death warrant, mister," the man who had been thrown onto the table promised.

His threat was punctuated by the sound of a Henry rifle cocking. "The first man who pulls a trigger gets my first shot," Clint warned. "Who's it gonna be?" Startled by the sudden appearance of the tall man in buckskins, his rifle leveled at them, there was a hesitancy to be the first one to pull the trigger.

They were made to consider the risk further when Spud stepped up beside Clint, his six-gun in hand, and promised, "The second one gets my first shot."

One of the men holstered his weapon and said, "I reckon there ain't no use for a killin' over this mess." He pointed at the broken table and bottle and glasses spilled on the floor. "But somebody oughta have to pay for the damage done here."

"I think you're right about that," Clint said and pointed his rifle at the original antagonist. "I reckon it oughta be him. He started the whole thing. He don't look too old to learn to mind his own business, but he ain't gonna last too many more years if he don't start to pretty quick." Clint and Spud watched them closely until the other two put their handguns away and started picking up everything that got scattered on the floor. Clint turned to Spud and spoke softly so they wouldn't hear him. "I expect we'd do well to leave here before they do. Are you ready to go?" Spud said he was. "How 'bout you, Leach?" Clint asked then, and Leach nodded and picked up the bottle he paid for. So while the three drifters were looking around on the floor for some money that had been on the table, Clint, Spud, and Leach walked quietly out the door.

Outside, they had about a mile to walk down the dark trail beside the river, knowing that the three men they had left behind them were most likely riding three of the horses they had seen tied at the hitching rail. Clint and Spud were both of the opinion that the altercation with the drifters back at the saloon might not be over yet. And they preferred to be the ones in ambush waiting for them to pass, rather than have it the other way around. They assumed that Leach felt the same; he didn't say. Regardless, they were about halfway back to the wagons when they heard the three horses coming along behind them in the dark. So they left the path and crouched just below the edge of the riverbank to let them pass. "We oughta caught 'em by now if they was walkin'," they heard one of them say. "They musta rode up there," another one said. "I was sure as hell hopin' to put a bullet in that damn gorilla that like to broke my back," a third voice complained.

They walked their horses on past the three hiding beneath the bank. And when they had passed, Leach picked up a dead limb, and sneaked up behind the last horse. Using the limb like a whip, he swung as hard as he could and swatted the unsuspecting horse across the rump. The horse squealed and jumped into a full gallop, almost knocking the other two horses off the path. "What the hell's the matter with you, Tom?" one of the men yelled after him, then they both chased after him at a lope. Clint and Spud exchanged incredulous looks with neither thinking of anything to say.

It was the last they saw of the three drifters as they walked on back to the wagons. When they split off to go to their separate wagons, Leach caught Clint by the elbow to stop him. "Clint," he said, his voice deep, like the croaking of a frog, "'preciate it. I owe you." He turned and walked toward Thornton's wagon, holding Bass's bottle of whiskey. Clint was too stunned to reply before he was gone.

"Well, if that ain't somethin' to scratch your head over," Spud commented. "Not only talked, he said a whole sentence. Sounded like a frog on a lily pad." They both thought of how long he had remained underwater at the Kansas River crossing and Levi's comment that they weren't ears on the side of his head, they were gills. "I see the social hour is still in swing. You gonna go visit for a while?"

"No," Clint replied. "Like I said, I'm gonna start out early in the mornin'. Goin' to see my Crow father, old Yellow Hand. Thanks to you lettin' me buy those supplies from you, it'll be a lot easier to get there and back in one day."

"Ain't no problem," Spud said. "I 'preciate you goin' to Jake's Place with me. I reckon ol' Leach is pretty glad you went with me, too."

That reminded Clint of something he had almost forgotten, what with the altercation Leach stirred up. "Just before that business with Leach, I looked at you and you were cryin'. Is everything all right, Spud?"

"Oh," Spud said, "yeah, everythin's all right. It just hits me once in a while when I have a few drinks. I get to thinkin' about the years I wasted when I was a young man and couldn't stay away from the bottle. Sometimes I get downright melancholy after I've had a few drinks and start thinkin' about things that coulda gone a different way. I got to where I was afraid to have more'n one or two shots when there was anybody with me but Scofield. He knows how I get. But he ain't gettin' away from Lulu Belle now—I mean, Lily. So I thought I'd get you to go with me. I figured it'd be all right if you knew about my problem. I hope you ain't mad."

"'Course I ain't mad," Clint said. "I didn't think nothin' of it. I'm glad you feel comfortable drinkin' with me." They came to Will's wagon then, so Clint said, "I'll see you tomorrow night when I get back."

# Chapter 8

He left before breakfast the next morning, planning to stop about halfway to the Crow village to rest his horses and make some coffee and maybe eat a piece of hardtack. The horses could easily go the full twelve miles to the village, but he thought he'd like to have his coffee before he got to the Crow camp. He was leading a packhorse, one of the three horses they had picked up from the attempt on Scofield's life at Leo's Road Ranch. Once he got into Spud's supplies, he kept adding things he was sure Mourning Song was probably without, until he needed some help for Biscuit to carry everything. He rode back up the trail they had walked on the night just past and when he went past Jake's Place, it was shuttered and closed, and he naturally thought about the events of the night before. The mystery of Roy Leach was one that he had no answer for. The man was absolutely unpredictable. And he didn't hesitate to take action without any concern for the results they might cause. He could have been shot last night had they not happened to be there, and again when he swatted the horse. *But he actually spoke enough to thank me,* Clint thought. *Maybe he considers me a friend now.* "I don't know that I need a friend like Leach," he confided to Biscuit.

He shook his head to clear it of thoughts of Leach, but they were replaced by thoughts of Spud Williams with big tears running down his face. He would have believed the story Spud told him behind the crying about anybody else but Spud. He always figured every bone in Spud's body was cynical. "Uncle Clayton never told me about Spud's cryin' problem when he got drunk," he complained to Biscuit. "I don't need to know everybody's problems. Now, I'm tellin' mine to my horse." After he stopped to have his coffee and hardtack, he alternated Biscuit's pace between a walk and a trot to shorten the final miles to the village. Consequently, he arrived there well before the sun was directly overhead.

The village was located in the same grassy meadow he found them in the year before. When he rode in, most of the women were down at the river's edge, doing the morning chores. They stopped to look at him and some of them recognized him from last year and called out welcome greetings. Hearing the women calling out, the few men left in the village, most of them boys, came out of their tipis to see who had come. "Crawls Through Fire," a young boy called in greeting. Clint remembered him from last year. His name was Brings Pony.

Then a young warrior closer to Clint's age came out of a tipi and walked briskly toward him. "Welcome, Crawls Through Fire," he said. "It is good to see you."

Clint dismounted, thinking the young brave looked familiar but he didn't remember seeing him in the camp the year before. Then it struck him. "Broken Wing! I didn't recognize you at first!"

"It has been a long time, my friend," Broken Wing said, beaming with pleasure at one who had been his closest friend when they were boys. "It looks like the years have been kind to you."

"And you as well," Clint returned. "You were not here last year. Have you decided to come back for good?"

"No, I am still working for the soldiers as a scout. I came back when I got word that Yellow Hand had died." When he saw the look of surprise in Clint's face, he paused. "You did not know?"

"No," Clint replied. "I didn't know. I came to bring Yellow Hand some more cartridges for a rifle I gave him last year, and some things I thought Mourning Song might need. When I was here last year, I knew it wouldn't be long, but I had hoped to say goodbye to him, since this is the last wagon train my uncle and I will lead."

A small crowd of people had gathered around them by that time and they parted to make a path for Mourning Song as she walked slowly, but still straight and tall, in spite of her age. "My son," she greeted him.

"Mother," he replied and they embraced. "I am truly sorry I didn't get here in time to say goodbye to Yellow Hand. I brought you a few little things you might need." He looked around him at the gathering, realizing it was noticeably smaller than last year. He looked back at Broken Wing then. "Maybe to share," he said. "I brought some flour and cornmeal, some coffee, some sugar and salt, rice, and some dried beans. I wish I could have brought more. I also brought more cartridges for the rifle I gave Yellow Hand."

"Brings Pony has the rifle now," Broken Wing said. "It is a good rifle. He has learned to use it well. It is good that you brought more cartridges. I think he is about out."

"Come," Clint said to the two young women who walked Mourning Song from her tipi, "help me unload these things from my packhorse." They responded at once and he untied his packs and they started carrying them inside the tipi. He handed Brings Pony the boxes of cartridges for the Sharps rifle.

When that was done, Clint unsaddled Biscuit and the pack-horse and let them go to water and to graze. "What are they going to do?" he asked Broken Wing. "They can't stay here much longer."

"They know that," Broken Wing answered. "Some of the young boys want to go up into the Absaroka Mountains to hide. But the older people are ready to go to the reservation in Montana Territory. I have told them I will take them there when they decide to go." They talked a while longer, then Broken Wing asked, "You will go to the far Oregon country?"

"Yes, as I said, I won't be going back to Missouri to lead the settlers out there after this trip. It is time I stayed in one place and thought about a family."

"Yes, you are getting pretty old," Broken Wing joked. "Do you have a wife out there?"

"No, no wife," Clint answered. "What about you?"

"Being a scout for the soldiers leaves me no time and no place to keep a wife. The Crow warriors have always been at peace with the soldiers, and many of us are working for them now, scouts for their battles with the Sioux and the Cheyenne. So I think that when the Sioux and the Cheyenne are beaten and moved to the reservations, the Crow scouts will be allowed to own land and live free with the white man."

"That would be a good thing for you and the other scouts," Clint said. He didn't tell him, however, that he seriously doubted that would happen. More likely, the government would send the loyal scouts to the reservations with the rest of the Indians. He hoped he was wrong, but he didn't think there was much chance that he was. He spent most of the day visiting with Broken Wing, reminiscing about the three years Clint had spent in the Crow village. The women cooked a big meal using the supplies he had brought with him. They ate and talked some more, and then he said his goodbyes, this time for good, and he turned Biscuit and the packhorse back down the trail toward Fort Laramie. He had a sad feeling, not for himself but for the uncertainty awaiting his friends in Yellow Hand's village. While they had talked, he had asked Broken Wing if he had seen any signs of Sioux hunting parties while he and Brings Pony were hunting. Broken Wing said that he had not and he had hunted in a wide area around the fort.

He managed to make it back to the circle of wagons by suppertime. For reasons no one was interested in investigating, Spud was feeling in a cooperative mood and had allowed Lily to help him prepare supper. He even admitted that she had a real knack for making pan biscuits. "Well, that is something," Clint allowed when Scofield told him. "I think he's startin' to mellow a little bit since he's gettin' close to retirin' from this business." He didn't mention the crying episode at Jake's Place.

"Spud told me about that little business you and him had at Jake's Place last night. He swears that Leach ain't no mute a-tall. Said he said a whole string of words to you and thanked you for steppin' in when he got into it with three fellows who didn't like his looks. Spud said he was set to take on all three of 'em. He didn't even know you and Spud were settin' at a table in the back until they pulled their guns on him and you stepped in. Was Leach wearin' a gun?"

"Uh-uh," Clint replied. "Maybe he didn't think they might shoot him if he picked the fellow up that got in his face and threw him on the table where his friends were sittin'. That's his trouble. He takes a notion to do something and he just does it. He doesn't take time to think about what trouble it might cause. And he's strong as an ox. Did Spud tell you about Leach whackin' one of their horses with a tree limb just to make 'em run?"

"Yeah, he told me about that," Scofield said. "Sure looks like he's used to doin' everything without thinkin'. Makes you wonder what Bass Thornton really plans to use him for, don't it?"

"Well, did you have a good visit with your Injun folks?" Scofield asked, changing the subject.

"Yes and no, I reckon you could say," Clint replied. "Yellow Hand, he was my Crow father," he said aside to Lily, who was listening to the conversation, "Yellow Hand was dead." Lily looked distressed at once, so he was quick to assure her that the cause of his death was old age and was expected for some time now. "My Crow mother, Mourning Song, is not far from joining Yellow Hand, but she looked fit." Talking directly to Scofield then, he asked, "When you came and got me from Yellow Hand's village, do you remember my best friend there? He was my age. Name was Broken Wing. Well, he was there and I hadn't seen him since that day you darn near kidnapped me."

"He's good at kidnapping people," Lily remarked.

"Both of you came willingly," Scofield maintained. "I don't know if I remember Broken Wing or not. I'm sure I wouldn't recognize him if I saw him today."

"I almost didn't," Clint said. "But we were pretty young back then. He's been working as a scout for the army here at Fort Laramie. I asked him if there had been any trouble with Sioux raiders on any of the few ranches hereabouts. He said they hadn't seen signs of any Sioux for quite a while."

"Yeah, that's what Seth Ward told me," Scofield said. "So maybe we won't have to worry about that this trip. 'Course when you don't worry about 'em, that's when they usually show up. Last year, they told us pretty much the same thing," he said to Lily. "And then we had some Sioux horse thieves try to run off all our horses the next night at Register Cliff. And we'll be campin' at Register Cliff again tomorrow night."

"Maybe we ought to camp somewhere else tomorrow night," Lily suggested.

"Then I might have a mutiny on my hands if I didn't stop there, so these folks can scratch their names all over that sandstone bluff," Scofield declared.

"Why do they wanna to that?" Lily asked.

"They get this stuff from readin' all those guidebooks about the Oregon Trail. Register Cliff is one of about three places where folks like to write their names and the date, so folks that come along behind 'em will know they passed there and when."

Lily chuckled. "Well, I can see why they might wanna do that. Where's the harm in that?"

"It's called defacin' nature," Scofield replied.

"You do that every time you cut down a tree," Lily came back.

"You tell her, Clint. You know what I'm talking about."

"Leave me outta this," Clint said. "I've got no opinion one way or the other. I think I'll go watch the dancin'. Maybe Levi Watkins will put on another show. I missed his first one."

"Well, let me tell you, it's the kind of performance you don't wanna see but once," Scofield remarked.

"At least I can listen to Tiny playin' the banjo," Clint said. "I believe the banjo is my favorite instrument." He paused, then thought to add, "Of course, I mean next to Uncle Clayton's bugle." He got up to leave. "You folks goin' to the social hour?"

"I don't know," Scofield answered. "If Lily wants to, I reckon."

"Well, I'll see you over by the fire, if you do." He walked out toward the center of the circled wagons.

"Your nephew is a fine young man, isn't he?" Lily commented.

"He sure is," Scofield agreed, "and he's the best scout in the business. My brother and his wife ain't had but one big worry and that was to get me and Clint both paired up with a good woman. Now, I've already took care of my part of the problem. So they'll both be on poor Clint when we get back to get him hitched. When they get that done, they'll be happy. They'll feel like they've done everything the Lord put 'em here to do."

"Does Clint know that?" Lily asked.

"I think he does, because he actually brought the girl home with us on the last trip. I know for certain the girl would marry him in a minute, but she ain't sure he's wantin' to get married. She's afraid he can't get by her past. So they're like best friends right now."

"You mean like you got by my past?" Lily asked.

"Hers is a lot different. She got married when she wasn't much more'n a child to a mean drunk who beat the hell out of her. Lucky for her, he got hisself shot, so she married Clint's friend, and they weren't married two months before he got killed. So she's totin' all that baggage and it was always Clint she ran to for help. Besides, you ain't got no past in my mind. As far as I'm concerned you weren't even born before that day you walked into this camp. If I know Clint, he'll feel the same way about her as I do about you. It don't matter what happened yesterday, we're gonna live our lives from the weddin' day forward."

"Why, Clayton Scofield, you big ol' teddy bear. I've a good mind to tell all these folks what a romantic cuss you are."

"You do, and I'll whup you good right out there at social hour, so everybody knows how things really stand."

"Now you're talking about a place that you really don't want to go to," she teased. "You think that Leach is an animal when he's riled, you ain't seen nothing till you get on my bad side."

# Chapter 9

The bugle screeched out at four o'clock the next morning as threatened the night before, and the travelers prepared to return to the grind of following the North Platte once again. At seven on the nose, the wheels turned and it was farewell to Fort Laramie and onward toward the Continental Divide at South Pass. It would be just one day's travel to reach Register Cliff. Clayton had told Lily that he always stopped to please the travelers, but it was a full day's travel and there was convenient water and lush grass for grazing. It was a little past the usual five o'clock stopping time when the pioneers actually rolled into the grassy valley by the river and got their first look at the massive sandstone bluffs that bore the name Register Cliff. The bluffs, on the south side of the river, stood about one hundred feet high, and the huge blank faces left the perfect place to register one's passage. It was easy to carve a name and date, and a message as well, into the soft sandstone face. So as soon as the wagons were circled and the livestock cared for, there was a rush to get to the bluff.

With the incident that happened here a year ago in his mind, Clint didn't unsaddle Biscuit right away. He told Scofield that he was going to take a little ride across the river behind the bluffs to pick up any sign of recent visitors. Scofield thought that was a good idea. So Clint crossed over the river and rode along the bluff until coming to a passage that led up and over to the other side of the massive cliff. Then he scouted the length of the bluff for about fifty yards in each direction from the passage before returning to the camp to report no sign of any recent visitors. "I reckon the reports of no Indian activity anywhere near the fort were on the money," Clint said. "I didn't see any sign that would tell me anybody had been checkin' on this campsite."

"Good," Scofield said. "Let's eat supper. Then we'll take a look around the wagons. Make sure there ain't no gaps between 'em like there was the night those Injuns tried to drive our whole herd out between Tyson's and Gilbert's wagons."

"Right," Clint replied, grinning when he remembered the incident.

"Pa!" Caleb Yocum blurted. "Lookee yonder! They's somebody gotta camp up ahead!"

"Where?" His brother Zach asked.

"Straight ahead, yonder," Caleb said and pointed straight up the wagon track they had been following all day. Now all three saw the faint rosy tint in the sky up ahead of them.

"They got a good-sized fire to light up the sky like that, ain't they, Pa?" Zach asked. "Maybe a good chance to swap these wore-out horses we're ridin'."

"I hope they've got some food," Caleb said. "I'm 'bout to starve to death."

"That's too blame big to be a campfire, you dang fools," Jesse Yocum told his sons. "Might be a bunch of Injuns camped up ahead. We'll just keep ridin' on this trail till we get close enough to see who it is. Then we might have to ride a wide circle around 'em." They had been lucky to run up on two trappers camped on the Bozeman Trail that morning, but they hadn't been much better off than he and his two sons when it came to food and horses. The only thing of value they had was a pack of beaver hides. So Jesse's sons traded them a bullet in the back of the head for their horses and the skins. Jesse figured he'd trade the skins at Fort Laramie.

As they gradually closed the distance between them and the pink glow in the sky, it suddenly struck Jesse where they were. "It's a damn wagon train. They're parked in that campground by that place where they carve their names in the side of that big bluff." He gave his tired horse a kick with his heels to encourage a little more speed out of him. The horse responded but for only a few strides before resuming its weary pace.

"I swear," Zach complained, "I was sure hopin' it was gonna be a chance to get somethin' to eat."

"Maybe it is," Jesse told him. "Yep, it's a wagon train, all right," he said when they got close enough to see the circle of wagons near the water. "We might get us somethin' to eat and swap these horses for some fresh ones to boot."

"How we gonna do that, Pa?" Caleb asked. "They's too many of 'em to fight."

"We ain't gonna try to fight 'em, you idiot, we'll just ask for a little Christian charity for us poor boys who are down on our luck." Then a thought struck him. "I hope to hell they're a Mormon wagon train."

"What's a Mormon?" Caleb asked.

"Never mind," Jesse said. "He's a feller who's gonna give us somethin' to eat and then let us slip off with three of his horses."

"Better make that four of his horses, Pa," Zach reminded him. "That packhorse is about ready to cash in, too. And we need them hides to trade with."

"That's right," Jesse said. "That's good thinkin'. You ain't as dumb as I thought you was."

"Thanks, Pa," Zach said.

"All right," Jesse said. "We're just gonna ride right on down there by that wagon on this end with the tongue pointed this way. You two keep your mouths shut. I'll do all the talkin'. Lookee yonder, there's a feller with a fiddle. Looks like they're gittin' ready to have a party. This is a good time to hit 'em. You boys try to look half-starved."

"That ain't gonna be no trouble," Caleb said.

"Well, Mr. and Mrs. Scofield," Tracy Bishop announced. "I see you are going to favor us with your presence tonight."

"We had to come in case Levi was scheduled to give another performance," Scofield answered him.

Tracy laughed. "I don't know if there's a chance of that or not. Ella might go after him with a broom. I don't think she liked it that much."

Seeing Scofield and Lily come to join the entertainment, Clint brought over a little short bench he took from Will's wagon and placed it near the fire for them. Henry Abbott stuck his fiddle under his chin and started playing around with a little reel, then suddenly stopped to stare toward Scofield's wagon. "What in the . . . ?" Tracy started but didn't finish when one, then two, then a third rider filed between Scofield's wagon and Tiny Futch's, who was last in line for tomorrow. The third rider was leading a packhorse. All the busy conversation stopped when everyone became aware of the rough-looking visitors riding horses that looked exhausted. Scofield got up from the bench and walked out to meet them. Clint followed him.

"Howdy," Scofield offered when the three pulled up before him and Clint. "You havin' some trouble?"

"Howdy, sir," Jesse returned. "My name's Jesse Yocum and these are my two boys, Caleb and Zach. And I've gotta tell you we're mighty glad to see some white Christian people. Me and my boys was jumped by a Sioux war party back on the Bozeman Trail, and we've been runnin' for our lives ever since. We've plumb wore out our horses, but them Sioux finally gave up and turned back. But we kept a-runnin' ever since this afternoon. Trouble is, they got our other two packhorses with all our food and supplies on 'em, so we ain't et nothin' since supper last night. I figured you folks musta just come from Fort Laramie, and maybe you're stocked up on your supplies. And maybe you might be interested in tradin' a little somethin' for me and my boys to eat for some prime beaver pelts. I'd offer you money, but we're plumb outta that. We're just lookin' for some grub for tonight. We oughta be able to get somethin' for our furs when we get to Fort Laramie tomorrow night. We was plannin' on stoppin' here for the night 'cause our poor horses can't go another mile." When he saw a bit of doubt in Scofield's expression, he said, "We'll make camp a little way down the river from you folks, so we won't bother you none."

"You ain't ate since last night, huh?" Scofield responded, still a bit skeptical. "Well, we ain't got much use for any beaver pelts, but we can spare some grub to keep you from starvin', so keep your pelts to trade at the fort."

"Why, that's mighty Christian of you, friend, but we didn't wanna come in here beggin' for a handout. It's just that these pelts is the only thing we've got to deal with since we lost our other packhorses."

"Keep your pelts," Scofield said. "You'd best go ahead and take care of those horses. You're right, they look like they've been wrung out. Make your camp and we'll scare up something to feed you."

"God bless you, sir," Jesse responded, then said, "God bless you all," since the other people had gathered behind Scofield and Clint and could hear the conversation. "My boys and I surely are grateful. We'll make us a camp right down yonder." He pointed to a spot just outside the bottom of the circle of wagons. "Is that too close? I'd kinda like to stay pretty close to you folks in case there's any more of them Sioux sneakin' about."

"Why don't you just let them stay inside the wagons, Clayton?" Ada Bishop suggested. "I can fix a cake of cornbread right on this fire we got going here."

"I can fry up some bacon to go with it," Wilma Aiken volunteered. "It would be a lot simpler if they just stayed inside the wagons." Several of the other women volunteered to provide some food as well.

"I don't know what to say," Jesse confessed. "I never expected this much kindness." He looked back at Scofield. "Is that all right with you, Mr. Wagon Master?"

Scofield glanced at Clint, but he only shrugged. The Yocums were a dingy-looking threesome, but maybe there was a reason for it, if what they said about a Sioux war party chasing them was true. It struck Clint that no respectable Sioux warrior would want any one of those greasy scalps. "Well, I can't think of any reason to say you can't sleep inside the wagons tonight."

"Well, thank you kindly," Jesse said. He looked around him at the way the circle was laid out. "We'll unroll our beds down there with our horses." He lowered his voice so only Scofield could hear him. "My boys ain't used to bein' around women and children, since their mama took sick and died when they was just little fellers. I wouldn't want none of these young'uns to pick up any bad habits from Caleb and Zach. You know what I mean. They probably won't, but they might, 'cause we'll be sleepin' out on the ground. We'll slip outta here before daylight, so we don't get in the way while you folks are gittin' ready to pack up and leave."

"We'll have a wake-up call at four o'clock in the mornin'," Scofield told him. "So we'll all be up before daylight. You and your boys might as well have breakfast with us before you go." He was thinking it was worth feeding them again, just to make sure they rode out of there with nothing more than they rode in with.

"I declare, there ain't no way I can pass that up." He turned to look at his sons. "How would you like that, boys? Have some breakfast before we start out in the mornin'. You don't like to get up in the mornin' till the sun does, anyway."

"That sure suits me," Caleb responded.

"Me, too," Zach said.

"Well, Mr. Scofield, is it?" Jesse said. "I'd like to thank you kindly one more time. We never knew what a lucky day this was gonna turn out to be, considering the way it started out. We'll go on now and set up our little camp for the night and turn these poor horses loose to graze."

"Shouldn't be long before these women bring you some supper," Scofield told him. "Three or four of 'em ran back to their wagons to fix it already."

"Yes, sir! Come on boys, let's go get these saddles off these horses." They led the horses down near the river where one gap had been intentionally left in the circle so the horses and cows could get to the water. The gap would be closed up when all the stock was brought in for the night.

"You feel like you might be makin' a mistake?" Clint asked when the three guests led their horses away.

"I am kinda uneasy about it," his uncle answered. "What do you think about 'em?"

"I think we'd better talk to whoever's got the guard duty tonight and tell 'em to keep an eye on those three," Clint said.

"The critical shift is the midnight till four o'clock one," Scofield said. "I looked at my notebook before I came out here and Jim Rayford and Vance Miller have got that shift tonight. So I'll go talk to them. The only thing to worry about is they might try to steal some of our horses to replace those they broke. What else could they do?"

"Nothin' I can think of," Clint admitted. "Maybe we're just worryin' about nothin'. They'll most likely go on their way after breakfast in the mornin', happy with the free food they got."

"I'm gonna talk to Jim and Vance, anyway," Scofield said. "It's my job to worry."

"You the feller pickin' the banjo, weren'tcha?" Jesse Yocum asked when Tiny Futch came up to their little camp. "Damn, you're a big'un when you come up close. Watchin' you pick that banjo with them other two fellers, I just thought they was little."

"Yep, that was me, all right," Tiny said. "I just come to tell you that I'd be walkin' by here from time to time tonight 'cause it's my night to stand guard. Just thought I'd let you know, so you wouldn't take a shot at me."

"Big as you are, you'd be hard to miss," Jesse said with a chuckle, although he was disappointed to find out they would post guards. That was going to make their horse trading a lot harder. "That's too bad you gotta spend your night guardin' all these wagons. That'll make for a long night."

"I won't be doin' it all night long," Tiny replied. "I've got the early shift. I just guard till midnight, then another fellow has the midnight to four o'clock shift. Then at four o'clock, everybody gets up. Well, I just thought I'd let you know what I was doing nosin' around this end of the circle. I've gotta go over now and help Watkins and Bishop close up that gap between their wagons, now that the horses are in for the night."

"You gonna need some help?" Jesse asked. "Them wagons are pretty hard to move, ain't they? Me and my boys'll give you a hand."

"We could probably use some help, if you don't mind," Tiny said.

"Me and my boys oughta do somethin' to pay you folks for what you've done for us," Jesse declared. "Come on, boys, let's go move them wagons."

They ended up with more manpower than was really needed to roll two wagons a couple of feet each, but Tracy Bishop and Levi Watkins thanked them all for their help. Then everybody said goodnight and Jesse and his sons retired to their camp. "That's how we're gonna leave this place tonight," Jesse told them.

"That ain't much of a gap, Pa," Caleb said. "How we gonna lead them horses between them two wagons without wakin' 'em up?"

"We ain't gonna lead 'em between them two," Jesse answered him. "We'll lead 'em behind the tailgate of that one wagon we pushed close to the other one. That's why I kept telling you to push on that wagon. 'Cause now there's a bigger space behind that one than there was before we started pushin' on it. It looked like it won't be no trouble to lead a horse through that gap, if you lead him real slow."

"When we goin'?" Zach asked.

"We ain't goin' till ever'body is asleep," Jesse told him, "after the new guard takes over at midnight. When he comes around here, we'll play like we're sound asleep, then maybe he won't bother checkin' on us no more."

"Everything's peaceful," Tiny said when Jim Rayford came up to the fire to relieve him at twelve o'clock.

"Good," Jim replied, "hope it stays that way. What about those three strays that wandered in last night?" he asked, referring to Jesse and his sons. "Scofield told me to keep an eye on 'em."

"I don't know why," Tiny replied. "Every time I've walked past them tonight, they were all asleep. I don't see why Scofield's worried about them a-tall. They even came over and helped close the gap between Tracy and Levi's wagons. I wouldn't worry about them."

"Well, that's good," Jim said, "but I reckon I'll check on 'em, anyway, to keep Scofield happy."

"All right, then, I'll see you in the mornin'," Tiny said. "There's about a cup or two of coffee left in that pot if you wanna risk it."

"Might as well," Jim replied. "Maybe it'll keep me awake." He stood there for a moment and watched Tiny walk away. Then he poured some coffee into the cup left there beside the pot. It proved to be every bit as rank as he expected it to be, but he forced himself to take a few swallows of it before he dumped the remainder on the ground. He put a couple of sticks of wood on the fire, then left to take his first walk around the wagons on the lower half of the circle.

When he approached the livestock, he thought it might be a good idea to let the three visitors know who he was, so he went over to their little camp near the horses. But when he got close enough to hail them, he hesitated to do so. They all three looked fast asleep to him. *I might check on them a little later*, he thought. *But it looks like the next sound they'll hear is Scofield's bugle. That oughta start their day off right.* He snickered at the thought.

Jesse Yocum raised up on his elbow and watched Rayford walking away. "Well, he's done took his first look and I reckon he thinks we're all asleep." When there was no response from either of his sons, he realized they were asleep. "It's a wonderful thing to have a simple brain, like a dog's got. When you lay down, you just go to sleep." He waited, but they didn't hear that either. "Dumber'n their mother. Wonder who she's sleepin' with to-night?"

He waited for almost a couple of hours before he woke his two sons. "It's time we got ourselves some good horses and say good-bye to this place," he told them. "We gonna take our saddles and that packsaddle and walk right in the middle of that herd of horses, pick us out a good'un and throw a saddle on him."

"Ain't you afraid that guard or somebody else will hear us over in the middle of their horses?" Caleb asked.

"Dark as it is, nobody in them wagons can see what's going on in that herd," Jesse assured him. "And that guard ain't been back by here in over an hour. This whole camp is asleep. The only place we gotta be extra careful and quiet is when we lead them horses between them wagons. Now, let's get goin'."

They rolled up their bedrolls and picked up their saddles, as well as the packsaddle, but they left the pack of beaver pelts there thinking it too much to carry with everything else they had. Jesse said they would pick it up on their way out. Moving slowly and calmly, they went into the middle of the herd and looked at the selection, each man picking one that he fancied. "Don't take all night," Jesse whispered. "Pick one and throw your saddle on him." He had picked his right away, so he picked out another to carry the packs. He was in the process of slipping a bridle on a sturdy-looking dun when he heard the voice behind him.

"What are you fellows doin'?" Jim Rayford asked.

"Oh!" Jesse exclaimed. "You gimme a fright there, feller. I didn't hear you comin' up behind me. Why, we was just gittin' our horses ready to leave right after breakfast. Don't have no idea what time it is, but I figured it must be gittin' close to gittin' up time."

"It ain't but two o'clock," Jim said. "You got a long time yet."

"No, I'm ready to go right now," Jesse said, pulled a Colt .45 out of his holster, and stuck it in Jim's face. "And if you make the first sound, I'm gonna put a hole right through your skull." Jim froze in fear. Aware then of their father's surprise visitor, his sons came to his aid. "Fetch me that rope off my saddle, Caleb. Pull that bandana off his neck, Zach."

Caleb went to get the rope and Zach asked, "Why don't you just shoot him, Pa?"

"And wake up the whole damn camp?" Jesse responded. "I ain't gonna kill him unless he tries to make a noise. And then if he does, I reckon, I'd just slit his throat."

"Why don't you just go ahead and cut his throat?" Zach asked while he pulled the bandana off the terrified man's neck. "And you wouldn't have to waste your rope."

"I swear, there ain't enough time left in my life to try to learn you and your brother nothin'," Jesse said, exasperated. "If we kill this pilgrim, there'll be somebody coming after us for sure. But if we just trade a few horses and leave, they ain't likely to come after us because they ain't wantin' to waste a day trying to get over the Rockies before snow falls. Hurry up, Caleb!" Jim Rayford, his eyes as wide as saucers, nodded rapidly in agreement at Zach.

Once Rayford was securely tied, hand and foot, his bandana stuffed in his mouth and tied with a short piece of rope, he was left on the ground in the middle of the horse herd. Jesse and the boys went back to pick up their pack of beaver pelts, then headed for the riskiest part of their escape plan. Jesse instructed Caleb and Zach to watch how he led his new horse and the pack-

horse between the two wagons, and to do exactly as he demonstrated. Walking the horses slowly across to the line of wagons
beside the river, he slowed up even more. He put his finger to his
lips, signaling them to be quiet, then pointed to two young children sleeping under one of the wagons. He slowed almost to a
stop when the horse had to step over the wagon tongue of the
wagon behind that one. He wanted them to make sure the horse
saw the wagon tongue on the ground. When his chosen saddle
horse was outside the circle, he led the packhorse through the
gap. This was the only part of their plan that really concerned
Jesse. It seemed his sons were born with a natural knack for making mistakes. For that reason, he was greatly relieved when
Caleb, then Zach, led their horses through the gap with no problem at all. Joyous, in fact, he climbed on board his new horse and
led his sons, using the bright moon as a light, down along the
bank of the Platte, leaving the silent wagon train behind them.
He planned to continue riding until well after daylight, counting
on Scofield's reluctance to delay his train another day.

# Chapter 10

At four o'clock on the dot, Scofield's bugle sounded the call for the start of another day and the sleeping wagon train came to life once again. Usually at five o'clock, the cattle and horses were rounded up after being allowed to graze all night. But there was no need for that on this morning because the livestock were kept inside the corral formed by the circle of wagons during the night just passed. Consequently, it was not until Maureen Rayford came to ask Scofield where her husband was that anyone knew he was missing. "He didn't come back to the wagon?" Scofield asked.

"Not so far, he hasn't," Maureen said, "and I need him to help me get ready to go."

"I don't have any idea where he is, Maureen, but I'll find him for you." He heard Clint yelling his name then and turned to see him signaling for him to come. He was at the horse herd with several of the other men. "Let me go see what Clint's hollerin' about, then I'll see if I can find Jim," he told her. He reached the horses in time to see Clint untying the last knots in the ropes around Jim Rayford's wrists while several of the other men watched.

"The Yocums decided not to stay for breakfast after all," Clint told Scofield when he walked up. "They also decided to help themselves to some fresh horses, but they were fair about it. They left their old broke-down nags in trade."

"Damn," Scofield swore. "We both had a feelin' about those three." He looked at Rayford then. "Are you all right, Jim?"

"I reckon," Rayford replied. "I checked on 'em like you said, and they were all asleep. At least, I think they were. But when I checked 'em again about two o'clock, they weren't there, so I went lookin' for 'em. Found 'em right in the middle of the horse herd, saddlin' up some horses. When I asked what was going on, the daddy, Jesse, stuck a gun in my face and said he'd kill me if I made a sound. Well, I don't mind tellin' you, I ain't sure I coulda made a sound, as big as that gun barrel looked right in my face. They got in a discussion over how to keep me from makin' any noise. His son wanted to cut my throat so they wouldn't have to leave the rope. But his papa said if they killed me, then you'd more'n likely come after 'em. But if they just took the horses, you most likely wouldn't waste a day tryin' to get 'em back."

"I reckon he was right about that," Scofield said. "I guess we can spare three or four horses, but we can't spare you. Matter of fact, your wife is looking for you now. She's wonderin' why you didn't come home this mornin'. I think she suspects you mighta found some cute little filly in one of the other wagons."

"She knows better'n that," Jim said.

"Well, go tell her you're all right," Scofield said.

Clint was still standing by, listening to the conversation between the two. Scofield was in such a carefree mood about the horse-stealing incident, he hated to spoil it. He knew his uncle had suspicious feelings about the Yocums and he was just feeling fortunate there had been a minimum of loss. When Rayford left to join his wife, Clint said, "I reckon I can go after those three and catch up with you on up the road somewhere."

"Oh, hell, no," Scofield responded. "You heard what I told Rayford. With all the extra horses we've picked up, we can afford to lose a few—a lot better than losin' a day gettin' to South Pass."

"One of those horses they stole was that Morgan of yours," Clint said.

Scofield's face blanched when he realized what Clint had said. "How do you know that?" he asked and started looking around him at the horses.

"'Cause he ain't here no more," Clint stated simply.

"Oh, hell, no," Scofield denied. "He's here somewhere." He started walking through the herd, looking right and left.

Clint followed along behind him. "I've already looked everywhere inside the circle, Uncle Clayton. Blackie's gone." He knew how much that horse meant to his uncle, so he knew there was no question about whether he should go after the horse. "I'll leave as soon as I can throw a few things together to eat while I'm gone."

Scofield looked as if he was going to be sick. Clint knew he was torn between his responsibility for the members of the wagon train, and his feelings for his faithful horse. "I can't let you go back after them," he finally blurted, knowing he had no one else he could responsibly send to help him. "There's three of them Yocums."

"I'll be careful," Clint said. "I was pretty good at stealin' horses, myself, back when Broken Wing and I stole our first ponies from a Sioux raidin' party." He could see his uncle trying to protest but having difficulty making the words come out. "I saw where they went out of the circle behind Tracy Watkins's wagon, and they left a trail down the riverbank. I'm gonna go saddle Biscuit right now, then I'll get some jerky or something from Spud to carry in my saddlebags, and I'll be gone."

"Doggone it, Clint, you be careful."

"I will, Uncle Clayton. I doubt I'll catch 'em before they get to Fort Laramie, and if I don't, I'll catch up with 'em there. You know they're gonna wanna trade those pelts they stole from somebody. Then they'll most likely spend the money at Jake's Place. Like Jim Rayford said, they don't think anybody will be chasin' 'em." When he saw Scofield trying to form one more objection to his going after them, he said, "I don't want them to have Blackie either. It's best that I go get him." He left then to get his saddle.

"You're jumpin' the gun a little, ain't you?" Spud asked, when Clint led Biscuit up to his wagon and dropped the reins on the ground.

"Biscuit and I are goin' huntin' and I wanna get some jerky or something I can carry in my saddlebags. I can't wait till breakfast is ready." He quickly explained what the big powwow at the horse herd was all about and where he was off to right away.

Like Clint, Spud knew how fond of that horse Scofield was. "Of all the horses they coulda picked to steal, they had to pick that one," Spud lamented. "I ain't even started to cook breakfast yet, but I can give you a cup of coffee right now. I've got some beef jerky and some crackers you can take with you. I ain't got nothin' else you wouldn't have to cook."

"That'll do," Clint said. "Just something to take the edge off is all I need." He stood by the wagon and drank the coffee while Spud collected some jerky and crackers for him.

"Good luck," Spud said when Clint handed him the empty coffee cup and climbed up into the saddle. "And look out you don't get shot."

"Thanks, I will," Clint said as he rode away. He picked up the obvious trail left by the three horse thieves where they came out between the wagons, then rode east along the riverbank. He was a little surprised when after a distance of about one hundred and fifty yards their trail went into the river. He only paused a moment or two to consider the reason. For he was convinced Jesse and his two sons would go to the only place they could sell those beaver pelts, and that was the post trader's store at Fort Laramie. So he had to think that the reason they chose to go into the river at that point was to confuse and slow down any immediate pursuit. He thought they probably did believe they were safe from pursuit if they didn't kill Jim Rayford and they had several hours' head start. He had no thoughts of trying to track them, anyway. His plan was to get to Fort Laramie as fast as he could and hope to catch them there before they decided to move on to somewhere else.

So he ignored the tracks leading into the river and continued to ride along the riverbank. In less than a mile, he came upon their tracks coming out of the water again, and they headed straight for the wagon road. It confirmed his assumption that they would take the road to Fort Laramie, the same road the wagon train had traveled from Fort Laramie. He felt sure if he needed any additional proof of that, he could dismount and search the road and he would eventually find a hoofprint headed in the opposite direction from those left by the wagon train. It was not that far to Fort Laramie, only one day by wagon. By alternating Biscuit's pace between a walk and a gentle lope, he should be able to make it to Seth Ward's trading post close to the time Seth opened up in the morning. Maybe things would fall into place like he was counting on, he hoped. Because if they didn't, he had no idea what an alternate plan for Jesse Yocum could be.

When he came to the small creek about half a mile west of Fort Laramie, he stopped to let Biscuit drink water and rest for a spell. It was difficult to do when he felt sure he had caught up with Jesse and his sons, but he didn't want to have to try to run on an exhausted horse, should things happen to break that way. So he forced himself to wait there for almost an hour before he climbed back into the saddle and proceeded on into the fort. "I know I shortchanged you, boy, but I'll make it up to you on the way back," he said to the Palouse. He pushed on into Fort Laramie, and as he expected, the morning was just getting underway at the blacksmith's and the various tradesmen. His eye was focused on the one sight, however, the familiar black Morgan horse tied at the rail with three other horses in front of the post trader's store. Although it was what he was hoping to find, it was almost too good to be true. With what he had in mind next, he had to be sure and he had to be quick.

When he pulled Biscuit up next to the four horses, Biscuit and Blackie exchanged greetings, so that told him the Morgan was, indeed, his uncle's. To be double sure he was not horse stealing, he dismounted and went to the door of the store and took a cautious look inside. Near the back counter of the store, he saw Jesse Yocum and both of his boys watching intensely as Seth Ward started going through the pelts. *Good,* he thought, *they're just getting started with the trading.* But still, he had to be quick.

Back to the horses then, he took the coiled rope off his saddle and tied one end to the back of his saddle. Then he uncoiled the rope all the way and laid it on the ground behind Biscuit. That done, he then went to Scofield's Morgan first and pulled the saddle off and dropped it on the ground. He untied the reins from the rail and re-tied them to the first of four large knots he had spaced out on his rope while he had been resting Biscuit at the creek. He repeated the procedure on the three remaining horses, knowing that if he was caught in the middle of it, he would likely be shot by one of the Yocums for a horse thief. By this time, with only the packsaddle left to be dumped, a small crowd of curious spectators had stopped to watch the brazen theft. It would have been so much easier had the young man wearing buckskins simply taken the reins of the four horses and ridden away, saddles and all. Still, riding with one hand with his other hand holding four sets of reins would have been unhandy. They had to admit that the lead rope with the four knots spaced a little distance apart looked like a good idea. Scarcely able to believe he was going to get away with it without exchanging gunfire, he tied the last set of reins to the fourth knot. He climbed on Biscuit then, gave the fascinated audience a two-finger salute, and rode away from the post trader's store, leaving the row of three riding saddles and one packsaddle lined up before the hitching rail. As he rode out of sight, he could not know that the little crowd of spectators he had attracted were still in place, patiently waiting for the owners of the saddles to appear.

He rode straight out the road to Register Cliff, thinking the same as Jesse Yocum had when he had the horses and was riding in the opposite direction, to put distance between them quickly. As he rode, he had the same thought that some in the gang of spectators had. Scofield would have said, "Just take all the reins and ride away with the horses, saddles and all. Why take a chance on getting shot while you're fixing up your fancy rope?" He would find it hard to explain to Scofield that he specifically wanted to take only what was his to take, the horses. And he also regretted the fact that he could not be there to see their reaction when they came out of the store to find their saddles lined up with no horses under them.

The reaction was nothing short of dramatic, as a matter of fact, providing the entertainment the small crowd, that had now doubled, anticipated. Walking out the front door of the store, chuckling over the cash money they had exchanged the beaver pelts for and arguing about what to spend it on, they stopped, surprised by the crowd of people waiting there. The crowd went completely silent then as the three walked out on the boardwalk. "What's all the . . ." was as far as he got when Jesse was stopped, dumbfounded. "What tha . . ." he started again, trying to believe his eyes were playing tricks on him as he stared at the row of saddles on the ground by the hitchin' rail.

Caleb and Zach were both too confused to speak for several long minutes until Caleb finally asked, "Where's our horses, Pa?"

"How the hell do I know?" Jesse roared. "Somebody stole 'em. Ask these people. They act like they know what happened to 'em." He roared at the spectators then. "Well, who took 'em? You all look like you saw who done it, and not a one of you come in the store to tell us."

"A young feller wearin' buckskins, ridin' a Palouse horse come and got 'em, pretty much like he was mindin' his own business," a gray-haired old man spoke up. "He didn't look like he cared if anybody saw him or not. He just rode up, took the horses, and rode away. I reckon he didn't want the saddles. They don't look like they're worth much at that."

"That sounds like that wagon train scout, Pa," Zach said.

"Shut up, Zach," Jesse barked, "don't be talkin' about that."

"A fine thing," Jesse addressed the crowd then. "A man and his sons come to trade pelts at a danged army post, and their horses are stole right out in broad daylight, and ain't nobody helped us."

"Why don't you go talk to the commandin' officer?" the old man suggested. "Maybe he'll make good your loss, if they was really your horses."

"We might just do that," Jesse said. "Pick up your saddles, boys, and let's get away from here before somebody steals them."

"I wouldn't worry about that," another voice commented, causing a wave of chuckles as Jesse and his sons picked up the saddles.

"We goin' to talk to the commandin' officer, Pa?" Caleb asked as they walked away from the post trader's store.

"Hell, no," Jesse said. "We're goin' to that harness shop and spend some of that money we just got on three bridles. Then we're gonna find out where the army grazes their horses and get us some new ones." He sighed and shook his head when he thought about it. "I'd sure like to find me another'n like that black one I just lost."

"I hope we find 'em pretty soon," Zach said. "I'm already tired of walkin'."

Scofield called a halt a little earlier than five o'clock on the second day out from Register Cliff to take advantage of a nice-sized creek, knowing the next good creek was too far to reach that day. They circled the wagons and let the livestock graze along the creek bank for a while before driving them inside the circle for the night. They were just about to round them up when

Clint rode into the open end of the circle on Biscuit, leading Blackie with three other horses loping along behind him. Scofield and Spud both ran out to meet him. "I ain't never been so glad to see somebody in my life," Scofield exclaimed.

"You're talking about the horse, ain't you?" Clint japed.

"Hell, yeah," his uncle returned in kind. "Where did you find 'em?"

"Right where I figured they'd be," Clint said, "inside Seth Ward's store sellin' those pelts they most likely stole."

"They didn't put up a fight?" Spud asked.

"Not a bit," Clint answered.

"Well, I'da never figured they'd just turn 'em over to you without no fight or nothin'," Scofield said.

"Well, to tell you the truth, when I got there, I looked in the store and they were so busy dealing with Mr. Ward that I didn't wanna interrupt just to tell 'em I'd come to take the horses home."

"You just stole 'em back?" Scofield asked, then roared with laughter. "Tell me exactly how you did it." So Clint told them the whole story, much to his uncle's delight. "So all those three bandits got from us was a little bit of food and a free ride to Fort Laramie. And now they're on foot with less than they had when they rode into our camp at Register Cliff. Sure as hell serves 'em right, don't it?"

"Well, they've still got their saddles," Clint said with a smile.

"You know you're pretty doggone lucky you got away with that without gettin' shot, don't you?" Scofield asked. His first reaction upon hearing Clint's account of the horse rescue having been wildly humorous, his second thoughts struck him now with how dangerous Clint's stunt actually was. "That was a crazy thing to do," he said then. "If they'da walked out and shot you down in the act of takin' those horses, nobody there woulda known the horses didn't belong to them. I swear, Clint, I'm mighty grateful to you for gettin' my horse back, but I don't want you to take crazy chances like that."

"Tell you the truth, Uncle Clayton, I liked my chances just takin' the horses and runnin' better than waitin' for them to get through with their tradin' so I could face the three of them with six-guns."

"He's got a dang good point there, Scofield," Spud said.

"Yeah, I reckon he has," Scofield admitted. "Glad you got back all right, Clint."

"I'll bet you're hungry as hell," Spud said.

"You'd win that bet," Clint said.

"Well, I'm gittin' ready to cook supper right now," Spud said, "so it won't be long. You need some more of that jerky to hold you till supper's done?"

"No, I can wait for supper," Clint replied. "I've got to take care of the horses first, anyway." He left them then to unsaddle Biscuit and release the horses with the others.

Spud uttered a little chuckle and said, "I woulda liked to have seen the look on ol' Yocum and his sons' faces when they walked outta that store and saw their saddles layin' in a row where their horses used to be."

"So would I," Scofield confessed. They both laughed.

# Chapter 11

The next morning, the wagon train started out once again on the dusty, wearisome trip along the North Platte River on a trail that gradually inclined as they approached the Rockies and the Continental Divide. They were often saved from drinking the brackish water of the Platte by the many small streams and creeks that emptied into the Platte. However, good green grass for the horses and cows was hard to find, replaced by dry prairie grass that grew waist high in some places. Buffalo they had counted on to supplement their food supplies seemed to have vanished from the high plains, leaving only their dried dung patties to be used for fuel on the treeless plains. The buffalo chips burned rapidly, unfortunately, requiring a couple of bushels of them to cook one meal. Collecting them became the primary role the children played at the end of each day on the trail. For the next week and a half, one day was not distinguishable from the next or the day before it, until finally a huge whale-like rock appeared on the horizon late one afternoon, and Scofield confirmed that it was, indeed, Independence Rock. "We'll be campin' there tonight," he told Lily. "I'll go back and pass the word, if they ain't already guessed it." He wheeled Blackie around and rode back along the line of wagons to let everyone know they were camping there that night.

Lifeless spirits were immediately regenerated with the reaching of Independence Rock, for a couple of reasons. The saying goes that, if you reach Independence Rock by the Fourth of July, you will have traveled halfway to your destination. And you would ordinarily make it through the Blue Mountains and the Cascades before the heavy snowfalls close the mountain passes. Since they were still in the latter weeks of June, there was reason to have a Fourth of July celebration a few days early. A second reason for celebrating the reaching of Independence Rock was that it was here they would finally say goodbye to the North Platte River and its brackish water and cross over to the Sweetwater, a river aptly named. They would now follow the meandering river to South Pass, a trip that Scofield said could take anywhere from ten to twenty days, depending on the weather and the amount of rain the area had received. "For the Oregon Trail crossed the Sweetwater nine times last year," he said. "They're normally not difficult crossings, though," he hastened to tell those he passed the word along to. "Nothin' like some of the rivers we'll be crossin' when we get to the other end of this journey. Not even as bad as the Kansas River crossin'."

"Good," Levi Watkins said. "Then we'll celebrate our country's birthday and get a head start on the rest of the country." He looked at Scofield again. "You said we was gonna take a day off, right, Capt'n?"

"That's right, Levi," Scofield answered him. "I think it'd be good for everybody. I was hopin' I might even get a chance to see that special dance of yours again."

"I hate to disappoint you," Levi said, "but that was a one-time performance. Ella made that pretty plain to me. She said I scared Tim and Molly. She said they thought their pa had caught the cholera."

When they reached the massive rock, they formed their circle and released the livestock to graze, but then most of the pioneers went over to the huge granite rock that stood about one hundred and thirty feet high, nineteen hundred feet long, and eight hundred and fifty feet wide. Like Register Cliff, there were names of emigrants and dates cut into the granite on almost every smooth surface. There were footpaths leading all the way around the gigantic rock, and already, fathers and mothers were pulling adventurous youngsters off the sides of the oddity. For as big as it was, every rambunctious kid knew it was climbable. Unfortunately for them, however, it was approaching suppertime, and the firewood was as scarce here as it was by the Platte. For the most part, the only trees were those lining the river. So if they wanted to eat, they were going to have to go hunting for buffalo chips. And the exploring and adventure was going to have to wait until tomorrow.

"It is big, though, isn't it?" Lily remarked while they were eating supper. "I'm happy we don't have any little ones to worry about climbing up on that rock and falling off."

Scofield chewed up a tough piece of bacon and washed it down with a gulp from his coffee cup, winked at Clint before he responded to her remark. "Yeah, darlin', I'm glad you brought that up. I've been meanin' to talk to you about that."

"Talk to me about what?" she asked.

"Young'uns," he answered. "I was thinkin' as how we're a little older than most folks when they get married, so we oughta get busy startin' our family right now. Ain't that what you think?"

"The hell you say," she exclaimed. "If you're thinking you wanna hear the patter of little feet around our house, you'd best see about buying you a dog. And you can take care of it, too."

Scofield pretended he was shocked. "Why, I never . . . I'm sorry Clint and Spud had to hear that. They know I always wanted to have a house full of young'uns."

"Spud, let me borrow that frying pan, will ya?" Lily replied. "I wanna hit him over the head with it." They all had a good laugh over it then. She reached over and gave Scofield a playful tug on his ear. Clint was convinced that his uncle had made a wise decision when he married Lily. He was happy for both of them. Then a random thought struck him and the picture of Ruby Nixon came to mind. He wondered if the two of them would be as good a match as his uncle and Lily seemed to be. Everybody at home in the Willamette Valley assumed that he and Ruby would marry, but that didn't mean it was the right thing to do.

The social hour was well attended that night in anticipation of the celebration of the country's independence from England, Clint supposed. This, even though it was not really the Fourth of July. In fact, it was not yet July. Bass Thornton, not a regular attendee of social hour, even came out of his wagon, with his young bride on his arm. What made it even more surprising was the fact that he brought an unopened bottle of expensive whiskey and offered anyone who wanted one to have a drink. "But," he added, "you'll have to go get your own glass. I didn't bring glasses for anybody. And when the bottle's empty, that's the end of it. This is the only bottle I've got." Levi, Tracy, and Tiny didn't hear his last two sentences because they were already running to their wagons to get glasses, much to the disgust of Ella, Ada, and Annie.

Ella and Ada were further surprised when Levi and Tracy both returned with not only a glass but also a bottle of their own. Although not of the quality of the whiskey in the bottle Bass brought, it was one of Jake Plummer's better brands from his saloon at Fort Laramie. When he was met with an accusing glare from Ella, Levi said, "Me and Tracy decided we'd tie one on if we ever got to the Willamette Valley. So we slipped up to Jake's Place the day before we left Fort Laramie. But I thought Bass has got a better idea, to salute the Fourth of July, so I dug my bottle out, too." He looked over at Tracy and grinned. "Looks like you had the same idea."

"Where did you hide that bottle in our wagon?" Ella demanded. "We ain't got room to hide anything."

"Now, hon," Levi replied, "if I told you that, I wouldn't have a place to hide anything again."

"What else have you got hid away?" Ella asked.

"All that fortune that you married me for," he japed.

"Well, I can believe that," she returned, "'cause that wouldn't take up no space a-tall to hide."

"You oughta be proud of me," Tiny said to Annie. "I came back with nothin' but a glass. And I think I'll take a drink outta Bass Thornton's bottle before it's empty." The word had spread rapidly, so there were already several men waiting for Bass to pour a shot for them. The obvious preference of their fellow travelers for the more expensive whiskey gave both Levi and Tracy the opportunity to have more than one drink from their bottles.

Still chuckling over Levi's comeuppance from his wife, Tracy took another drink from his bottle and turned around to find Ada standing right behind him, her hands on hips and a look on her face that required no words. "Ah, honey," Tracy protested, "don't you start in on me. It's just one little ol' bottle of whiskey. It ain't worth makin' a fuss in front of everybody like Ella did."

"You're right," Ada told him. "I don't want our children to see how intelligent their papa is. If we get caught by a winter storm before we get through the mountains and we're all starvin' to death, at least it'll be good for the kids to know that their daddy bought himself a bottle of whiskey with our food money."

"Oh, for goodness' sakes, Ada, I told you, it ain't but one cheap little ol' bottle of likker. Here, Jim." He handed the bottle to Jim Rayford, who was on his way to help empty Bass Thornton's bottle. "Help yourself."

"Don't mind if I do," Jim said and took the bottle from him and kept walkin', stopping every few seconds to take a drink right out of the bottle.

"There," Tracy said to Ada, "it's done gone. You can find something else to bellyache about now." She didn't bother to respond, just turned and walked away. "Well," he muttered to himself, well aware of the mood she was now in, "it ain't like we was on no honeymoon, anyway." He looked around to see where Jim Rayford had gotten to with his bottle and saw him arguing with

Vance Miller over it. So he stepped up behind Tiny in Bass Thornton's whiskey line. He was in time to hear Bass turn Tiny down for another drink.

"I'm sorry, Tiny," Bass told him. "There isn't but one shot left in this bottle and I promised Leach I'd save him at least one shot of whiskey."

Tracy decided to make another try at his own bottle. Jim and Vance appeared to be having quite a discussion about it. He walked up in time to hear part of their discussion. It may have been about the bottle to begin with, but it had now progressed to something further. "Maybe if you'd had a few snorts of whiskey that night we both had the midnight guard shift at Register Cliff, those three outlaws wouldn't have rode off with Scofield's Morgan," Tracy heard Vance say.

"Maybe if you hadn't been hidin' somewhere takin' a nap, you mighta seen I coulda used some help, seein' as how there was three of them," Jim retorted.

"Why, you SOB," Vance blurted. "You got a lotta gall accusin' me of hidin' when you didn't even know they were leavin' until after they'd already saddled four of our horses."

"You'd best watch who you're callin' an SOB," Jim responded. "You're liable to find yourself eatin' those words."

"If it was anybody else but you, that might worry me, but I expect you'll handle it the same way you handled Jesse Yocum," Vance said, "all curled up on the ground." His remark earned him a hard right hand flush on the nose.

"Whoa!" Tracy blurted involuntarily, as Vance staggered two steps backward to regain his balance.

"Why, you lowdown . . ." was as far as Vance got before he roared, enraged. He charged into Jim, his head down like a bull, with his fists swinging blindly. He backed Jim up, swinging away, leaving Jim with no targets for his fists but Vance's back and the back of his hard head. Meanwhile, Vance, bent over like he was, could only pummel Jim's hips and stomach, causing frustration more so than real damage. They tussled like this for a couple of minutes before anyone but Tracy noticed the fight. When the others realized the two of them were going at it, they immediately circled them to watch the action, the other men naturally spurring them on. Finally, with no real damage having been done aside from Vance Miller's bloody nose, they both became weary. And totally frustrated by Vance's bent-over defense, Jim grabbed him by the back of his collar and yanked him toward him as hard as he could. Then he stepped aside as he plunged past him and gave him a kick in the seat of his pants. Surprised to find Jim no longer right in front of him, Vance stood erect then and looked back at him. "You had enough?"

"I ain't had any," Jim answered. "You won't stand up and fight."

"I fight the way I fight," Vance countered. "I think you mighta broke my nose," he said, wiping it with his shirt sleeve. "You wouldn'ta done that if you hadn't cheated, and we'da started the fight fair."

Late to get there, Scofield arrived at that point, having just been alerted that there was a fight going on at the social gathering. "Who's fighting?" he wanted to know, and when he was told it was Vance and Jim, he was amazed. "What about? If there is a dispute between any of the wagons on this train, you agreed when you signed on that you would bring it to me and we'd settle it fairly. So what's the dispute?"

"Can I answer that for you, Capt'n?" Maureen Rayford spoke up.

"Why, I reckon so, Miz Rayford," Scofield answered.

"My husband and Mrs. Miller's husband were trying to demonstrate to all our children that are standing around watching how not to try to settle an argument. So that when they see how childish it looks, they won't copy them. They'll just sit down and talk it over." She looked over at Vance's wife standing there and asked, "Ain't that about what they were trying to do, Edith?"

Edith Miller smiled. "Yes, Maureen, that's what the whole performance was about. That we all should try to act grown-up."

Scofield found it hard to keep from grinning. "So there ain't really nothin' to talk about then. Is that right, Jim, Vance? 'Cause we can't have any bad blood between any members of this wagon train. We're liable to have to rely on one another before we get through the second half of this trip." Men and women, they all assured him that there was no bad blood between the Millers and the Rayfords. "Good," Scofield said. "I know I told you we would stay over here an extra day so you could celebrate the Fourth and get a few things fixed on your wagon boxes since we're gonna be crossin' so many rivers in the next few weeks." He paused, then said, "It's gonna be the same river, but we're gonna cross it many times. But if you don't want to stay here that extra day, we can move on in the mornin'. So let me know if you wanna stay or keep moving." He got an overwhelming vote to take the day off. "All right, that's what we'll do."

Will Tucker told Clint about the fight between Vance and Jim when Clint came back to his wagon to go to bed. "I know you were with your uncle and Spud when that thing started. I went out there to listen to the music and I happened to be sittin' close by." He told Clint that it had started over a bottle of whiskey but progressed to a crack Vance made about Jim getting jumped by Jesse Yocum and his sons at Register Cliff. "Jim hauled off and smacked Vance on the nose and it wasn't much of a fight. The women were right. It looked like the kind of fight you'd see between two kids in a schoolyard." Then he demonstrated Vance Miller's fighting stance. "The only lick that meant anything was the first one Jim took to start it off. And that was before Vance bent over and started swingin' his fists and hopin' Jim would walk into one."

Clint chuckled over the image Will painted for him. "I'm glad you saw it," he said. "I'll tell Uncle Clayton tomorrow so he'll know we most likely don't have a real feud startin' up between the two of 'em."

After the day of rest and relaxation, they left Independence Rock, following the Sweetwater River. One day's travel brought them to the Devil's Gate, another easily identified landmark on the Oregon Trail. It was another example of nature's power, for the Sweetwater River had carved a V-shaped trough right through the granite rock, which was about three hundred and seventy feet tall at the top and about fifteen hundred feet long. They had to drive their wagons around it because the base of the trough was only about thirty feet wide. So there was not enough room to drive the wagons beside the river and follow it all the way through the trough. Clint rode out before the wagon train as usual, but only to be able to warn Scofield if he sensed some kind of danger. Scofield knew where he wanted to park the train, so he led them to a camping spot he had used before that was close to the point where the river entered the canyon. He found Clint waiting there for him. There was good grass there for the livestock and some remains of a sizable trading post that had operated there many years before. Scofield told Lily that he had heard stories about a handcart train of Mormons some years back who had gotten caught by an early snow and had to camp there. The old trading post was gone but the buildings they built were still standing. The Mormons burned half the buildings to keep warm. "Did the Mormons make it out of here all right?" Lily asked.

"I don't have no idea," Scofield replied. "I didn't ask. I don't even remember where I heard that story, but it's supposed to be a fact."

"I declare, Clayton, don't tell me a sad story like that if you don't know the ending. For goodness' sakes," she huffed.

"Now that I think about it," he chuckled, "I think they said they lived happily ever after." She made a fist and threatened him.

Like Independence Rock the day before, the emigrants were fascinated by the gigantic cleft the river had carved. So, many of the travelers walked back to experience the power of the seemingly gentle river as it was now forced through the narrow confines at the base of the trough. They could hear the sound of the water all the way back where the wagons were circled. And when they walked back inside the passage, they found the noise almost deafening, as the river crashed through the rocks on the bottom.

The next morning, Clint rode out before the wagons got started, so he could check the river crossings coming up. Sometimes severe weather brought flooding and washing out of normally used crossings, causing him to find other suitable ones. The next landmark would be a granite mountain with a split in it that resembled a gunsight. It was appropriately called Split Rock, but it would take three and a half to four days to reach it. He was thinking about some trouble they had the previous year at Split Rock. It had involved Indians, but it was started by the son of one of the people on the wagon train. He had fancied himself a fast gun and he thought all Indians were fair game. Clint said a word of thanks that there seemed to be no one of his kind on this train.

The next few days passed without any disruption of the daily routine when they went into camp at Split Rock. They were in the first days of the month of July now, and Clint and Scofield's concern was for the river crossings ahead of them. Sometimes June was a rainy month in this part of the country, and Three Crossings, in a place called the Narrows, was just two days farther. There were steep hills so close to the river there that the trail was forced to cross it three times within a distance of two miles. The third crossing was the worst because it was the deepest, and worst again because the deep part was next to the other bank. Clint would not wait until the wagons were approaching the Narrows. He would have to ride on a day ahead of the train to evaluate the crossings and see if the water was too high to cross. In that event, he would ride back to tell Scofield they were going to have to take the alternate route south of the Narrows. It was called the Deep Sand Route and was about eight miles longer than the crossings route, and four of those miles were through an area of thick sand that made it extremely hard on the horses to pull the wagons. But it was sometimes the best way because the wagons could be subjected to considerable damage if the water was too high in the river. Sometimes the wagon boxes had to be raised up six or more inches off their beds when the water level was over the wagon wheels. All these factors were the total topic of discussion between Clint, Spud, and Scofield at the end of the first day's travel after leaving Split Rock. Clint was planning to leave early the next morning and ride all the way to Three Crossings. And if, in his opinion, it would be too risky to take the Three Crossings route, he would ride back in time to turn the wagon train south to take the Deep Sand Route.

# Chapter 12

He got up at the sound of Scofield's bugle at four o'clock as usual and went out with the other men to round up the horses and cattle, which had been allowed to graze all night, since they had seen no sign of Indians about. That thought sparked another one, and it occurred to him that they were halfway along the trail to Oregon and they had seen no sign of Indians so far. That was unusual, past Register Cliff, to see no Indians, friendly or hostile.

On most mornings, Clint helped Spud get his horses and Scofield's Morgan as well as his own saddle horse. On this morning, he also picked out a horse to take with him as a packhorse. He was just going to be away from the wagons for a day and a night while he scouted Three Crossings, so he could get by without a packhorse. But he decided to take one this time and let it carry his coffeepot and frying pan, some flour to make johnny-cakes, and some bacon. He remembered how much he missed his coffeepot when he rode back to Fort Laramie to rescue his uncle's horse. And he preferred not to have a lot of supplies and cooking paraphernalia hanging on his saddle. So he selected a packhorse.

"You gonna wait till I get some breakfast fixed?" Spud asked when he saw Clint throwing his saddle on Biscuit.

"No," Clint replied. "I'm gonna ride all the way to the Narrows today, so I'm gonna go ahead and get started. Then I'll stop and fix something to eat when I rest Biscuit."

"You'd best watch your topknot," Spud said. "Just because we ain't seen no Injuns don't mean there ain't no Injuns. I reckon you already know that, since you used to be one."

"I'll do that, Spud, and when you get started on the trail this mornin', if you see me comin' back, ridin' flat out for glory, you'll know I made contact with some Indians, and I'll be bringin' 'em back for you to handle."

"Ha," Spud responded. "I'd appreciate it if you hightailed it in another direction."

His horses saddled, Clint led them out into the circle of wagons to let Scofield know he was leaving. "You ain't gonna eat before you go?" Scofield asked.

"That's the same thing Spud asked me," Clint said with a chuckle. "What's the matter? Am I startin' to look like I'm starvin'?"

"Lily told me I should start lookin' after you a little better," Scofield japed.

"Well, tell her I'm gonna go ahead and get started. I'd like to reach Three Crossings before dark so I can get a look at it tonight."

"That's a good idea," Scofield said. "Then if the crossings are too fouled up by the weather or whatever, you'll have plenty of time to head me off before we get too far up that trail through the Narrows." He stepped back then to give Clint room to step up into the saddle. "You be careful, young fellow."

"That I will," Clint returned and let Biscuit know, with only a slight pressure of his heel, it was time to go. The big Palouse started off at a comfortable lope, the sorrel packhorse following behind. He enjoyed being able to ride for a day not being restricted to the speed of the wagons. He and Biscuit could comfortably reach his destination that night, a distance that the wagons would need two days to make. He and his uncle had thought that their wagons might be the first ones starting out from Independence, but Seth Ward told them when they reached Fort Laramie that there was one wagon train that had already passed through. Upon leaving Devil's Gate, they began to see more tracks left by another train, so maybe they were catching up to them. He should be able to tell if they had any trouble at Three Crossings.

When he left Split Rock, he rode for what he estimated Scofield and the wagons would travel by the end of that day, so he started looking for a good campsite for them. He picked one he liked with room to circle the wagons and good grass between them and the river. So that was where he stopped to rest his horses and have his breakfast. When he finished eating, he washed out his coffeepot and his frying pan. Then he took his hand axe and cut off a stout limb from one of the trees on the bank. He whittled one end of the limb to a sharp point and then drove it into the ground with his axe, right beside the trail. Scofield was sure to see it and know it was Clint's suggestion for his camp. When he thought his horses were ready, he climbed back into the saddle and continued on to Three Crossings, which he figured to be about another twelve or thirteen miles.

Alternating Biscuit's pace between a walk and a lope, he managed to maintain a good steady speed, and by the time he was feeling hungry again, he could see the hills that crowded the river a short distance ahead. He followed the river around one tight curve he remembered to be just before the first crossing. But when he rode around the curve, he suddenly reined Biscuit back to a stop. He quickly scanned the river back and forth before returning his eyes to look at the single wagon, burned almost completely up. The contents of the wagon, at least those that were evidently considered worthless, were scattered about on the ground. The bloated and burned bodies of two mules were still in the traces where they had been shot. An obvious Indian attack, but what was a single wagon doing there alone? Was it with the wagon train he had seen tracks of just recently? The poor folks in this wagon must have dropped behind for some rea-

son. Questions he figured he would never know answers for, but
the most important thing now was whether or not the war party
that struck this wagon was still close by.

He pulled his rifle from the saddle sling and scanned the riverbanks on both sides. He could see no sign of life, so he walked
Biscuit slowly toward the burned-out wagon. There were no
bodies in the wagon, and there were no burned skeletons. So the
occupants were either taken out, or they escaped. Then he noticed marks on the ground beside the wagon, as if something, or
someone, was dragged from the wagon. He felt sure by then that
the war party responsible for the attack was no longer around, by
the simple fact that he had not been shot at. So, he dismounted
to take a closer look at the marks on the ground. He decided they
were definitely dragging marks. His guess was that someone had
pulled a body from the wagon, so he followed the trail with his
eyes and decided they led to a clump of trees close to the river. It
was not a wolf or coyote because, if it was a body, it would have
been eaten right there.

Leading his horses, he followed the marks on the ground until
they disappeared into the trees between two gooseberry bushes.
He dropped Biscuit's reins then and cocked his rifle. Then he
pushed the branches of the bush aside with the barrel of the rifle
and stopped dead still, shocked by the sudden scream of the
young woman hiding there. "Whoa! Lady! Lady! I'm a friend.
I'm not gonna hurt you. Calm down. You've got nothing to be
afraid of from me." She stopped screaming, but she was still terrified. She pressed back against the bushes behind her, the tears
streaming down her face, afraid of what he might do to her. He
realized that the way he was dressed was not at once reassuring to
the frightened woman, so he tried to calm her. "My name is Clint
Buchanan. I'm a scout for a wagon train about a day behind me.
I'd like to help you if I can."

She seemed to relax a little after that, so he looked around her
in the bushes. Then he saw a man's body behind her and beyond
that the start of a hole she had been digging, evidently meant to

be a grave. "Is that your husband?" She didn't speak but shook her head. "Your father?" Clint asked. She nodded rapidly. "I'm really sorry, miss. Was it Indians?"

She nodded again and he wondered if she was a mute, but decided she was still just too scared to talk. To prove him right, she said, "Yes, Indians."

"Was there anyone else in the wagon with you and your father?"

"No," she managed. "My mother died from cholera. We buried her."

"I swear, I'm sorry to hear that, miss. You've had more than your share of bad luck. Is that why you and your father are not with a wagon train? They make you drop back because they were afraid of the cholera?"

"No," she answered, no longer afraid that he meant her any harm. "We dropped back to bury my mother."

He nodded his understanding, but he had to ask, "How did you manage to escape the Indians?"

"In the water," she answered, then started tearing up again as she recalled it. "I was at the river, washing our dishes when they shot my father. He knew he was dying." She had to stop when she sobbed in recalling the moment.

"Just take your time," he said. "I don't mean to rush you. We can talk about it later, if you want to."

She shook her head, determined to control her emotions. "No, I'll be all right. His last words to me were, 'Go in the water.' I knew what he meant. He knew I was a good swimmer. So I slid down into the river and swam under the water across to that patch of reeds over there." She pointed to a crop of reeds growing out of the water on the other side of the river. "I hid in those reeds while they took everything they wanted from the wagon and destroyed the rest. They shot the poor mules and scalped my father, then left him to burn when they set the wagon on fire. Then they searched these trees on this side of the river for a little while, looking for me but finally gave up. When they left, I came back to bury my father."

Clint was amazed by the woman's story. Little more than a girl apparently, she didn't look to be physically capable of doing all she said she had. But it accounted for her bedraggled hair and still wet clothes. "You must be one helluva swimmer," he commented. "I ain't sure I could swim that far underwater, especially with a heavy dress like that."

"I guess you don't know what you're capable of until you have no choice," she said. "When I look at it now, I don't think I can swim that far holding my breath, either. And I thought it was all for nothing when you came. I thought it was them coming back."

"I'm sorry I scared you," Clint said. "Which way did they ride away from here?"

"That way," she said and pointed toward the south.

That led him to believe that the war party had gone to check the alternate trail around Three Crossings, and possibly they were not through scouting for other stragglers like the girl and her father. He didn't tell her that he felt sure the Indians would come back to look for her, knowing she was running, terrified, for her life. He walked back and led Biscuit and the packhorse into the trees where they would not be seen. Then he asked, "How many were in the war party?"

"There were four of them," she said.

That wasn't especially good news, but it was better than hearing it was a full-sized war party of ten or more warriors. "Did they all have guns?"

"I don't know," she answered. "I don't know which ones were doing the shooting. I'm sorry."

"No, that's all right. I just thought you might have noticed. What is your name?"

"Melody Meadows," she answered.

"Well, Melody, the most important thing on my mind right now is to make sure I keep you safe until a train of twenty-eight wagons gets here. That's too many guns for four Indians to take on. But they won't reach this point until tomorrow afternoon, late. So we're gonna move from here, get away from this wagon, but we'll finish buryin' your father first." He looked over beyond her again. "Doesn't look like you got very far with diggin' the grave."

"I'm afraid not," she confessed. "I was trying to dig with a stick. There's a shovel on the side of the wagon, if the handle didn't get burned up. But I was afraid to crawl back out to the wagon to get it. I was expecting them to come back and catch me the whole time I was dragging poor Papa's body back here."

"I'll go see," Clint said. "The sides of the wagon are still mostly standin'." He went back to the wagon and found the shovel, singed but otherwise useable. He went to work immediately, grateful she had started on a spot with soft dirt.

"I should help do some of the digging," she said, aware that it was taking a lot of time that might be best used for something else.

"I'll tell you how you can help. Keep your eyes open in case those Indians come back. And maybe you best look around out there to see if you can recover any of your clothes. You'd most likely feel a lot better if you could get on some dry clothes." When she hesitated, as if still afraid to go out near the wagon again, he said, "If they were anywhere close by, they would have taken a shot at me."

"I guess you're right," she said. "It would be better to get out of these wet clothes."

While he worked to dig a suitable grave as fast as he could, he was thinking about the reason he had come here. He still had a responsibility to Scofield and the wagon train to test the crossings and get the word back to them in time to turn them toward the Deep Sand Route around the Narrows, if that was his decision. He decided he would finish the grave as fast as he could, then look for tracks leading into the first crossing. He had asked Melody if the train she and her father had been part of had, in fact, made the crossings. She, of course, had no idea, since they had dropped too far behind to know which way their train had gone. So, he would have to rely on there being recent tracks leading into the river to determine if they had even tried. The tracks should tell the story, both entering the water and coming out.

When he finished digging the grave, he still had enough daylight left to at least scout the river crossings, so he told her that he thought it best if he put her father to rest, and she graciously accepted his offer. "It's best you remember him as he looked before he was killed and forget what he looked like after. Maybe you'd like to change into those dry things you found to wear." She thanked him for his thoughtfulness. When she went farther down the river to change, he took the opportunity to examine her father's body. He saw the bullet hole in his forehead that no doubt was the kill shot, but he looked for other wounds as well. He found another bullet wound in his side, but he also found multiple wounds caused by arrows. This told him that maybe as many as two of the four did not have guns. Satisfied that the odds may have improved in his favor, he dragged the body over to fall into the grave and quickly covered it with dirt. When she returned, he told her to hang her wet clothes on some tree limbs and she could come back to get them when they had dried. "Come with me now," he said. "There is something I have to do while I still have light enough to see. We'll take a short ride." He climbed on his horse.

She didn't know what he was going to do, but she had no option other than to do his bidding. So, when he took his foot out of the stirrup and extended his hand down to her, she took it, put her foot in the stirrup, and he lifted her up behind him. He rode up the bank to the first crossing, but he did not dismount, for he was satisfied to see the recent multitude of wagon tracks entering the river. So the wagon train Melody had been with did come this way. "This is where we usually circle the wagons and cross over the next morning," he told her. He turned his horse, left the wagon trail, and rode through the trees along the bank of the river until reaching a point where he could ride back to the wagon road and the exit of the first crossing. He saw nothing in the riverbank that would indicate the wagons had trouble leaving the water, nor did he expect to. For the river was not high. He saw no reason for a crossing any different than a normal one. He rode a mile ahead to take a look at the second crossing. He saw no trouble there, either, and decided to gamble on the third crossing being in the same shape. It was beginning to get dark by then, so he knew he had to turn his attention back to the young lady riding silently behind him.

"We're gonna make camp now, Melody. I've got a little bit of food that'll maybe keep us from starvin'. So we're goin' back closer to your wagon and build us a fire before it gets too dark to see what we're doin'."

She was alarmed at once. "Shouldn't we go somewhere else, away from our wagon? I'm afraid they'll come back to look for me."

"I can almost promise you they'll come back lookin' for you," Clint said. "The reason they've left you for this long is because they don't think you have any means to go very far. But we need to put a stop to their searchin' for good and all. You trust me?"

"I trust you," she answered uncertainly, seeing no other option.

Like the country they had been traveling since following the Sweetwater, there were no trees except those that crowded the winding riverbanks. So Clint rode back to the wagon, where they dismounted and he had Melody help him pick up any items of clothing still scattered on the ground. "And that half-burnt quilt there," he said. "Pick that up." When they had a couple of armfuls, he said, "That oughta do it." Then he walked into the trees where he had found her, past her father's grave, and about twenty yards beyond until he found a partial clearing just the right size for a small camp. He unpacked his coffeepot and bacon and the flour to make johnnycakes. "Sorry I didn't bring something more, but I didn't know I was gonna have a guest."

"Oh, I don't know, Clint . . . that's what you said your name is?" He nodded and repeated it. "Well, I don't know if I could eat anything right now, so I don't care what you brought."

"Maybe you'll drink some coffee then," he suggested and started collecting some wood for a fire. "We're gonna have to share my cup, though." She continued to look more and more dismayed as he casually filled his coffeepot and set it next to the fire he was in the process of starting. Once it was going for sure, he took the half-burned quilt, put some of the odd pieces of clothing they had picked up on the quilt, then rolled it up and laid it on one side of the fire. He took a walk up to the edge of the trees to take a good look around before picking up some more wood and returning to his fire. "That coffee oughta be just about ready," he said. "Pour you a cup?" he asked. She shook her head, so he poured the cup for himself.

"That's pretty good coffee," he said, "even if I have to say so, myself." He poured another cup. "Here, you carry this, we've gotta go now." When she asked where, he said, "We need to move the horses away from here and make our camp. This one's yours. That's you wrapped up in your quilt there." It was an old, well-known setup for an ambush, but he was confident that it would still work in this situation. He was confident that the four Indians had no idea of his existence and they would have no reason to believe the terrified woman could be baiting a trap for them. The success of the ambush would still depend upon his ability to strike quickly and accurately enough to severely cripple their efforts. His intent was simple, to kill them before they had a chance to kill him and Melody.

At last, Melody was fully aware of his intentions and she was not sure she wanted that. While she wanted the Indians punished for the murder of her father, she had hoped that Clint would take her on his horse, instead, and run as far away from there as they could manage. She could hold her tongue no longer. "Why don't we run away from here, instead of you risking your life against four of those savages?"

"A couple of reasons, I guess," he answered. "They deserve to be punished for killing your father and what they still intend to do to you. If they are not eliminated, they will continue to attack and kill other helpless victims. I'm going to leave you with the horses, in a cold camp, I'm afraid, because I don't wanna set another fire to draw 'em to you. I'm gonna leave my extra pistol with you, so you'll have some kind of weapon. Then if I lose this contest with these Sioux murderers, and I think that's who they are, you can take the horses and run. And if you have to do that, try to run back the way you came in the wagon and you'll eventually run into the wagon train I'm with." He studied her face as he told her all that, and her wide-open eyes, staring at him, told him of her bewilderment. "Don't worry," he said. "I think my chances of comin' back are pretty good."

"I think I will drink this coffee after all," she said.

He reached into his saddlebag and pulled out a little bundle wrapped in a cloth. "How 'bout a piece of jerky to go with it?" She took one piece. "That all you want?"

"Yes, thank you. I still don't have my appetite back."

He picked her up and set her in the saddle, then he led his horses along the riverbank, finally settling on a spot he felt a safe distance from the false camp. There was one of the river's many curves between the two spots, and looking across the bend they could see the faint glow of the fire he had built. There was nothing left to do now but tie the horses so that Biscuit wouldn't follow him when he went to the ambush. He got his extra pistol out of his saddlebag and gave Melody a quick lesson on how to fire it. In a little while he figured he'd best get into position to receive his guests. So he told her he was going to get set now, and if it happened like he expected, she would hear a lot of gunfire. "Don't get upset, most of it will probably be comin' from me."

"How will I know if you got them, or they got you?" She was not at all comfortable with what he was planning to do.

"You'll probably be able to tell," he told her. "Anyway, you know which way to run if you have to." He left her then and walked back through the trees crowding the riverbank to pick his spot. Although he had a strong feeling about the four raiders, he had no real way of knowing they would return to look for the girl at all. He just thought they would because she seemed like such a harmless risk. He might be getting set to sit there all night watching an empty trap. That thought was quickly discarded in the next few minutes when he caught sight of the four silhouettes against a rising moon as they left their horses by the burned-up wagon and disappeared into the trees along the bank. His Henry rifle already cocked and ready to fire, he aimed it at the edge of the circle of light provided by the fire. He had positioned himself at a perfect range for his rifle. He could hear the triumphant shout of the first warrior to step into the firelight when he saw the rolled-up quilt. Clint held his fire, waiting until the second warrior stepped into the light behind the first, who was yelling commands at the quilt. He could see part of a third warrior and he knew he could wait no longer. So he quickly set his sights on number three, since he could see enough to make the shot count. He pulled the trigger, cranked another cartridge into the chamber and dropped number two, who had been startled by the shot, but unaware that the warrior behind him had been hit. The first man in the circle, who was in the act of jerking the quilt up from the ground when the first two shots were fired, turned to run. Unfortunately for him, he turned right into a clean shot in the chest.

Three of the four raiders dead, but he had hoped for a miracle to give him all four, so it was not to be. Now it was a question of hide-and-seek. One thing for sure, he had to move from this spot. The fourth warrior had no doubt located his position from the muzzle flashes, so he cranked another cartridge in the cylinder and moved quickly to chase the last survivor. His intent was to cut him off before he could escape to his horse. When he found out he had guessed wrong, it was too late. He heard the warrior's blood-curdling battle cry only a split moment before he felt the impact of his body upon his shoulders and knew he had been outsmarted.

# Chapter 13

"Well, he never came back," Spud commented to Scofield as the wagons rolled out of the camping spot Clint had suggested with the limb he had driven in the ground beside the trail. "So I reckon that means we're drivin' 'em straight through Three Crossings."

"Reckon so," Scofield replied. "Suits me just fine. It's awful tough on the horses drivin' that Deep Sand Route. I reckon he's settin' up there waitin' for us, but I hope he takes a notion to go huntin' while he's waitin'. I could sure enjoy some fresh venison for a change. I reckon I'll ride on up ahead for a ways since Clint ain't here, just to make sure there ain't nothin' blockin' the trail."

"Right," Spud replied as Scofield rode on ahead, and thinking he could see there wasn't anything in the road for a quarter of a mile, just sitting right there in the wagon seat. *He's trying to make Lily think he's always a busy man*, Spud thought. As Spud would have predicted, there wasn't any problem in the trail straight through the morning. And it was after the nooning when they were back on the trail, and Scofield was riding along beside the wagon again before they were met with anything out of the ordinary. Again, it was Spud who called Scofield's attention to it. "There's a rider comin' this way," he alerted him.

They watched as the rider gradually came closer. "I swear, it looks like a woman and she's leadin' a packhorse," Scofield said.

"Ridin' a Palouse." He suddenly became more alert to that happenstance. "That looks like Clint's horse and that sorrel he took with him." More than a little concerned now, he didn't wait any longer to find out, gave the Morgan a kick with his heels and rode out to meet the woman. She pulled the Palouse to a stop when she saw the man on the big black horse coming toward her. The imposing figure he made caused her to become a little concerned as to what manner of man he might be. Scofield pulled right beside her, looking the horse over carefully as well as the saddle. "Howdy, ma'am," he said. "Mind tellin' me where you got the horses?"

"They're Clint's horses," she answered. "I can't remember his last name."

"Buchanan," Scofield supplied. "How'd you come by 'em?"

"Clint told me to take them and ride to meet you, if something happened to him. Are you Mr. Scofield?"

"I am. What happened to Clint? Is he all right?"

"No, sir, the Indians killed him. That's why I took the horses and came to meet you."

Scofield was stunned. "What Indians?"

"The ones that killed my father and burned our wagon," she said. "Then they were trying to find me, but Clint found me first. He saved my life."

"Are you sure Clint's dead?" Scofield asked. He was still numb from her shocking news and he couldn't think of what to say.

"Yes, sir, I heard the Indian scream out like a wild animal when he killed him and Clint didn't shoot anymore after that." When she saw how much trouble he was having digesting the news of Clint's death, she said, "I'm sorry to bring you this news. I guess Clint was a special person."

"Clint was my nephew," Scofield replied, "and one of the finest young men you'll ever get a chance to meet." He pulled himself together then. "But I apologize for my bad manners. It's just that you hit me with the last news I wanted to hear. You must be worn out and hungry. Clint told you to come back here because he expected us to take care of you. It ain't time for us to stop for supper yet. I kinda planned to stop at Three Crossings for supper. But we can take care of the horses and you can ride in my wagon. My wife can find something for you to eat."

"I hope Clint's horses are all right," she said. "I never rode a horse that far before. And when I hid for a while last night, I didn't take the saddle off the horse and I know you're supposed to do that. But I was afraid I couldn't put it back on when I started again this morning."

"Never you mind, miss, Biscuit's a strong horse. He'll be all right. That's his name, Biscuit. S'cuse me again. You already know my name, Scofield, Clayton Scofield. I never asked you yours."

"My name's Melody Meadows," she said, "and thank you for takin' me in. I can certainly work for my passage. I don't expect to go along without helping out."

"Don't you worry about that," he told her. "We'll find a place for you."

By this time, the wagons were approaching them, so Scofield rode out in the middle of the trail and signaled a halt. Then he came back to Melody as Spud pulled his horses to a stop. Lily, who had been walking, came up to join them. "This is Melody Meadows," Scofield told them. "She's gonna join our company here. Melody, this is my wife, Lily, and this is Spud Williams. Lily, I'd appreciate it if you could help Melody settle with us temporarily till we find her a permanent place."

"Of course," Lily said. "I'll take care of you, honey."

"I'm gonna throw Clint's saddle in Will Tucker's wagon along with the packsaddle and I'll turn the horses loose with the others."

"There's somethin' you ain't tellin' us, Scofield," Spud said. "Is it bad news?"

"The worst," Scofield replied. "I just got pieces of the story from the girl. But her father was killed when four Injuns attacked 'em. Clint found the girl and had to fight the four Injuns. She thinks he killed three of 'em." A black cloud immediately descended around the wagon and no one spoke for several minutes, unable to think of anything appropriate. Melody realized the high regard everyone seemed to have for Clint, and she was at once sorrowful that she had to bring them the news.

Spud, never one to shy away from awkward questions, finally spoke. "You say Clint killed three of 'em. What about the fourth one? Is Clint dead?"

"That's what she said," Scofield answered. "Clint told her to take the horses and run if he got in trouble."

The magnitude of the shock registered on Lily's face. Spud, incapable of showing deep emotions, nevertheless uttered, "Dang, that's sorry news."

Wiley Jones, whose wagon was second in line behind Scofield's wagon that day, walked up to see what the stop was about. Like Scofield and Lily, Wiley found it hard to believe Clint was dead, the news all the more strange when seeing the messenger. Scofield didn't take the time to give him the full story at that point. "We can't stay parked here," he said. "We've gotta keep movin'." He took the reins of Biscuit and the packhorse and rode back down the line to Will Tucker's wagon while Wiley walked back to his. With Will's help, he loaded the saddles into Will's wagon. Will didn't say anything, he just stared at Scofield for confirmation when he heard the message that Clint was dead passing back from wagon to wagon. Scofield simply said, "I'm afraid so, Will." He turned the Palouse and the sorrel loose to join the horse herd and rode back to his wagon to give the signal to roll.

It was a rather solemn train of wagons that finished out the day's travel. Clint Buchanan had been a well-liked and admired young man. And perhaps one of the more sorrowful ones was the young lady who knew him the least but was the unfortunate messenger of his death. Melody walked with Lily for a major portion of her trip back to the place where her world had been totally turned upside down. She found Lily to be a friendly and gracious person and soon the two became friends. They talked about the recent passing of Melody's mother, then the horror of her father's brutal slaying at the hands of raging savages. Then Melody confided that she and her parents were traveling west to not only create a new life, but also for the wedding of their daughter. "You're on your way west to get married?" Lily asked, fascinated. "Is he someone you've known a long time?"

"No," Melody answered. "I've never met him. The marriage was arranged by our parents. His name is Worthy Davis. I had a picture of him, but it was in with some things that got burned up in the wagon."

"And that's all right with you?" Lily asked. "I mean, traveling way out there to marry someone you don't even know?"

Melody shrugged and answered, "I guess so. I didn't have any prospects where we lived in Missouri. And he seemed like a nice person in the letter he sent me, and my folks wanted it."

"Well, you'll certainly have a story to tell when you get there. I hope he appreciates what you're going through to get to the wedding." She cocked her head to one side and said, "Worthy, huh? I hope he is worthy after what you've just been through."

"I feel so bad about Clint, though," Melody lamented. "I'm so sorry I brought you folks that awful news."

"If you hadn't, we might have never known," Lily told her. "Melody, you didn't kill Clint. You just brought us the news. Nobody here thinks you were the cause of it."

"But I was," she protested. "Those four savages came back to get me, and if Clint hadn't stopped them, I'd be dead instead of him. And maybe that would have been better all the way around. Then I'd be with my mother and father, and Clint would still be guiding this wagon train."

"My, my," Lily clucked, anxious to head the young girl off before she put herself in a dark hole. "That woulda left poor ol' Worthy looking in an empty bag, wouldn't it? And all those poor little babies that are waiting for you to have 'em."

Melody couldn't suppress a giggle. "They coulda found another mama. That woulda been all right with me."

* * *

It was a little before five o'clock when they reached Melody's father's wagon, the bloated, half-burned bodies of his mules lying in the harnesses. "Where's the ambush camp you said Clint set up?" Scofield asked Melody. She pointed toward the trees along the riverbank. Scofield stared at the place she pointed for a long moment, then said, "I'll come back and take a look. We'll drive on up toward the first crossing. There's a big enough place to circle the wagons up there." He waved the wagons on and rode ahead of them to make sure nothing had changed since crossing there last year. When he rounded the last curve before reaching the grassy camping area, he pulled Blackie to a sudden stop, startled by a vision of Clint sitting, Indian style, at the head of the meadow. Frozen, for at first he thought it was an illusion, and then the illusion spoke. "I thought it was about time you showed up. Did Melody reach you with my horse?" Clint asked as he got up on his feet.

"Clint!" That was all Scofield could manage for a few seconds until Clint started walking to meet him. Then he turned around and yelled back to the wagons pulling in, "It's Clint!" His announcement was answered by a ragged group cheer from the wagons who were close enough to hear him.

Their outburst startled Clint, causing him to stop before continuing to walk to meet his uncle. "What's all the cheerin' about?" he asked when he approached his uncle, who was fairly beaming with the joy of seeing his nephew alive.

"We thought you was dead," Scofield said.

"That crossed my mind," Clint admitted. "Did Melody find you?" he asked again. "When I went back to get her, she was gone and so were my horses. I thought she just got scared and took off." He started to ask again if she brought his horses back but stopped when he saw her jump down from Scofield's wagon and come running toward him. "Well, I see she found you." He smiled at her as she ran up to him, expecting her to stop, so he was forced to take a couple of steps backward when she threw herself in his arms.

"I'm so glad to see you," she gushed. "I'm so sorry I rode off and left you. I thought you were dead."

When he recovered his balance, he asked, "Why'd you think that?"

"Because I heard that savage yell out that bloody scream that sounded like a war cry or something, and you didn't shoot any-more after I heard that. I knew you told me to run if anything happened to you, so I ran. I'm so sorry. Please forgive me for leaving you here."

"All right," he said. When he said no more than that, she looked concerned. So he smiled and said, "I forgive you. I'm glad you found the wagon train."

She relaxed then. "They've been so nice to take me in." But then she thought of something else. "Now, what kind of person will they think I am for running away and leaving you?"

"It doesn't make any difference what they think," Lily Scofield spoke out as she walked up to join them. "We know what happened and we'll set 'em straight. Won't we, Clint?"

"That we will," Clint said with a chuckle. "To tell you the truth, I thought I was dead, too, when I let that last one get around behind me. I didn't know he was there until he let out that war cry. And he was already in the air when he screamed. The next thing I knew, he landed on my back and we both went down. I lost my rifle when he hit me and he lost his knife. It was dark in those bushes. After it was all over, I found my rifle, but I didn't find his knife till the sun came up the next mornin'."

"How'd you kill him?" Spud wanted to know, having just pulled the wagon up beside them.

"I didn't lose my knife when we went down," Clint said. "It was still right there on my belt." Seeing the look of nausea on Melody's face, he quickly changed the subject. "Did my horse treat you all right?"

Her expression cleared up at once. "Yes, he did," she answered.

"He didn't even complain when I made him wear his saddle all night. I think he knew I didn't know how to put it back on him in the morning."

"He probably did. He'll let a lady do things that he wouldn't let me get away with," Clint told her.

"I expect we'd best get these wagons circled up and get on with our chores," Scofield announced. He was feeling very satisfied with his world again, now that Clint had returned from the dead. For the last half of the day he had been worrying about being the bearer of the news to his sister-in-law, Irene, and Ruby Nixon, who were determined to get Clint married to Ruby when they got back. At least, he amended, Irene was determined. Ruby was just hoping. The way Melody threw herself in Clint's arms just now would make a romantic think there might be a spark there, he thought, if Lily hadn't told him about Melody heading west to marry some fellow named Worthy. He shook his head and reminded himself, *It's a long way between here and Oregon.*

Before the social hour after supper was over that night, everybody but the children made it a point to let Clint know how glad they were to see him among the living again. And there was a show of sympathy for the newest member to the company, Miss Melody Meadows, for the loss of her father and mother. Due to already crowded conditions in all the wagons, it was going to be somewhat of a problem to find a permanent place for Melody. The only wagon with a space for her was Will Tucker's. And Clint had moved into Will's wagon when Scofield married Lily. There were some who thought it unthinkable for the young woman to move into Will's wagon, even though Will was thought to be a man of the highest character. But surely she could not move in with both Will and Clint. This was especially so when it was learned that Melody was on the Oregon Trail with her parents for the purpose of marrying a man, one Worthy Davis, who was anxiously awaiting her arrival. The problem was finally solved to everyone's satisfaction when Scofield donated his sleeping tent to Melody, since he and Lily seldom used it. Then Will and Clint could sleep in, or under, the wagon, depending on the weather. Melody, in return, volunteered to do the cooking for Will and herself. Clint would continue to eat Spud's offerings.

The river crossings started first thing the next morning with Spud driving Scofield's wagon into the first crossing. As Clint had predicted, it was accomplished with no more trouble than he had expected, so the others followed in order. Those first three crossings were so close together that Scofield and Clint were directing the first wagons in line across the second crossing while the wagons at the end of the line were still facing the first crossing. The canyon was so narrow that at one point the wagons left the river on a trail that was only as wide as the width of one wagon. The granite wall on the side of the narrow trail provided yet another place for the emigrants to leave their names and the date. Scofield was intent upon keeping the wagons moving as quickly as possible, but it was difficult to maintain a decent pace. South Pass was around one hundred miles away along the winding Sweetwater, with either nine or ten crossings, depending on the amount of rain June brought that year. So that segment of the trip could take anywhere from ten to twenty days. As it turned out, it was fourteen days before they reached South Pass, the gradual rise to cross the Continental Divide. To those anticipating a magnificent gateway to cross the Rockies, it was quite a big disappointment when they got their first look at South Pass. A seemingly endless sagebrush-covered plain with not a tree in sight. It was a dead-looking land and hardly seemed capable of influencing all the rivers on one side of it to flow into the Atlantic Ocean, while all the rivers on the other side flowed into the Pacific. As far as Scofield and his nephew were concerned, the only real importance held by South Pass was that it provided a gradual grade to cross the Rocky Mountains without risking the climb through steep Rocky Mountain passes. It would prove to be a long dusty drive, especially for those wagons near the back of the train. The sagebrush was so prolific that it covered everything except the single wagon ruts across the plain. It made it especially difficult for the women and children who made up the majority of walkers. Because the sage was right up to the wagon tracks, the walkers could not walk wide of the wagons to escape the dust. So the fashion of the day was to wrap a bandana around your face.

Eighteen miles past the Continental Divide, they came to the Parting of the Ways, where the single wagon road split to become two choices. The right-hand fork went due west toward Fort Hall, while the left-hand fork led southwest to Fort Bridger and Salt Lake City. The right-hand fork was sometimes called Sublette Cutoff. It would shorten their trip by about seventy miles if they went that way. Scofield always told his people about the cutoff, and every year someone always asked why they didn't go that way. This trip it was Tiny Futch. "Because," Scofield explained, "it may be shorter, but there's a stretch of desert about forty or more miles wide with no water and no grass. You got a good chance of losin' some of the livestock. That's always been reason enough for me to take the original route by way of Fort Bridger. Besides that, Fort Bridger is a good place to replace exhausted supplies and make repairs if you need 'em."

"So, there's water and grass if we take the long way. Is that right?" Levi asked.

"That's right," Scofield said. "Oh, it ain't like when we was followin' the Sweetwater, but there's water along the way and there's willow wood for your fires, too."

So they went into camp that night beside a creek called Little Sandy. They had to cross it to intercept Big Sandy River but Scofield said there was no need to cross it that night. It was only about ten feet wide and two feet deep, not problem enough to even slow the wagons down. And the grass was better on the side where they circled the wagons. So after the animals were taken care of, the women and Spud cooked supper, and the musicians cranked up after supper.

Scofield and his lady came out to the social hour, and in a little while, Clint joined them. "How's a man as big as Tiny Futch learn to pick a banjo like that?" Clint asked when he knelt down next to them. "His fingers are so big, I don't see how he can get 'em between the strings."

"I don't know how he does it, but he can sure make that banjo talk, can't he?" Lily remarked.

"How come you don't ever join 'em and play your bugle, Uncle Clayton?" Clint asked.

"Same reason you don't sing with 'em," Scofield came back.

"Oh," Clint replied. "Well, I reckon I can understand that."

"How are things gettin' on at the Will Tucker wagon?" Scofield asked. "Miss Melody has been with you two young men a pretty good while now."

"It's more like she's been with Will for a while," Clint said. "I really don't see her that much. She sleeps in that tent you gave her. I sleep under the wagon if the weather is good. If it ain't, I sleep in the wagon with Will. And you know I eat with you folks. But from what I get from Will, I think they're doin' just fine. She's doin' the cookin' for him, and anything else that needs doin', like sewin' up holes in his shirt, washin' dishes, or whatever. Poor thing, she feels guilty that she hasn't got any money and she wants to pay her way by workin'. Will tells her not to worry about it, that he's glad to have her stay with him."

"Well, who would expect her to have any money?" Scofield asked.

"It's good she's got pride," Lily said. "She's a fine little lady. You think there's a chance she and Will might get to be really good friends?"

Clint shrugged. "Shoot, I don't know. I never thought about it."

"Does she know anything about Will's late wife?" Lily asked. "I mean he must have some of Angel's clothes somewhere in that wagon, and maybe some baby clothes."

That was as far as he could let it go before having to make a comment. "Ain't that just like a woman?" Scofield asked. "Al-

ready tryin' to match 'em up. Will mighta got messed up so bad
by Angel that he don't wanna take a chance on another woman."

"Meetin' a nice girl like Melody seems to me is the cure for
what's ailing Will," Lily said.

"Sounds to me like you don't care a-tall about poor ol' Worthy," Scofield said.

"I don't," Lily replied. "If he was serious about marrying
Melody, he woulda gone to Missouri and got her."

"Come on, Lulu Belle," Scofield whispered so only she would
hear. "I think it's time we went back to the wagon." He pulled
her up on her feet. Then he reached down, grabbed her around
her legs, hefted her up on his shoulder and marched off toward
the wagon amid a chorus of cheers, whistles, and attaboys. Ever
the spunky one, Lily just smiled and waved to the crowd.

# Chapter 14

Seven o'clock on the money, Scofield's wagon, with Spud in the driver's seat and Lily beside him, rolled across the shallow creek and the wagon train started out to strike Big Sandy Creek. They would follow Big Sandy all the way to its confluence with the Green River, a distance in the neighborhood of seventy miles. Scofield planned to make it in five to five-and-a-half days. The night just past, at the social hour, before he had carried Lily off caveman-style, he had reminded those who were there that they would be paying a ferry toll to cross the Green River. "It's gonna take us about five days to get there, so you've got plenty of time to dig the money outta all your hidin' places." It was no surprise to anyone who had read the articles of agreement they had all signed before leaving Independence. But he thought it always good to remind them. He also told them that, if it was the same as in prior years, there would likely be more than one ferry operating at the river. "The one most people use is one operated by the Mormons. It's a reliable one, but sometimes their charge is a little high, especially if the river's way up and the crossin's more dangerous. They was askin' fourteen dollars last year, and I've heard that ain't as high as they have charged. So we went a couple of miles south of the Mormon Ferry and did business with a fellow named Lewis Robinson. He charged ten dollars, seemed like a lot, but it was better'n fourteen and he done a good job of it, so I reckon we'll go back there."

"Why don't we ford the river, just like we did all the way up the Sweetwater?" Bass Thornton asked.

"The Green River's bigger'n any river you've come to so far. It's a little too deep and a little too wide," Scofield answered. "It's usually high this time of year and the current's pretty strong, too. There's lots of folks tried swimming 'em, or floatin' 'em across, but there was a lotta wagons lost tryin' it." He grinned at Bass and then added, "And Leach ain't nowhere near tall enough to push your wagon up from the bottom of the Green River."

So the wagon train continued on its southwest course, following Big Sandy Creek, a strong creek that turned away from the established wagon trail often, but always returned to provide camping sites with water and wood. Each day on the trail seemed pretty much like the day preceding it until, finally, Clint rode back to camp one night after the wagons were circled and the cook fires started. "The Green River's about five miles up ahead," he reported to Scofield. "There's another wagon train camped there at the Mormon Ferry. Didn't look like they'd even started takin' any of 'em across yet."

"We got here sooner than I expected," Scofield said. "I figured maybe tomorrow at noonin' time. You didn't ride on down to the Robinson Ferry, right?"

"No, I didn't," Clint said. "It was already gettin' late and I knew you were goin' there, anyway."

"You coulda found out if Robinson was still there," Scofield said with a grin.

"I guess I could have, couldn't I?" Clint admitted. "I reckon I was too hungry to think straight. I'll find out for you in the mornin' before you get there."

"I reckon that's that wagon train we started catchin' up to back at the Narrows. Couldn't be anybody else." Then it occurred to him. "That's the wagon train Melody Meadows and her parents started out with."

"That's right," Clint replied. "I didn't even think about that. You reckon she might wanna go back with them?"

"She might," Scofield said. "I don't know why, though. Although," he reconsidered, "they might have made friends with some of the other families and she'd like to go back with them. We'll tell her about it, and she can do what she wants." He paused to think about it a little more, then decided, "I'll tell Lily about it and let her talk to Melody. They're pretty friendly, and if I go talk to her about it, she'll most likely think I'm wantin' her to go. And I don't want her to think that."

"Good idea," Clint agreed.

Lily thought it was a good idea, too. So after supper, she looked for Melody and found her at the creek washing the dishes. "How's everything at the Will Tucker wagon?" Lily called out cheerfully. "You haven't kicked those two worthless men out yet?"

Melody laughed. "If you've come to help me wash dishes you're too late. They're already done."

"Clint just rode back before supper, and while we were eating, I heard him telling Clayton that we caught up with that wagon train you started out with. And I thought you'd like to know that."

"Oh," Melody responded with no show of excitement. "Is that so?"

"Yep, we've almost reached the river, and they're camped there waiting to get ferried across. I thought I should tell you, in case you wanted to go back with the folks you started out with."

"Oh, that's all right," Melody replied. "I'm happy where I am. Does Mr. Scofield want me to leave?"

"No, not at all," Lily quickly replied. "He wasn't even gonna say anything about it. But I thought you ought to know, in case you have some close friends on that train."

"No, I'm all right where I am," Melody said, seemingly concerned. "Do the folks on this train wish I would go back?"

"Good heavens no, girl. Where do you get ideas like that?"

"You've been a good friend to me, so I have to tell you the truth. I can't go back to that other wagon train. When Clint found me, I didn't tell him the whole truth." She captured Lily's rapt attention right away. "He asked me if they asked Papa and me to drop out of the train because Mama had cholera. And I told him they didn't, that we dropped back to bury Mama. Well, that wasn't really true." Tears began to gather in the corner of her eyes when she continued. "Lily, Mr. Selmond put it to a vote, and everybody on the whole train voted for Papa and me to drop out of the wagon train because they were afraid we had cholera, too." She could no longer hold back the tears. "I was afraid Clint would leave me, too."

"Well, bless your heart," Lily said, "I hope you know Clint better than that now."

"Lily, I'm not sick. Papa and I never got sick."

"How do they know your mama had cholera, anyway? Is there a doctor on that train? Your mama mighta had pneumonia." She bit her bottom lip and shook her head. "Well, that settles it. I don't want you back with those people. If you can stand it with Will and Clint, then that's where you'll stay."

"Thank you so much for saying that because I am very happy in Will's wagon. Will has been so sweet to me—just like you and Clint and everybody else on this train."

"I think you're right where you ought to be, and it might make you even happier to know we're heading for a different ferry. So you don't even have the chance to accidentally see any of those people. Come on, I'll carry some of those things back to your wagon for you."

That night at the social hour, Scofield announced that they would be in for a short ride the next day. "We're only about five miles from the river and about seven miles from the ferry that's gonna take us across. You're still gonna get the four o'clock bugle and we'll pull outta here at seven as usual. But when we get to that ferry, we're still gonna have to set up camp. It'll take a good part of the day to ferry all twenty-eight wagons across, and then all the livestock. They can't take but one wagon at a time. And to save some money, all the women and children will swim across." He waited for the outburst he expected, then said, "I was just jokin' about that. We ain't gonna make the children swim." He received a few more howls. "So enjoy the rest of the evenin'."

He sat back down next to Lily again as the musicians assaulted another old familiar tune. Every night it was the same old favorites they played, but everybody patted a foot in time and some even sang, if they knew the words. Lily tapped him on the arm to draw his attention toward the wagons to see Will and Melody coming to join everybody. Will was carrying a box for Melody to sit on. "It might be kinda hard on Will when we get to Oregon and he has to hand her off to her betrothed," Lily said.

"Reckon so," Scofield said. "But it's a long way from here to the Willamette Valley." He grinned at her and added, "And you know how women are."

She punched him on his shoulder. "No, I don't. How are women?" He held his arm and pretended like it was injured.

They both looked up then and realized Clint was watching them. "I ain't sure I wanna see any more of this," Clint said, then turned and walked over to join Will and Melody.

Just as he had informed them the night before, Scofield blew a series of ear-piercing noises through his bugle at four o'clock sharp to start the day for their short drive to the river. Shortly before reaching the Mormon Ferry, Clint appeared in the trail ahead and signaled Scofield to bypass it. Then he rode over to the alternate trail and waited for Scofield to come to him. "Robinson is operating and there's no one waiting to be ferried across. Looks like our timin' is right this year."

They continued the short ride down to the ferry and went into camp on the riverbank, the wagons lined up to go one wagon at a time. Robinson was delighted that they had passed up the more popular ferry to give him their business. And to prove it, he made them a rate of eight dollars per crossing. As usual, the operation was started with Scofield's wagon starting the parade. The plan was to ferry about half the wagons across and then start transporting the livestock across before ferrying the rest of the wagons. That way, there would be someone to take care of the horses and cows left on the one bank as well as someone to tend to them when they arrived on the opposite side. Since Scofield went across with Spud on the first crossing, Clint decided to stay behind until the last wagon was safely on the ferry.

It was a time-consuming process, even though Robinson and his men worked at a steady pace. Soon the noon hour arrived and the cook fires started at the wagons on both sides of the river.

There were still four wagons left to cross when the war party of a dozen Cheyenne warriors broke from the trees beside the river, screaming their war cries and firing at the wagons. Clint reacted immediately. He yelled for the women to get the kids into the wagons. Then he pulled his rifle from the saddle sling and knelt beside Roy Leach behind the wagon belonging to Bass Thornton. Realizing that Leach was not armed, he drew his pistol and tossed it to him. Leach grinned in response. Taking dead aim then, Clint methodically starting picking off the leaders of the charging war party, one by one. He was fortunate in that one of the other four wagons was Tiny Futch's, and Tiny, seeing Clint's response, was quick to do the same. The last two wagons belonged to Vance Miller and Jim Rayford and Clint was gratified to hear rifle fire coming from both wagons. The immediate response turned the Indians' charge into a suicide attack, for half of their force was cut down and the other six scattered, heading for cover. In a matter of seconds, it seemed, the whole incident was over and hard to believe it had actually happened.

The sudden surprise of the unexpected attack could have been disastrous for the unprepared four wagons, however, had not Clint's natural reactions dictated his response. "Anybody hurt?" he yelled when the last of the Indians disappeared. There was no answer, so he yelled, "Everybody all right?" This time, he heard from all four wagons. When he was satisfied that no one got hit, he went to the edge of the water where he found two of Robinson's men lying on their bellies beneath the bank. "It's all right," Clint told them, "they're gone. Signal that ferry back over here and let's get these last wagons across." He could see Scofield and the other emigrants on the bank across the river, alarmed by the sudden attack. So he waved his arm in the air to say they were okay.

When he went back to the wagons, everybody but the children were out of them, examining the bullet holes that had been ripped into the sides of the wagon boxes. Leach grinned again when he handed an empty six-gun back to Clint, much like a child who had been allowed to play with a new toy. "I reckon we showed those damn savages who not to pick on," Jim Rayford exclaimed.

"We sure as hell did!" Vance replied.

"Why did they attack us?" Bass Thornton asked, having just climbed out of his wagon. "I was told the Indians seldom struck a wagon train of this size, since there would surely be too many guns to fire back at them."

"That's generally true," Clint replied. "But those Indians didn't attack a whole wagon train. They waited till all but four wagons had crossed the river. I counted a dozen of 'em and I reckon they figured they could swarm over the folks in four wagons while all the rest of the wagon train was helpless on the other side of the river. Looks like they picked the wrong four wagons. They were a little too greedy."

"They mighta had better luck if you hadn't been on this side of the river," Tiny said. "I swear, every time I set my sights on one of them in the lead, he'd drop off his horse before I pulled the trigger. Blamed if I don't believe you play that Henry faster'n I play my banjo."

"You're forgettin'," Clint said, "Jim and Vance was shootin' at 'em, too, and so was Leach. He was at a disadvantage 'cause all he had to shoot with was my pistol." He looked at the simple soul, still with the childish grin on his face. "Good job, Leach," he said, and the childish grin completed the trip across his rough, craggy face from ear to ear. "Mr. Thornton's wagon goes next and I see the ferry comin' back. So you can drive your wagon on down there." Leach hopped back up in the driver's seat and waited for Bass to get back on the wagon. When he drove away, Clint said to Tiny, "I know your wagon's next in line, but if you don't mind, I'd appreciate it if you'd let Miller and Rayford go next. That's just in case those other six Indians decide they've got a better chance against one or two wagons." He knew Tiny understood why he asked him to stay back, so he said, "If you want to, you could send Annie and the kids with Rayford or Miller, just to play it safe."

"I doubt Annie would go without me," Tiny said. "If it gets down to you and me against them six Indians, I'll bet on you and me."

"I 'preciate it, Tiny." So with rifles ready, they waited for the ferry to drop Thornton's wagon off and return for Miller's, all the while keeping a wary eye on the trees where the six Cheyenne warriors had disappeared. Although Robinson's two employees were anxious to get the last of the wagons across, it seemed to Clint and Tiny that each crossing was taking longer than the one before it. When Rayford's wagon was taken across, and no sign of the Indians, they pretty much figured the Indians felt it not worth the risk to attack one wagon. "If they came back now, it would just be for the sake of avenging the deaths of their fallen. So maybe that's the last we'll see of them." Even as he said it, he had uncertain feelings about the possibility, for he knew how deeply this disastrous defeat had shamed them. He should have suspected there might be a meeting of the six survivors behind the screen of trees along the riverbank.

"I cannot return to our village and tell them of the dead brothers we have left on this riverbank without the scalp of the man with the medicine gun that shoots all day without reloading," Lame Otter declared. "Why do we hide here, waiting for darkness so that we might sneak out to pick up our dead? It is early in the day. It will be a long time before darkness."

"I feel the shame, just as you do," Crooked Arrow said. "We could attack the one wagon that is still there, but the medicine gun is waiting. He wants more kills."

"I think the warrior who kills that man will surely gain his powerful medicine and the gun that shoots many times," Little Buffalo said.

"I cannot leave my wife's brother out there for the buzzards to eat," Lame Otter said. "Stay here if you will. I am going to go get his body. The white men have gone down to the water now."

"I will go with you," one of the other warriors said. "We must not leave them."

Down at the ferry dock, Tiny prepared to drive his wagon onto the ferry. "Look!" he exclaimed to Clint. "They're comin' outta the woods!"

Clint automatically cranked a cartridge into the chamber of his rifle but then hesitated, for there were only two Indians that came out in the open campground. He watched for a few seconds then realized, "They're only picking up their dead. Go ahead and get your wagon on the ferry. I'll keep my eye on the Indians."

The two men who operated the ferry on that side of the river were not too comfortable when they heard the Indians were back. They moved Tiny on as fast as they could. Lewis Robinson had built a ferry long enough to take the wagon with a team of two horses still in harness, but there was no room for Clint's horse, too. "Are you gonna be all right by yourself till they come back for you?" Tiny wanted to know because another Indian joined the first two in retrieving the bodies.

"Looks like they're just after their dead," Clint said. "Just don't take too long," he said to one of the ferry operators.

"Mister," the man replied, "we ain't coming back, not with

them damn Indians coming outta the woods again. Me and my partner are going back with this wagon, so you'd best come on board, too."

"It doesn't look like you've got room for my horse on that ferry," Clint said.

"That's a fact," the man said. "We can't take your horse, but we can take you. You stay here by yourself and you're a dead man. And you can find you another horse. So come on, we're ready to go."

"Mister," Clint said, "you've obviously never had a horse that's saved your life before. I'm not leavin' my horse for those Indians to take."

"That's just crazy," the man said.

Through talking to him, Clint turned to Tiny and said, "Take these over for me, Tiny. All right?" He then took off his gun belt and handed it and his rifle to him. "I don't want them to get wet. Biscuit and I are goin' for a swim."

"Clint," Tiny exclaimed, "are you crazy?"

"Most likely," Clint answered. "I'll see you on the other side." He climbed up into the saddle and rode down the bank and into the river.

In the trees beyond the campground, Little Buffalo dropped the body he had carried from the open field. He turned toward the river again and stopped. "Lame Otter, look! The medicine gun is crossing the river on his horse!" Lame Otter did not hesitate. He grabbed his rifle and ran out into the clearing and screamed out his anger when he saw the man on the horse already out past the point where the horse had to swim. He inserted a cartridge into the chamber and closed the bolt as he ran toward the riverbank.

On board the ferry, Tiny saw the Indians running down to the riverbank. He took a quick look at Clint's progress and saw that he was not yet in the deepest part where the current was strongest. So he picked up his rifle and aimed it at Lame Otter, who was in the lead, and fired a couple of shots, but the ferry was crossing through the strongest current so his base was not solid and his shots kicked up dirt on either side of Lame Otter. They did nothing to discourage the infuriated Cheyenne warrior. He aimed his rifle at the man on the horse and fired, just as Biscuit hit the swift current of the river and was swept sideways as he struggled to reach the other shore. Lame Otter was desperate now in his efforts to eject the spent cartridge and insert another, for the strong current was sweeping Clint and his horse farther and farther away from him. The frustrated warrior ran along the riverbank, trying to keep up with the current. But when he stopped to take another shot at Clint, who was fully in the water, hanging onto Biscuit's saddle, he was staggered by the impact of Tiny's shot. Startled, the warrior dropped to his knees and looked down at the hole in his deerskin shirt. Confused now, he continued to stare at the hole until the impact of a second shot caused him to fall over on the ground.

No longer concerned with shots from the Indians, Clint still had the river to fight as his struggling horse fought to make it to the opposite side, gradually making progress. On the south bank of the river, most of the men and boys of the wagon train were running along beside the river, trying to keep up with the current. Leading them was Scofield, riding his horse. When finally Biscuit's hooves struck the bottom of the river, Clint swung back into the saddle and the horse waded ashore to the cheers of those waiting for him. When Biscuit climbed up on the bank, Clint dismounted to give the exhausted Palouse some rest. "Well done, Clint!" someone cried out as he stepped down.

"I expect it's more like well done, Biscuit," Clint remarked. "He's the one that got us across. And well done, Tiny." While he was in the middle of the river, he was aware of some shots that seemed to be coming from the ferryboat and he figured they had to come from Tiny.

"Have a little trouble gettin' across the river, partner?" Scofield asked with a grin, looking down at him from the saddle.

"Some," Clint answered simply. He knew his uncle was greatly relieved to see him safely across. He led Biscuit up the bank. "I hope you got a fire built somewhere. I need to dry out my saddle blanket and these clothes."

"Well, no, we ain't," Scofield said. "Tiny's pullin' his wagon off the ferry right now, and he's all we was waitin' for. We're ready to roll. We've still got three hours left before supper."

"I reckon I'll just have to hang my pants and shirt on the back of Will's wagon. I'll take Biscuit's saddle off and throw it in the wagon, my moccasins, too. And we'll just ride bareback and barefooted till suppertime. It's a good thing it's still summer."

Levi Watkins said, "Glad to see you didn't get shot by the Injuns, Clint. Vance and Jim have already been tellin' everybody how they turned 'em back when they tried to attack."

"That's right," Clint said. "They were both doin' some shootin'."

"What Injuns you reckon they were," Scofield asked, "after we got this far without seein' a one?"

"Can't say for sure," Clint said. "Most likely Cheyenne or Arapaho. Don't make much difference, one'll kill you just as dead as the next."

He led Biscuit to the wagons and went directly to Will Tucker's where he found Will and Melody getting everything ready to pull out when Scofield gave the signal. "Hey, Clint," Will greeted him. "I'm glad you made it across all right. I told Melody you were swimming across the river and that's what the last shots were about."

"Yep, we made it all right," Clint replied. "I've gotta pile Biscuit's saddle in the wagon and I'm gonna need to use the wagon for a couple of minutes to change into my dry shirt and britches. Then I'll get outta your way."

"I'll get out of your way," Melody said. "You did get soaked, didn't you?"

"I sure did," Clint said. "I won't take long." He didn't take but a minute, then he went to Tiny's wagon to get his weapons and ammunition.

"I was comin' to look for you as soon as I got my wagon in

line," Tiny said. "Helluva way to end a river crossin', wasn't it?" He couldn't help grinning at Clint, riding his horse bareback with no boots or moccasins on his feet.

"I wanna thank you for gettin' that last Indian off my back," Clint said as he strapped his gun belt back on and took his rifle from Tiny. "I knew it was you that stopped him."

"I reckon those were the two best shots I've ever made," Tiny confessed. "I shot at him when he was runnin' down to the river and missed him every time. I'm blamin' it on the way that ferry-boat was bobbin' up and down when we hit the roughest part. But when he was aimin' at you when you was in the water, I knew I better not miss."

"Well, I'm obliged," Clint said. "I'm glad it was you that had to take the shot."

Tiny was too touched to respond, so he just nodded. So Annie said thank you for him.

# Chapter 15

In short order, the wagons pulled away from the Green River, angling to intercept the southwest trail they would follow to Fort Bridger, another five-day drive, approximately. Will's wagon was halfway back in the line; Clint's wet buckskins were hanging on the back flap. So were his moccasins, and Biscuit's saddle blanket was lying on the canvas cover.

There was no sign on the trail of the recent passage of another wagon train, so they could assume the train that Melody started out with was now behind them. Even in his present state of undress, Clint was insistent upon performing the job his uncle hired him to do. So he rode out well ahead of the wagons to find a place to camp that they would reach in about three hours' time. The spot he settled on might push them a little past the usual five o'clock quitting time, but it was far superior to the first one he considered. That one was a fairly busy stream with some firewood and poor grazing. But it was the best he had come upon in a stretch of mostly dry, treeless plain. When he decided to look a little farther, he was surprised to find a full-flowing creek with more than ample grazing. He could tell that Biscuit preferred it by far, so he decided it to be the official campsite for that night.

Since he was quite a way ahead of Scofield and the wagons at that point, he decided to explore the creek even farther. So he rode downstream until coming to a small, wooded area where a stream emptied into the creek. He suspected it was the stream he originally thought he was going to have to settle for as the campsite. It caused him to think of Ash Hollow back on the Platte. For like Ash Hollow, this little oasis at the confluence of the stream and the creek offered a refreshing surprise from the dusty, dry trail between the Green River and Fort Bridger. He couldn't understand why it was such a surprise. And the more he thought about it, the more he realized he had been there before. They camped there the year before. How could he forget it? He had killed a deer there. Only one thing could make it perfect, he thought.

"I expect we oughta be seein' Clint about now," Scofield said to Spud. "The time's about right to call it a day, and that line of trees up ahead looks like there's water of some kind." They continued on with still no sign of Clint as they neared the line of trees. Scofield gave his horse a nudge and loped on ahead of the wagon to discover the stream. He turned the big Morgan around in a complete circle as he looked in every direction for his nephew. Then he rode back to the wagon and pulled up beside Spud again. "It's a stream. Ain't very deep, but it's wide. I reckon it'll do for the night. I expect we can go ahead and circle 'em up. Hell, it's time to quit for the day. I just don't know where Clint is. He oughta be here. I hope he ain't fell off that horse," referring to his lack of a saddle.

Spud recognized it as a joke, but he suspected Scofield was a little concerned. He was not as concerned, himself, so he made a suggestion. "If I was you, I'd just keep right on goin' and figure we just ain't got there yet."

"You think so?" Scofield asked. "Maybe you're right, but you know, we ain't passed many places where we could camp, and I remember this little stream. We might be comin' back to this stream." He decided then. "See that line of hills about a quarter of a mile ahead? If we don't see him by the time we get to those

hills, we'll turn around and come back here." Spud shrugged in-
differently.

So, when the wagons reached the stream, they kept right on
going, heading for the hills beyond. Just before they reached
them, Clint rode out of the gap that the trail passed through and
waved them on. Scofield and Spud looked at each other and
grinned. "I never doubted it," Scofield said, and he rode on
ahead so he could see where he was going to circle the wagons.
When he approached, Clint wheeled Biscuit around and led him
to the creek that flowed along the line of hills. "We camped at
this creek last year," Scofield said when they stopped beside it.
"I swear, I had forgotten it was here. I must really be gettin' old."

"Then I reckon I am, too," Clint said, " 'cause I forgot about it,
too. You remember I killed a deer here last year?"

"Yeah, that's right, you did," Scofield answered. "I remember
that." When he noticed Clint was grinning at him, he started to
ask why. But Clint turned his head and nodded downstream.
Scofield followed the direction with his eyes and saw the deer
propped against a tree, halfway gutted.

"I was trying to get him skinned and gutted before you got
here, but I didn't have time. I woulda hung him up, but I don't
have any rope. It's lucky I had my belt on, so I at least had my
knife."

"Well, I'll be . . ." Scofield started, then paused to chuckle.
"Just like last year. Let me call Spud in here and get my wagon in
place, then he can jump on that deer with you and we'll have
fresh venison for supper."

As he said, Scofield went back and directed Spud into position, and when he told him Clint had a deer, Spud responded immediately to help with the butchering while Scofield directed
the other wagons into place. While Spud took over the butchering, Clint released Biscuit to graze with the other horses, then
went to Will's wagon to get his moccasins. "Hey, Melody," Will
called to the wagon. "Clint's here to get his moccasins."

Melody came right out of the wagon. "Oh, hello, Clint," she said, all smiles. "I guess your feet must be pretty sore by now."

"No, not too much," Will said, "but it will be a lot better with 'em on."

"Didn't Will tell you?" she asked.

"Tell me what?" Clint asked.

"Will, you said you would tell him," she said to him.

"What?" Clint demanded impatiently.

"Well, Clint," Will started, "we ain't got no idea when, but somewhere between here and the Green River those moccasins fell outta the back of the wagon. We feel really bad about it but we didn't have no idea they fell out. You can see, your saddle blanket is still on top and your shirt and britches are still hangin' on the wagon. We were worried about them, didn't think we were in any danger of losin' your moccasins. Maybe you can buy some boots at Fort Bridger."

Clint didn't say anything for a long moment. He just looked at Will, then looked at Melody. Melody tried, but she couldn't hold it and suddenly started to giggle. When Clint continued to stare at her, she pointed to Will and said, "It was his idea."

"Well, we had you for a minute there," Will said. "You gotta admit you were thinkin' about goin' to Fort Bridger barefoot."

"Okay, I admit it," Clint said, with no show of humor. "Now, can I have my moccasins?"

Seeing his apparent reaction to their little joke, Melody was at once alarmed. "We just thought it would be funny to play a little joke on you since you don't have any other shoes. We didn't mean to make you mad." She looked at Will then and said, "See, Will, he didn't think it was funny at all."

When she looked back at Clint again, he continued to fix an angry stare at her until she started to fluster with concern. Then he suddenly broke out a big smile and said, "Admit it, I had you for a minute there."

"Doggone you, Clint," Melody replied. "I wish I hadn't cleaned up your ol' moccasins now."

"She cleaned up your moccasins and dried 'em out as best she could with an old rag I had in the wagon." Will chuckled.

"I declare," Clint said to Melody, "you shouldn't have bothered with them. If I'da thought you would do something like that, I wouldn't have left them in the wagon."

"Why don't you eat supper with Will and me tonight?" Melody asked. "You can miss Spud Williams's cooking for once, can't you?"

"I guess I could," Clint answered, "but only if I get to pick what I want to eat."

"All right," she said, "what do you want?"

"I'm in the mood for some fresh venison," Clint replied.

"Ha!" Will responded. "I reckon we all are. I'm sorry, we're fresh outta deer meat tonight."

"Then I reckon I'll have to bring some with me," Clint said. "If you two buzzards hadn't tried to play a trick on me, I mighta brought enough for . . ."

"You shot a deer?" Will interrupted.

"Well, he practically begged me to put him out of his misery. I left Spud back there by the creek, finishin' up the butcherin' I started. If you'll give me my blame moccasins, I'll get back there to make sure he don't give it all away before I get the cuts I want."

That was all it took for Melody to bring him the moccasins forthwith. He thanked her for her efforts because they were almost completely dry. He left then with a promise that he would return with fresh meat. When he got back to his deer, Spud had hung it from a limb and was well along with the butchering. Clint told Spud that he was going to take a portion to cook with Will and Melody. And after Spud took what he wanted for Scofield, Lily, and himself, they could just portion it out as far as it would go, just like they did at Ash Hollow.

"You know, Spud," Clint remarked while he was cutting away the deer's backstrap meat. "When I left Will and Melody just now, it felt like I was leavin' a young married couple. You know what I mean?"

"Yeah," Spud replied. "I know what you mean. The two of them has been livin' together for a pretty good while now. And you live with somebody close up, like in that wagon, for a while, you either end up likin' 'em or hatin' 'em. I expect it's gonna be pretty hard on 'em when we get to Oregon country and they have to part. I don't expect what's his name, Worthy? I don't expect Worthy to be too tickled either, if he finds out how she traveled out there."

"Wouldn't surprise me none if Melody might change her mind about livin' up to her folks' arrangement with Worthy," Clint said.

Much like the last time Clint killed a deer, he and Spud cut the meat up in portions and offered it to anyone who wanted it. In a very short time, every part of the deer that was edible was taken. No one got all the venison they wanted, but a good portion of the people on the wagon train got a modest serving. The company was generally in good spirits in camp that night when the musicians struck up a cheerful tune. They had crossed the Green River with no casualties other than a wet guide, and Scofield said they would reach Fort Bridger in four more days at the most. Clint and Will roasted fresh deer backstrap over the fire while Melody put a pot of beans on the fire, since there was firewood plenty enough to boil water. That was not always the case in so many of their camps. To go with the beans and venison, she made some pan bread with Will's dwindling supply of flour. But there was no worry on his part because he could stock up on all his supplies at Fort Bridger. Clint was back in his comfortable buckskins, and Biscuit's saddle and blanket were dry. Nothing to do but enjoy the music and watch the dancing, so that's what Clint did until it started getting close to bedtime and he said goodnight to Will and Melody. Then he took his usual look around the outside of the camp to make sure no horses or cows were left outside the corral formed by the circle of wagons before he closed it up for the night.

He signaled to Scofield, who was talking to the night guards before they went on duty. He wanted to let him know he was going to be outside the circle to take a look along the creek to make sure no livestock was still out. Scofield acknowledged with a wave of his hand. So Clint jumped on Biscuit's back and went out between Thornton and Bishop's wagons, the designated gate for that night. Riding bareback again, he took the Palouse gelding for a brisk walk beside the silent waters of the creek in the growing darkness of the night. After a walk of around fifty yards, he turned around to check in the other direction, thinking none would stray much farther from the herd than that.

"It's him!" Little Buffalo exclaimed in a whisper. "It's the Medicine Gun!"

"Where?" Crooked Arrow responded excitedly.

"There!" He pointed to Clint riding through the trees on the opposite side of the creek. "It's him! He rides the spotted pony the Nez Perce breed! I knew we would find him! Now we will avenge Lame Otter and the others who died at his hand." After they had helped their brothers gather the dead from the river attack, Little Buffalo and Crooked Arrow were not satisfied to let the white men go on unharmed. The long line of wagons was easy to follow and they knew they would not travel far before stopping for the night. He immediately raised his rifle to aim across the creek, but the trees blocked a clear line of sight. "I can't see to get a clear shot at him. There is a clearing up ahead of him. When he reaches that we can get a shot at him. Come." They followed as quietly as they could, leading their horses through the brush and willows on that side of the creek.

"Do you think that maybe he might be trying to trick us?" Crooked Arrow speculated.

"What do you mean?"

"All the other white men are inside the fort they made with their wagons," Crooked Arrow said. "But the Medicine Gun rides out by himself and rides up and down on the spotted pony, daring us to shoot. Maybe his medicine is so strong that it will turn our bullets away."

"No," Little Buffalo said. "I think he came out because he doesn't know we wait to kill him. That is what I think. I think the medicine is in his gun, and whoever has the gun will have its medicine. To prove it, I will shoot him and take his scalp, and I will tie his scalp to the medicine gun. He is making it easy for us. After I shoot him, all of the other white men are inside their wagons, none of their horses ready to ride. We will have plenty of time to take his scalp and get on our horses and ride away from here with the medicine gun. Come, he is getting close to that clearing."

They hurried now, thinking their chances even better because the clearing was farther away from the circle of wagons. Clint decided that all the livestock was inside the wagon corral, so he reined Biscuit back just before entering the clearing ahead of him and wheeled the Palouse around and started back. "He knows!" Little Buffalo blurted. "Shoot him!" They both raised their rifles and fired at him, even though their line of fire was partially blocked by the trees. Clint felt the impact of the bullet that spun him around, causing him to come off Biscuit and land hard on the ground. His rifle went flying through the air to land several yards away from him. "We hit him!" Little Buffalo crowed. "Quick! He has lost the medicine gun. Let's get his scalp and get away from here before the others come out to see what happened!"

Still leading their horses, the two Cheyenne warriors ran through the creek toward the body lying unmoving on the ground. "I will take his scalp," Little Buffalo said. "Pick up the medicine gun!" Crooked Arrow ran to the Henry rifle, anxious to get the powerful medicine in his hands. Little Buffalo pulled his scalping knife from the sheath on his belt, grabbed a handful of Clint's hair and yanked his head back, raising him just enough to give him room to pull the Colt six-gun from his cross-draw holster.

Little Buffalo was startled to see the barrel of the weapon right before his eyes before it discharged into his face, killing him instantly. Startled as well by the sight of pieces of Little Buffalo's head flying in the air, Crooked Arrow aimed the Henry rifle at Clint and pulled the trigger. But there was no cartridge in the chamber. He pulled the trigger again, horrified when still nothing happened, while Clint took careful aim and placed a bullet in his chest.

When the second Indian fell, Clint tried to look around to see if there were any more, but the pain he felt made him drop back flat on the ground. *Hell*, he thought, *if there were any more of them, they would have already shot me.* So he tried to relax and figure out how badly he was wounded.

The first person to reach him was Scofield, yelling his name. Spud was right behind him, carrying a lantern. "Over here," Clint called out.

"Oh, my Lord," Scofield blurted when he saw him. "Make sure they're dead!" He instructed Spud behind him. "How bad is it, Clint?" Scofield asked then.

"They're dead," Spud sang out.

"I don't know for sure," Clint answered his uncle's question. "It hurts like hell, and it's bleedin' a lot, but I don't feel like there's nothin' gone wrong inside me."

"Spud, bring that lantern over here, so we can see where he's hit." Spud held the lantern down close to Clint. Scofield pulled Clint's shirt open until he could actually see the wound. "All right," he declared. "You were lucky. It's in your shoulder. Can you move your arm?"

"Yeah, I had to move my arm to draw my pistol," Clint said.

"That's lucky, too," his uncle said. "That means it ain't broke your collarbone or nothin'."

"I'll take your word for it, but I'll tell you, I don't feel lucky right now." By this time, some more of the men had joined them, having heard the shooting, but they had waited until they found out that Scofield had gone out of the circle to investigate. And there were no more shots fired. "Help me up, Uncle Clayton," Clint said.

"No," Scofield said. "You'd best lay right there. You're bleedin' a helluva lot. We'd best carry you back. You try walkin' and you're liable to lose more blood." He turned to look at the collection of men who had now come out to see what happened. Clint was not a small man, so Scofield was looking to pick a sizable man to help him carry him. He didn't notice Leach, who had come up behind him. Leach took one look at Clint, then stepped in front of Scofield, bent down and picked Clint up as if he was a newborn colt.

"Where you want him?" Leach asked.

Startled by the ease with which the otherwise mute curiosity picked Clint up, Scofield said, "My wagon." He knew that Lily had doctored some gunshot wounds in her time as Lulu Belle when she was at Leo's Road Ranch. Leach turned and carried Clint back inside the circle of wagons. Scofield and Spud followed him while most of the other men remained to gawk at the bodies of the two dead Indians. Forgotten at that point, Biscuit dutifully followed Clint back inside the circle of wagons.

Back inside the circle, Leach walked straight to Scofield's wagon. When Lily saw him coming, she ran out to meet him. "Clint!" she gasped. "What . . . ?" she started to ask, but Leach walked past her, since Scofield said to take Clint to his wagon. Clint gave her a helpless look as he was whisked by. She turned to question Scofield, who was right behind. "What happened?"

"It's a shoulder wound," Scofield told her. "I wanted you to take a look at it and see what you think."

"All right," she said, "but who shot him?"

"I ain't had a chance to find out yet, but it looks like it mighta been a couple of them Injuns that attacked the wagons back at the river crossin'. He killed both of 'em."

As concerned as she was for Clint, she couldn't help asking, "How'd you happen to get Leach to carry him here?"

Scofield gave her an incredulous look. "You'd do better to ask if there was any way I coulda stopped him." He took her elbow and turned her around. "Now, we'd best go after him. He might just drop him on the ground."

They hurried after Leach to catch him by the time he reached the wagon. "Let's lay him on the tailgate, Leach," Scofield said. Leach waited while he lowered the tailgate, then he laid Clint gently on it.

"Thank you, Leach," Clint told him. "I appreciate it." Leach didn't reply verbally, but he nodded his head and his lips parted slightly. Clint interpreted that as a smile, and the silent hulk of a man turned and walked away. It called to mind that night on the bank of the Laramie River when he and Spud were walking back from Jake's Place with Leach. He had surprised both him and Spud when he spoke enough words to express his thanks to Clint for stepping in to help him in the saloon that night.

"'Preciate it, Leach," Scofield called after him, causing him to pause long enough to look back at him to see if he wanted anything else, then he continued on to Thornton's wagon.

"Let's sit you up, so we can get that shirt off," Lily told Clint. "Can you do that?" Clint said he could, so he sat up while she took his shirt off. "Yep," she said, "it's in that muscle right by your armpit." She looked at his back then. "It didn't go straight through, so I expect it would be best if I see if I can get to that bullet. I wish I had something to give you to help with the pain, but we drank up the last of that whiskey we had. We're supposed to get to Fort Bridger in three or four days. I don't know if they've got a doctor there or not. Do you know, Clayton?"

"They did at one time," Scofield answered, "when the army took it over after that little war they had with the Mormons. I swear, I don't know if there's still one there or not. But at least we could getcha drunk while she worked on it."

"As long as I'm sittin' here, why don't you just go ahead and poke around in there and I'll see how long I can stand it," Clint said.

"All right," Lily said. "It's your funeral—oops! I didn't mean to say that."

"Damn," Clint said. "Maybe I shoulda asked Leach to dig it outta there. Let's get started."

They spread a blanket on the tailgate for Clint to lie back on. Scofield got a couple of buckets of water from the creek while Spud built up the fire. He filled the kettle with water and set it in the fire to heat up. Lily washed her sharpest knife again, although it had been washed since she last used it. After she cleaned most of the blood away, she warned Clint that she was coming in, and he braced for it. He bit his lip to keep from yelling with her first probe in the wound. She started to withdraw when she saw his reaction, but he told her not to stop. "Go after it!" He managed to say, hoping he would pass out, then she could go in and dig it out without hesitation. But he couldn't pass out, so he held on for all he was worth, while the tune of an old square dance song drifted over the wagon from the musicians at the social hour.

When it reached a point where he thought he was going to have to tell her to leave the bullet in there, he felt her withdraw and figured she'd reached the same conclusion. "To hell with it," he said. "I won't be the first man to walk around with some extra lead in their bodies."

In answer, she held the bullet up to show him. "Want me to put it back in?"

"Hallelujah!" he blurted. "You got it!" He looked at Scofield, who was grinning at him, and said, "Let this be a lesson for ya, Uncle Clayton. Don't ever get shot."

"I'll try to remember that," Scofield said.

"Slap some kinda bandage on that thing and I'll thank you for your gentle services," Clint said, anxious to be on his way.

"All right," Lily said, "but I need to clean it up a little bit after all the probing I did to start the bleeding again. Then, to do a good job, we ought to cauterize it, so it doesn't get infected."

"Right," Clint said with some hesitation. "I don't reckon we could get by without doin' that."

"Won't take but a second," Lily said. "Spud's already got a knife in the fire."

"Thanks, Spud," Clint said, sarcastically. "And here I was, kinda proud I'd gotten through this whole operation without yellin' out some word you shouldn't say with a lady present." He shook his head and said, "Well, let's get it over with."

"Okay," Lily said, "I'll let you know when, so you can get set. I'll count to three." She took the knife from the fire and nodded to Scofield.

"I swear, Clint," Scofield said, "did you take a close look at this bullet? Look at that markin'."

"I can't see any markin'," Clint started, but then yelled out a word that was definitely not fit to be said in a lady's presence when Lily slapped the red-hot knife blade on the wound.

"Dang!" Clint blurted. "I'm sorry, but you said you were gonna count to three."

"I did count to three," Lily said. "I didn't say I was gonna count out loud."

# Chapter 16

The days that followed the incident with Little Buffalo and Crooked Arrow were awkward days for Clint. While the wound he suffered was only a shoulder wound, it made ordinary movements difficult, because it was his right shoulder. He was grateful for the fact that they encountered no more hostile Indian activity on the rest of the way to Fort Bridger, for he could not comfortably rest the butt of his rifle against his shoulder. He could draw his pistol if he had to, but it was painful for him to do so because he had to take his arm out of the sling that Lily had made for him. Consequently, it was a relief to arrive at the fort on Blacks Fork of the Green River that Jim Bridger had established originally as a fur trading post. The fort, now a military post, was surrounded by green pastures, ideal for the wagon train's camp, with plenty of water and grazing. Scofield ended up leading his company to camp in the same spot he had picked the year before. It was handy to the fort, especially the sutler's store, which was operated by a man named William A. Carter, who was a pleasure to trade with. Consequently, the emigrants did a lot of trading with him. There was a doctor assigned to the post at this particular time, and Scofield suggested that Clint might want him to check out the wound that Lily had doctored for him. Clint decided the wound was healing nicely, so he said he was satisfied with the work done by Dr. Lulu Belle. Since several of the wagons needed some repairs and quite a few horses needed shoeing, Scofield decided to stay over an extra day and even then it was a busy couple of days for the post's blacksmith and farrier. Since the wagon train was not moving out the next morning after they arrived, it allowed for an extended social hour that first night.

Clint thought his shoulder was feeling well enough to do without his sling, so he left it in the wagon when he finished supper and decided to join the folks at the social hour. He saw Will and Melody sitting on the bench that Will had made out of two wooden boxes, so he walked over to join them. "We were wonderin' if you were gonna show up tonight," Will said in greeting. "You bein' a cripple and all," he added.

"I just came out tonight because I thought maybe you and Melody might get out there and show these old folks how the young folks dance," Clint replied.

Will laughed, then looked right and left to make sure Levi nor Ella Watkins were in earshot before he spoke. "If I got out there and tried to dance, you'd think Levi Watkins was a professional dancer."

"Now I know I'd like to see it," Clint said and sat down on the ground next to their bench.

"It's kinda nice camping here," Melody remarked. "Did your uncle say anything about staying here longer than another day?"

"No," Clint answered. "Why? Are you anxious to get movin'?"

"No, indeed," she replied. "I just think it's nice here and I remember my father talking about the long, dry country we'll go through when we leave Fort Bridger."

"We'll go through some more rough, dry country for about a couple of weeks when we leave here. But we'll cross some mountains and be travelin' through some beautiful country, rivers and streams. I wouldn't call it dry."

"Well, it's desert, isn't it?" Melody insisted. "And aren't deserts dry and sandy?"

Clint looked at Will, but Will looked as puzzled as he was. "What makes you think we'll have to drive these wagons through a desert?" Clint asked.

Melody shrugged. She was becoming as confused as they seemed to be. "In the letters my folks got from Worthy Davis, he said we would be traveling through some desert country shortly before we got there."

"Where does Mr. Davis live?" Will asked.

Melody gave him a look of disbelief, shrugged her shoulders again and shook her head. "Salt Lake Valley," she said.

Clint and Will were both caught with their mouths open and speechless. They looked at each other dumbfounded. Finally, Clint asked the question since it was obvious Will was not going to. "Melody, are you a Mormon?"

"Yes," she answered impatiently, as if she assumed they knew. "Did you think this wagon train was goin' to the Salt Lake Valley?"

"Isn't it?" She answered innocently.

"Melody, this train is turning north when we leave here, heading for Oregon. Why would you think it was goin' to the Salt Lake Valley?"

"The wagon train Papa and I were on is headed for the Salt Lake Valley. And this wagon train is traveling on the same roads as that train is. Isn't it? We keep catching up behind them, and now Will says we're ahead of them, since we crossed the Green River. So, it seems to me that we must all be going to the same place."

Finding the situation hard to believe, Clint looked to Will for an explanation, thinking surely they would have talked about it. "You never said anything about Melody being a Mormon."

"She never said anything about it," Will replied. "We never talked about religion and stuff like that."

Clint looked at Melody again. "Didn't you ever wonder why nobody on this train ever said anything about goin' to church meetin's and stuff like that? Whatever Mormons do?"

"Well, I did wonder a little bit, but I liked the way you folks did things," Melody said. "I thought everything would change once we got there."

Clint and Will could not help looking at each other, perplexed, and completely at a loss at the moment. "Melody," Clint said, "when that wagon train you were on gets here, they're gonna head outta here to the southwest. We're gonna head northwest toward the Bear River country. We're still a thousand miles from the Willamette Valley in Oregon. I need to talk to Uncle Clayton about this, but I expect you'll have to stay here and wait for that train behind us. I reckon it was just plum lucky that we got ahead of 'em. Otherwise, there's no tellin' how long you woulda had to wait for another Mormon train."

Melody listened to what he was saying, a deep frown etched on her face. She didn't say anything for a long time after he finished. When he started to ask her what she was thinking, she spoke first. "I don't want to go back to the other train."

"There's no tellin' how long you might have to wait here for another train goin' that way," Clint repeated, in case she hadn't really grasped that probability. "There's a telegraph here, maybe we could telegraph Worthy Davis that you're stranded here. Then maybe he could arrange to come and get you." He didn't want to point out to her that she was penniless as well, and he wasn't sure how much the people on this wagon train could afford to donate to support her until her betrothed came to get her.

Totally distressed at this point, she shook her head. Then, after a long pause, during which they all three stared at each other, she replied almost in a whisper, "I don't want to leave this train."

"Will you marry me?" Will blurted.

"Yes," she said, nodding vigorously as she stepped into his arms.

"Whew." Clint exhaled, exhausted. "I thought you were never gonna ask her." He gave Will a pat on the back and Melody a quick hug. "I was afraid you two were too blind to see what the rest of the whole wagon train knew was the right thing. Uncle Clayton can marry you but only on one condition."

"What's that?" Will asked.

"That I get to be the best man," Clint said.

Will grinned and asked Melody, "Is that all right with you?"

"I guess so," she replied, "if I can have Lily as my maid of honor. Do you think she would?"

"I think she'd be tickled to be your maid of honor," Clint said. "When do you want the weddin'?"

"Well, I don't have anything on my schedule for the rest of the night," Will said. He grinned at Melody. "Are you busy?" She giggled shyly and shook her head.

Watching the two, Clint didn't believe they could be any happier than he was for them. He thought about the nightmare that Angel had brought down on Will and the hell he had to suffer with the insane slaying of his wife and child. For a long time he wasn't sure Will had the strength to recover from what he went through. He wondered how much of that Will might have told her. He hoped Will had opened his heart to her, leaving nothing for her to wonder about. Looking at the two of them now, he couldn't help wondering if Melody had been sent here by someone higher up who handles things like that. "If you're both ready to tie the knot right now, I'll go get Uncle Clayton and Lily," he said.

They looked at each other and nodded. "I think we're ready," Will said.

"I'll go get 'em before you change your mind," Clint said and left straightaway. When he got to Scofield's wagon, he found his uncle and Lily sitting by the fire, drinking the last of the coffee from supper. "Hate to disturb your peaceful evenin'," he said, "but we've got a problem out there that needs you to fix it."

"Can't you handle it?" Scofield asked, thinking it must be really bad, if Clint couldn't take care of it.

"Nope, I ain't qualified to take care of this problem. It takes the wagon master." He glanced at Lily and said, "I'm gonna need you, too, Lily."

Concerned now, Scofield asked, "What is it? What's the problem?"

"Will Tucker and Melody Meadows wanna get married. I'm gonna be the best man, and Melody wants Lily to be her maid of honor."

"Well, I'll be . . . ." Scofield started. "You're foolin' with me." Clint shook his head, grinning. "When?" Scofield asked.

"Right now," Clint replied. "They're waitin' out at the social hour."

"Well, I'll be . . . ." Scofield repeated while Lily chuckled delightedly. "That's the best news I've heard all day. Come on, Lily, let's not keep 'em waitin'. Bring the broom. We'll make sure they're good and married."

"Uh-oh," Levi said to his wife when Scofield walked out and asked the musicians to stop playing. "I hope this ain't bad news. I was just gettin' comfortable."

"'Scuse me for interruptin' ya, boys, but I've got a little piece of important business to take care of, then I'll let you get back to the entertainment." Then he directed his attention to Henry Abbott. "Henry, can you play the weddin' march on that fiddle?"

Big smiles broke out on all the musicians' faces and they all started looking around, trying to spot the couple, the obvious suspects being Will and Melody. "I surely can," Henry said. "You just give me the signal when you want me to start."

Scofield went back to the bench where Lily and Clint were talking to Will and Melody. "All right, are you folks ready?" They said they were. "Will, you and Clint come with me. Lily, you and Melody come when Henry starts playin' 'Here Comes the Bride'. And I'll tell the folks what's goin' on."

"Right," Lily said. "I think they'll know if they start playing that."

The three men walked out in front of the largest of the several gatherings of the emigrants. "Folks, I'm gonna interrupt your visitin' for just a few minutes, then you can get back to your socializin'. As wagon master of this company, there are some official duties I have to handle, and this is one of those times." He looked over at Henry Abbott and nodded. Henry was quick to respond, and in a few seconds, he forced the familiar strains of "Here Comes the Bride" out of the old fiddle. The crowd caught on almost immediately, and soon cheers and whistles rang out when Melody and Lily started walking proudly toward the three men. Clint stepped over to the side, and when he did, Will stepped over with him. Clint turned him around and sent him back to stand before Scofield.

"Flip a coin to see who has to do it," Levi Watkins called out.

"Shut your mouth, Levi," Ella scolded.

"See what you got comin', Will?" Levi responded.

Scofield held his hand up to get everybody's attention and nodded to Henry to stop the music. "All right, folks, two of our young folks have decided to be united in marriage. In my capacity as wagon master, I am authorized to perform the ceremony." He then gave his brief version of a wedding ceremony and asked Will if he took Melody as his lawful wedded wife, till death do you part. Will said he did. Scofield then asked Melody if she took Will under the same circumstances, and she agreed. "If anybody has any reason to object to this weddin', keep your mouth shut. I now pronounce you man and wife. And to make it a double tight deal, the couple will step over this broom together." Clint and Lily held the broom a few inches above the ground, and Will and Melody stepped over it. "You may now kiss the bride," Scofield said, "and anybody else that'll let'cha."

The crowd gave the newlyweds a big hand and a rousing cheer. It was a popular union, especially since they were all witnesses to the end of Will's first marriage. Lily gave Melody a big hug and told her she had married a fine young man and wished them the best of luck. Then she took her broom from Clint and took hold of Scofield's arm. "You just went plum poetic tonight, didn't you?" she teased, "especially that part about kissing the bride."

He laughed. "I was just havin' a little fun," he said. "I was so glad to see that young man find himself a nice girl like Melody. It's a rare but nice thing when everything seems to be goin' the right way."

Leaving the happy couple to receive all the congratulations and well wishes from all the folks who had witnessed the marriage, Clint walked back to the wagon with Scofield and Lily. As they were passing the little group where Levi and his wife were sitting, Levi called out, "Hey, Clint, you wanna come sleep under my wagon tonight? It might be a sight quieter than Will's."

"I guarantee you it'll be dead quiet for the next month, Mr. Smart Mouth," Ella remarked.

Clint didn't bother to reply to his remark. He figured Levi's wife had answered it sufficiently. As they walked back to the wagon, Clint said, "Well, you're caught up on the important news about Will and Melody, but you ain't gonna believe what led up to Will poppin' the question. Melody's a Mormon." When they digested that surprise, he went on to tell them what he and Will had found out that night.

"You mean to tell me this fellow, Worthy Davis, has a place down in the Salt Lake Valley somewhere? And all this time, she thought that's where we were goin'?"

"That's a fact," Clint said.

"And you said she was a Mormon?" Scofield asked. Clint nodded. "Is Will gonna drop out of this train and hook up with the Mormons behind us?"

"Nope, Melody said she didn't wanna leave our wagon train. She's goin' to Oregon."

"Well, then, everything's turnin' out like it's supposed to," Scofield said.

There was no bugle blast at four o'clock the next morning, since the wagon train was going to remain at Fort Bridger for another day. As a matter of habit, Clint woke up shortly after four, anyway. He had slept soundly with no disturbances from the wagon over his head. The thought of that caused him to smile. As he usually did, he pulled his moccasins on, strapped on his gun belt and made a visit to the clump of trees designated for use by the males of the wagon trains. Then he paused a couple of minutes by the river to splash some cold water on his face to thoroughly wake himself up. After checking on Biscuit, he went to Scofield's wagon where he knew Spud would already be cooking breakfast. Like many of the emigrants on the train, Scofield and Lily were still sleeping, taking advantage of the rare opportunity to do so. He poured himself a cup of coffee and sat down next to the fire to talk to Spud.

"How's the shoulder?" Spud asked.

"Comin' along just fine," Clint replied, moving it back and forth to demonstrate. "It's still a little bit tender around that wound, but not like it was a couple of days ago. Oughta be just fine by the time we get to Big Hill."

"I'd just as soon you hadn't mentioned that place," Spud said. "Spoils my breakfast just thinkin' about comin' down that hill."

"You're right, sorry I brought it up," Clint said.

"Have any trouble sleepin' last night?" Spud asked. "Seein' as how you was sleepin' by yourself under that wagon last night. 'Course, since them two decided to get married, maybe you was already used to sleepin' under that wagon by yourself."

"You oughta be ashamed of yourself for thinkin' things like that about that young lady," Clint scolded. "I can tell you for a fact, last night was the first night Melody didn't sleep in Uncle Clayton's sleepin' tent since she joined us."

"So it was a real honeymoon then, weren't it?" Spud responded with a grin.

Eager to change the subject, Clint said, "I hope Uncle Clayton told everybody how important it is to get any repairs done to their wagons, if they need something fixed. 'Cause from here on to Oregon, they're gonna be put to the test."

"That is a fact," Spud agreed.

"What is a fact?" Scofield asked when he joined them at the fire.

"Clint's already talkin' about goin' over Big Hill," Spud said. "And I told him it gives me a pain just talkin' about it."

"That reminds me," Scofield said, "I'll have to talk to the folks about the Thomas Fork Crossin'. There'll be the usual complainin', but I told 'em in the agreements about all the tolls they could expect. I don't think but about half of 'em read the whole thing. I reckon you can't blame 'em for kickin' about it."

"I sure as hell don't blame 'em," Spud declared. Clint agreed. The crossing of the Thomas Fork of the Bear River came just a short distance from the Hill. It was a dangerous little crossing, but quite a few years back, some emigrants had built two bridges across it, which made it an easy crossing. But it wasn't long before some enterprising men took possession of the bridges and started charging a toll to cross them. Their argument for the toll was the fact that they had to maintain the bridges. That seemed fair enough in exchange for a reasonable toll. But they charged a dollar a wagon, which was hard to swallow to cross a waterway that was little more than a creek. The alternative was to take an eight mile detour, so Scofield had to determine beforehand if his present charges were willing to pay the toll, or if they would choose to take the alternate route.

# Chapter 17

At close to the noon hour, the Mormon wagon train pulled into Fort Bridger and went into camp at the far end of the stockade, leaving a wide expanse of pasture between the two trains. Will Tucker asked his bride if she would like to visit the camp to say goodbye to any friends she might have made when she and her father were members of that company. "No," she told him. "I don't believe I have any friends in that company. The few people I thought were my friends all voted for my father and me to drop out of the train. So all my friends are with this train." She squeezed his hand. "And the only one I really need is sitting right here beside me." So the only contact between the two camps was the random contact made at the sutler's store, or one of the craftsmen's shops. That night, at the social hour, there was a definite increase in the level of enthusiasm of the musicians. Clint interpreted that as a determination to make sure they could be heard by any entertainers in the Mormon camp. Even a couple of the other men who had guitars brought them out that night to back up the regular players. At times, on some of the old favorites, it made normal conversation difficult. When finally Scofield thought it time to get to bed, he thought he was going to have to shoot his pistol in the air to get everyone's attention. But they got quiet to hear his announcement when he drew the weapon. He reminded them then of the toll on the bridges at

Thomas Fork and how expensive they were the previous year.
"We'll have about a week and a half before we reach it, so you
folks talk it over and decide if you're gonna pay the toll and make
it an easy crossin', or you druther drive eight miles farther to go
around it. Makes no difference to me. I just need to know before
we get there."

"What happens if most of are willing to pay the toll and move
on, but there are a few who vote no to paying an excessive toll?",
Bass Thornton asked.

"If they can't afford the extra payment, or they just won't,"
Scofield said, "then the rest of you can go on across the bridges,
but I'll go with them to show 'em the way to get back to the right
road."

"Then you'd have to catch up with the rest of us," Thornton
said.

"No," Scofield replied. "You would just set there on the other
side of the river and wait for us to get there."

"That doesn't make any sense," Thornton said. "We pay the
toll and lose the time we paid to pick up."

"Unfortunately, that's a fact. But you see, Mr. Thornton, I ain't
leavin' any of this party behind. The folks who run into real
Injun trouble are the stragglers and the ones left behind. You can
ask Mrs. Melody Tucker about that. She can tell you. I'm gonna
do my damnedest to get every one of you folks to the Willamette
Valley, and our best chance is to stay together." He got a round of
applause and a few cheers from the women for his declaration.
When it died down, he said, "You folks talk it over. You might decide to take the long way around." He started to go to his wagon
but remembered one more thing. "We won't set no guards again
tonight, since we're settin' on the army's doorstep, same as last
night."

Levi, never one to pass up an opportunity, piped up. "I swear,
Capt'n, we need 'em more'n ever tonight to guard against Mormons tryin' to steal our women." His remark was followed by the
sound of a slap on the back of his head and, "Damn, Ella!"

"Why would he think Mormons would want to steal the women?" Melody whispered to Will.

"Because he ain't got no sense," Will told her. "Pay him no mind."

Seven o'clock the next morning saw the wagons pulling out of Fort Bridger on a road leading northwest toward the mountains and valleys of Idaho Territory. Their daily travel for the next week and a half would be much like country they had traveled since crossing the Green River. As the distance to the Thomas Fork Crossing diminished, there was more and more talk about the toll at the crossing, with quite a few of the emigrants against it. They argued that there were more tolls to pay later that might not be avoided, so they should save wherever they could. The issue was finally put to rest a day before reaching the fork of the Bear River. Bass Thornton told Scofield they would all cross on the bridges and he would pay the toll for all the wagons. "A dollar a wagon," he said. "I'll give the man twenty-eight dollars and we'll all go across, instead of losing the time to go around."

Scofield was astonished. He knew that Thornton was in a hurry to get out to the Oregon country, but he had never shown any signs of being a generous benefactor to anyone. He had always been a bit of a mystery from the time he showed up on the final day before leaving Independence. Dressed more like a lawyer, doctor, or gambler than one seeking to farm a piece of land, he was hard to figure out. And so far, no one had. Violet, his wife, was an attractive woman who seemed to have no capacity for serious thought and looked to be about half his age. His wagon was brand-new and appeared to be reinforced to haul heavy loads; the fact that it was hauling a heavy load was confirmed at the first river crossing they had come to. Since it was now obvious he was transporting something heavy, naturally everyone started to wonder just what it could be. But no one had the courage to ask him what was in the wagon. And now, he was willing to pay the bridge toll for every wagon in the train, just to save eight miles' time, out of a thousand left to travel? "Well, that's a mighty generous thing to do, Mr. Thornton," Scofield finally remarked. "A man could buy a lot of supplies with twenty-eight dollars. But if you rather spend it on bridge tolls for the whole train, I can't think of nothin' to say but much obliged."

"Good," Thornton said, "so that problem's taken care of, and we'll be able to roll right over those bridges and continue on, right?"

"That's right," Scofield replied. "You seem to be in an extra big hurry to get to Oregon."

"Yes, I guess I do," Thornton said, but offered nothing more.

Scofield waited for him to state his reasons, but Thornton remained silent. "I reckon I need to warn you," Scofield thought it best to tell him. "After we cross at the Thomas Fork, we'll strike what they call Big Hill in just a few miles. We're gonna have to cross Big Hill to get to the Bear River Valley. And that ain't something you do in a hurry. It's steep and it's dangerous, a helluva pull to get up it, but more dangerous comin' down the other side. And there ain't no way to get around it. You've got to go over it. And it always takes a lotta time before I get all the wagons over it." Then in an effort to encourage him, he said, "But once we get over it, we'll be able to make some better time."

Thornton did appear to be somewhat troubled to hear of the extra time it would take to climb over Big Hill but decided to take Scofield's word that there was no alternate route to avoid it. "I guess sometimes you just have to play the hand you're dealt," he said, turned and silently signaled Violet, who was watching some children playing. Turning at once, she came to him and they went back to his wagon.

Scofield watched them walk away. "Sometimes you just have to play the hand you're dealt," he repeated. *He must be a professional gambler*, he thought. *I bet that's what he is.* He went back to his wagon then to tell Lily about the conversation with Thornton and see if she didn't agree with him. He put a lot of stock in Lily's opinions, especially when it came to reading people. She had a world of experience dealing with all sorts of people when she was working for Leo Sterns at Fort Kearny. He was disappointed, however, when he got back to the wagon and related his whole conversation with the strange Mr. Thornton. Lily didn't have a guess as to what line of work, or crime, Bass Thornton might be involved in. But she was definitely of the opinion that he was not a professional gambler, even when Scofield repeated the phrase he used in parting.

"Anybody coulda said that," Lily contended. "He just doesn't strike me as a gambler. He's hauling something awfully heavy in that wagon, though. You said you thought Leach was gonna drown when he lifted that wagon off the bottom of the Kansas River."

"Well, he damn-near did," Scofield said. "If you'da been there and seen how long that man was underwater before that wagon came outta that river, you'da thought he was a goner."

"We are talking about Leach," Lily reminded him. "Nobody's figured out what kind of animal he is. I wouldn't be surprised if he ain't got some alligator in him from somewhere down his family line. I wonder where Thornton found him."

"I'd give a dollar to know what he's carrying in that wagon," Scofield said, getting back to the subject of concern, "and how much trouble we're gonna have gettin' him over Big Hill."

"Maybe he's hauling a wagonload of gold," Lily fantasized. "You said he's gonna pay for everybody to cross the toll bridges. Why don't you offer to take some of his load in our wagon?"

They reached the Thomas Fork Crossing in the afternoon, and when the emigrants got their first look at it, they understood why it was such a difficult crossing for wagons. Little more than a stream, there were steep, muddy banks into the water and coming out on the other side, making it extremely hard for the horses to pull the wagon out. The bridges made it a simple crossing, and it was Scofield's intention to cross over before stopping for the night. He wanted to give Big Hill the whole day the next day if it was needed, so they would tackle it right after breakfast. When he halted the wagons at Thomas Fork, he noticed the sign was still up with the toll still one dollar per wagon. He stepped down from the saddle and walked up on the bridge where a man was standing, awaiting him. "I see you ain't lowered your price none since last year," he said to William Floyd, who was the gate-keeper that day.

"No, we ain't," Floyd replied. "But we ain't gone up on it, nei-ther. You wantin' to go over the bridges?"

"That's a fact," Scofield replied and pulled the roll of paper money Thornton had given him out of his pocket. "I've got twenty-eight wagons crossin', and there's twenty-eight dollars I got right here." He showed him the money. "I'd like to get started right away."

"What about those extra horses and cows following along with you?" Floyd asked.

"What about 'em?" Scofield responded.

"You have to pay for them to come across the bridges, too," Floyd said, "a nickel a head."

"Your sign don't say nothin' about paying for extra livestock," Scofield insisted. "It just says one dollar for each wagon. That means it includes whatever extra stock you brought with you."

"It don't matter whether it's on the sign or not," Floyd said. "A nickel a head is what it'll cost you for them horses and cows to come across the bridge."

"You just lost yourself twenty-eight dollars," Scofield said. "I'll take my wagons around the other way."

"It's eight miles farther that way," Floyd reminded him.

"But it's twenty-eight dollars cheaper," Scofield remarked. "And eight miles don't make much difference when you got about a thousand to go. But twenty-eight dollars makes a big dif-ference when you ain't got a lot of money to spare." He turned around and called back to Clint, "We're gonna take 'em around the other way, Clint."

"Right!" Clint called back and stepped back up into his saddle.

"Good day to ya," Scofield said to Floyd and turned to get back on his horse.

"Hold on!" Floyd exclaimed. "I'll let you take the livestock across at no charge. I just hope my partner don't hear about it."

Scofield waved Spud forward, then turned around, went back and handed the money to Floyd. When he walked back to his horse, he met Bass Thornton, who had walked up from his wagon to listen to the negotiation between Scofield and Floyd. "Well done, Mr. Scofield," Thornton said, then did an about-face and returned to his wagon.

Clint and Scofield sat on their horses and watched the wagons cross over the bridges. Even though the bridges simplified the crossing, it still took some time before all the wagons could lumber across. When the last wagons were rolling across, Scofield said, "I reckon we can get the rest of the livestock across now. You ready to do some cowboyin'?" Clint said he was, so they got in behind the major portion of the extra horses and herded them toward the bridges. At this point, it was only the horses lagging behind. All the cattle they had were milk cows and almost all their owners led them across with the wagon. Clint and his uncle herded the biggest portion of the extra horses onto the bridges and the strays followed along behind them. Then it was on to prepare to climb the eastern Sheep Creek Hills and specifically Big Hill, where they camped for the night.

Once the wagons were parked in position for the night, most of the people took some time to just stand and gawk at the steep line of hills towering over them. "I ain't sure my horses can pull my wagon up that slope," Tracy Bishop remarked. "That thing looks straight up."

"Maybe this ain't the place we'll be goin' up in the mornin'," Henry Abbott said. When Clint walked by, Henry called, "Hey, Clint, where are we gonna drive up this mountain in the mornin'?"

"Right in front of you," Clint answered. "You're lookin' at the trail."

"You're japin' us now," Tracy said. "Ain't no way we're gonna drive these wagons up that slope there. There's gotta be a better place to go over that thing."

"I'm afraid not," Clint told him. "I hate to tell you, but this is the only place we can get a wagon over, and we have to cross over it to get to the Bear River Valley. Look up that hill, you can see wagon tracks on the side of it. Your horses will make it. And that steepest part near the top, we'll use an extra team of horses to help yours make it up that grade."

"I hear what you're sayin', Clint," Henry said, "but I'm afraid my wagon's gonna be standin' on its tailgate by the time we make it to that part."

"We've gone over these hills right here every year we've been makin' this trip," Clint assured him. "It's the same place wagon trains have crossed Big Hill ever since they started comin' this way. We'll make it up. That's the easy part. Makin' it down again, that's where the real fun starts."

"Thanks for cheerin' us up, Clint," Levi called after him as he walked on.

The normal routine was followed the next morning, starting with Scofield's jagged-edged notes from his bugle piercing the deepest sleep of his charges at four o'clock. The stock was taken care of and the breakfast cooked and eaten, and the first wagon, which was always Scofield's, was ready for the assault on Big Hill. Clint went up first, walking an extra team of horses to be used if necessary, his gunshot wound no longer an impediment. All those lined up behind Spud watched anxiously to see his progress. He started slow, his horses already straining against the steepness of the incline. Then they settled into the slope and maintained a steady climb. Behind Spud, Levi started up next with much the same results. Soon there was a line of wagons on the side of the hill, moving slowly upward as their horses struggled to gain solid footing in the steep slope. Finally, Spud reached an incline that stopped his progress altogether, his horses driving but not able to move the wagon. Clint hitched the extra team to the wagon and the four horses pulled Spud on up to the top.

Clint unhitched the extra horses while Spud started tying the wheels of his wagon together to keep them from turning, in preparation for the long, steep descent to the valley below. Had he not tied them, the wagon would have tried to run over the horses and likely ended up on its side or turned upside down. Clint wished him good luck, then hurried back to help Levi up the steepest part. And so it continued for a total of seven hours. All those who could preferred to climb the hill on foot instead of taking the hazardous trip in the wagon. With their wheels tied together, the wagons slid all the way down the long, steep descent. Several wagons swerved and threatened on the way down, but only one came dangerously close to disaster. And that was the one wagon Clint and Scofield were concerned about to begin with.

It was obvious that the wagon was overloaded when Leach started Thornton's wagon up the beginning of the climb. For the horses were straining from the first to move the wagon slowly up the foot of the hill. They managed to maintain that slow pace for only so long and Clint had to come to the rescue when Leach was not halfway up the hill. With the help of the extra two horses, the wagon was moved along at a little faster pace but was slowed down to a crawl when they reached the steepest part of the hill. With Leach laying heavy on the reins and Clint urging the extra horses on, they somehow reached the top of the hill.

Clint told Leach to tie the wheels strong because if they started to turn going down the steep side of that hill, everything would be lost. So Leach tied them tight and with another wish of good luck, Clint sent him down the hill. Even sliding, the wagon proved too heavy for the steepness of the hill. Although the wagon tongue kept the wagon from running over the horses, it became a question for Leach, namely, how much could the tongue take before it broke. So he tried to turn the horses in an effort to make the wagon zigzag. That resulted in causing the wagon to skid sideways against a small tree and hang there. Although stopped, the wagon began to lean dangerously toward the side. He realized it was starting to slowly tip over on its side. Leach being Leach, he jumped out of the driver's seat but not on the side to escape the wagon's momentum. He jumped under the slowly falling wagon and braced himself to catch it. The amazing part that would be talked about afterward, and added to the mystery about the man, was the fact that Leach actually held the wagon in its tilted-over position. Clint rushed down the slope with his extra team, tied a rope on the side of the tilted wagon and pulled the wagon upright again.

With the wagon temporarily at rest on the steep slope, Scofield and several of the men waiting their turn to cross the hill came up to Thornton's wagon with ropes. They tied their ropes to the back of the wagon, preparing to hold back on the wagon. There was a brief pause, however, when Tiny Futch exclaimed, "Injuns!" That immediately grabbed everyone's attention and they looked to see him pointing to a group of six Indians on horseback, gathered on the top of the hill, some thirty-five or forty yards distant. Caught without weapons, their first inclination was to abandon the wagon and run back for their guns.

"Hold it!" Scofield barked. "They're Shoshone. They're friendly. They musta got the word that a wagon train was crossin' Big Hill and they came out to watch the fun. I expect they'll visit our camp tonight to see if we wanna do any tradin'. They're most likely bettin' with each other on whether we get this wagon down the hill without turnin' it over. So let's give 'em a show." They took his word for it and tied their ropes onto the wagon. Then with Leach back in the driver's seat, the descent continued and the wagon finally reached the valley floor, with the wheels sliding and dragging four men straining to hold it back.

Having walked over the hill with a group of the women and children, Bass Thornton watched the harrowing descent of his wagon from the safety of the valley floor. It was the first time any of them could recall seeing the normally confident man actually sweat. "You could see the drops of sweat popping out on the side of his face," Ada Bishop told her husband that night. "And when that wagon went up on two wheels and started to tip over, he made funny little noises to himself, like he was talking to somebody. Ella Watkins said he musta been talking to his ape 'cause Leach jumped off the wagon and ran under it and held it there till Clint pulled it upright. Ella asked him then what in the world he had in that wagon to make it so heavy. And he said it was just some things they needed to start a new home with." Up to this point, halfway along on their journey, there were no real mysteries to cause speculation, other than the possible parents of Roy Leach. Now, the reigning mystery would be *What is Thornton hauling in that wagon?* The first guess was always gold.

Having started at seven o'clock, the crossing over into the Bear River Valley was completed at a few minutes past two o'clock that afternoon, two hours past nooning time, so everyone was ready to eat. Scofield asked them to tighten their belts for a little longer, for he had a campsite in mind just a couple of miles farther along the trail, and they would stay there for the night. He said it was a popular campsite for all the wagon trains after successfully crossing Big Hill, called Clover Creek. "You'll have everything you need there for your horses and your cook fires."

Spirits were high as the wagons got underway once again for the short trip. It was almost impossible not to feel elated over the contrast they now experienced on this side of Big Hill in comparison to the windy and dry, sagebrush-covered, desertlike conditions they endured for days leading up to Big Hill. "See, Melody," Will said to his new wife, "Clint told us we'd be travelin' through some beautiful country soon, and he wasn't lyin'." At Clover Creek, they found it was also like Scofield had promised, with grass and water, and trees for firewood. Along the creek, there were flowers and berry bushes. It was like they had come to a different world.

The extra time in the Clover Creek camp was spent making any repairs they could fix that were made necessary after the rough passage over Big Hill. Scofield told them that any repairs beyond their capability could be handled at Fort Hall, which was not that many days away. Many in the company made it a point to ask Bass Thornton if anything had gotten damaged during his wagon's crossing. He answered all with the same response, that nothing was harmed. Thinking they might find out more from Violet, they found that her standard answer was, "Bass said nothing got hurt."

That night at the social hour, Scofield told them that in the morning they would follow the Bear River to a place called Soda Springs. "Following this trail on the bank of the river, I'm hopin' we'll be able to make more miles than we've been gettin' and get to Soda Springs in two days. It'll be a place like you ain't ever seen before. There's all these different springs of hot soda water, hot enough to wash your clothes in. You can drink it, too. Has a taste kinda like drinkin' beer. You ladies oughta like that." He left them with that to talk about for the rest of the evening.

Wiley Jones poked his wife with his elbow to get her attention. "What?" she responded, annoyed.

"I wonder what that sly old dog is haulin' in that wagon," Wiley said.

"Why?" Maggie asked. "It sure as hell ain't got nothin' to do with you."

"I bet it's got somethin' to do with that sweet young thing he's callin' his wife," Wiley commented, ignoring Maggie's grumpy disposition.

"Why don't you ask Leach about it?" Maggie suggested. "I bet he'd be tickled to talk to you about it."

# Chapter 18

As always, the wagons started out at seven o'clock the next morning, following the Bear River in a northwest direction. The day was uneventful, with no delays, and another day just like it brought them to Soda Springs where they went into camp, anticipating some extra time the next day to enjoy the novelty of the natural carbonated water. They found the springs to be a place of natural beauty as well. When Scofield assured them that it was all right to drink it, they sampled the water that night. Since the springs were a favorite place of the Shoshone Indians, and they had come close to a possibility of conflict the previous year when they camped there, Scofield had the wagons circled and the horses and cows brought in for the night. He planned to stay at least half a day before starting out for Fort Hall the next day, because it was such a rare opportunity for the folks on his train to take advantage of hot water. It was also the only place where they could enjoy the novelty of the soda water. As a precaution, he and Clint would both patrol the camp in addition to the men who were on guard duty that night. Their concern was more the attempt to steal the horses rather than an attack by a large band of Indians. Generally speaking, the Shoshone were friendly with the white man. But with the increase in recent years of the emigrant trains bringing more and more people into the Shoshone hunting grounds, there had been reports of some attacks. Clint planned to take a look around the springs in the morning in an effort to determine if there was evidence of recent Shoshone visits.

The night passed peacefully, and as soon as it grew light enough to see, Clint rode Biscuit out of the circle of wagons and looked for any signs left by horses or men. There were tracks of unshod horses, but none that looked recent. And most of the tracks he found were leading into the springs or going away, which indicated the rider was visiting the springs, not watching it. After covering a complete circle, he went back to eat breakfast and give Scofield his report. "Nobody recently," he said in answer to his uncle's inquisitive look when he walked up to the fire.

"That's good," Scofield said. "Then maybe these folks can enjoy the bubble water for a little while before we head on up to Fort Hall."

"I wanna take a pail and fill it up with that soda water," Lily commented. "I'll bet it'd be just the thing to make biscuits with. It'd be like havin' yeast in 'em."

"Most likely wouldn't be fit to eat," Spud said. "I wouldn't waste the flour on it."

Lily gave him an impatient smile. "Well, I'm gonna waste a little bit of flour on it, and I'll replace it when we get to Fort Hall. I just wish I had a good oven to bake in, instead of a frying pan."

It didn't take long for the kids to find that the odd-smelling water was not too hot to swim in. And their mothers were quick to take advantage of it with a bar of soap and a washcloth. After that, they washed the dirty clothes and soon the willow trees around the various springs were draped with drying clothes. Most of the men spent considerable time sampling the different springs. Scofield told them that one or more of the many springs was reported to taste like beer. He had been told that the first white men to discover the springs had originally named them

Beer Springs. Then somewhere down the line the name was changed to Soda Springs. He figured the women probably had a hand in that. At any rate, it was truly a holiday for the weary travelers, and it extended beyond the half-day that Scofield had planned, because he didn't have the heart to spoil their fun.

Clint hoped there were no Shoshone hunting parties anywhere close by. He was afraid they might be inclined to try to drive them out of this sacred area. So he made it his business to scout the area out away from the natural springs. He was rewarded for his efforts while scouting a little way up the trail the wagon train would be following the next day, when he saw a half dozen antelope crossing a wide stream. He was fortunate that they were crossing to the side where he was. One shot from his rifle felled the hindmost antelope. When he returned to the camp, it reminded Spud that Clint had done the same thing the prior year at this same place. "Antelope must lay around all year and wait for you to come back," Spud japed.

Clint and Spud butchered the antelope and selected the usual parts they saved for their wagon, and now for Will and Melody as well. Then the rest was given away on a first come, first served basis. It was a proper supper for this occasion and made for good eating, especially when served with Lily's pan-baked bread, which was as light as if it had been made with yeast. Even Spud admitted as much.

The social hour was especially casual and laid-back, and unusual in that many of the men sat around listening to the performers and drinking spring water from a fruit jar. Scofield briefly reminded everyone that they would be back on the regular routine in the morning when they would say goodbye to the Bear River and head for Fort Hall. With the guard roster set for the night, he returned to his wagon to catch a nap before returning for the midnight changing of the guard.

At midnight, Scofield returned to the fire in the center of the circle of wagons, empty now except for the men who had guard duty that night, and to Scofield's surprise, Clint. "What are you doin' here, Clint?" Scofield asked when he approached. "Noisy wagon?" he japed, referring to Will's wagon that Clint slept under.

Clint laughed and answered, "Nope, I just had a feelin', so I thought I'd stay awake a while longer tonight."

"Uh-oh," Scofield responded at once, well aware that Clint's "feelings" were oftentimes for legitimate reasons. "About what?"

"Well, nothin' for sure." Clint hesitated. He didn't want to get Scofield worked up over something he wasn't sure about, himself. "The fact of the matter is I took another ride around this place after supper. Up on that ridge, north of us, I found fresh tracks, unshod hooves of two horses. Looks like they just stayed there a while, watchin' us, long enough, anyway, for one of their ponies to leave his callin' card. I didn't wanna worry you if it was just a couple of hunters takin' a look. I'll stick around a while tonight and keep my eyes open. You got Pete Welker and Cecil Trainer comin' on after midnight. You might tell 'em to keep their eyes open for any Indians trying to get to the horses."

"Yeah, I'll do that," Scofield said. "You sure you're gonna be all right? You've been keepin' some long hours."

"Yep, I'm all right," Clint answered. "I ain't sleepy, anyway. The three of us oughta be able to keep an eye on the horses. I think those tracks I saw was just some curious Indians, stoppin' to take a look at the crazy white folks."

"You're most likely right about that," Scofield said. So he went to the fire where Welker and Trainer were having a cup of coffee before going on their patrol. "You two all set to take over?" Scofield asked when he walked up. They said they were.

"Is Clint gonna hang around?" Welker asked. A short, solidly built man in his early forties, Pete Welker and his wife, Gladys, were seldom seen at the nightly social hour, but they were both friendly people and their three children were always polite.

"Yep," Scofield answered. "He's gonna hang around a while. He often does when we're camped in Injun territory, just in case he's needed."

"Good," Welker said. "He's a good man to have in that case."

"He can take my place, if he wants to," Cecil Trainer volunteered. "And I'll go back and crawl in bed with my wife. I was just gettin' into some of the best part of my dreams when she woke me up to go on guard duty. Maybe I could get back to where I was before she shook me awake. It weren't with her." He laughed, thinking about it. In contrast to Pete Welker, Cecil never missed the social hour. He and his wife, Mavis, fancied themselves quite the dancers.

Scofield shook his head in response. He couldn't imagine two different personalities to be paired on the same night for guard duty. "Well, you've both pulled guard enough to know what you're supposed to do," he started to tell them.

"Right," Cecil interrupted, "keep the Injuns from stealin' the wagon train."

"What we're concerned about when we're parked in Injun territory, like we are tonight," Scofield continued, "is to make sure no horse thieves sneak in between the wagons and get away with some of our horses."

"Or my cow," Cecil remarked.

"Or Trainer's cow," Scofield said. "But if that happens, I don't expect you to try to stop them by yourself, but you need to fire your pistols and make sure you wake up the rest of us, so we can all stop 'em. Trainer, you take the south half of the circle, and Welker, you take the north half. Don't pay no attention to Clint if he disappears. He comes and he goes. Have a good evenin'." He left them with it and returned to his wagon.

Clint figured it would be a good idea to let the two guards know what he had in mind, so he wouldn't suddenly startle them and wind up getting shot. So he caught them before they left the fire to start their walking rounds. "Scofield probably told you we ain't got any reason to think anybody will be after our horses tonight, but we're gonna keep an eye out just in case, right?" They both said that was so. "Well, while you two are watchin' things inside the circle, I'm gonna look around a little bit outside the circle to see if I see any weak places in the corral. I'll let you know it's me, if I think I'm gonna surprise you." They both said they understood and they would make sure it wasn't him if they had to shoot at somebody.

"It is Rides Ahead!" Two Deer exclaimed. It was the name they had given Clint since they had followed the wagon train after it left Clover Creek. They called him that because he always rode out in front of the wagons. "He goes to talk to the other two. He may be trouble."

"Maybe he will not stay," Bloody Moon said. During the several nights they had watched the wagon train, they had learned that there were different guards watching the horses every night. More important, they soon realized the guards were not warriors or soldiers. They were the men from the wagons, and not men like the big chief, or Rides Ahead. They were the farmers who sought to settle on the Shoshone and Bannock hunting grounds. To steal the horses, they would have to drive them through the gap between the wagons around the circle. And to do that, they were going to have to open the gap by turning the wagon tongue either in or out to get it out of the way. After watching the nightly routine every night, they discovered something else. The farmer who took his turn as guard always came from one of the wagons. So that meant there was only a woman and maybe some children left in the wagon. And that would be the wagon to move out of the way, for the woman and children would most likely be sound asleep. So that was their plan. They saw the wagon that Cecil Trainer had left. They would move back away from the wagons now and wait until the guards became weary of their rounds and the woman and her children were fast asleep.

"Good," Two Deer said, "Rides Ahead goes back to his wagon."

"No," Bloody Moon said. "Look! He went between the wagons. He is on the outside! We must back away from here. Go back to our horses!" They pulled back away from the circle of wagons. "If he sees us, we must kill him, and then our chance to steal horses is gone."

From a safe distance back up the hill, they watched Clint as he walked around the outside of the corral of wagons. Finding no big gaps like the one that Jesse Yocum and his sons had created at Register Cliff, Clint went back inside the circle to his bed under Will's wagon to wait a while before taking another look around. He reasoned that if there was going to be any attempt on the horses, it would come in the wee hours of the morning. He started to close his eyes for a moment to rest them but opened them again right away. Scofield was right when he said that he had been keeping some long hours. He'd best just keep his eyes open. So he rolled out from under the wagon and sat up facing the horse herd. He would concentrate on watching the horses.

He suddenly jerked his head up, realizing he had been asleep. He felt immediately panicked. He had drifted off, but for how long? He blinked his eyes rapidly, trying to clear them, as he stared at the horse herd. *Some lookout*, he reprimanded himself. But the horses appeared to be calm. He had no watch, so he had no idea if he had dozed off for seconds or hours. Staring out toward the middle of the circle, he hoped to see one of the guards, but evidently they were both at opposite ends of the circle. He decided he would be better on the move. At least he could stay awake, so he went back outside the circle, planning to take another walk around the wagons.

Halfway around the circle, he was startled to find two horses tied to a low bush no more than ten yards from the wagons. He saw right away that they were Indian ponies, but there was no sign of their riders. Then he saw that the wagon tongue of one of the wagons had been pulled away from the tailgate of the one in front of it. He knew immediately what the riders of the two horses had in mind. They planned to kill the two guards, then quietly herd some quantity of horses out of the gate they had made. His first impulse was to fire a couple of shots into the air to alert the wagon train, but then he reconsidered. If he did that, Trainer or Welker, or both, might suddenly be shot, if they weren't already dead. And the two Indians would run for their lives. His best chance to save the guards would be to catch the stalkers before they caught the guards. *Not much chance*, he thought as he sprinted toward the south end of the circle, since it was closer.

Cecil Trainer pulled his watch out of his pocket, squinting to read it in the darkness. "Damn," he muttered, "still almost two hours before Scofield blows everybody outta bed with that infernal bugle of his." Unaware of the silent shadow behind him, he put the watch away and took out his tobacco pouch and proceeded to fill his pipe. As he started to strike a match, his head was suddenly jerked back by a hand on his forehead and he saw the brief glint of the long knife blade.

Stunned, Bloody Moon dropped the scalping knife when, in one swift move, his head was jerked back by the hair and his throat was opened wide by Clint's skinning knife. With no time to waste, Clint didn't take the time to wipe the blood off his knife. "Make no noise or you might kill Welker!" he told Trainer and sprinted toward the other end of the wagon circle, looking right and left as he ran, desperately hoping he was not too late. Past the horses in the middle of the circle, he still saw no sign of Welker or his stalker. He was afraid he was too late, but just as he thought that, he saw them. Welker was at the very front of the circle, close to Scofield's wagon. Behind him, Two Deer was closing fast. Clint knew he could not get to him quick enough.

Welker paused, thinking he might have heard something behind him. But before he could turn around, his head was jerked back and he briefly glimpsed the knife blade in the warrior's hand as it opened with the sharp crack of the Henry rifle, and the knife dropped to the ground. Welker's knees threatened to fail him as he turned around to see the body behind him, then looked up to see Clint standing some fifteen yards away, his rifle in hand. Welker looked back down in stunned silence at the dead warrior at his feet, then back at Clint again. And then the silence was shattered by the explosion of the wagon train's sudden awakening to the sound of the rifle shot. The first on the scene were Scofield and Spud, since it happened right beside their wagon.

"Are you all right, Mr. Welker?" Clint asked before he talked to Scofield.

"I guess so," Welker answered, still thoroughly shaken by his near-death experience. "I'm still standin' here. Is Trainer all right?"

"Yes, sir," Clint answered. "He was when I left him. Here he comes now." They looked then to see Trainer coming their way along with a number of the other emigrants.

Scofield waited, knowing if there was still a crisis, Clint would have said so. "Everything all right now?" he asked when Clint turned to him.

"Yep," Clint answered. "I'm sorry I had to wake everybody up, but I couldn't get to Welker in time to do it quietly." He nodded toward the body lying there. "He already had his knife ready to cut Mr. Welker's throat."

"He's right, Scofield," Welker said. "He sneaked up behind me and jerked my head back. I saw his knife right in front of my face. I thought I was gonna die."

Scofield bent down to check Two Deer to see if he was dead. "Shot him in the side," he said. "Right under his arm, bullet went through his ribs and musta struck his heart. He's dead." He straightened up again and said, "Just like you'd shoot a deer, right behind his front leg."

Trainer hurried up to join them then. "Pete, you all right?" he called out when he saw him standing there obviously unhurt. "I swear, I thought I was a dead man back there for a split second, and when I heard that shot, I was afraid you might be."

"Did you have an Indian attack you, too?" Welker asked, since he had heard no gunshot before the one that killed the Indian at his feet.

"I sure as hell did," Trainer answered. "Sneaked up behind me, he did, just like an Injun would, grabbed me by my head and started to cut my throat. But Clint, there, sneaked up behind him and cut his throat first. And I mean from ear to ear, awful lookin' thing. Then he told me not to make no noise and took off lookin' for you. Hell, I couldn'ta made a sound if I'd tried to. I'd done swallowed my vocal cords before that." He turned to Clint then and asked, "Why didn't you want me to make no noise?"

"I didn't wanna take a chance on spookin' this one that was goin' after Mr. Welker," Clint told him. "He mighta just shot him and took off."

"Just the two of 'em?" Scofield asked.

"I'm pretty sure that's all," Clint said. "There's two horses tied outside the wagons and there wasn't any sign of any others. I figure it's gotta be the two whose tracks I kept findin'. I reckon they were plannin' to run off with a bunch of our horses, and not just a couple. Probably figured if they killed the guards without makin' any noise, they might have half the night to lead our horses outta here."

"Makes sense to me," Scofield said. "Gotta give 'em credit for bein' so ambitious. I'm kinda surprised they didn't wanna cut some of their other Shoshone brothers in on the deal."

"They might not be Shoshone," Clint suggested. "They might be Bannock. You know, they're up here in this territory, too."

"I suppose you're right," Scofield said. He looked at his watch and announced, "You folks have a little over an hour before the day officially starts, so you might wanna crawl back under your blanket for a little while." Back to Clint then, he said, "I reckon we oughta get rid of the bodies before the women and the children see 'em."

"I'll go get those two horses tied out there and load 'em on them," Clint volunteered. "Then I'll take 'em off somewhere and dump 'em."

"I'll help you load 'em," Scofield said. So Clint went out the gate Bloody Moon and Two Deer had opened with Trainer's wagon tongue and led the two horses inside the wagons. He and his uncle threw Two Deer's body on one of the horses, then went down and picked up Bloody Moon. Clint led the horses back outside and picked a spot about a quarter of a mile from the river and dumped the bodies. Then he took the roughly constructed Indian saddles off and dumped them on top of the bodies. When that was done, he jumped on the back of one of the ponies and rode him back to the wagons, leading the other one. When he got back, he turned the horses in with the herd, then went back and closed the wagon tongue gate. The wagon train had settled down by then, so he crawled back under Will Tucker's wagon and closed his eyes, not sure how much time he had to sleep, if any. "If there's any more horse thieves out there," he muttered to himself, "they're welcome to as many head as they want. I won't try to stop you."

Morning came way too early and Clint debated whether or not to get up when he was shaken awake by Scofield and his bugle. *Maybe I'll just lay here until Will drives his wagon from over me*, he thought. Then he sighed, knowing his uncle depended on him to help get the wagon train on the move every morning. So he rolled out of his blanket and pulled it out with him when he crawled out from under the wagon. He folded up the blanket and threw it over the tailgate. "Mornin', Clint," Will called from inside the wagon.

"Morning, Clint," Melody's tiny voice echoed.

"Mornin'," Clint answered back and headed to the bushes to answer nature's call.

The popular topic of conversation around all the breakfast fires was naturally about the uninvited guests who called in the wee hours of the morning with the intention of murdering Pete Welker and Cecil Trainer. There was a great deal of admiration for the performance of their young scout in saving Pete and Cecil's lives. Gladys Welker and Susan Trainer each made sure to find Clint that morning before the wagons rolled to personally thank him for his heroic efforts in saving their husbands. There was also some discussion among some of the men regarding Clint's handling of the situation, this mostly springing up from Cecil Trainer's account of Clint's method of dealing with the two savages. They were somewhat fascinated by the fact that this seemingly good-natured, respectful, and polite young man had a side of him that was not normally exposed. As Levi Watkins put it, "You think about that polite young man sneakin' up behind that wild savage, grabbing him by the hair, and slashin' his throat open from ear to ear, just like the savage was gonna do on Cecil. Then, when that other Injun had Pete Welker's head bent back and his scalpin' knife right at his throat, our polite young scout raised his rifle and shot that damn Injun dead before he could use the knife." He shook his head then and said, "There's a lot we don't know about that young feller."

"There's one thing we know about him," Tracy Bishop said. "He's on our side, and I'm mighty glad of that." He received a few *hear hears* and a couple of *amens* for his comment.

At seven o'clock, Scofield gave the signal to roll, and the wagon train left Soda Springs and the Bear River when the river made a dramatic turn back toward the Utah desert. On a road heading in a northwest direction now, Clint rode as much as a quarter mile ahead to make sure the way was clear and passable. This would be their route for the next several days.

# Chapter 19

The wagons rolled into Fort Hall at the end of the day, close to suppertime. The fort, located on Spring Creek since 1864 when the original fort was washed away by floodwaters of the Snake River, was a welcome sight to the weary travelers. They would stay over an extra day for some much-needed wagon repairs and horseshoeing. The fort also provided an opportunity to replenish supplies in preparation for the long haul required to follow the Snake River across Utah Territory from Fort Hall to Farewell Bend. It was a journey that Scofield figured to take about eight or nine weeks, depending on the weather. So far, there had not been enough rain to make any of the river crossings since leaving the Green especially hazardous.

After the wagon train was circled up and the animals were watered and set to graze, Clint went to Scofield's wagon for supper as usual. His uncle and Lily were already eating. "I was wonderin' if you was gonna show up," Spud said in greeting. "Thought maybe you was dinin' tonight with Mr. and Mrs. Tucker, after I cooked up the rest of my rice and the last of that bag of beans I got at Fort Bridger."

"Why would you think I'd be eatin' with them?" Clint asked. "I always eat here."

"After what you done for that young lady, and seein' as how

you and Will are such good friends, I'da thought she'd invite you over for supper pretty regular."

"I hadn't thought about it," Clint commented, wondering what set Spud off on that subject. "Besides, they're newlyweds and they don't even know there's anybody else in the world right now."

"Shoot," Spud replied, "they been married ever since Fort Bridger. They ain't newlyweds no more. I expect they've been married long enough now to be good and sick of each other."

"You mean like Wiley and Maggie Jones?" Clint asked, since they came to mind right away.

"Well, I weren't thinkin' about them, but they are a good example. He paused and nodded toward the couple seated by the fire, eating. "I was thinkin' about Clayton and Lily over there."

"Ha!" Clint barked. "They're more like newlyweds than Will and Melody. What's got into you tonight?" He was really beginning to wonder about Spud until Spud's next question, and then he told himself he should have recognized the symptoms.

"You know," Spud started, "I've had me a cravin' all day for a drink of corn likker. It's been a good while since I've had a drink. How 'bout you? You wanna go with me after supper and get a little shooter? What's the name of that place about a mile from here?"

"Lucky's," Clint answered. "When I talked to some people about it last year, some called it Lucky's River Club and some called it Lucky's River House. So it's just Lucky's, I reckon. You didn't go there last year when we were here?"

"No, I reckon I didn't have a cravin' when we was here last year. But I remember you and Cal Nixon went there to fetch Ruby's husband."

"It's nothin' but a hog ranch," Clint said, "but I expect it's still the only place you can get a drink of whiskey." He was thinking about the last time Spud got one of his cravings and how it ended up. That time it was Fort Laramie at Jake's Place, and they walked back to the wagons with Roy Leach.

"How 'bout it?" Spud asked again. "Scofield used to go with me, but Lily's got him locked up."

Clint was not at all interested in going to Lucky's. In fact, he had purposefully intended to avoid the place. And in addition to that, he had no desire for a drink of whiskey. But he knew now that Spud didn't want to go by himself, and he suspected it was because the emotional reaction he had to the drinking at Jake's Place had not been an isolated occurrence. He found it hard to turn him down, however, because he knew that Spud asked him to go with him because he felt he wouldn't make fun of his crying problem and tell anybody else about it. "Okay, Spud," he said, as cheerful as he could manage. "But you know I ain't much for drinkin' whiskey. So I'll have one, maybe two, and that's it for me."

"That's fine by me," Spud said, "whatever you feel like. I just hate to sit around drinkin' by myself, you know? People think you're a drunk."

"Yep," Clint said dryly, "that's what they usually think. But at Lucky's hog ranch that ain't thought to be a bad thing."

So after Clint ate his beans and rice, with a slice of sowbelly and a cup of coffee, he sat down to wait for Spud to clean up his pots and pans. Lily told him to go along and get his drink of whiskey, she'd clean up the dishes. Clint asked Scofield if he wanted him to bring anything back. "Just Spud," his uncle said with a chuckle. Then Scofield gave Lily a questioning look and she shook her head. "Reckon not," Scofield said then, and winked at Clint.

*Doggone you*, Clint thought.

So, Clint and Spud walked up the path behind the fort that led to the two-story log house that was Lucky's River Club. Owned by a man named Ike Ennis, it was built on a steep embankment beside the Snake River. Clint remembered from the year before that Ike's standard practice for handling unruly and trouble-making customers was to haul them out the back door and drop them off the porch. The drop was a high one and the embankment so steep that a body could easily roll right down into the river. They started up the path at a leisurely walk, but as they got far enough up the path to see the lights from the windows and hear the sounds emanating from inside the building, Clint noticed that Spud's pace kept increasing. When they reached the front porch steps, Spud was leading Clint by a couple of strides.

"Before we go in this place," Clint saw fit to warn Spud, "there's something I oughta tell you. It's been a year since I was in there, and maybe they won't remember me. But if they do, I might not be welcome." His statement captured Spud's attention right away, so he continued to try to refresh Spud's memory. "The last time I was here was when Cal Nixon and I came here lookin' for Ralph Tyler and found him dead."

"I swear, I forgot all the details about that," Spud said. "This was where he died. Well, maybe they won't remember that."

"Maybe not," Clint said. "But they might remember that Cal killed a man that pulled a gun on him and we had to back outta there holding our guns on them and threatenin' to shoot the first one who made a move."

Spud stroked his chin thoughtfully while he considered what Clint had just told him. "It's been a year," he finally said. "They ain't likely to remember you." He would have been more correct to assume that a tall young man wearing a buckskin shirt and moccasins, and carrying a Henry rifle, they would not likely forget.

Inside, the main saloon was fairly busy, even this early in the evening. Most of the customers were soldiers, but there were a few cowhands or drifters, which accounted for the few horses tied at the rail out front. Clint had been told last year that the soldiers who had been sent to Fort Hall originally to protect the miners and the settlers had been called back when the Civil War started. And the soldiers who were at the fort now were a detachment of volunteer Union soldiers who were supposed to be moved away from Fort Hall to a new location. Fort Hall would remain under the operation of the Hudson's Bay Company, however, and would still be an important stop on the Oregon and California trails. When it came to Clint and Spud, this was mildly interesting, but was of no real concern to them because this was to be their last journey on the Oregon Trail.

Benny Thatcher, bartender, glanced toward the door when Spud and Clint walked in and paused to look the room over. In the dim light of the doorway, Benny thought at first glance that Clint was an Indian and carrying a rifle to boot. Just before going to intercept them when they walked on into the room, he saw that Clint was not an Indian. Still, something looked familiar about him. He continued to stare at him, trying to determine what was triggering his mind's struggle to recall. He looked at the man with him and knew he had never seen him before, so he returned his concentration to the man with the rifle as the two walked up to the bar. "Whatcha drinkin'?" Benny asked, his question aimed at Clint, but Spud answered.

"Corn whiskey," Spud said, "and I believe I'm gonna need a bottle of it."

"You really do have a cravin', don't you?" Clint asked. "I'm just gonna have a shot. You want me to pay you for a shot outta your bottle, or get it from the bartender?"

"You don't need to spend your money," Spud said. "Just get you a glass."

"You might need to take that bottle back to the wagon with you," Clint said and put some money on the bar. "Just pour me a shot," he told Benny.

"I got it now!" Benny suddenly exclaimed. When Clint mentioned the wagon, that was the spark that ignited his memory. Clint had come into the saloon looking for a drunk from the wagon train. He then told Clint as much. "That was, hell, a year ago at least!"

"Yeah, you're right," Clint confessed. "That was a year ago and now my friend and I are just lookin' for a drink of whiskey."

"This ain't the feller who was with you that night," Benny continued, still intent upon recalling the incident that turned volatile before the shooting and the exit with Clint and the man with him backing out with guns drawn and threatening. He put two glasses on the bar and filled one of them for Clint while Spud uncorked his bottle and poured his own.

"No, that fellow ain't with us this trip," Clint said. "Only me and Spud this trip and we just came in to get a peaceful drink of likker."

"I remember you," a hoarse female voice at his elbow declared, surprising Clint. She had slid silently in beside him in time to hear some of the conversation with Benny. "I'm Sally Switch. You remember me?"

"Sure do," Clint lied. "How you doin', Sally?" He wondered briefly what her real name was but was not interested enough to ask her.

"I'm doin' what pleases you most," she replied. "Why don't we go upstairs and have a little visit?"

"That sounds mighty nice," Clint lied again, "but I'm afraid I'm dead broke. I just gave Benny my last quarter."

She poked her lips out in what she considered a pretty little pout. "Your friend must have some money. Won't he lend you some?"

Spud grinned from ear to ear. "Sure, Clint, I'll loan you some money to take her upstairs."

*Dadgum you, Spud*, Clint thought, *and after I came up here with you, so you could get drunk.* "Oh, that would be mighty nice," he said, "but I know you're testin' me." He looked at Sally and explained. "You see, I've got a problem holdin' on to money, and the boys have been tryin' to help me break the habit of borrowin' money when I ain't got no way to pay it back. He's just funnin'. He wouldn't really loan me the money. I reckon he can go upstairs with you, though." He looked back at Spud and grinned. "I'll hold your bottle for you."

Sally Switch didn't attempt to hide the disappointment in her expression even before Spud claimed that, "Unfortunately, those days are long gone for me. It's one of the penalties for livin' too long." Sally didn't waste another second on the two of them. She turned abruptly and went back to scouting the tables.

"Let's go set down at that table in the back there," Spud said then, pointing to an empty table with only two chairs. He picked up his bottle and headed toward it without waiting for Clint to agree or object. Clint picked up his drink and followed him. "Here's to all the hardworkin' whores in Utah Territory," Spud said when Clint sat down at the table, then Spud tossed his first drink down.

Clint threw his whiskey back as well, clenching his teeth till the burn subsided. Spud poured himself another, then hovered the bottle over Clint's empty glass. "Just once," Clint said, and when he tossed that one down, he turned his glass upside down. "That'll do," he said. While he watched Spud pour another shot, someone came into the saloon through a door behind them and walked past their table on his way to the bar. When he turned at the bar to talk to Benny, Clint recognized him as Ike Ennis, the owner. He and Benny talked for a few minutes, then they both turned to look in his and Spud's direction. Ennis turned back to say something more to Benny. *Now come tell us to get out*, Clint thought as Ennis turned in their direction and walked directly toward their table.

"Well, I see you're back," Ennis said. "You with that wagon train that just pulled in today?"

"That's a fact," Clint answered.

"You ain't lookin' for no runaway pilgrim this time?"

"Nope, just came in to give you a little business."

Ennis nodded his head slowly. "Then you'll be pullin' out of here tomorrow," he stated.

"Or the next day," Clint answered.

"That fellow you killed when you were in here last year was a regular customer," Ennis said. "He was in here every day. I hated to lose him as a customer."

"He was? What did he do for a livin'?" Ennis didn't answer, so Clint reminded him. "You remember? I didn't shoot your regular customer. He was just dumb enough to pull his gun on a man that was about three times faster than he was."

"That's right," Ennis said, remembering then. "You were the one with the rifle. Where is that other fellow? Will he be in tonight?"

"Nope, sorry, he ain't with us this trip." He didn't tell him that Cal was dead, didn't want to give him the satisfaction. "Look, Mr. Ennis, I reckon I can understand why I might not be welcome here. But my friend, here, didn't have anything to do with that unfortunate business that happened here last year. So, how 'bout if we just sit here nice and quiet till he has a couple of drinks and then we'll leave? Would that satisfy you?"

Ennis smiled. "Why, what makes you think I want you to leave? Like you said, that business last year was unfortunate, but you weren't the one who pulled the trigger. You weren't the one who killed my brother-in-law. You just made sure his killer got out of here alive. No, you fellows stay as long as you like. I'm glad to have your business." He left them then and went back out the door he came in.

"Brother-in-law?" Clint repeated. "Did he say brother-in-law?"

"That's what he said," Spud answered.

"That fool that pulled on Cal Nixon was his brother-in-law?" Clint repeated. "All of a sudden, I don't feel comfortable sittin' here with my back to that door. Whaddaya say we move over to another table?" He pointed to one in the opposite corner, facing that side of the room.

"Whaddaya say we just get the hell outta here," Spud countered. "I got my bottle. I don't need to stay here."

"That would work, too," Clint said. "Let's just get up kinda casual-like and walk through the middle of the room between all the tables." He wanted to discourage Ennis from taking a shot at them in the middle of his customers, if, in fact, he was crazy enough to take a shot at them.

So they got up from the table and made their way through the middle of the room. They happened to pass right by Sally Switch, who was hovering over a card game. When Clint went by, she grabbed his elbow long enough to say, "You missed a real thrill tonight."

"You don't know the half of it," he replied and kept walking. When they got close to the front door, he cranked a cartridge into the chamber of his rifle and turned to keep an eye on the bartender and those standing at the bar. Then he quickly turned and followed Spud through the door. When they got outside, he didn't have to tell Spud to hurry. When he caught up with him, he said, "I'm sorry your drinkin' got messed up, but we did the right thing gettin' outta there. The trouble is you don't know who you have to worry about back there. And I got a feelin' we ain't seen the last of them yet. At least I ain't. The only problem you've got is bein' with me. At least it's good and dark on this little path now. I think it'd be a good idea to get off it if anybody comes along."

"Right," Spud said, suddenly very sober. They walked quickly for only a minute or two when they heard someone approaching on the path. "Over there!" Spud whispered and pointed to a clump of trees off to the side.

Puzzled by his reaction at first, Clint said, "We don't have to hide from anybody on their way to Lucky's."

"Oh, right," Spud said, pulled the cork from his bottle and took a slug from it as two soldiers walked past them on their way to the hog ranch.

They weren't halfway down the path when they heard the horse coming up behind them. "Now we need to hide," Clint said. "Come on, follow me." He ran down the side of the slope the path ran along, into the trees that covered the slope. Then he stopped to watch the rider pass by. In the dark, they could make out the shape of the rider. *Good*, Clint thought, *only one*. To Spud, he said, "Might just be somebody goin' home from Lucky's. Ain't but one way to find out for sure." He paused, then said,

"Well, there's two ways, but one of 'em will get us shot. So we'll take the other one."

"I hope to hell you know what you're doin'," Spud said, "'cause I ain't even wearin' a gun."

"Well, if we're lucky, you won't need one," Clint told him. "That path leads right into the back of that fort. I don't think that was a soldier goin' back from Lucky's 'cause most likely he'd be walkin' instead of ridin' a horse. Anyway, if the fellow on the horse is lookin' for us, he's gonna be waitin' for us to come walkin' down that path. He knows he shoulda caught us before we got to the end of the path, so he knows we heard him comin' and hid. So he'll be sittin' at the end of the path waitin' for us to show up. And that means we've got to stay off the path and go back in the trees beside it. Don't that make sense to you?" Spud didn't answer right away. He was obviously still trying to sort it out. So Clint said, "If you rather, you can just stay hid here while I go on to see if that fellow's lookin' for us or not."

"Hell, no!" Spud quickly replied. "I'm goin' with you."

"Okay, well, let's not keep the man waitin'." They made their way through the trees on the side of the slope, walking parallel with the path until Clint whispered, "There he is. He came back down the path a ways." He could imagine if the man was a killer sent to even a score for Ike Ennis, he would most likely prefer not to do his job right in an entrance into the fort. His plan would probably be to shoot him on sight, then gallop away up the path to Lucky's before anyone in the fort came to investigate the shot. "You wait right here," he told Spud, "while I go see if he's lookin' for us."

"Damn it, Clint, you be careful," Spud said.

"I will," Clint said, "but if anything happens to me, you know you ain't but about a hundred yards from the wagons, right?"

"Right, but you be careful," he repeated.

"I will," Clint said again and took off through the bushes beneath the trees, clutching his rifle, which was still cocked from their exit from the saloon. When he was even with the man on the horse, he could see that he was also holding a rifle, ready to fire. There was little doubt that he was an assassin sent to kill him. So he continued through the trees a little farther, then came up on the path behind the horse. He felt almost one hundred percent sure the man had come after him to kill him. There was no reason not to play it safe and shoot him in the back while he sat unsuspecting on his horse, but if he was wrong, it would be outright murder, and he knew he couldn't take that chance. So he asked, "You lookin' for me?"

Startled, the man wheeled his horse around to face Clint, and when he recognized him, he didn't hesitate but raised his rifle to fire, only to be struck in the chest by Clint's bullet before he could get a shot off. The man fell forward on the horse's neck, dead or alive, Clint didn't take the time to see. He turned the horse back around and gave it a swat on its rump, and it started back up the path at a trot. "Let's go, Spud!" Clint yelled.

"Did you kill him?" Spud asked anxiously when he appeared out of the trees.

"I don't know, I think so. Let's get away from here before somebody comes lookin' to see what that shot was about. Reckon we oughta pick up that rifle layin' on the ground, though." He walked a little way down the path and picked up the rifle. When he turned around again, Spud was already on his way back to the wagons, so he hurried to catch up with him.

They could hear the music coming from the social hour as they approached the clearing where the wagon trains parked, but they went back to Scofield's wagon. They found Scofield and Lily sitting by the fire, drinking coffee. "Didn't expect you two back here this early," Scofield said.

"Didn't expect to be back this early," Spud grumbled. "I gotta find me another drinkin' partner."

"Oh?" Scofield replied and glanced at Clint. "He ain't much of a drinker, is he?"

"No, he ain't," Spud said, "but that ain't the worst of it. He's snakebit when it comes to goin' in a saloon. Last time he went with me, I thought I was gonna get shot and I ended up walkin' home with Leach. This time, the feller who owns the saloon sent somebody after us and Clint had to kill him." He shook his head slowly. "I swear, I'm stone-cold sober. Is there any more coffee in that pot?" Lily volunteered to make him a fresh pot.

Scofield looked back at Clint again for an explanation. "We heard a shot just a little while ago. Was that you?"

"Yes, it was," Clint answered. "I shouldn't have gone there tonight. The fellow that owns that place remembered me. He remembered I was with Cal that night when Cal shot that gunslinger. Turns out that gunslinger was the owner's brother-in-law." He went on to tell him about the conversation he had with Ike Ennis and what it eventually led up to. "I didn't see as I had much choice when the man came after me. I just hope the fellow I shot tonight didn't marry the brother-in-law's widow."

# Chapter 20

The next day was spent replacing spent supplies and repairing wagons for the long drive along the Snake River. With no idea if Ike Ennis would make another attempt on his life or not, Clint tried to keep a low profile. This came after some strong urging from his uncle and Lily. In truth, he had no desire to go after Ennis; he much preferred to simply ride away and forget the whole thing. He did ride Biscuit in to see Ned Blanchard, the blacksmith, to get new shoes, however. Biscuit could have waited a little longer, but Clint remembered the excellent job Ned did for the Palouse gelding the last time they were in Fort Hall. Ned appreciated the compliment and did another careful job for him. "Thank you for the business, Clint, come in and see me next year." Clint told him that as of that moment, he wasn't planning to make the trip again, that he and Scofield were going to raise horses and cattle on the land his two uncles owned in Oregon. They wished each other good luck and Clint spent the rest of the day inside the wagon circle.

At seven the following day, the wagons pulled out of Fort Hall on the start of a long, dry, and dusty trail to Three Island Crossing, a trip of around one hundred and seventy-five miles of mostly barren-looking land. The end of the first day found the emigrants about seven miles short of American Falls. The next day, they stopped for the nooning near the falls, where the Snake

dropped some fifty feet to smash against the rocks and forma-
tions in the channel of the river with such velocity that the roar-
ing could be heard for miles. The following morning saw them
approaching a cruel passage through an area of massive rocks and
boulders that Scofield called the Devil's Gate. He said it was
called that because some years back, a wagon train was attacked
by Indians there and many were killed. The passage was barely
wide enough to allow a wagon to pass through the rocks and it
was another place where the emigrants had written their names
on the boulders with axle grease.

The first point of concern for Scofield and Clint was reached
at nooning on the fourth day after leaving Fort Hall. It was the
crossing of the Raft River and the reason Scofield had studied
the morning sky every day, looking for signs of coming rain.
Thankfully, there had been none in that time, so the rivers were
not running high. The Raft River, so named because of the depth
of it and the requirement to build rafts to float the wagons across.
Scofield and Clint both rode out into the river to check the depth
of the water and the solidness of the bottom, looking for a solid
bed that ran all the way across. After riding back and forth several
times to determine the path for the wagons to drive on, they
marked it on both banks. And although it was time for the noon
rest, Scofield ordered the crossing to begin. "We'll rest and eat
dinner on the other side," he said. "It's still summertime and a
thunderstorm can come up pretty quick. If that happened while
we were settin' around on this side, we might have to raft the fool
river."

So they proceeded to cross the river. The water came up to the
wagon boxes, but the horses never had to swim, and the crossing
was successful with no time loss building rafts. The nooning was
later than usual but enjoyed more than most. The Raft River was
where the emigrants following the California Trail left the common trail and headed in that direction. Only the folks heading for
Oregon continued along the Snake River toward Three Island
Crossing, which was now one hundred and twenty miles distant.

Leaving the Raft River, the wagon train traveled the dusty road for the next five days, passing Cauldron Linn rapids and crossing Rock Creek before reaching Shoshone Falls. It was here that Scofield took pity on his charges and took a short detour to the north in order to let the emigrants see the spectacular waterfalls. His gesture was well received and appreciated by the people on his train. It was a brief holiday away from the dusty trail, and at the social hour that night there was much discussion about the boredom of their meals, and how nice it would be to have something like fish for a change. Scofield listened with great interest because he had more surprises up his sleeve for them. He let them fantasize on a change of diet for a while, then he made his announcement. "Well, folks, can you hang on for about three more days? 'Cause if you can, we oughta be rollin' into Upper Salmon Falls. And, folks, they named it that for a dang good reason. That's where all these Indians in these parts, Shoshone and Bannock, too, catch all their salmon. And when we get there, you might see as many as a hundred Indians catchin' salmon. When we pull up there, they'll be all over us with salmon to trade for anything you've got to trade."

"He ain't just pullin' our chain, is he, Clint?" Levi asked.

"No, sir," Clint answered. "He's not exaggeratin', either. And they'll all be big fine-lookin' salmon, too."

"Shoot," Tracy remarked, "let's get started tonight. Give Clint a lantern and we can follow him right now."

Salmon was the conversation for the rest of the evening. Lily asked Scofield afterward why he didn't wait to tell everybody about the salmon until they got a little closer to Salmon Falls. "Well, seemed to me like everybody was draggin' a little bit and needed something to pick 'em up. So I gave 'em that to look forward to. Looked to me like it did the job."

"You know, I guess you're right. I can't wait to eat some of that salmon, myself," she admitted.

\* \* \*

It was early afternoon when the wagon train reached Upper Salmon Falls and the travelers discovered right away that Scofield had not exaggerated his description of the welcome that awaited them. There were close to fifty or sixty Indians spearing what seemed to be thousands of salmon tackling the waterfalls. The emigrants were met by scores of Indians even before they could unhitch their horses and tighten up their wagon corral. They were holding up strings of freshly caught salmon and asking, "You trade?" In spite of Scofield's warnings, very few of the folks had their trade items ready, so they were rummaging through their wagons to find any article of clothing or knick-knack of any kind they thought they could do without. The salmon looked too good to pass up. One of the clever Indians even came with salmon that had been cleaned and smoked. "You keep long time," he said. He was only the first, however, for there were many more who came with smoked salmon, anticipating the travelers' need for food they could keep for a longer period. Lily expressed her surprise that the Indians kept so much smoked salmon on hand when there was so much fresh salmon to eat. Scofield explained that the Indians knew the wagon train would be there in a few days by word of scouts. "Most likely when we stopped at Shoshone Falls," Scofield said. "A scout probably rode ahead from there to tell everybody here to get ready."

Melody Tucker was quick to open Angel's trunk that held the rest of Will's late wife's belongings. After selecting the few pieces of clothing she could use, Melody would have left the rest beside the trail after she and Will married, but Clint had advised her to keep it because there would be a use for it later on. Now, she realized why he urged her to hang on to the clothes. In addition to fresh salmon, Angel's things bought her and Will smoked salmon enough to last for weeks.

It was still early enough in the afternoon for some of the folks to walk over to the falls to watch the Indians catch the salmon.

They were surprised to see most of the fishermen using spears to catch them. There were a few nets being used. They were small nets, for a net of any larger size would fill so quickly it would be difficult to pull it out of the water. "The blamed salmon are so thick that those Injuns ain't even takin' aim," Levi claimed. "They just throw the spear in the water anywhere and pull it back with a fish on the end of it."

Like Will and Melody, Scofield and Clint had brought some things with them for the specific purpose of trading for salmon. And after he swept Lulu Belle away from Fort Kearny, Scofield had advised her not to throw away any clothing she might have discarded. The net result was that there was fresh salmon enough for every family's cook fire that night, even those who had nothing they could trade.

Once the wagons were set in place and the horses and cows let out to water and graze, the most popular spot was one stretch of riverbank below the falls where everybody was cleaning salmon to cook for supper. One of those looking for a spot to clean a couple of fish was Wiley Jones, he having been the loser in a coin toss with his wife, Maggie. As he walked along the row of fannies, most of them women's, he spotted a vacancy on the riverbank next to one he had admired before. So he quickly dropped to his knees and moved in beside Violet Thornton. "This looks like the best spot to clean my fish," he said as he laid the pan of salmon down at the edge of the water. Violet looked at him with a shy smile. "Doggone if I don't believe this is the first time I've ever seen you anywhere without your husband right beside you." She responded with nothing more than a soft giggle. Determined to make her talk, he said, "I reckon I don't blame ol' Bass. If I had a young, good-lookin' little filly like you, I wouldn't let her run loose, either." When she still didn't say anything in return, he asked, "He tell you not to talk to anybody?"

She giggled again but answered. "He didn't tell me that. He just likes to keep me close to him."

"He'd most likely be mad if he knew you was down here at

the river talkin' to me," Wiley said. "Sweet thing like you, I wouldn't wanna cause you to get a whippin'."

She blushed. "He don't whip me. He treats me nice, like a little princess."

"That sounds like he wants to be your daddy 'stead of your husband. Ain't that about right? You're daddy's little girl?"

"You shouldn't oughta be talkin' to me about things like that," she said. "What would Maggie say, if she knew you were talkin' like that?"

"She'd probably raise hell and that's why I ain't gonna tell her. She don't have to know everythin' I talk to other women about. I don't ask her what she talks to other men about. Ain't that the same way you look at it? You ain't gotta tell ol' Bass what you're talkin' to me about. That's just between me and you."

"He wants me to act like a lady," Violet said, "and he treats me like one."

"But he ain't down here cleanin' fish, is he?" Wiley replied. "How'd you two ever get together in the first place? Where'd you meet him?"

She looked concerned by that and hesitated before she answered. "I'm not supposed to talk about that," she finally answered.

"You don't have to worry about that when you're talkin' to me," he told her. "'Cause I ain't gonna tell another soul what goes on between me and you. You can talk to me anytime you need to talk to somebody who ain't old enough to be your daddy. And don't worry about Maggie makin' any trouble about it. I don't tell Maggie about my private feelin's. What we got is more a business agreement just to get out to Oregon than it is a marriage."

"I better get back to the wagon," Violet said. "I'm done with this fish, and Bass will be wonderin' what's takin' me so long."

"Well, I wanna thank you for talkin' to me, Violet," Wiley said. "I'm just like you. I ain't had nobody I could really talk to. And I've been admirin' you ever since we left Independence."

Totally confused, she didn't know what to say, so she just smiled and nodded as if she understood. Then she took her pan of fish and hurried back to the wagon. He turned around and watched her until she disappeared inside the circle of wagons. "That's the way I like 'em," he muttered to himself, "young, good-lookin', and dumb as a knot on a tree." He was sure he had a pretty good idea how she ended up with Bass Thornton. "He bought her," he muttered again. And if he had to guess, he would have said she was probably working in a house of prostitution when Thornton found her. "He bought her, just like he bought that big ape that drives his wagon, although I don't know where the hell he had to go to find him—maybe the circus." He wasn't sure if he had made any real progress with the young woman or not. *But I gave that little brain of hers something to think about*, he thought. Then he started cleaning his salmon.

When he got back to his wagon, Maggie asked, "What the hell have you been doin'? Didn't I tell you I wanted to cook it for supper tonight while it was still fresh?"

"Maybe you oughta clean the next one yourself, if you ain't satisfied," he answered her. "There was plenty of the other women down there cleanin' their fish."

"Yeah, well, I ain't like the other women on this damn train," she said.

"Boy, that's the God's honest truth," Wiley agreed.

"You keep talkin' and you're gonna find yourself cookin' your own supper tonight."

With bellies full of salmon and some smoked for later, the emigrants returned to the trail that would hopefully lead them to their new lives in the Willamette Valley. They looked forward to a two-and-a-half-day trip to Three Island Crossing, where they would cross the Snake River. It was one of the few places where a crossing of the powerful river could be made, since the river carved its way through deep canyons for much of its length.

Weather was critical, however, for if the river was high, it was too dangerous to risk a crossing and the alternate route along the south bank would have to be taken to Fort Boise. That would mean a hot, dry and dusty drive of around one hundred and twenty miles of sandy terrain that was taxing on horses and emigrants alike. In contrast, by crossing over to the north side of the river, there was plentiful water and grass all the way to Fort Boise. It was Scofield's decision to make and he decided the river was low enough to warrant the risk of a crossing.

They arrived at the crossing early in the afternoon and Scofield signaled for the wagons to circle up for the night, rather than start the crossing at once. He wanted to have a full day to complete the crossing, knowing it a good possibility it would take that long. "Use this extra time this afternoon to get your wagons ready to cross in the mornin'," he told them. "Even low, like it is now, the river's pretty deep. But I don't expect any trouble till we cross from the last island to the north bank. That's where the water is deepest and the current is strongest. And I expect that's where your wagon is gonna float a little way before the wheels strike bottom again. It'd be a good idea to hang everything you'd like to keep dry from the top of your wagon."

So, with those brief instructions, the people did what they could to prepare for the crossing in the morning. As they had at the Raft River, Scofield and Clint rode out into the river in an effort to locate the gravel bars that ran the width of the river to establish the path of the crossing. They saved the final crossing from the third island to the north bank until last, and Scofield waited on the island while Clint tested the crossing. Biscuit maintained contact with the bottom until reaching the center of the channel. Then he had to swim, but only a couple of yards before striking bottom again. The current swept him sideways until he got his footing again. When he climbed up on the north bank, Clint wheeled him around and called back to his uncle, "It ain't gonna be easy."

"It never is, is it?" Scofield called back.

"I think I'll just stay here," Clint joked, "and the rest of you can come on over in the mornin'."

"I expect you're gonna get mighty hungry by the time Spud gets over there in the mornin'," Scofield returned.

"I expect you're right. Come on, Biscuit, let's go get dry."

Having decided the line the wagons would follow in the morning, they went back to the camp and the fire that Spud had built, to try to dry off a little and change into their spare trousers. Clint had taken his moccasins off beforehand and ridden across barefoot, so he dried his feet and slipped the moccasins back on. During the crossing the next day, he would be working too hard to go barefoot. But at least he would be comfortable this night.

For supper, Spud served the last of the smoked salmon. "This is it," he announced. "You're gonna have to go huntin' if you wanna eat anythin' besides bacon from now on."

"When we get across this river where there's good grass and water, there oughta be something to hunt," Clint told him. "And I'll gladly go hunt for it."

There was a good showing at the social hour that night with everyone either excited or frightened about the crossing in the morning. Bass Thornton seemed especially concerned about the possibility of wagons being swept downstream by the swift current in the river. "Why not take the dry route?" he asked Scofield. "If there's any chance at all you could lose a wagon, wouldn't it be wise to take the safer route?"

"Well, I reckon there's always a chance for some bad luck on any river crossin'," Scofield replied. "And, if there had been a lot more rain upriver this summer, there wouldn't be much choice. We'd have to take the dry route to Fort Boise. But believe me, when I say the dry route I'm talking about a hundred and twenty miles of sand, dust, and heat. But the river's down enough to let us across without more than a little bit of trouble. After we leave here, we'll be crossin' more rivers that can be a problem if you don't mind what you're doin'. Like I said, there's a chance for some bad luck at any river crossin.'"

Clint knew his uncle was thinking about this very crossing the previous year when they were attacked by a Ute war party. Just like the attack at the Green River this time, the Utes had waited until all but a couple of wagons had started across before striking those two. And for that reason, he would be with the last wagons to cross tomorrow, and Scofield had lined Tiny Futch up last. Tiny had proved to be willing to help protect the wagon train and the families trusting their lives to Clayton Scofield and Clint Buchanan.

"I heard stories that some of the wagon trains crossing here chained their wagons together," Thornton continued, "making one long chain of wagons, so that they all pulled together and no one could be lost."

"That's a fact," Scofield replied. "I think the trains you're talkin' about were teams of oxen, four to a wagon. And it sounds like a good idea to do that. Up to fifteen wagons at a time all chained together, is what I heard. But like all the rest of us here, you ain't got but two horses pullin' your wagon. And if you chain 'em together, whaddaya gonna attach the chains to? 'Course, we ain't got no chains, anyway. And if we had that much rope, I'm afraid we might get the horses tangled up in the rope. So the only way I know to cross this river is like I've always done it before, and up to now, I ain't ever lost a wagon here." He paused, then said, "Maybe that overloaded wagon of yours will be the first one."

"I beg to differ with you," Thornton replied. "I assure you my wagon was built to carry a substantial weight and is not over-loaded."

"I'll take your word for it," Scofield said, "'cause I don't wanna lose your wagon any more than you do, and we'll do what we can to get everybody's wagon across and on the way to Fort Boise tomorrow." He received a small patter of clapping for his intentions.

"I'm sure that you will," Thornton allowed and sat down.

Sitting beside him, Violet turned to glance to the side and was startled to find Wiley Jones looking at her. He smiled and nodded. She looked quickly away. *Yeah, but you turned to look at me,* he thought. He turned his head back toward the front and found Maggie staring at him. "You're wastin' your time, Romeo. That witch is goin' with the money. You're stuck with me."

"Whaddaya talkin' about, you crazy goose?" Wiley snarled.

"Talkin' about you makin' eyes at Bass Thornton's little honey. Bass Thornton's used to havin' trash like you to polish his boots. If she looked at you, it'd be because she was lookin' for a place to spit."

*Yeah, but she did turn around to look at me,* he thought. "How 'bout stickin' your tongue out, Maggie? I wanna see if it's forked," he spat back.

Tiny picked a few notes on his banjo then, and Henry Abbott took the cue and sawed out the next few notes of the familiar tune on his fiddle. Lucien Aiken struck the chords on his guitar and they were off and running. Several couples got up to dance. Wiley looked at Maggie, shrugged his shoulders, and asked, "You wanna dance?"

"Yeah," she answered, "but I don't see nobody here I wanna dance with."

# Chapter 21

At seven o'clock sharp the next morning, Spud drove Scofield's wagon into the first part of the crossing with Lily sitting on the driver's seat beside him. They followed Clint, on Biscuit, as he led them on the proper path across the gravel bars that had built up on the river bottom. Next in line, Will Tucker moved his wagon in position and entered the river to cross the wide expanse of water before reaching the first of the three islands. Then one after another, the rest of the wagons moved slowly forward in the long line. The second expanse of water was not nearly so wide as the first and proved to be no real problem with the water coming up no higher than the top of the wheels. The horses had solid footing and pulled the wagon up onto the second island with no trouble at all. From there to the third island offered a bit deeper water, but nothing that wasn't manageable, although the current did seem to be a little stronger.

Spud followed Clint across the third island, then waited while he rode Biscuit across the final part of the river. "Right there is where his horse started swimmin'," Spud said to Lily. "See how that current took him to the side before he got his feet on the bottom again? He didn't swim very long, so at least the horses and the wagon ain't gonna be floatin' at the same time." He gave Lily a wink. "We oughta make it all right. It's gonna be hard on the horses to swim and pull the wagon, but it ain't gonna be for long." He popped the reins on their rumps and drove them into the water. It was as he had told her: When the horses had to start swimming, the wagon slowed down almost to a stop but picked up again as the horses found footing again. And when the wagon got to the deepest part, it began to float and the swift current moved it to the side before the horses pulled it to solid ground, a drift of only a few feet. Then the horses pulled the wagon to the bank.

"Well, we got the most important folks across safely," Clint joked. "Now, I'll go back to the end of the line and see how they're doin'." He rode Biscuit back into the river and met Will and Melody approaching the deepest part. "They won't swim but a few yards," he called out to Will. "Your wagon might float a few feet downstream, but it oughta straighten right out."

"Right!" Will yelled back to him, and Melody waved.

Clint continued back across the three islands, passing the line of wagons and answering their questions about conditions ahead of them. When he got back to the south bank he found his uncle waiting for him. "Spud and Lily have any problems?" Scofield asked.

"Nope, no problems," Clint answered. "They're high and dry and waitin' for you. Did you tell Tiny why you put him last in line?"

"No," Scofield answered. "He didn't ask, didn't seem to care, so I didn't bother. He's been runnin' around here playin' hide-and-seek with Levi's young'uns. He's so dern big, he can't hide hisself too good, so they find him every time."

"I'll stay back here till everybody starts across," Clint said, "if you wanna ride on up the line to keep everybody movin'." He knew that's what Scofield usually did on a crossing. "Don't worry, if we get a visit from the Utes again this year, I'll tell 'em they have to wait till you get back here."

"I druther you just take care of it," Scofield replied as he climbed up into the saddle and turned Blackie toward the water.

He rode along beside Tracy Bishop, who was just entering the river.

"How's it goin', Clint?" Tiny greeted him when he walked back to his wagon. "Anybody havin' any trouble?"

"Not so far," Clint answered. "You all set to go?"

"Yep. I did everything I could think of to keep the water outta my wagon bed."

Clint nodded. "If there's a place to get in, the water will find it." He paused while he decided whether or not he should tell him about last year at this crossing. "You might wonder why you got last place at this river crossin', like you did at Green River."

"I hadn't thought about it, to tell you the truth," Tiny replied. "Why? Is there a reason?"

"Well, there wasn't any particular reason at the Green River crossin', but because of you and your rifle, Scofield, and me, too, wanted you at the tail end of this crossin'."

"Is that a fact?" Tiny responded, pleased but trying not to be obvious about it.

"That's right," Clint said. "You see, last year at this crossin', we got jumped by a Ute war party. And they did it just like those Cheyenne did at Green River." He went on to tell Tiny about the attack and how the Utes waited until all but a couple of wagons were left to cross. "Now, I sure hope to hell we ain't unlucky enough to have the same tribe of Indians attack the same wagon train again. But if they do, Uncle Clayton feels better havin' you back here with me, and I know I like the idea a helluva lot."

"Well, I'm mighty glad I can help out," Tiny responded, "although I am surprised a little bit. I woulda thought your uncle would druther have Vance Miller and Jim Rayford on the tail end of the train." They both had a chuckle over that thought.

The crossing continued with no major problems as wagon after wagon followed in the path designated by Clayton Scofield as the morning wore on. Finally, there was only one wagon left to begin the crossing. And when Tiny climbed up into the driver's seat of his wagon and snapped his reins, Clint breathed a sigh of relief. Common sense had told him the odds of a similar attack again this year were enormous against it. But he was convinced that crossing was just plain bad luck and he didn't rule it out. He went on ahead of Tiny to the first island, then continued on up the line until he found three wagons at a standstill on the third island. He rode up to the first of the three wagons to ask why he was stopped. It was Henry Abbott, and he didn't have to ask, for he saw the wagon ahead of Henry's in the deepest part of the channel, its rear end turned downstream by the current. There were several ropes on the wagon with half a dozen men on each rope, straining to deny the river the horses and wagon. "Who is it?" Clint asked Henry, for he could see no driver.

"Bass Thornton," Henry answered. "And it looks like they're about to lose it."

"Where's Leach?"

"I can't see him now," Henry said, "but when it looked like the horses couldn't hold the wagon against the current, he jumped in the river. Bass and Violet are still in the wagon."

Totally alerted now, Clint looked the situation over quickly, then he gave Biscuit his heels and the big Palouse went into the water and started across to the bank where Scofield and the gang of men were fighting to keep Thornton's horses from being pulled back into the deep water with the wagon. Clint saw right away that the river was winning, and he knew what had to be done. He jumped down and took his rope from the saddle. Scofield ran to him and Clint handed him one end of the rope. "Hang on to this!" he told him. "We've gotta work with the river, not against it! Get some of them to help you hold it!" He took the other end of the rope and dived into the water and let the current take him to the wagon. He then held on and inched around to the back of the wagon. "Thornton, you in there?" He yelled as he hurriedly tied the rope to the back of the wagon.

"Clint! Yes! We're in here. Can you save my wagon?"

"I'm gonna try," Clint answered. "You got any rope in there?"

"Yes, one coil," Thornton replied and frantically started throwing things out of his way to get to it. "Here it is!" He inched his way carefully toward the back of the wagon until he could reach out and hand it to Clint. Clint took it and quickly tied one end to the side of the wagon opposite the side he tied the first rope to. "You folks just hang on," he said and swam straight to the riverbank with the other end of the rope.

As soon as he hit the bank, he scrambled out of the water and ran back to Scofield and the men helping him hold the rope. "Some of you! Over here!" he yelled at a group of spectators. They willingly obeyed. Scofield could see that Clint had taken charge, and since he looked like he knew what he was doing, he gladly followed his orders. "What you're gonna do," Clint told the two groups on the ropes, "is make sure the tail of that wagon stays right where it is. That bunch holdin' on to the horses is gonna turn those horses downstream while you're keepin' the rear end of the wagon right there. That'll line the wagon up with the horses and then they can pull it downstream."

"Right, Clint," Scofield said. "Let's just do what he says."

Clint ran up the bank to the men holding the horses in the shallow water. "We've been tryin' to figure a way to hitch another team of horses to pull 'em out," Levi told him. "But so far we ain't been able to come up with a way to hitch 'em."

"We don't need another team," Clint said. "See those men over there with Scofield. They are gonna hold the back of that wagon right where it is, while all of you are gonna walk those ropes you're holdin' downstream without lettin' 'em get any slack in 'em."

"We're goin' in the river?" Levi asked.

"No, damn it," Clint replied impatiently. "But you have to keep those ropes tight, so those horses don't get pulled back in the deep water with the wagon. You're gonna walk on the bank, headin' downstream. And when you do that, you're gonna turn the horses downstream. With those fellows holding the back of the wagon right where it is, the wagon will straighten out and the horses can pull the wagon out, going downstream."

"I see what you're doin' now!" Levi said. Then to the rest of the men holding on to the ropes, he said, "We gotta make sure we don't get no slack in these ropes. We're gonna walk right down the riverbank till the horses and the wagon are headed downstream. Then we can help the horses pull on out."

"Right!" Clint exclaimed. "But when that wagon gets straightened out, don't try to pull the horses straight up the bank right away, or the damn wagon will double up again. Pull the horses out at a slant, and they oughta be able to pull the wagon out." He walked around in front of the men hanging onto the ropes. "Start walkin' those ropes now and follow me." He started walking along the riverbank, and when he saw that they understood what they were doing, he told them to keep walking in that direction, and he was going to the wagon to help turn the horses.

Back in the river again, Clint waded in water up to his chest to get to the two frightened horses. The first thing he did was try to calm them, then he would see what he could do to help turn the wagon. He was frankly amazed that the wagon had not rolled over with the current as strong as it was. He was startled moments later when what looked to be a boulder behind the front wheel suddenly straightened up and a head appeared above the water. "Howdy, Clint," he said after he took a big gulp of air.

"Leach!" Clint exclaimed, having forgotten all about his disappearance. "What were you doin' under the wagon?"

"Keepin' it here till you got here," Leach answered. "I knew you'd come."

Clint was amazed and wondered if maybe the simple brute might have had some influence on the wagon having not rolled over. "Well, Leach, you did a good job. We're gonna try to turn the wagon around and pull it out downstream." He quickly explained how they meant to do that. "I need to have you back up on the wagon, so you can drive the horses, once they get straightened out." Leach dutifully climbed up on the driver's seat and, picked up the reins. Clint was glad Leach was still there because he had figured that he was going to have to drive the horses. Now, he could remain in the water and work directly with them.

He continued to try to calm the horses while he waited for his team of men to walk far enough along the riverbank to pull the horses in that direction. Finally, the horses, helped by Clint, began to turn in the downstream direction. When they did, the front wheels of the wagon began to straighten the wagon until it lined up in the direction Levi and the other men were pulling in. Clint signaled Scofield to release the ropes holding the back end of the wagon. Then he yelled to Leach. "All right, Leach, drive 'em outta here! Hold 'em on that same line!" Leach understood, and with further help from the ropes, the weary horses pulled Thornton's wagon through the shallow water until gradually rolling out onto the bank.

Back up the bank a good way, Scofield stood in a group of cheering men, with a wide grin on his face. He then walked back to the edge of the bank and yelled, "Whaddaya waitin' for, Henry? Come on! We're wastin' time." Not anxious to follow the example of Thornton's crossing, Henry nevertheless did as instructed, for he knew he had no choice. So he committed his wagon to the Snake. Like all the wagons before Thornton's, and all wagons afterward, he made the crossing with little or no trouble at all.

As soon as Thornton's wagon pulled to a stop on dry land, he jumped down and hurried back to Clint, who was walking toward the wagon, coiling his rope as he walked. Bass extended his hand as he approached. "I hope you'll permit me to shake your hand, young man," he said. "I want to thank you for saving my wagon. That was a fine piece of work."

Clint shook his hand and said, "We're just doin' what our contract says, to do the best we can to get you to Oregon safely. I think you oughta thank your man Leach, too. I think he's the reason your wagon didn't get swept out into that channel before I got there."

"I will," Thornton said. "I'll tell him you said that." He paused then said, "Odd thing, before Leach jumped in the river, he said he had to hold the wagon until you got there. Of course, Leach is an odd man. He very seldom says anything at all. But I thought it unusual that he thought you would be the one to help us."

"I think he did a helluva job down under that wagon to keep it where it was," Clint said as he untied Thornton's rope from the other side of the wagon and started coiling it up for him. It occurred to him as strange that Thornton was so thankful for the saving of his wagon, but never said a word of appreciation for the safety of his wife. Clint looked back at the wagon to see Leach busy between his horses, untying the ropes that were thrown to him when he was stopped in the river. "When he gets through untyin' all the ropes, you can have him drive your wagon on up there with the others. It's so close to nooning time, I expect Scofield will just call for it right here."

Clint was accurate in his prediction, for Scofield called for the nooning as soon as Tiny Futch drove his wagon up onto the riverbank. It was another meal when Clint sat by the fire with half his clothes off, while trying to dry the other half. Scofield saw fit to announce to Lily and Spud that, thanks to his nephew, he was going to retire from the wagon train business never having lost a wagon at Three Island Crossing. "Helluva job, Clint," he said. "Wish I had something stronger than this coffee to salute you with."

"You're right, Scofield," Spud said. "And as a matter of fact, I still have a couple of drinks left in that bottle I bought at Lucky's back at Fort Hall." He went to the wagon to get it. When he came back, he said, "I believe I can get four drinks outta this bottle." He paused and looked at Lily. "I'm assumin' the lady wants to salute you, too."

"I do," Lily said with a chuckle. So they held their coffee cups out and Spud very carefully splashed a little bit in all four cups. Then he poured a tiny bit in each cup again and looked to judge how much was left in the bottle. He took the final pass and emptied the bottle.

"Here's to keepin' your record clean on the rest of the rivers ahead of us," Clint proposed, "especially the Deschutes."

"I'll drink to that," Scofield said and tossed the whiskey down.

After the noon meal there was a great deal of visiting to talk about the crossing just completed, and the major topic was naturally the near disaster with the Thorntons' wagon. When Bass and Violet joined the others, they were bombarded with questions about their ordeal. Bass was frank in confessing his fear that all was lost and eloquent in his praise of Clint Buchanan. Violet, as usual, had very little to say, other than the fact that she was terrified for the entire time. While Bass was describing exactly how they came to be snared by the current, Wiley Jones found Violet off to the side and managed to impart a short message to her. "I'm glad to see that you're all right, Violet. I was worryin' about you the whole time. I just wanted to let you know that." She looked at him, not knowing what to say, then she looked back down quickly when Bass turned toward her. But he was stopped again by someone else's question. And when Violet looked up again, Wiley was gone.

"What did you say to her?" Maggie demanded when Wiley came over to the other side of the fire.

"What did I say to who?" Wiley asked.

"You know who," Maggie insisted, "that skinny child bride of Bass Thornton's."

"I was tryin' to be polite to him because they near 'bout got sucked under in that dang river. But everybody kept talkin' to him, so I give up. And she was just settin' there, so I said we, both of us, we hoped she was all right. I was just tryin' to be polite."

"You tryin' to be polite," Maggie scoffed, "that'll be the day."

"You know, you oughta be thankin' your lucky stars you get to tell folks you're married to me. Ain't nobody handled that river crossin' better'n me. Your fanny was nice and dry when you got across. Next river, I'll let you drive the wagon."

"I gotta admit, you can drive the wagon," she allowed. "I reckon I don't give you enough credit for the things you're good at. If I can think of somethin' else you're good at, I'll give you credit for that, too. Right now, I can't think of a blame thing."

When the nooning time was over, the wagon train started up the Boise River Valley and they did not have to travel far before the travelers became aware of the reason for risking the difficult crossing just accomplished. The difference in the terrain they now traveled was as profound as when they crossed over Big Hill and descended into the Bear River Valley. For the next seven or eight days they would travel the north side of the Snake, where there were trees and grass and plenty of water.

For their first night's stop, Scofield had in mind a nice little creek about seven miles from Three Island Crossing, so Clint rode ahead to make sure it was all right. He found the spot pretty much the same as when he had last seen it, making allowances for a year's growth on the trees and the bushes. He rode down to the creek and let Biscuit drink. Always with an eye or an ear out for the presence of game, he lingered there for a while, listening to the quiet. But there was nothing to alert him, not even the rustling of a rabbit in the bushes. *Sorry, Spud*, he thought, *no fresh meat for supper*. He turned Biscuit away from the creek and rode back up on the grass, stepped down from the saddle, and dropped the reins on the ground. The Palouse gelding took it as a sign that he was going to be there for a while and started grazing on the healthy grass. Clint was in no hurry. Scofield and the wagons were coming along behind him, so he just felt like taking a few moments to enjoy the peaceful valley after the day he had just had with the river and Thornton's wagon. He had no doubt that the trouble had to have been caused by the extra heavy load

Thornton had in the wagon. He wondered if this today would be enough for Scofield to demand to know what Thornton was hauling. If not, he wondered if he shouldn't suggest it to his uncle. He picked up Biscuit's reins and started walking back toward the wagons. He just felt like walking. It was a beautiful valley, peaceful and wide. After about fifteen minutes, he came down out of his mood, stepped up into the saddle, and started back to meet Scofield and the wagons.

He caught sight of the wagons when he was about halfway back, so he pulled Biscuit up to a stop and waited. When Scofield saw him, he loped ahead of the column of wagons to hear his scout's report. "Just like it was last time we saw it," Clint told him.

"Good," Scofield said. "One of my favorite campsites. I reckon it's because we hit it first thing after leavin' the south side of the river. I always called it the wash house."

"I know," Clint interrupted, "'cause everybody seems to wanna take a bath after we cross the Snake, and wash off the dust and grime from the south side." Scofield said the same thing every year when they reached this creek. "I ain't so sure I need the creek this time," Clint went on. "I had a pretty good soakin' in the river this year."

Scofield laughed. "Yeah, I reckon you did. Well, maybe the women will wanna take advantage of the wash house. They usually do."

When the wagons caught up to them, they continued on to the campsite and Scofield had them form the circle as usual. Although the valley looked so friendly and peaceful, there was still the need to take precautions. Over a hundred miles up the valley where the original Fort Boise was, is where they would cross the Snake again. It was a fur trading post operated by the Hudson's Bay Company, but it was no longer there. Some years back, however, due to Indian attacks upon settlers and gold miners, the army built the new Fort Boise about fifty miles east of the old fort. So, Scofield and Clint were always aware of the potential for trouble.

After the camp was set and the animals were taken care of, Scofield told everyone about the clear, clean water in the creek and the privacy provided by the heavily wooded banks. "The way we did it in years past was the ladies used the creek down to the sharp bend, and the men went past that and on around the bend. The bushes are thick right down to the water, so the men can't see anybody down in the water when they're walkin' downstream to their piece of the creek. The bushes down around that bend ain't quite as thick as the ones where the ladies bathed, but nobody wants to look at the men, anyway." He received a mixed chorus of cheers and jeers in response to his announcement. "That's just a suggestion that worked pretty well for the trains before you. You do what you want. It's gonna be gettin' pretty dark back under those trees pretty soon now, anyway. So some of you shy ladies won't have to worry about anybody seein' anything they ain't supposed to."

Those interested in bathing or just washing some clothes, male and female, took a walk down the creek to get a look at the areas Scofield talked about. Much to Wiley Jones's delight, Violet Thornton was one of the ladies who started down the path. Bass didn't bother, and neither did Maggie. So it was a perfect opportunity to see if the shy young girl was as taken with his attention as he thought. He followed close behind the group of women Violet was walking with, and when they came to the thick clump of bushes that Scofield said was the end of the ladies' section, he stepped up close behind her back. "Down on the other side of these bushes is the perfect place for you to wash up," he whispered, causing her to jump, startled. She turned to look at him as he smiled at her and walked on toward the bend in the creek. *She'll know what to do*, he thought.

# Chapter 22

Many of the ladies and girls were excited about a chance to clean off some of the soil and sweat they carried all the way from Fort Hall. For that reason, supper was pushed ahead a little in those wagons. Wiley took the plate Maggie handed him and sat down on a wooden box he used for a chair beside his wagon where he could watch the other wagons, especially Thornton's. "Uh-oh," he suddenly muttered when Violet Thornton stepped down from their wagon carrying a couple of towels, then proceeded to go between the wagons and walk briskly toward the creek. He stuffed the last of the fried cornbread in his mouth and forced it down with the rest of his coffee. *Can't keep the little darlin' waitin'*, he thought. *She might get scared and run back to the wagon.* He took his plate back to the fire and dropped it in a bucket of water Maggie put there for the dirty dishes.

"You want some more of this cornbread?" Maggie asked.

"Uh-uh," he answered and dropped his cup in the bucket as well.

"You don't want no more coffee?" Maggie asked, surprised. "What's wrong with you?" When he ignored her questions and grabbed his hat, she demanded, "Where are you goin'?"

"Damn it, woman, I got to go to the bushes right now," he said, "unless you want me to drop my drawers and squat right here by the wagon."

"Go on and git," she barked, then she couldn't resist adding, "and be careful, that's where your brains are—what little bit you got."

He wasted no time beating a path down beside the creek. The sound of one or two feminine voices giggling on the other side of the thick bushes was enough to set his mind racing as he tried to visualize the tender young maiden awaiting his pleasure. At last, he reached the last big clump of bushes before the bend. *There won't be no doubt about it now if she's hidin' in them bushes*, he thought. *I'm tempted to tell Maggie about it. Then hear what she's got to say.* He paused there for a few seconds to look both ways on the path to make sure no one saw him go through the bushes. It was already getting dark under the trees, but there was plenty of light to see what he was looking for. "Anybody in here?" he called out softly. There was no answer, but he heard something moving straight ahead of him. "I hear you movin' in there, sweet thing. Ain't no use to be shy. I just come to visit. Just you and me. Ain't nobody else's business." The motion in the bushes stopped. Grinning now, he reached out and pulled one large branch aside to gaze into the emotionless face of Roy Leach.

Wiley was paralyzed with fear, his arms and legs unable to function as he gazed directly into the cold eyes of the ape-like creature, while his internal organs proceeded to operate, making his excuse to Maggie no longer a lie. He wanted to run but could not command his legs to do so. No one would ever know the extent of Wiley's beating but Leach and Wiley himself, up to the point when Leach's fist smashed Wiley's face in and put his lights out. But that was after he was mauled and thrown around like a great ape slams a jungle cat.

Wiley didn't return to his wagon, even after Maggie took the supper dishes down to the creek to wash them and get water in the pot for coffee in the morning. It didn't worry her, but it did irritate her because she was suspicious of his interest in Violet Thornton. But Violet was at the social hour that night with her husband, so Maggie figured he'd show up sometime, and she couldn't wait to hear his excuse. She wasn't jealous over his constant ogling of Bass Thornton's young wife. She was just irritated by it. She only claimed to be married to Wiley to get a ride out to the Oregon country, anyway. When it was time for bed, and he still hadn't returned, she could have told Scofield or Clint that Wiley was missing. But she decided to just go to bed, and if he didn't show up by seven o'clock, she'd drive the wagon herself, and wish him the best of luck. That was not to be, however, for the camp was alerted by the scream of Pearl, Henry Abbott's wife, when she filled her coffeepot the next morning at around four forty-five. Spud commented later that day that it was the first pure note he ever heard Pearl hit. It was strong enough to summon several of the men to find what was left of Wiley Jones.

He was alive, so they carried him to his wagon, where Maggie was unable to do anything but stare in horror at the crushed face until Ada Bishop and Ella Watkins helped her clean him up a little. A couple of the men reluctantly volunteered to remove his trousers and clean him up down there. One of them commented to Scofield later that it looked like he had literally had the crap knocked out of him. Wiley himself was of no help when asked what happened. He didn't remember much about the night just passed, only that he was attacked by some monster. "Looks like maybe a bear," someone suggested. Wiley wasn't sure, but he said that may have been what attacked him. All he was sure of was that he felt like every bone in his body was broken. They made him as comfortable as they could in the back of his wagon, and when Scofield told Maggie he'd see about getting someone to drive it, she told him she'd drive it herself.

It won't be the first time I drove a wagon," she assured him. "And we'll be ready to roll at seven o'clock."

Clint went down to scout the spot by the creek where Wiley was found. He reported back to Scofield that there was plenty of evidence of a whirlwind in those bushes near the water. But there were no bear tracks, no wolf tracks, no deer or elk. The only footprints were boot prints. He left it at that and let his uncle come to his own conclusions. As far as he was concerned, he could only attribute the attack to one man, only one man he knew who might be capable of such a violent attack. But that was just his guess. The sign told him what happened, but could not tell him why it happened, nor who the perpetrator was. Only Wiley could say for sure, and at the moment he appeared unable or unwilling.

"What do you think happened?" Scofield finally asked Clint.

"I'd rather not say," Clint answered. He shrugged. "I can't prove it, anyway."

"You know damn well there ain't but one man on this wagon train coulda throwed him around like that," Scofield said. Clint shrugged again. He knew his uncle was struggling with the decision to charge Leach with the assault on Wiley Jones, or simply let it go. Scofield, like Clint, did not believe Leach would attack unless in reaction to some harm done to him. What made it more difficult, however, was the fact that it was hard to believe that even Wiley was dumb enough to accost Leach. Finally, Scofield decided to talk to Maggie again before deciding to take any action against Leach.

A little before seven, Scofield went back to Wiley's wagon to see if Maggie was all set to drive when he gave the signal. She was, she said, and when he asked about Wiley, she said he was resting as best he could in the back of the wagon. "Has he told you anything more about what happened to him?" Scofield asked.

"No," Maggie answered. "Either he can't remember, or he don't wanna say." She had her own theory about what happened to him down at the very end of the ladies' bathing area. She wondered why nobody ever questioned what he was doing in that part of the creek in the first place. "Look here, Mr. Scofield," she finally told him. "I know you probably feel like you need to punish somebody for bustin' Wiley up like that. But if you're worried about me gettin' all upset about it, just forget it. I already have. I think he most likely knows what he ran into, but he don't wanna

talk about it. Who knows? Maybe it'll teach him a lesson. Whaddaya say we forget about it and let's go to Oregon."

"Whatever you say," Scofield replied, glad to leave the matter
there at the creek. He climbed up on Blackie and rode back to
the head of the wagon train where Spud was waiting to start his
horses. A couple of painful cries from the tormented bugle and
the wagons started up the Boise River Valley.

For the next week and a half, they traveled up the valley to
reach old Fort Boise and what would be the final crossing of the
Snake River. On several days of that part of their journey, Clint
spotted Indian scouts watching the passing of the wagon train.
They made no attempt to approach the wagons, but Clint figured
it would be no surprise to the Indians at old Fort Boise and the
river crossing when they finally arrived. That last crossing was
typically a regular crossing for the wagons. But since the Snake
was a river of many moods, sometimes it was not of a disposition
to receive the wagons. The local Indians counted on this and
were ready to ferry the wagons across on bullboats made especially for the purpose, for a reasonable fee.

On the day of their arrival, the weather was still very friendly,
so the river was fordable and about half of the wagons decided to
pay the fee to have their wagons ferried across on the bullboats.
It was a surprise to no one that Bass Thornton was the first to decide in favor of the bullboats, and Maggie Jones was a close second. They influenced more of the others, even though their
horses would have to swim across with the rest of the livestock.
As usual, Spud led the wagons into the river after Clint and Biscuit determined the best path. Then Clint returned to make sure
none of the livestock were left behind.

After leaving the last Snake crossing, they traveled another
day and a half before reaching another river to cross. This one,
the Malheur River, was not a difficult crossing, however, and
Maggie Jones handled it as easily as any of the drivers. Her passenger complained of every bump that jolted his broken bones,
however. His facial profile, once displaying a prominent slender

nose, was now of a flat nature, so as to not be recognizable by those who knew him before. He still claimed to have no memory of the cause of his injuries, saying at one point that he thought maybe his horse had thrown him and he landed face-first against the trunk of a large tree. That seemed a possibility until Maggie told him that he wasn't riding a horse.

They struck the Burnt River a day and a half after leaving the Malheur at a place on the trail called Farewell Bend, so named because it was the last they would see of the Snake River. The mighty river turned away from the Oregon Trail and headed north, leaving the emigrants to follow the Burnt River up the Burnt River Canyon. Even though Scofield had prepared them beforehand, they were not prepared for their first look at the canyon. All the high bunch grass had been burned up, leaving smoking ash that covered the ground and the trees. Climbing the worst roads they had encountered thus far, they found passes barely wide enough to negotiate. In some places, the road was cut into the side of a mountain and several of the men would hang on one side of a wagon to keep it from turning over until reaching a more level stretch. Not only was the canyon a strain on the horses, it also provided a dead, eerie sense for the emigrants. For the whole canyon was burnt, the ground black, the air still smokey, and it was like nothing was living in the canyon. Scofield said he believed the local Indians, the Snakes, set fire to the high bunch grass that covered the canyon because everywhere the grass was burned, new green grass came up. "There's other tales, too," he said. "Some people think they burn all the grass to discourage folks like us from drivin' through their country."

"I believe that story," Levi said. "They didn't leave any grass anywhere."

Morale soon dropped to a low point, for every day was an ordeal to be endured until nighttime. And then nighttime found them with no decent place to camp as they continued to climb up the canyon. At least they had the Burnt River for water. Then, after four hard days, the river turned sharply away from the trail,

leaving them with four more days of burnt earth and searching
for streams and creeks. Scofield and Clint tried to keep the spirits up by telling them they were almost to Flagstaff Hill and that
would be the end of the burnt earth. And then one day they left
the canyon and drove around Flagstaff Hill. They stopped there
briefly while some climbed up Flagstaff Hill to look out over the
Powder River valley and to get their first glimpse of the Blue
Mountains in the distance.

With spirits renewed upon seeing the distant mountains, they
descended the hill into a valley with grass and water to end the
day's travel. The days that followed led them into the mountain-
ous terrain of the Blue Mountains, but there was grass and water
and wood for their fires as they left the valley and started a long,
hard, and oftentimes dangerous climb up toward Emigrant Hill.
Upon reaching Emigrant Springs, Scofield called for an early
camp. It would be the last good camping ground until they descended Emigrant Hill. And they could take advantage of the opportunity to replace or refresh all their water supply from the
nearby springs before moving on up the winding trail called Dead-
man Pass. The pass was named that because a teamster driving a
wagon up the pass was attacked and killed by Bannock Indians.
It was remembered by Scofield and Clint because of an attempted ambush by Nez Perce Indians the year before. Consequently, Clint scouted the trail the next morning before the
wagons moved on. The low clouds that hovered over the mountains had released a light drizzle during the night that left the
rocky trail slippery in places, which made the climb more difficult. After gaining the top of the hill, the long, winding trail down
to the Umatilla valley was even more treacherous than the climb
up. As Scofield liked to phrase it, "Like a damn snake waitin' for
a chance to bite you."

To everyone's surprise and admiration, Maggie Jones drove
her wagon down the treacherous hill like an experienced teamster. The ride down was as nerve-racking as Scofield predicted
and was incentive enough to inspire Wiley to get out of the

wagon and walk down the second half of the descent. Up to that point, no one thought he had recovered enough to walk. When asked about his attack, he still claimed to remember nothing about it. Noticeable, however, was the definite change in the once brash young man's personality to one of quiet withdrawal. Most agreed that it was an improvement.

In the days that followed, they crossed the Umatilla and the John Day River. They were both easy river crossings, but they were the only water of any quantity the travelers saw as they crossed the Columbia Plateau. For it was a dry and dusty journey of over a hundred miles with only a single tree here and there before they got their first sight of the Columbia River. As in years before, Clint and his uncle witnessed the sheer disappointment in the faces of the travelers as they gazed down at the Columbia from the high tableland of the plateau. Weary and parched from the journey across the dead-looking plateau, the sight of the river was far from what they had pictured. Spirits improved a little, however, when Spud led the wagons down to the river and set up the camp beside it.

That night, there was a renewed interest in the social hour, which Scofield was glad to see. "I was beginning to think you folks weren't gonna make it to Oregon City," he told a group of the folks. "You've already got through the worst part. But it's gonna be more like you pictured it from now on. In the mornin', we'll drive along beside the river for about five miles before we strike the Deschutes River. Now, I'll be honest with you . . ."

"Well, it's about time," Levi interrupted, drawing a laugh, including one from Scofield.

"The Deschutes can be a rough crossin'," Scofield continued, "especially in bad weather. But we're lucky this year 'cause we got good weather. It's still a tricky crossin' 'cause it's right where the river joins the Columbia. It's about a hundred and fifty yards wide and the bottom has a lot of big rocks that get moved around 'cause the current's strong, especially when they've had bad weather. Now, there wasn't nothin' in your guide about payin' a fee to get ferried across, but you can pay the Indians about ten dollars to ferry your wagon if you want to. But I'll be fordin' the river with my wagon because there's some of the Indians that'll help you across for two dollars. I always use an Indian named Jim Two Hook and I give him the two dollars plus a good horse. And he leads the wagons on a path across the river where we won't hit any rocks and the bottom is solid. Like I said, you can pay the Indians to take you across, but we'll ford it just like we did the Snake at Fort Boise." He chuckled then and added, "Give you something to think about."

"I don't have to think about it," Maggie Jones piped up. "I'm gonna follow you."

"I swear," Levi said, "that sounded like a challenge to all us men, didn't it?"

"Well, it ain't one to Bass Thornton," Maggie answered him. "I think he oughta pay to have his wagon took across."

"What does your husband say about it?" Ada Bishop asked.

"I don't know," Maggie answered. "He ain't here right now. But he ain't had a lot to say about anything for a while now."

"Ain't he any better, Maggie?" Ella Watkins asked. "I saw him out of the wagon, walkin' down Emigrant Hill. But I ain't seen him walking ever since."

"He looks to me like he's all right," Maggie said, "but he says he ain't. So, I don't know. He's eatin' all right, when I've got somethin' to cook."

"Somethin' sure as sand hit him mighty hard to have knocked his brain loose like that," Vance Miller said. "There ain't no tellin' what lives in those trees back down that creek we was camped beside." Scofield glanced at Clint and caught him glancing back at him.

The next morning after breakfast, Clint rode out of camp, leading a bay gelding. He went on up the Columbia to Celilo Falls and the Indian village there and rode into the center of the village to a shack with a small corral behind it. There was a paint

horse in the corral with another older-looking sorrel. Clint recognized the paint. He stepped down as Jim Two Hook came out to
meet him. "Buchanan," Jim greeted him and came to shake his
hand, his eyes on the bay horse Clint was leading.

"Howdy, Jim," Clint said. He nodded toward the paint in the
corral. "I see you didn't sell the paint."

"No sell," Jim replied. "Good horse. I keep. Scofield with you?"

"Yep, he'll be at the river in just a little while. He sent you this
horse as a gift and asks if you will guide us across the river."

"I guide," Jim said. "I put new horse in corral, then I go with
you." Clint led the bay into the corral and left the bridle on it.
Jim smiled and nodded his appreciation. Then he threw his saddle on the paint and they rode off to meet the wagons.

When the wagons arrived at the river, Scofield found both
Clint and Jim Two Hook on horseback on the small island in the
middle of the river. Upon seeing the wagons approaching, they
entered the water again and returned to the east bank of the river
to meet them. Scofield dismounted and shook hands with Jim
Two Hook. The Indian thanked him for the gift of the bay horse,
then told him what a good horse the paint was that he was now
riding. "You lucky this time," Jim told him. "River not angry this
time. You have no trouble. I lead you across."

"I knew that you would," Scofield said. "You are a good friend."

They wasted no time after that. Since the river was not angry,
as Jim said, Scofield committed Spud and his wagon right away.
Jim had already selected the proper crossing route to avoid the
many rocks on the river bottom. So the rest of the wagons lined
up to follow Spud into the rapidly flowing river. Meanwhile,
Clint made arrangements with two of the other Indians gathered
around the wagon train to assist in moving the livestock across.
One wagon was floated across on the ferry, to no one's surprise,
since Bass Thornton no longer wanted to risk his wagon. Leach
swam across with his team of horses. The rest of the morning was
taken up with the crossing, but there was still the task of climbing up on the high bluff on the western side of the river. It was a

tremendous strain on the horses, immediately following a long, swift river crossing. Scofield gave Jim his thanks along with two dollars for guiding them safely across while Clint paid the two Indians the same amount for helping with the animals. Then they turned their attention to climbing up the bluff.

There was a good spot on top of the bluff for the nooning and Scofield started Spud up the steep slope right away. Judging by the difficulty Spud had with his wagon, Scofield had a double team hooked up to Thornton's wagon when it was Leach's turn to start up the incline. It turned out to be a wise decision, for the four horses struggled to gain the top of the bluff, once again igniting a discussion on what he might possibly be hauling in that wagon. "Whatever it is, he sure figures it ain't nobody else's business," Tracy Bishop commented.

"That's his right," Ada told him. "Why do you care what he's carrying across the country, anyway? Nobody's asked us what we're carrying in our wagon."

"That's because all the rest of us are toting the same things, beddin', cookin' stuff, some furniture and supplies. But it looks like Thornton is carryin' a load of rocks or something heavy enough to damn near sink his wagon at every river crossin'. I thought for sure we'd lost him and Violet at that Three Island Crossin'."

"And Leach, too," Pearl Abbott remarked. "He disappeared for so long Henry and I thought he was dead."

"You don't have to worry about Leach," Levi told her. "He ain't gonna drown. He's got gills. If that wagon had got away, he'da most likely just swum on up the river to mate with a female ape."

"Shut your mouth, Levi! Here they come!" Ella scolded when Bass and Violet joined the group.

"Yep, here we come," Bass said, having overheard Ella's remark. "Are we the topic of discussion today?"

Not one to play coy, Maggie Jones answered him. "Everybody's wonderin' what you're carryin' in that wagon that weighs so much," she said. Ella Watkins cringed, but she was eager to hear Bass's answer as much as the others.

"Why do you want to know what we're carrying in our wagon?" Bass responded. When no one answered that question, he asked another one. This one he aimed at Maggie, since she had been so outspoken. "What are you carrying in your wagon?"

Not at all intimidated, Maggie answered without hesitation. "Just whatever provisions we need to get by on, plus a few sticks of furniture." She grinned and added, "And right now, one empty-headed passenger who ain't quite sure where he's going or where he's been." The women tried not to laugh, but the men gave her a chuckle.

Bass smiled politely at her. "Well, there's not a whole lot of difference in my wagon and yours, then, but one. My wagon empty is a lot heavier than your wagon empty, and that was because I had it built that way to better survive this two-thousand-mile trip we all decided to take. I guess I should have thought more about occasions when I had to use it as a boat. But as far as what we have in the wagon, not a lot different than most of you, I suppose. We have some family heirlooms from my family as well as some from Violet's family, plus we are carrying all of her brother's belongings—nothing, I'm afraid, would interest any of you."

Everyone was quiet after he finished. Someone had finally asked Bass the question that had them all guessing, but he answered telling them no more than they knew before. Feeling the silence awkward and in an effort to make polite conversation, Henry Abbott broke the silence. "You said you were carrying all of your wife's brother's belongings. Where is he? Is he waitin' for you out in the Willamette Valley?"

Bass looked at Violet and chuckled before he answered Henry. "That would be some kind of a miracle," he said. "The last time I saw him, he was over by the wagon."

His statement brought another hush over the group, this one caused by confusion as everyone replayed his answer in their minds. Levi was the first to ask. "You mean Leach? Are you sayin' Leach is Violet's brother?"

"I assumed that you all knew that by now," Bass answered.

"Wait a minute," Levi said. "When you joined the wagon train on the last day in Independence, I remember askin' you who Leach was, and you said he was just some fellow who wanted to go to Oregon but had no wagon. So you hired him to drive your wagon."

Bass chuckled again. "That's right, I did, didn't I? That was Roy's idea. He thought he would like it better if you folks thought he was just a hired hand. That way, he wouldn't be expected to take part in things like the social hour or do visiting of any kind. People easily get the wrong impression of Roy. They think he's a little slow when it comes to the mind. But Roy's not slow. He's just different. He prefers to keep his own company. Roy and Violet are all the family they've got. Their parents were both killed in a hotel fire when Violet was just a small child and Roy's been taking care of her and protecting her ever since. So you can understand why Violet and I weren't going to go to Oregon and leave Roy behind."

# Chapter 23

Later that afternoon, when Levi told Scofield and Clint about the story behind Bass Thornton's association with Leach, it was as surprising to them both as it had been to those present at the time. Overhearing, Lily commented, "Well, I'll be . . ." she started. "So her maiden name was Violet Leach. Who woulda thought that? There sure isn't any resemblance to her brother. She can thank her lucky stars for that bit of fate."

"It don't seem fair, though," Spud remarked. "You have two young'uns and give one of 'em all the pretty, then give the other'n all the ugly."

There were many conversations similar to the one at Scofield's wagon as the train moved away from the Deschutes River, heading for The Dalles. There was some concern, mostly from the women, that Violet might have overheard the many references to Leach as an ape or a monster with gills who could live underwater. But for Maggie Jones, the true identity of the brute, Leach, was a case of two plus two adding up to a solid four. This seemed especially relevant when she had heard Thornton say that Leach had protected Violet since she was a small child. "And he's no doubt still protectin' her now," Maggie said to herself as she drove her wagon toward The Dalles. She turned her head to look back inside the wagon at Wiley, lying in his blanket. And she had to wonder, does he really not remember what happened to him? Or does he know that he was the target of Leach's wrath for stalking his sister? It sure made for a believable explanation for Wiley's terrifying experience. There never was an answer for what Wiley was doing in that little clump of trees at the end of the ladies' bathing area. If he was cramping up and had to relieve himself, as he claimed, there were a great many closer places to do so, rather than go all the way down there where he was found.

She was well aware of Wiley's fascination for the young girl who was Bass Thornton's wife. Wiley was not very clever in hiding it. There was no question of jealousy on her part, for she herself cared not a fig for Wiley. Her relationship with him was from the beginning a business deal, a partnership to enable both of them to afford to travel out to Oregon. They claimed to be married because that was what Scofield's contract specified. She and Wiley had agreed to go their separate ways as soon as they reached Oregon City. So she was not jealous of his lust for Violet Thornton. She was disgusted with Wiley Jones for his stupidity and conceit.

"I'm gonna find out just how sick you really are," she vowed to herself. She had an idea that Wiley knew exactly what he ran into that night at the creek. "If I have to beat it outta you with a broom handle, I'm gonna find out how much you know." She slapped her horses with the reins. "Or my name ain't Maggie Mayfield."

Bouncing along in the back of the wagon, Wiley tried to sleep, but found it impossible. "Crazy cow," he muttered to himself. He could hear her talking to herself about something but could not understand a word of it. He wanted to get out and walk, but he didn't want her to know he was physically recovered from the beating he suffered at the hands of that half man, half ape. She would likely expect him to drive the wagon and do all the work that she was now doing. He didn't want anybody to know he remembered any part of that night. Then one night before they reached Oregon City he would find the opportunity to put a bullet into the ape's brain.

* * *

They reached The Dalles at nooning time the next day. It was a surprise to the emigrants for they didn't expect to see a couple of stores, a hotel of sorts, a blacksmith, and several other small shops. There were even a few small houses built near the little settlement, with cultivated fields. They circled the wagons as usual so they could corral the livestock, but Scofield planned to move on as soon as the horses were rested. They would have time to refresh water supplies and pick up any provisions they needed for the last part of their journey, which would take them around Mount Hood. Scofield had told them that when they reached The Dalles, they would have completed what is officially thought to be the entire Oregon Trail. The Dalles was considered the end point because at this point, the original settlers were faced with Mount Hood and the Cascade Range, which were insurmountable objects for wagons. There was no room for wagon trails within the deep gorges and canyons where the Columbia River flowed. To go forward in the early days of the wagon trains, the emigrants had to pay barge operators to float their wagons down the Columbia. Then they walked the path along the bank or drove their livestock over Lolo Pass, a narrow mountain pass ten miles northwest of Mount Hood. The fees were exorbitant and the risks were enormous when barges were caught in a whirlpool or strong current. But the Barlow Road offered a safer and cheaper choice of routes to Oregon City.

The route was not without its hazards, however, for the climb up to Barlow Pass was a steep and dangerous segment with no way down into the valley except an almost impossible descent down Laurel Hill. The name Laurel Hill held a special meaning for both Clint and his uncle. It was there that they left a good friend behind the previous year, buried in a little graveyard plot at the bottom of the hill. Cal Nixon was a victim of his own wagon, crushed when a line lowering the wagon broke. Bad weather had been a contributing factor to that particular tragedy. Scofield and Clint were hoping that the good weather they had been blessed with for the past couple of weeks would continue, at least until they got past Laurel Hill.

After the nooning, they set out on the one hundred and twenty mile Barlow Road, heading south toward the Tygh Valley, enjoying seven miles of trouble-free driving before going into camp for the night. With water and wood abundant, spirits were high as the travelers sat around the community fire and socialized that evening. "It'd be nice if the road all the way to Oregon City was as nice as it was today," Ada commented.

"According to what Scofield told me," her husband said, "it'll be pretty much the same for the next day and a half, and then we'll start climbin'. That's when the hard part starts. And that's the real Barlow Road, Scofield said, eighty miles right up the foothills and up to the pass they named after this Barlow. Scofield said climbing up in the pass is gonna be slow goin' and some places we might have to use a double team of horses to make the climb. But goin' back down is gonna be the hard part."

"You sure know how to ruin my good mood," Ada remarked, "just when I was thinkin' how much I enjoyed the walking today."

"Speakin' of needin' to double-team the horses," Tracy said, "here comes somebody who's gonna most likely need some extra help."

Ada turned her head to see Bass and Violet approaching the fire. "You'da thought they woulda brought Violet's brother along with 'em tonight," she said facetiously. "I declare, I shoulda spotted the family resemblance."

"Meowww," Tracy drew out, and she struck him on the shoulder with her fist.

"Everybody looks comfortable out here tonight," Bass Thornton offered in greeting as he situated a small bench for Violet and him to sit on.

"Welcome to the Barlow Road social club," Tracy responded. "We'll have the band strike up your favorite tune, if they ever get started."

"You should bring your brother with you sometime, Violet," Ada suggested. "I feel like we haven't been very neighborly to him."

There was a definite pause in the general conversation immediately following her suggestion, with Violet clearly not sure how to respond. So Bass responded for her. "Oh, that would take some doing. Wouldn't it, honey? Roy's awfully shy about meeting people." Violet smiled, embarrassed, and nodded her head rapidly.

"It don't surprise me that he might be shy about meetin' this crowd of people," Tracy said, in an effort to defuse the awkward moment Ada's comment had caused. "It takes me a little while to work up the nerve to come out here every night, myself."

"I know what you mean," Bass said and chuckled in appreciation for Tracy's efforts. He was not anxious to get into another discussion about Leach, a topic that was difficult to explain.

There was another discussion just beginning in one of the wagons that involved Leach, this one with a somewhat ulterior motive. "How are you feeling tonight, Wiley?" Maggie asked as she put the supper dishes away. "I noticed there ain't nothin' wrong with your appetite."

On the defensive at once, Wiley gave her a painful frown and declared, "I'm 'bout the same, I reckon. Still ain't got a nickel's worth of strength yet. I was fixin' to tell you how much I 'preciate you doin' for me since I ain't been able to do for myself."

"No trouble a-tall," Maggie replied. "I'm kinda glad to find out I don't need nobody to help me. I hope you'll be able to get your strength back pretty soon 'cause we ain't that far from the end of this ride, and you'll be on your own. You say you ain't got your strength back yet. How 'bout your memory? You remember what happened to you that night?" He shook his head slowly and frowned as if he was trying to remember. She studied his expression for a few moments, then said, "Do you know that Leach is Violet Thornton's brother?" She let that sink in while she watched his reaction. His face went blank, so she figured he had not heard yet. "Bass Thornton told us that," she continued. "He said Leach has been lookin' after Violet ever since she was a little girl, protectin' her from anybody givin' her any trouble." Wiley didn't say anything, but she could tell that every word was sinking in despite his attempt to maintain a blank expression. So she decided to try to push him all the way out with it.

"That's what happened back at that creek that night," she went on. "Big brother Leach, protectin' his helpless little sister when some evil-minded saddle trash came sniffin' around her." She watched his eyebrows knot up in anger as she went on, so she asked straight out, "How did it feel when that damn ape smashed your nose flat? I bet it hurt like hell."

He was too angry to answer her, but she could tell that she had pushed all the right buttons. In fact, he couldn't really tell her how bad it hurt when Leach struck him, for it knocked him unconscious. He only remembered how badly it hurt when he woke up later that night, lying in the bushes by the creek, when he hurt all over his body, so much that he couldn't move. No, he didn't remember the impact of the blow that knocked him out. But he remembered the terror he felt moments before the knockout when he pulled a branch aside and looked into the deadly face of a monster looking back at him. And that was the memory he could not rid his mind of. Of course he had thoughts of vengeance and he hoped to have a chance to take that vengeance with a shot to the back of Leach's head. In the meantime, he was clinging to the claim that he didn't know what had happened to him, and he didn't want to admit that it was because of his fear of Leach. He reasoned that Leach must have thought he was dead when he left him, and the only thing that was stopping Leach from coming to finish the job was his story that he couldn't remember what had happened to him. And now this with Maggie. Her mouth might cost him his life. Maybe Maggie should have an accident.

She might have read his mind, for she said, "Be careful what you're thinkin'. I'm a light sleeper and I sleep with my pistol in my hand."

"You talk like a crazy woman," he finally said. "Whaddaya say things like that to me for? I thought we was partners."

"Right," she replied sarcastically. "You plannin' on doin' something about Roy Leach, partner?"

"Nothin'," he said. "I still don't remember what happened, I was blindsided. I can't go on what you're guessin' happened."

She looked at him for a long moment, then just shook her head. "I'm goin' to the social hour," she finally said, turned and left him standing there.

He watched her walk away and mumbled to himself, "Right, enjoy yourself, partner, because I expect you're gonna have an accident before we get to the other end of this road." Their partnership agreement called for a fifty-fifty split of everything when they reached Oregon City. He gets one horse. She gets one horse. They sell the wagon and split the proceeds. But now, he realized he's going to need every penny he can get his hands on. To begin with, he thought they might work it out together, but they soon found they didn't like each other that much. "And I sure as hell don't need her lip," he mumbled. From the description Scofield gave them of the road through Barlow Pass, there should be plenty of opportunities for an accident for a young woman who gets careless. As far as Leach was concerned, his death was going to have to be a death of opportunity. If an opportunity occurred, he wouldn't hesitate to take it.

In the morning, they continued south to the Tygh Valley, where the road took a more southwest heading, crossing the Tygh and two other creeks before fording the White River. Starting the climb northwest along Barlow Creek, they had not gone far before having to hook up an extra team of horses to Bass Thornton's wagon. Since his was the only wagon that had to have the extra horses, they left them hitched to his wagon until the descent of Laurel Hill later on. The road led around the south side of a large butte to a place called Summit Meadow, where they stopped to rest the horses. The meadow was a swampy area that served as a watershed for Still Creek. After the horses were rested, they drove on, passing an area where they were amazed to see forty-five abandoned wagons. Scofield explained that back in 1849 a small regiment of soldiers were taking the road from The Dalles to Oregon City. They had rough weather and rougher luck on their journey, ended up losing two-thirds of their horses and having to leave forty-five wagons behind. He said the emigrants had given the place the name of Government Camp. The wagon train arrived at Laurel Hill a little early for the usual five o'clock quitting time, but Scofield said it would not be wise to start any descents this late in the day. He said it was good they got there early enough to see the task awaiting them in the morning. There was no room on the narrow trail to circle the wagons, so they went into camp sitting right where they were.

Scofield, Clint, and Spud made their way down the steep road on foot to see what kind of shape it was in. "Don't look much different from last year," Spud declared, "except it ain't got no little sheet of ice layin' on top of it. Ought not be no harder'n last year."

"Maybe so," Scofield said, "but I'll like it a whole lot better after we get that dang cannonball Thornton's drivin' down to that creek."

"That's something nobody's guessed yet," Clint remarked. "Maybe Thornton's shippin' a wagonload of cannon balls out to Fort Vancouver." The other emigrants on the wagon train had guessed about everything other than that.

"We might as well tie our ropes around the same trees we tied 'em on last year," Scofield said. "Might as well go ahead and do that tonight. One less thing to do in the mornin'."

When they settled that, they walked a little way along the trail at the bottom of the hill to see how the little graveyard patch had survived the year. "Well, there ain't been nobody else killed since we was here," Scofield said. "And it don't look like anything's bothered the grave, so you can tell Ruby everything looks just like we left it."

"Except the bushes has growed," Spud commented. "That was a helluva thing, him gettin' in the way of that wagon like that."

Clint thought about the sudden tragedy that took Cal Nixon's life. In the short time he had known Cal, they had become good friends. Cal was the kind of man who seemed so much in control of his life that it seemed impossible he could have been taken in a freak accident from a frayed rope. *Some things are beyond explanation,* he thought. He looked up then to find his uncle staring at him as if studying him intensely. "What?" Clint asked.

"Nothin'," Scofield answered, "but sometimes things happen for a reason. It might not seem like it, but it has to happen to make things come out right in the long run."

Clint exchanged glances with Spud and they both raised their eyebrows. Back to Scofield then, Clint said, "I swear, Uncle Clayton, you're doin' some real deep thinkin'. We better tell Lily to check you to see if you've got a fever."

"Yeah, and it's a waste of time tryin' to talk to young people about it," Scofield said. He didn't think it was a good idea to tell Clint that he believed Cal was taken in order for Clint to end up taking care of Ruby. And it was all done by whoever is in charge of things like that. But there were some things he didn't feel comfortable sharing with his nephew. So he said, "It's about time for you to start cookin' supper, ain't it, Spud?"

"Yeah, I reckon," Spud said, "if I can climb back up that hill." He started back up the steep trail to the wagons above, passing some of the other men on their way down to see what they would be faced with in the morning.

"Hell," Levi declared when he saw Clint and Scofield, "you call that a road? That ain't no road, that's a cliff."

"You just need to drive down it real slow," Scofield japed, "so your wagon doesn't pass your horses on the way down."

Levi gave him a look, then turned and took another look at the trail down Laurel Hill. "We gonna try to drive our wagons down that road?"

"You can't drive a wagon down that road, Levi," Tracy said. "We've been talkin' about lowerin' the wagons down Laurel Hill for the past couple of days. Ain't you been listenin'?"

"That's right, Levi," Scofield said. "You'll be bringin' your horses down here. Then we'll lower your wagon on ropes. We've found the best way to do it is to turn it around and back it down. That way, the wagon tongue won't be in the way, and with a rope on it, we can guide the wagon if we need to. We'll have to lower one wagon at a time, and when we get it down, you hitch up your team and move it outta the way for the next wagon. That's why we'll most likely spend the day here tomorrow."

"I swear, this is just like Ash Hollow," Lucien Aiken commented, "lowerin' the wagons on ropes."

"Maybe a little bit worse," Tiny Futch said. "There ain't no Garden of Eden at the bottom of this one. I think I better go eat my supper." He started back up the steep incline. The rest of the group thought it a good idea as well and started up after him. Clint and his uncle followed up after them, knowing how hard the task was certain to be.

# Chapter 24

The work began right after breakfast the next morning with Spud driving his wagon in the one clearing at the top of the hill that gave his horses room to make a right turn, then backing the wagon onto the road. Spud unhitched his horses at that point and walked them down to the bottom of the hill. The rest of the men tied the heavy ropes to the front axle as well as the front of the wagon box. The last rope was tied onto the wagon tongue by Clint, since it was his job to make sure the tongue trailed harmlessly and helped to keep it on a straight path. Two key men, picked for the job by Scofield, were the men who manned the ropes tied to the front axles. The ropes were wrapped round and round two stout trees and the two men were responsible to hang on to the loose ends of the ropes and let the ropes gradually unwind from the tree trunks. For this job, the men had to be strong, so Tiny Futch was on one tree, while Roy Leach was on the other. Scofield decided that he would substitute for either of them when it was time to lower their wagons. He gave his two strongmen a word of caution to keep an eye on the condition of their ropes. He told them that the grave at the bottom of the hill was there because the man minding one of the ropes failed to notice it was fraying and getting ready to break.

And so it began. Scofield's wagon was successfully lowered to the bottom of the hill, where Spud untied all the ropes, hitched up his horses and moved the wagon down the Sandy River trail, out of the way of the next wagon. One after another, the wagons were lowered to the bottom of the hill. There were plenty of bodies ready to jump in to help on the ropes tied to the wagon boxes, and by noontime almost half the wagons were on the road at the bottom of the hill. Since the horses did not require any rest, the operation was suspended for a brief dinner period before resuming again. There were only six wagons left atop the hill when it was Bass Thornton's turn to descend. Scofield took Leach's place on the rope while Leach pulled the wagon in place, then unhitched the team and walked them down to the bottom of the hill.

Beads of sweat were clearly visible on Thornton's face as he nervously stood ready to assist on one of the ropes if it became necessary. Tiny gave Scofield a worried look as the wagon began to back slowly, for he could already feel a difference in the strain on the tree trunk. An image of his tree being uprooted and flying through the air flashed across Scofield's mind as the unwinding rope began to burn grooves in the tree trunk. He stared at the taut rope and imagined he could see it stretching thin. *Just get on down the hill*, he thought as the heavy wagon inched its way about halfway down the steep slope. He glanced over at Clint, holding on to the wagon tongue rope, trying to hold back on the pull of the wagon as well, but rapidly losing the battle as he was gradually dragged down the slope with the wagon, along with the two gangs of men hanging on to the ropes tied to the wagon box.

Scofield looked again at his straining rope, wondering which was going to fail first, the rope or the tree? Would it be his rope that failed first, or Tiny's? He got his answer a few short seconds later when he clearly saw the rope start to fray. He yelled the warning at the same time the rope popped in two. The wagon, fully three-quarters of the way down the hill, lunged sideways. Tiny, reacting instinctively, immediately released his rope from the tree to prevent the careening wagon from turning over on its side. In response to Tiny's actions, Clint tried to turn the front wheels with the tongue and managed to turn them enough to keep the wagon from rolling over. With less than a fourth of the incline left to travel, the wagon was left to rumble wildly down the hill, dragging the few souls who had not let go.

Waiting patiently at the bottom of the hill with a team of horses, Leach watched the heavy wagon as it rolled slowly down the slope toward him. When the rope broke, his first instinct was to catch the wagon. But even he realized he would be swatted on the back of the wagon like a fly, so he yelled and slapped the horses, chasing them up the Sandy Creek road. Then he scrambled out of the wagon's path as it clattered past him and found a place to settle, halfway off the road.

Everyone at the top of the hill ran down to assess the damage done, Bass Thornton among the leaders and Scofield right behind him. When they reached the wagon, Leach was checking the wheels and axles, looking for any damage that needed to be fixed right away. Bass untied the back canvas and opened it just enough to stick his head in to look inside. Scofield, frustrated at this point with Thornton's mysterious heavy wagon, took a less than subtle approach. "Everything all right?" he blurted bluntly, then pulled a rope loose that held the canvas cover to the front corner of the wagon box and stuck his head inside. He didn't say anything for a few seconds as he continued to stare at the heavy iron contraption. "Thornton," he finally demanded, "what the hell is that?"

Thornton shrugged casually, but it seemed to Scofield that he was clearly annoyed that he had taken a look inside his wagon. "That's a printing press, Mr. Scofield. That's what it is."

"Well, it's a big one," Scofield said. "Doesn't leave you much room for anything else in that wagon, does it?" He stuck his head in and took a longer look. "I can sure understand why your wagon is so doggone heavy. That thing's solid iron, ain't it? I reckon you're plannin' to go in the printin' business in the Willamette Valley, or start a newspaper?"

"I'm thinking about both," Thornton said.

"Why were you keepin' it such a big secret? Everybody on the wagon train has been tryin' to figure out what you're haulin'," Scofield said with a chuckle. "A lotta guessin', but I ain't heard anybody guess a printin' press. You coulda told me in Independence that you were gonna haul a printin' press in your wagon."

"I was afraid you'd tell me I had to hire it out to a freighter to take it out there," Thornton said. "And that would have doubled my expense. I'd still appreciate it if you didn't say much about it to everyone else."

"All right," Scofield said. "I won't announce it, but I'm surprised you don't wanna advertise it."

"I've got my reasons," Bass said.

"Whatever you say," Scofield replied and stepped aside when Leach brought the horses up to be hitched. "After you move your wagon outta the way, Leach, come on back up the hill. We've got five more wagons to get down here and we're gonna have to fix you up with a new rope. I broke your old one."

The rest of the afternoon was spent lowering the last five wagons down Laurel Hill. As tricky and difficult as all the wagons had seemed before it had been Thornton's turn, his descent made the last five no trouble at all in comparison. The last wagon to be lowered was Wiley and Maggie's, and Maggie waited at the bottom of the hill to hitch the horses up again while Wiley watched from above. He stood on the side where Tiny was snaking the rope down the hill. Once Maggie got her team hitched and ready to go, Scofield announced that they were only going to drive about five miles before they reached the Barlow Road toll gate. "I know you're all anxious to pay for the privilege we've had to travel on this road." He waited for all the hooting and the groans to die away, then he continued. "It'll be time to quit for supper, anyway, so we'll just stop right there for the night. There's wood, water, and a little bit of grass there."

While there were still enough of the people around to hear

him, Wiley called out to Maggie, "Since it's only five miles, I'm gonna see if I can walk it. Try to see if I can build up my strength again, so I can take the load offa you."

"Well, now, that's a good idea," Maggie responded. "You just hop on if you get tired. Tell you the truth, I hadn't noticed I was doin' any extra chores, anyway."

When the wagon train started out again, Clint rode Biscuit up beside his uncle on Blackie. "It's sure good to be on this side of that damn hill, ain't it?" Clint asked.

"It sure as hell is," Scofield answered. "I thought for a little while back there that we finally succeeded in losin' Thornton's wagon. Lord knows we've tried enough times."

"I saw you stick your head in his wagon," Clint said. "Did you see what he's haulin'?"

"Yep, I did," Scofield answered. "I told him I wouldn't tell nobody what he's totin'."

"Well, you can tell me," Clint insisted. "I ain't gonna tell anybody."

Scofield chuckled. "He's haulin' a great big ol' printin' press. Solid iron, it must weigh a ton."

"Well, I'll be . . ." Clint started, obviously disappointed. "Why didn't he want you to tell anybody that?"

"Beats me. He said he had his reasons."

It was quite a bit past the usual five o'clock quitting time when the wagon train reached the Barlow Road toll gate and the cabin built there to house the men who manned the toll gate. Since Scofield was planning to camp there, anyway, he suggested to the man in charge of collecting the toll, a large man named Everette Sartain, that they could just wait until morning. Sartain was in favor of the suggestion because he was in the process of cooking himself some supper, and it would take some time to take the toll from each wagon. Scofield told him that his people were also going to fix supper and afterward he was invited to listen to the musicians at the social hour. Sartain said that was to his liking and he looked forward to it.

Clint, standing beside his uncle, had other ideas about the supper hour. The toll gate was built beside a shady creek that came down from the mountain above and looked to be a natural attraction for deer. So he asked, "You get any deer around this creek, Mr. Sartain?"

"I'd say so," Sartain replied. "They come down almost every night to see if I've planted any new onions in a little bed I've got out back of the cabin. Matter of fact, that's what I'm fixin' to cook for supper."

"Well, you won't get upset if I walk back down the creek a ways and see if I can get a shot at one, would you? We ain't had fresh meat in quite a while now."

"You go right ahead, young feller," Sartain said. "The deer are thicker'n ticks on a dog's back in these mountains."

"Much obliged," Clint said. He knew he didn't need the man's permission to hunt the deer, but it was always a polite thing to do to avoid annoying someone.

So they went into camp and while the women were fixing supper, Clint took Biscuit to water and took his saddle off, then left him to graze while he took a walk back the way they had come, carrying his rifle. It was starting to get dark and he had a feeling there would be deer coming down a narrow game trail he spotted earlier that led from the mountain above to the creek. "Where you headin', Clint?" Tiny called out to him when Clint walked past the end of the wagons. "You goin' back to Laurel Hill?"

Clint laughed. "No, I'm gonna go down the creek a ways and see if I can get a deer."

"Be careful you don't shoot none of them two-legged deer I just saw standin' in the laurel bushes down there," Tiny warned.

"I'm goin' a little farther down the creek than that," Clint assured him. The game trail he had spotted was quite a bit farther than where the men were going to relieve themselves.

"Clint Buchanan," Wiley Jones mumbled to himself, contemptuously. "The big hunter, all the women think he's really somethin' just because he shoots a deer. Anybody can shoot a deer." He was sitting on the wagon tailgate, waiting for Maggie to fix supper. Since their wagon was the last to come down the hill, it was at the end of the line to pass the toll gate in the morning. While he had been sitting there, he had seen a steady line of men heading for the privacy of the bushes. "Shoot," he scoffed, "in a few more minutes, it'll be dark enough. I'll go right here beside the wagon."

"What are you mumblin' about?" Maggie yelled from the front of the wagon by the fire she had built to cook on.

"Nothin'," Wiley yelled back. "Just talkin' to myself."

*One fool, talking to another one*, Maggie thought and turned her attention back to the simple supper she was preparing.

Still seated on the tailgate, Wiley thought again about Clint going deer hunting. *Maybe I oughta go see if I can get a shot at a deer. It'd be something to eat besides bacon for a change*, he thought. *Must be deer around here, if the mighty hunter thinks so. And I'm just as likely to get one as he is.* "But then I'd have to skin the damn thing and butcher it," he mumbled and decided he'd just eat the bacon. Then something else caught his attention and he felt his body begin to tense up. *Roy Leach!* He came from Thornton's wagon and was heading down the creek where the other men had gone. *He ain't wearing a gun!* The thought struck him at once. This was the opportunity he was hoping for. He scrambled back into the wagon to get his rifle.

Hearing him rumbling around in the wagon, Maggie called out, "What are you doin'?"

He popped his head out the front of the wagon long enough to say, "I'm goin' huntin'. I'm gonna go see if I can get us a deer." Not waiting for her response, he crawled out the back of the wagon, dragging his rifle behind him.

Finding it hard to believe what she had just heard, Maggie ran around to the back of the wagon in time to see Wiley trotting back along the creek, rifle in hand. She was too late to question him, but watching him hustling toward the woods inspired her to think he didn't look as lame as he claimed to be. "If he does get a deer, he'll expect me to skin it and butcher it 'cause he'll be too feeble again. Well, I'll be damned if I'm gonna go get it for him if he does shoot one." She paused to think about that for a moment. Some fresh venison would be mighty good. Then she had another idea. "I'll ask Leach to tote it out for me and invite him to supper with us." The thought tickled her to the point of giggling.

The object of her scorn was even then stalking his prey, but it wasn't a deer. Moving as cautiously as he could, Wiley continued down the creek, determined this time not to walk blindly into an ambush. At least this time he knew he was stalking Leach and not Violet Thornton. It was not difficult to see where other men had gone by the bent and broken bushes. Obviously, Leach was modest in his private functions because he evidently went much farther down the creek. Even better, Wiley thought, because that put him closer to wherever Clint Buchanan had gone to hunt. His plan was simple. At first sight of Leach, he would lay the front sight of his rifle on his back and pull the trigger. He would worry about his story to Scofield and the others after he made sure Leach was dead. No one could prove it wasn't an accident. And Maggie could tell them he had gone deer hunting. It would be even better if everybody thought it was Clint Buchanan's stray shot that killed Leach. As he continued moving through the ever-darkening woods, he realized that he had come too far. No one was modest to the extent they would have walked this far to do their business. Somehow, he must have passed him. Frustrated to the point where he wanted to yell out his anger, he held it inside, however. He turned around to return to the wagon, only to stop, dead still, when several yards in front of him, the unmistakable form of Roy Leach appeared, walking away from him. Wiley realized that he had evidently walked past Leach, who had gone off to the side for his privacy. And now, Leach had come back out of the bushes to present his back as a broad target on his way back to the wagons.

Seeing his prayers answered, Wiley raised his rifle to sight on Leach's back, but he forgot about his plan to simply pull the trigger. He realized how much he wanted Leach to know who killed him and the satisfaction of the sweet revenge. So he called out, "Leach!" The ape-like man stopped and turned slowly around. To Wiley's disappointment, he showed no visible emotion at all. So Wiley said, "You remember me, don't you, you dumb ape. Did you think I was gonna let you live after you jumped me like you did? Why don't you make a move to stop me? See if you're quicker than this bullet with your name on it." Enjoying his tormenting of the helpless man, Wiley said. "I'm gonna give you a chance to see how fast you are. I'm gonna pull this trigger on the count of three. You can try to get to me before I say three, or you can try to run away. But make up your mind because I'm startin' to count now. One, two . . ." The crack of the Henry rifle ripped through the still night air as the .44 slug struck Wiley's chest before he could utter *three*.

Leach dived to the ground to avoid Wiley's reaction shot that went up through the treetops as Wiley fell backward, dead. Seeing Wiley on his back then, Leach got to his feet and walked over to make sure he was dead. Then he turned to see his benefactor coming up from the creek. "Clint," he muttered simply, "you always come when I need help. He followed me and I didn't have no gun."

Clint was sure he already knew the answer. He and Scofield had pretty much agreed on it, but he decided to ask Leach, anyway. "Leach, why did Wiley start to shoot you?"

"I gave him a whuppin'," Leach answered without pause.

"Why did you give him a whuppin'?" Clint asked.

"'Cause he come on to Violet and Violet's married, and I had to make him stop."

"That's what I thought," Clint said. "You were protectin' your sister, weren't you?"

"Am I in trouble now?"

"I don't think so," Clint answered honestly. "I'll talk to Scofield for you, and I'll tell Maggie what happened here tonight. It would have been better if it hadn't gone this far, and we'd settled it before he tried to kill you. But don't you worry about it. Wiley's the one who tried to kill you. I'm the only one who shot anybody. I'll make sure everybody knows the truth. You go on back to your wagon. I'll take care of Wiley's body. All right?"

"All right," Leach said and started back to the wagons but paused after a few steps to turn back and say, "You're a good friend, Clint." Clint wasn't sure how to respond to that so he just nodded and smiled. He was almost tempted to ask Leach to carry the body back to Wiley's wagon because the brute could probably do it without breathing hard. But he didn't know yet what kind of reaction he was going to get when he broke the news to Maggie. She might take a shot at Leach. Maybe he should tell Scofield first, so the two of them could tell Maggie. "Hell," he thought out loud, "she might take a shot at me for shootin' her husband when he was taking revenge for the cripplin' beatin' he took from the brute." *I definitely better tell Uncle Clayton first, and he can go with me to tell Maggie*, he decided.

"Damn," Scofield swore when Clint finished explaining what had happened down near the creek. "I was hopin' you were gonna be tellin' me that one rifle shot I heard meant I was gonna have some fresh venison tonight." He shook his head slowly while he thought about taking that news to Maggie. "Where's his body?"

"Right where it fell," Clint answered. "I thought I'd better tell you before I did anything else."

"Well, let's go tell Maggie what happened," Scofield said.

When they walked up to Wiley's wagon, they found Maggie sitting on an upside-down bucket beside the fire, eating supper. Mildly surprised to see the two of them visiting her wagon, she greeted them with, "If you're lookin' for Wiley, he ain't here. He took his rifle and said he was goin' deer huntin'. I heard a shot a little while ago, but he didn't come back with a deer, so I reckon he missed."

"That shot you heard is what we came to talk to you about," Scofield said. "I'm real sorry to have to tell you, Maggie, your husband's dead. Wiley was shot tonight."

She looked from one solemn face to the other, saying nothing in response until finally asking, "You're japin' me, right?"

Scofield and Clint exchanged puzzled glances, surprised by her reaction to such tragic news. "Maybe we ain't makin' ourselves clear," Clint said. "Wiley's dead. He was about to shoot Roy Leach, so he had to be shot to keep him from murderin' an unarmed man."

"Well, I'll be damned," Maggie drew out, scarcely able to believe that Wiley had somehow managed to solve her problem without her having to split everything up upon arriving in Oregon City. Everything was hers now. She wanted to shout hallelujah, but she knew it would be less than dignified to greet the news that way. "That is terrible news to have to hear after all we've been through and all the plans we had to . . ." She stopped abruptly, unable to pull it off. "Who shot him?" she asked, rendering them both dumbstruck by her less than grief-stricken response.

"I shot him," Clint confessed and braced himself for the moment when she finally realized this was all really happening.

"Well, I'm just gonna be honest with you, Clint. You just rid the world of a genuine worthless man."

They were both stunned, but Scofield had to say, "You must have felt differently about the man at some point, or you wouldn't have married him and started out on this journey to build a life together out here."

"You might as well know the true story now, Mr. Scofield. We've come too far for you to send me back. Wiley and I were never married. We had a business deal to make out like we were. That was the only way either one of us could afford to get out here. We were fixin' to split up as soon as we hit Oregon City." It was obvious to her that they were still having trouble accepting her stone-cold version of her husband's sudden execution, so she put it as plainly as she could. "Look, in the beginning when we first decided to talk about this arrangement, we didn't know each other very well at all. And I'll admit that we left that door open when we agreed to go out here together. Well, I don't mind tellin' you, it didn't take long before any permanent arrangement between us as man and wife was thrown out the door, and I told him so. He was comin' back to the wagon close to breakfast time while we were still waiting there in Independence, after a night of visitin' the dance halls and whorehouses, and God knows what else. He tried to tell me he was just blowin' off his last days of bachelorhood, and it would all end as soon as we started rolling." She paused to judge their reaction and could see they were both still uncomfortable. "I ain't tellin' you I'm any better person than he was, but I do keep my word when I give it to someone. He was sniffin' around the little gal Bass Thornton says is his wife before we were on the road two days."

Scofield interrupted her at that point. "Maggie, you don't have to go on talkin' about that mess. We just wanted to make sure you knew that Wiley didn't give Clint no choice in the matter of his killin'. And there ain't no need for you to worry about gettin' on out to Oregon City. We're gonna see that you do. Right, Clint?" Clint nodded in response.

"I was meanin' to tell you that I knew it was Leach who tore ol' Wiley up, and I knew why. Wiley never would admit it, but I knew it couldn'ta been nobody but Leach, and he caught him goin' after Violet down at the creek."

"We'll take care of the body for ya," Scofield said. "Figure anything we find on him is rightfully yours. So we'll turn it over to you. All right?"

"That's more than fair," she said. "Maybe he's got enough on him to pay the toll in the mornin'."

# Chapter 25

They bid farewell to Everette Sartain the next morning as each wagon rolled past the crude little shack that served as the Barlow Road toll gate. The toll was five dollars for each wagon plus ten cents a head for livestock. Everyone knew before leaving Independence that they would have to pay that toll. But Levi could not resist complaining that after coming this far on the road, Sartain should be giving them a cash award for making it to the toll gate.

Sartain chose not to respond. Instead, he commented to Clint, "I heard a rifle shot last night, but I didn't pick up the smell of roast venison. I figured you mighta got a shot at one and you missed."

"Nope," Clint replied. "I never saw the first deer before I was kinda interrupted by something that needed shootin' more than the deer. I was gonna talk to you about that, but I was waitin' for Scofield to come explain it with me."

When Scofield joined them again, he told Sartain about the unfortunate shooting of one of the emigrants, but that it had been the only way to prevent that emigrant from murdering one of the other members of the wagon train. "We took the body away from your place here and buried it," Scofield told him. "The man was a troublemaker right from the first day, and his death last night was the first blessin' his poor wife, Maggie, has had ever since she agreed to come out here with him. She's a spunky gal, though, and she'll be drivin' her wagon herself, just like she has been." He nodded slowly in confirmation of his assessment of Maggie. "So, I'd best get up there and get the first of this column movin'. If one of your boys runs up on a new grave down past that creek a ways, you'll know who it is."

"Much obliged for tellin' me," Sartain said. "And much obliged for usin' the Barlow Road. I can guarantee ya, it's a better way to come than boatin' down the river."

"I already knew that," Scofield replied. "Good day to you."

Sartain nodded to Clint, then stood and watched as both he and his uncle trotted their horses off to the front of the column. He went back to the toll shack where his oldest son, Elmore, was collecting the tolls. He waited there for five more wagons to pass through before he saw the wagon with the woman driving the horses. Maggie pulled her team to a halt and reached inside her coat for her purse. Sartain walked up beside Elmore. "I'll take this one, son." He walked up beside the wagon seat and asked, "Your name Maggie?"

"Yessir," Maggie answered. "And I've got your money. Five dollars and I ain't got no other livestock."

"Put it away," Sartain told her. "Your money ain't no good here."

Misunderstanding, Maggie became immediately upset. "It's genuine government-printed money. There ain't nothin' wrong with it."

"I'm sure it is, ma'am," Sartain quickly explained. "I'm just sayin' I ain't chargin' you to use the road. Mr. Scofield told me what happened here last night, and the least I can do for you is let you go through free of charge. It ain't much, but I'm happy to do it. Spend that five dollars on somethin' useful in Oregon City."

Maggie was at a loss for words for the first time she could remember. Maybe these people out here in Oregon country were a finer cut from the folks she left back east. "Why, bless your heart, mister. I sure will find something useful to spend the money on and I'll always remember your kindness. Getty-up!" She slapped her reins across her horses' rumps and pulled out after the other wagons.

The wagon train continued on along a road leading north and west, following Camp Creek to the Sandy River, where it crossed to the north bank. Continuing on to Marmot, they then made their way down a long steep ridge, called the Devil's Backbone, back toward the southeast, until they crossed back over the Sandy River again. Passing Eagle Creek, they had one more river to cross before the relatively easy road on into Oregon City. That river was the Clackamas, and there were three crossings to choose from. Scofield's preferred crossing was one called Feldheimer's Ford. It provided a wide rocky shore to enter the river and a forgiving bank on the other side. In most seasons, the river was deep enough to force the horses to swim a short distance before gaining footing again. In light of Bass Thornton's bad luck with river crossings, Scofield favored Feldheimer's for another reason. In recent years, Feldheimer had added another feature to his crossing, a ferryboat. Thornton seemed to have the money to take advantage of all manner of expenses, so he thought he might like to ferry his wagon across this last crossing.

The wagon train arrived at the east bank of the Clackamas at suppertime after a full day of driving through a steady rain, leaving them to set up for a wet camp. The travelers set up their sleeping tents as half shelters for their small supper fires, then returned to their wagons to eat a simple meal of bacon in most cases. Scofield and Clint walked down to the river's edge to judge the conditions of the crossing. The river was up, they decided, but not to the extent that it should cause trouble. While they were discussing it, Bass Thornton joined them. "Whaddaya think, Mr. Scofield?" Bass questioned as he approached. "Is all

this rain we've been driving through gonna make any major effect on the crossing?"

"Can't say for sure," Scofield answered him. "There is a deep
channel in the middle of this river, and some wagons might take
a little water in their wagon boxes. But if we keep the wagons
movin', we might keep that to a minimum."

"What do you know about the ferry across here?" Bass asked
then. "Are they pretty reliable?"

"I'm afraid all I can tell you about the ferry is that it's used
quite a bit," Scofield said. "Ain't none of the folks I've brought
out here ever used it. And nobody ridin' with us this trip has said
they wanted to take the ferry. You're the only one that ain't had
the best of luck at the river crossin's." He paused to watch
Thornton ponder the situation, then he suggested, "Why don't
you wait and see what the river looks like in the mornin'? I noticed the rain seems to have been tapering off in the last hour
or so."

"I expect that's a good idea," Thornton said. He flicked a
droplet of water off his hat brim just before it started to drop, and
gave them a tired smile. "I reckon everybody on the train knows
I'm coming out here to establish a printing company, and possibly, a newspaper. I don't know why I've tried to keep that a secret. Don't want the competition to find out, I suppose. But you
can see why I can't afford to lose that big press I'm hauling."

"Can't say as I blame ya," Scofield said, "but I didn't tell anybody but Clint and Lily about the press. When we get started in
the mornin', if you decide on the ferry, all you have to do is ring
that big bell hangin' in that pine yonder." He pointed out the
tree. "And they'll send the ferry across to take you back."

"Are you sure the ferry is still in business?" Thornton worried
aloud.

"I expect it is," Scofield said. "Most likely, they already know
we're here." He paused then when he heard Henry Abbott suddenly saw off a challenge on his fiddle. Henry didn't get far before Lucien Aiken answered the challenge with his guitar,

followed a few minutes later by the sound of Tiny Futch flailing away on his banjo. Scofield chuckled as he held his hand out, palm up. "No doubt about it," he said, "it's quit rainin'. If he didn't know before, I expect Feldheimer will know we're here pretty soon now." When the three of them turned around and went back to the circle of wagons, there were already several of the men dragging wood into the center of the circle for a big fire. Clint was happy to see it because he hadn't seen many happy faces during the perilous ride down the Devil's Backbone, especially when it was necessary to use ropes to help lower the wagons down the steep tail end of the backbone.

It was actually the first social hour the folks had celebrated for a couple of nights, so it was good to get everybody's spirits up for this one last river crossing. Ordinarily, Scofield and Clint expected the celebration to come after they crossed the river tomorrow, if there was to be one at all. This must surely be a good sign that the emigrants were eager to take on the river, they decided. Scofield went back to his wagon to talk Lily into joining the impromptu social hour. Always the practical person, Lily wanted to know why they should celebrate crossing the river before they had actually accomplished it. "I shoulda left you at Fort Kearny," Scofield joked, "and took one of them younger gals that worked for Leo Sterns."

"It's a good thing you didn't," Lily returned. "By now, Clint and I woulda had to float you across the river like Thornton's wagon." She grabbed her bonnet in case the misty rain had not completely stopped and started toward the fire coming to life in the middle of the circle of wagons.

The rain did stop, indeed, and the social hour promised to be one of the most memorable for all who participated. The Watkinses and the Bishops took advantage of what many of them were certain would be the last celebration of its kind. Levi even threatened to demonstrate his exclusive buck-and-wing moves, if perchance someone might have managed to smuggle a bottle of whiskey this far in their journey. To his disappointment, no one confessed to having saved any spirits to survive this far. "What can I say?" Levi shrugged and asked. "I reckon it's just your loss."

"More like our gain," his wife, Ella, declared.

"I thought maybe Bass and Violet Thornton might join us tonight," Lily commented to Scofield as they walked toward the group. "Is he gonna take his wagon across with the rest of us? Or is he gonna try that ferry they got here?"

"I don't know," Scofield replied. "When Clint and I talked to him a little while ago, he was thinkin' it over."

"I don't see how you can blame the poor man for worrying about losing that press," Lily said. "He's taken a tremendous gamble on what he plans to do in the Willamette Valley. If he loses that press, I don't see any way he can make out here. Unless Violet and Leach are one helluva pair of farmers. You can tell by looking at Bass, he ain't familiar with a rake and a hoe. He looks more at home in a bank or a law office."

Lily's assessment of Bass Thornton was dead on the money. And by coincidence, Bass Thornton had been a person of interest about three thousand miles east of the little social hour beside the Clackamas River in Oregon. His name had come up in a mystery involving the disappearance of four sets of plates for the Treasury Department's "greenback" currency in ones, fives, tens, and twenties. The incident happened months ago around the end of March and it appeared to be a dead issue after so long with no clues.

Before the Civil War, the government hired the large New York Bank Note Company to finance the war, paying them large amounts of interest. As the war progressed, it became increasingly apparent that the bank note companies were unable to meet the demand. The result of this was the creation of the Bureau of Engraving and Printing within the Treasury Department.

The banks surrendered the printing plates used to print and engrave the money, and the Treasury Department printed their own money after that.

The transition took some time, but a careful record was kept to ensure that all printing plates for the government's currency were recovered from the individual banks. However, Spencer Clark, the founder of the Bureau of Engraving and Printing, confirmed that there were still four sets of plates missing. So he immediately launched an investigation. After thoroughly checking the meetings with each bank's representatives and checking the signatures left on the transfer papers, there arose one questionable transaction. The return of the forms from the Bank of New York was signed by Clark's representative as well as by Bank of New York's Bass Thornton. The problem was, there was no evidence that the actual plates were logged in with the others. A minor problem, no doubt, Clark assumed, but when he contacted the bank, he was told that Bass Thornton had resigned his position there and had left no forwarding address.

Properly alarmed at this point, Spencer Clark ordered another inventory of the plates. Certain that the plates were in fact missing, he reported the incident to Salmon P. Chase, the Secretary of the Treasury, who immediately called upon the U.S. Marshals Service to find Bass Thornton. Unfortunately, all checking of Thornton's previous addresses had brought the marshals no closer to the missing suspect. "I'm afraid we're not going to recover those plates if we don't find this Thornton fellow," Clark reported to Salmon Chase. "The man just disappeared, and I think that's just what he intended to do. That was back in March or April. There's no telling where he is today."

"First of April," Chase said, halfway joking. "Maybe he left on a wagon train with those stolen plates. Maybe we should have sent marshals to search the Independence area." He paused when he saw the dumbfounded look on Clark's face. Without further hesitation, he ordered, "Get on the telegraph to the marshals service in that area!" That was all the instruction necessary to send Clark running. To the amazement of them all, the marshals in the Independence area were familiar with Peter Moreland, a lawyer who was very much involved in the organization of wagon trains. In his files, he was able to show that a Mr. Bass Thornton had contracted to accompany a wagon train, headed by a Mr. Clayton Scofield, their destination Oregon City, Oregon.

"But that was on the first of April," Clark said. "That wagon train might already be there by now."

"But even if it is," Chase declared, "they ought to be easy to find. Telegraph the closest place to that Oregon City where there's a marshals service and send a couple of marshals to apprehend Thornton. It's worth the trouble and the cost to keep Mr. Bass Thornton from printing all the money he needs at the expense of the Bureau of Engraving and Printing. I just hope we ain't too late."

"You wanted to see us, boss?" Marshal Avery Booth asked Chief Marshal Tom Pullman as he and his partner, Deputy Marshal Sam Sawyer, walked into Pullman's office in San Francisco.

"Yep," Pullman answered. "I've got a little job for you that just suits the likes of you two."

"Uh-oh," Avery declared at once. He looked at Sam and said, "Right offhand, that don't sound like any job we'd want."

"This is right up your alley," Pullman insisted. "You and Sam have got more experience in this business than all the other men in my troop. This is a special request from the Secretary of the Treasury. It don't get much more important than that, so I thought of you two right away." He went on then to paint the picture for them and the seriousness of the government property Bass Thornton had stolen.

"I swear, Tom," Avery finally commented, "I thought you was serious at first, but you're just japin' us, now. Ain't you? You're tellin' us this Thornton feller stole some money plates, then got on a wagon train outta Independence, headed for Oregon City. And you don't know if that train has ever got to Oregon City or not. You know how far me and Sam have to ride to get to Oregon City from here?"

"Doggone it, Avery," Pullman said. "The wagon train is led by a man named Clayton Scofield. So you ought to be able to find out if the train has gotten there or is still on the way. Whichever, find out where this Thornton feller went, and take possession of him and the plates."

Sam interrupted at that point. "I just wanna be sure, boss. When you say he's got some printin' plates, you're talking about the kind you could put on a press and print legal money off of. Right?"

"That's right, Sam," Pullman answered. "So you see why it's important to catch him before he has a chance to go to work."

"Well, I ain't never had a chance to take a look at that country," Avery said. "So we might as well go see if we can find the money man. And you want him brought back here?"

"That's a fact," Pullman said. "And I'm authorized to advance you some expense money since you've got a long ride just to get there."

"We'll start first thing in the mornin'. Right, Sam?"

# Chapter 26

As expected, the emigrants of Clayton Scofield's wagon train to the Willamette Valley greeted the morning of their last real river crossing with the enthusiasm of seeing their long, arduous journey finally over. Most of the travelers were up before hearing Scofield's four o'clock assault on his bugle, and breakfast fires were already underway. As a result, the first wagon committed to the Clackamas rumbled across the gravel-covered east bank well before the usual starting time of seven. Spud drove his horses into the water following a line of sight with Clint, who was waiting on the other side. When Clint had first crossed over to test the footing for the horses, he had found that the river was a little higher than usual due to the recent rains. The wagons were going to have to float for a short distance until the horses found footing again. It was of no real concern to any of the wagon owners, with the exception of Bass Thornton. He watched as the wagons followed Spud across, taking special interest in the wagons' reactions when they reached the deepest part and had to float. Some of them veered sharply when subjected to the current at that point. But all recovered. "I'm not gonna risk my press, now that we're this close to our final destination," Bass announced to Scofield.

"Can't say as I blame you," Scofield replied. "Just ring that bell hanging on that tree over there, and they'll send a ferry across to getcha."

When the ferry arrived, Bass was disappointed to find that it was a small flat barge-like vessel that could ferry his wagon and his horses, but not at the same time. So the reasonable fee quoted was not quite so reasonable when he had to pay for two crossings. Still, he reasoned, it was not too much to pay to get his wagon across safely. Leach went across with the horses first to wait on the west bank while the ferry went back to get Bass and the wagon. Meanwhile, the other wagons continued to cross with no trouble in the deep part of the river more serious than a suddenly skewed wagon when it no longer had a sound bottom beneath its wheels. The horses found solid footing soon enough to pull the wayward wagon out of the current and back in line before it could drift very far.

Although a flimsy craft in appearance, the ferry was pulled to the other side of the river with no apparent issues and Bass Thornton's horses were led off onto the bank by Leach. As was his custom, Leach, in his natural sense of responsibility for guarding Thornton's property, tied a long rope to the horses' reins and walked them along the bank to be in position to hitch them to the wagon as soon as it landed.

Seeing the ferry with Thornton's wagon aboard approaching the channel of the river, Maggie Mayfield estimated they both might reach the strong current at the same time. To avoid a possible collision with the ferry, she pulled her horses sharply upstream, slowing her crossing considerably. Unfortunately, no one of them could have known that Mother Nature would take an interest in the game at this point. To add to the pot now stewing in the middle of the river, she dislodged a sixty-foot pine tree that the storms had uprooted and sent it barreling downstream like a giant spear past Maggie's wagon. It was on a course to broadside the ferry boat. There was no way to avoid a collision between the ferry and the pine tree.

With no other option available to them, the two men operating the mule-driven windlass that pulled the ferry back from the other side could only whip their mules to pull as hard and fast as they could. Their efforts appeared to be paying off, and everyone cheered as the ferry picked up speed, only to stop in the middle of the current when one of the ropes snapped in two. The hurtling pine slammed into the left rear corner of the ferry, taking out a quarter of the platform the wagon rested on and dropping the back of Thornton's wagon off the shattered ferry. It was the nightmare that Thornton could not let himself imagine. With no chance to prevent his total loss himself, all he could do was to scramble to the bow of the ferry with Violet and watch the wagon slowly sinking.

Leach, however, had no intention of giving up his master's wagon. He went into the water immediately and disappeared under the dark ripples. The only other reaction to Leach's effort was by Clint Buchanan when he saw the rope leading from Thornton's horses. Not sure he would be there in time to make a difference, Clint nevertheless did what he could. He unhitched Spud's horses and drove them down the bank to head the ferry off. Into the dark, chilly water he went with one end of a rope that Spud had now tied to his team. He almost bumped head-on into the murky form of Roy Leach. Clint would swear to Scofield and Spud when reliving the incident later that night that Leach was grinning happily.

When the two men came out of the water, they were met by more teams of horses ready to help pull the half-submerged wagon out of the river. Others were there to help Bass and Violet off the crippled ferry to a good fire with some warm blankets. There were still wagons to make the crossing, so Scofield stayed with them until all were successfully across the river. Then he announced that they would go into camp there to give the Thorntons time to recover. Even though it was a fairly short day and a half to their journey's end, no one objected to the delay.

"I guess I should have just trusted you to get my wagon across this river," Thornton confessed to Scofield.

"I'm glad we were able to save the wagon," Scofield told him. "What about your printin' press? I see it's still in the wagon. Can it still be used?"

"Yes," Thornton replied. "I'll have to take it apart and clean and grease every part, but we saved the press."

"Half your tailgate was smashed out," Scofield said. "Lucky your press wasn't settin' there. It mighta gone right outta the wagon through that hole."

"It might have at that," Thornton said. "I think that was where that damn tree struck the wagon."

"Well, I'm glad you didn't lose your printin' press, but I'm a lot happier to see we didn't lose any people."

"Yes, that's the most important thing," Thornton said in agreement. He was not enthusiastic in his response, however, because he was well aware of the crate heavy enough to have torn half the tailgate away when the ferry suddenly collapsed beneath his wagon. At this particular moment, his thinking was that the printing press might just as well have gone to the bottom of the river, too. On the other hand, he paused to speculate, maybe this was God's way of telling him it was in his best interest to seek an honest way of making a living. He still had money left and a young wife. Maybe he could teach Leach to run a press.

"You fellows need some more coffee?" Ernie Givens approached the table where Avery Booth and Sam Sawyer were eating breakfast.

"No, thanks," Avery answered. "I'm about coffeed up."

"I'll take one more splash of it," Sam said, "then I reckon that'll do me."

They were seated at their usual table by a window that offered a good view of the Abernethy Green, a large pasture beside Oregon City where the arriving wagon trains camped when they hit town. On this morning, the green was empty, as it had been ever since the two law officers had arrived. To Avery, it was beginning to look like they had missed the wagon train they had been sent to apprehend. "You sure about this fellow, Scofield?" he had to ask again.

"I'm sure," Ernie answered. "Clayton Scofield has been bringin' emigrants into this town for years. And we ain't seen hide nor hair of him. If he started out another train from Independence, then he oughta be showin' up any day now." He shook his head slowly and remarked, "I just can't believe you two fellows rode all the way over here to meet him. He ain't never had anything but a fine reputation around here with everybody who knows him."

"We go wherever they tell us to go," Avery said. "But there ain't no problem with Scofield. We're lookin' for a man who might be travelin' with his wagon train. That's all."

"Well, today might be your lucky day," Ernie said. And when neither Avery or Sam appeared to understand what he was implying, he called their attention back to the window and the first wagons of a train pulling onto Abernethy Green.

"Well, I'll be . . ." Avery started before pausing. "Is that Scofield's train?"

"I ain't sure yet," Ernie replied, staring at the arriving wagons now. "Yep, it's Scofield. I don't see him yet, but that's his guide, young Clint Buchanan, leadin' 'em in." A moment later, Ernie said, "Yonder he is, big man ridin' the black horse, that's Scofield." The two marshals jumped to their feet at once. Leaving money on the table, they went out the door and headed toward the green where Scofield and Clint were in the process of lining the wagons in a circle.

Scofield wheeled his horse around to meet the two riders coming directly toward him. His first thought was that the town might have closed Abernethy Green to arriving wagon trains. "They shoulda put up some signs," he mumbled to himself, with no intentions of moving the wagons.

"Clayton Scofield?" Avery asked when he and Sam pulled up to face him.

"I am," Scofield replied.

"Mr. Scofield, I'm U.S. Marshal Avery Booth." He showed his

badge. "This is Deputy Marshal Sam Sawyer. We're lookin' for a man who might be on this wagon train. He's a person of interest in a case involving the Secretary of the Treasury, Mr. Salmon Chase." Avery could see that his statement had definitely taken Scofield by surprise. "There was enough evidence to suspect this man might be traveling with your train," Avery continued. "He may or may not be traveling under a different name."

"I swear," Scofield mumbled. "What did he do?"

"Right now, we just want him for questioning. His real name is Bass Thornton. But since he may be using a different name, it will be necessary to talk to every wagon owner."

"Bass Thornton," Scofield repeated. "You won't have to talk to anybody else. That's Thornton's wagon right over there, the one with half the tailgate torn away. Come on, I'll go over there with you." He didn't wait for their reply, in case they preferred he didn't go with them, turned Blackie's head and loped across the green to Thornton's wagon. Left with little choice, they followed.

"Bass, there's a couple of U.S. Marshals that wanna talk to you about something," Scofield said when he pulled up beside Thornton's wagon.

"Oh?" Bass replied, obviously surprised. "Talk to me about what?" He had assumed that joining the wagon train was the best possible way to disappear. To find two marshals waiting for him in Oregon City was devastating.

"You might prefer to talk in private," Avery said, glancing at Scofield.

"No," Bass said. "I have nothing to hide from Mr. Scofield or anyone else. What is it you want?"

"To start with, we're gonna have to search your wagon," Avery answered.

"Help yourself," Bass said. "What is it you're looking for? Maybe I can help you find it." He lowered the damaged tailgate. "Violet, honey, I'm gonna have to ask you to come out of the wagon so these fellows can search it." She scrambled out onto the ground.

"Ma'am," Avery greeted her politely.

"What tore up your tailgate like that?" Sam asked.

"About a sixty-foot uprooted pine," Scofield answered for him. "He was lucky he didn't lose his wagon."

The two lawmen stared at the printing press taking up all but a little of the space inside the wagon. "What in the world is that?" Sam asked.

"A printing press," Bass replied. "Is that what you're looking for? Because I can show you the papers that show that I bought it. I'm planning to start a printing company and maybe a newspaper out here." Avery said that wouldn't be necessary, since a press was not what they were looking for. Bass was at once relieved because he had no such proof of purchase.

Booth and Sawyer took a brief look at what else was in the wagon. They both had a good idea of the object they sought, having had it described as an extra heavy crated container that would be hard to miss. And there was no such object. Finally, when frustration set in, Avery declared, "Well, they ain't here."

"Can I ask you exactly what it is you're looking for?" Bass asked.

"Plates," Avery answered, no longer concerned about them.

"Plates?" Bass asked, although he knew what he was referring to. "You mean dinner plates, like fancy china or something? Why would anybody think I had something like that? They'd most likely all be broken to pieces by now, if I did have them."

"He's talkin' about the kind of plates you put on a press like that and print money with," Sam finally explained.

"Oh," Bass responded. "Because I used to work for the Bank of New York, right? I was just the man who handled the paperwork. I didn't have anything to do with the actual printing plates. Besides, they were all turned back over to the Treasury Department before I left the bank." He looked over at Scofield and chuckled. "I wish I did have a couple of plates for some greenbacks. It'd make it a lot easier to get my printing business up and running." He shook his head and added, "I would have thought the Bank of New York would have had a higher opinion of me than that."

"Gentlemen," Avery finally stated, "I'm sorry to have bothered you with this nonsense. If it ain't in your wagon, then you obviously ain't got it. Come on, Sam, I need a drink."

"No trouble at all," Bass remarked. "I'm just sorry you had to come all the way over here for nothing." He now realized he had no choice but to pursue an honest living. It was hard to explain, but for some reason, he thought he was already feeling a sense of good fortune. In his mind's eye, he could picture the massive crate that tore off half of his wagon's tailgate as it now must lie at the bottom of the Clackamas River. Looking skyward, he mumbled to himself, "Somebody up there must be looking after me."

"What did you say, honey?" Violet asked.

"I said I think I might teach your brother how to run a printing press," Bass said with a wide smile. It obviously pleased her.

# Chapter 27

Except for the surprising visit upon Bass Thornton by the U.S. Marshals, the rest of the day was typical of the arrival of another wagon train of weary but happy emigrants to reach their destination after months of obstacles thrown in their way by man and nature. Lines were formed at the land office to study the maps of land parcels still available down the Willamette Valley. And parcels of land were purchased right from the plat on the wall. There was no more free land offered to those willing to work it, but the emigrants were happy to find that last year's price of $1.35 an acre had not gone up.

It was a busy day for the entire wagon train, a good part of it involving the "settling up" with Scofield upon his successful delivery of each wagon to the agreed-upon destination. As was his usual custom, Clint made it his business to help out the new arrivals in any way he could. In Maggie Mayfield's case, however, he wasn't sure how he could be of any help. As far as he could see, she had no potential to support herself. Touched by his apparent concern for her welfare, she confided that she would support herself as she always had, practicing the world's oldest profession for women.

Many friendships were forged on the challenge that was the Oregon Trail, and they vowed to stay in touch in the coming years, but Scofield knew that was not very likely. Even as close as the Bishops and the Watkinses had become, time had a way of removing all thoughts of anything other than working the land. Except for a few wagons, the camp remained there on the green for the night, but next morning, all final farewells were exchanged as the remaining wagons pulled out of Oregon City and headed down the valley. Satisfied that his work was done at that point, Scofield announced that it was time to take Lily to meet her new family. "Well, this oughta give 'em something to think about," Lily commented. "We're liable to both be lookin' for a place to sleep. What are your brother and sister-in-law gonna think when you walk in with me?"

"Hell," Scofield said, "Irene's likely to jump for joy. For years, she ain't liked the fact that I wasn't married. She was always afraid Garland was envious of me." Clint had to laugh. It was going to be one helluva surprise for the whole family.

"You'd best start peelin' some more potatoes," young Robert Scofield stepped inside the kitchen door to announce. "I think Uncle Clayton's home." That brought his mother, father, and sister, Janie, rushing to the door to see.

Ruby Nixon remained by the kitchen table, reluctant to run to the door to see for herself. "Yep," Garland Scofield confirmed. "It's Clayton and Clint all right, and it looks like there's a woman settin' in the wagon seat beside Spud." That was not good news for Ruby to hear. Last year, she was the young woman Clint brought home with him. She walked to the kitchen door then when the others walked down the steps to meet them, but she remained at the top of the steps. When Spud pulled the wagon up to a stop, Clayton stepped down from the saddle and walked over to the wagon to help Lily down.

When Lily was halfway down, Clayton didn't wait any longer. He swept her off the wagon wheel into his arms and carried her to the foot of the kitchen steps. "I'd like to introduce all of you to Mrs. Clayton Scofield! Lily, this ragged bunch of folks is your new family." Properly shocked, they all gathered around her to welcome her. At the top of the kitchen steps, Ruby's heart started to beat again. Clint motioned for her to come down.

He dismounted and when she came to him, he asked, "Do you still have the key to my cabin?" She nodded solemnly, reached into the pocket of her apron and produced the key. "I was hopin' to find a decent ring to swap you for that key, but the only thing I was able to come up with was this bone ring my Crow mother made. She gave it to me and told me to put it on your finger. I shouldn't hit you so sudden with it, Ruby, but if you'll have me, I want to marry you. I think we could make a go of it. I couldn't think of nothing but gettin' back to see you the whole time I was gone. I'll understand if you don't ever want to get married again, after being widowed by two husbands. And I'll understand if you can't think of me as anything more than a friend. I promise you that won't ever change. I'll always be your friend."

She put her arms around his neck and kissed him. "I was afraid you would never believe me, but it has always been you. Even when I agreed to marry Cal, it was because I thought you wanted me to." They embraced, oblivious of the looks of approval from everyone gathered around the wagon.

"Looks to me like we're gonna have to have a king-sized weddin' cake," Garland said to Irene.

Visit our website at
**KensingtonBooks.com**
to sign up for our newsletters, read
more from your favorite authors, see
books by series, view reading group
guides, and more!

**BOOK** **CLUB**

**BETWEEN THE CHAPTERS**

Become a Part of Our
**Between the Chapters Book Club**
Community and Join the Conversation

**Betweenthechapters.net**